WHEN
HEARTS BLEED

A BOOK OF ADULT HORROR/SUSPENSE
SHORT STORIES

GW00537355

When Hearts Bleed

A Book of Adult
Horror/Suspense Short Stories

B.J. Lawyer

2021
Goat Hill Books

Library of Congress Cataloging-in-Publication Data: Has been applied for

ISBN # 978-1-7378975-2-1

Book Cover Design: Unique Graphic Art.com
Bradley Peterson
br.peterson@gmail.com; www.bradpetersonart.com

Editorial Services:
Jennifer Murgia
Jennifermurgia8@gmail.com; www.jennifermurgia.com

Janet M. , jpmcurated, owner at jpmcurated.com

Illustrations:
"The Meteor Crater" Stephen Leonardi, Published 12/07/2020, Unsplash
"Mississippi Shadows" Wang Yan, Unsplash
"The Colorado Escape" www.pexels.com, cottonbro, Saint-Petersburg, Russia
"Allison's Eyes" Mohammed Alherz, Unsplash
"Forrest Creatures" Public Road, Unknown
"The Indian" Copyright @ image "Sees Behind" by Kirby Sattler
        sattlerartprint.com 713-445-7033
"The Gambril House" Bradley Peterson, Unique Graphic Art.com
"A Good Trip Gone Bad" Anthony Intraversato, Unsplash
"That Deluxe Shine" Author, B.J. Lawyer
"The Cabin" JP Valery, Pub. 07/009/2018, Unsplash
"Sweet Revenge" Vincentas Liskauskas, Unsplash
"The Vacation" Paul Gilmore, Unsplash
"Kay's New Cat" Author, B.J. Lawyer
"DNA Don't Lie" Denys Nevozhai, Unsplash
"Due Cause" Unsplash, Unknown, used by permission
"A New World" Shoeib Abolhassani, @shoeibabhn, 06/26/2019, Unsplash

Contents

Author's Acknowledgements

I must say, the creation of this book has taken me for quite a ride. I couldn't have written these stories alone, so it is now that I'd like to gratefully acknowledge and humbly thank the poor victims who helped me along to the end of this journey.

My beta readers, Kellie Geiger Mora, Samantha-Tyler Sirk, and Daniel Breeze, all of your advice and suggestions were invaluable. Of course, my Editor, Jennifer Murgia for her kindness and patience throughout this whole process. Mallory-Dalton Eden for putting up with my lack of computer skills and late-night telephone calls. A huge shout out to Janet M. for her last-minute efforts in catching my mistakes and helping me get this book finalized. Your insights truly made this book a better read! Last, but not least, James A. Sawyer who cooked a great deal of his own meals while never complaining as I often barricaded myself behind closed doors most evenings and nights for well over a year. His insights and ideas were also greatly appreciated and valued, not to mention his bartending services and homemade cookies and milk deliveries.

Again, thank you readers for purchasing this book and I hope you will enjoy reading it as much as I've enjoyed writing it.

It would also be nice if you'd all stick around for the next one.

DEDICATION

This book and the stories in it are for my dad, Glenn Carroll Lawyer "Bill". Dude, you never got the credit or the respect you deserved. I sure am looking forward to seeing you again in the clearing at the end of the path. I hope you know that I miss you, every day.

Also, for baby Casey. I can't wait to share ghost stories with you around the campfire, show you how to catch lightening bugs, and most of all, teach you to never – ever chase red balloons.

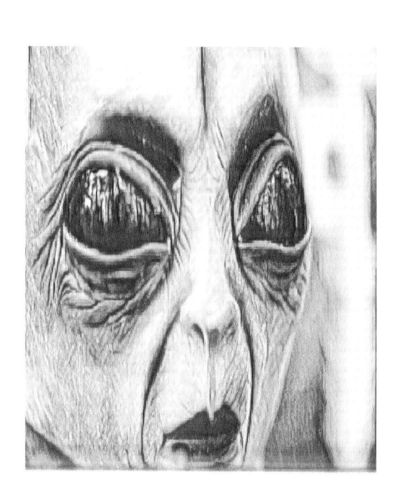

THE METEOR CRATER

CHAPTER I

I've lived in Arizona all my life. Winslow to be exact, and in Winslow, word gets around about stuff. Sure, there are secrets; there are secrets in any town. But in Winslow, secrets stay hidden. Secrets stay hidden or people die, and in Winslow nobody kids around about shit like that.

Winslow is a small desert town about a hundred miles west of the New Mexico border. It's hot in the summer and the winters are usually uneventful. We have one high school in town, which had less than four hundred students in the graduating class of 2020. Most students are Navajo, live on the reservation nearby and get bused into town. Hell, nearby isn't the right word. The "Res" is basically next door, and most kids walk. The buses are old and very unreliable, but when they run, they will pick up those who want the ride. If you throw up a wave, Carol Dunn, the driver on the east side, will smile and stop every time. She's one of the best drivers the district has, and they value her to no end. That goes for school kids, as well as the women headed to the grocery store. County regs don't always apply to the Winslow School District #22. How many towns can say that?

There is a lot of history in Winslow, and it seems most everyone respects it. For the most part, we aren't wrapped up in politics, religion is everyone's free choice, and we couldn't give a shit about what kind of car our neighbors drive or the amount of money the council members spend every week on booze. The people of Winslow are, and always have been, what you'd call real people, through and through.

The best part about our town, is how we look out for one another. We care about our neighbors, our elderly, and our pets. The last thing anyone wants to see is a stranger coming into town and disrupting the peace in our community. In fact, strangers don't seem to want to stay long. You see them once or twice, then their faces fade and they just turn into memories.

After that Eagles song came out back in the 70s, things picked up around here. Everyone noticed cars and pickups riding through town with out of state plates. Percy's Diner got so busy they had to hire on two new waitresses and another cook. Eventually, the town council took a vote and erected a fancy light post and sign on the corner of Main Street just so the visitors had a place to stand and take their pictures. We all got a kick out of it, and you better believe the stores enjoyed cashing in the profits. The Navajo also profited by selling their wares of "Genuine Navajo Jewelry, Pottery and Serapes", among other "can't live without" overpriced items.

In case you didn't know, Winslow is in the middle of a whole lot of nothin' on I-40. If you didn't live here, there was absolutely no reason to get off the exit, and that was exactly how the town folk wanted it.

Chapter 2

A few months ago, a man in a black suit and a yellow tie drove into town in a Land Rover with what looked like all the bells and whistles the manufacturer offered and stopped at Percy's Diner just off the main drag. He settled into a booth and ordered the lunch special with a side of French fries. He practically demanded that they be "real soft". He said he hated the crunchy ones because they hurt his mouth so much, and not to forget the ketchup. The guy knew what he wanted; I'll give him that.

He seemed rather fidgety, but when the food came, and after being appeased by Maria Shaffer-Longo, who the town folk considered to be the world's most amazing waitress this side of the Mississippi, he warmed up about thirty degrees or so. He still pretty much acted like a giant dickhead, but Maria had an unusual knack for handling dickheads, as well as other customers who needed special attention. In fact, Maria once sat on the Town Council and had the admiration of the entire town. Women wanted to be like her, and the men didn't want to fuck with her. But that was in the old days. Nowadays, you drank her coffee and ate her eggs, and you'd walk out of the diner happy or else.

During his lunch, he had made a passing comment about the health of the town and had asked if Maria or her friends had been burdened with ill health recently. He mentioned he was thinking about purchasing some property in the Winslow area and wondered if the water was okay.

As far as Maria knew, she, as well as her family and friends, have always been healthy and happy and felt Winslow was a wonderful place to settle. "If you like the desert life and lack of cosmopolitanality." She laughed and added, "If that is even a word!"

They both chuckled at the sentiment, and as he finished his meal, she began to clear his dishes and prepare his final bill. He wished her well and they both said good-bye.

Later that evening, Maria wondered why he brought up health and water issues. After all, those matters were on public record at the city office building in town. As she rolled over and turned off the light, she mumbled something about how he was just like all the rest. With a deep sigh she closed her eyes and drifted off to sleep.

Chapter 3

The closest tourist attraction to Winslow is the Meteor Crater which is about twenty-six miles west on I-40. It draws a lot of people and there are lots of stories behind that crater. The old timers don't like to talk about it and when the topic is mentioned, they usually change the subject quickly or leave the room altogether.

Folklore has it, there have been many unexplained animal deaths close to the crater. Winslow was the first established town next to it and in years past, it's been said that families have moved closer to the crater, to work the land and raise families. But no one has been able to last even a year before some type of tragedy occurs. Some say there is something in the water that causes people to go insane and simply wander into the desert while others say it's a type of cabin fever. A lot of people just can't handle being so far away from things. Sooner or later most just quietly disappear as though they had never been in Winslow at all, especially the vagrants.

The Navajo believe that no one can live close to the crater because the crater holds the spirits of the life forms killed when they hit Earth. They say the white man created the story about it being a meteor that hit, but they believe it was a whole lot more than just a meteor. Although the meteor crater has always been on Navajo land, the Navajo refuse to go near it. When it was taken over by the United States Government, the Navajo, who had always defended their land and objected to having their property taken from them, never fought the government on this point. It was as if they were glad to be rid of it.

About two weeks after the man in the suit appeared, the weather changed in a way that was totally out of the normal temperature ranges. The sky grew very dark, and the wind became so strong it felt like a tornado was going to hit. Monsoons are common during the mid-to-end of the summer months, but it wasn't even quite early summer yet.

Chapter 4

The man in the Land Rover, Charlie McKenney, happened to show up in the lobby of the La Posada Hotel on 2nd street as the skies turned black. He wanted the best room he could get that faced the pool. He practically demanded four pillows, not two, and wanted to make sure the floors were carpeted. "I hate a cold hard floor. If you don't have carpet, I'll go down the street, so tell me now." He said so in a way that let you know he was used to getting what he wanted.

The girl at the front desk assured him they had carpet—and new carpet to boot. "All the rooms had carpet upgrades three months ago whether they needed it or not. The last owner had installed this weird, pinkish color carpet and the new owner wouldn't have it, so he had all the rooms redone. You'll love it, Mr. McKenney," she said. "Do you have any pets with you today?" she added.

"Not a one. It's just me."

"That's fine, please sign at the X. Here is the code for the Wi-Fi." She scribbled it on the receipt. "Will you be needing a wake-up call, Mr. McKenney?"

"I'll call down in a bit if I do, I'm still arranging my schedule," he said.

"Excellent. There is a continental breakfast from 6:00 to 9:00 in the dining room on the first floor, and the pool hours are from 10:00 to 10:00. Enjoy your stay, sir. I'm Bev, Bev Markwood, and I'll be here at the front desk, until 8:00 a.m. Feel free to let me know if you need anything."

He nodded as he turned and walked away, appreciating her pleasant attitude, and carefully folding his room receipt and tucking it in his front coat pocket. He always saved his receipts for tax purposes and thought people would be amazed if they only knew how much money they could save if they just held on to them.

Within moments, he was driving around to the side of the hotel where his room was located and began searching for a good parking spot. He never chose the closest spot because there were always too many hard cases that liked to squeeze in too close around him. A door ding would be grounds for a huge confrontation and possible legal issues, which is never any fun for anyone, especially Charlie. Therefore, he picked the safest spot he could towards the rear of the lot, grabbed his bag of clothes and toiletries, and the bottle of Jim Beam he purchased prior to arriving at the hotel, and climbed out of the Rover.

He fumbled for the plastic room card, wondering why in God's name hotels stopped using regular door keys. He mumbled something about how "these days everybody has to reinvent the fucking wheel" and let himself into room 237.

McKenney was obviously a hard-working guy, but he was also a tad on the extreme side. By that, I mean he was the kind of man that would do anything to get what he wanted. He wasn't necessarily brave, but he could surprise you under the right circumstances. He, for lack of a better word, could be very danger-ous if he needed to be. Those that knew Charlie would all have the same opinion. He was wound too tight and since his wife left him, he was about as unstable as a three-legged chair.

McKenney woke up about 8:30, showered, dressed, and wandered down to the lobby to grab a toasted bagel with about a pound of cream cheese balanced on top. When he wanted a bagel or for that matter, anything else, he wanted it his way. After he was finished, the food bar usually needed to be restocked because he was a big guy and couldn't care less if there was a line of people behind him. He was going to satisfy himself. If he happened to take all the little cream cheese packets, who cared. The rooms were all overpriced in the first place, so this was him getting even and he was fine with that.

Charlie McKenney had been married for about ten years when his unhappy wife realized she had been cleaning the house with no help from him, cooking nice meals he would barely eat because he wouldn't be in the mood for whatever she made at the time, and love making was impossible due to his unfortu-nate shortcomings in that area. His wife left him graciously and with all the best wishes for him to have a wonderful new begin-ning and didn't ask for a single penny. Although most men in the world would consider that a blessing, Charlie was appalled, and considered his wife to be the most ungrateful bitch he ever knew. In the end, it didn't matter because she was gone, and he was single.

That next day Charlie drove up to the meteor crater. He wasn't expecting all the commercial drama but wasn't surprised either. He paid the money to enter and had packed a lunch, so he was able to sit on the platform that hovered over the crater and think and reflect about his new beginnings and ambitions in Arizona.

As he sat, he noticed a weird smell. It became so strong that he had to hold his shirt over his nose. "What the heck?" he thought. The other tourists didn't seem to notice and as he observed his surroundings, he concluded that some poor desert dog or other unfortunate creature must have curled up and died under the viewing platform. He didn't particularly care and he wasn't about to let that stop him from enjoying the view or his meal but was surprised that no one had come to cart off the carcass.

He couldn't believe he was finally here. It blew his mind when he thought about a meteor with the impact energy of twenty megatons striking the very spot at which he currently sat over 50,000 years ago.

The crater was huge, as he expected, and he tried to imagine what it must have felt like to witness the meteor as it crashed to Earth. The impact had to be breathtaking as well as deadly. It was said that when the meteor struck, according to astronomy.com, a website which Charlie visited often, it killed any human-sized life for up to four miles, and due to the sharp change in pressure, the shock wave would have produced severe lung damage up to seven miles of the impact. That and the 900-mile-an-hour winds any lifeform was unfortunate enough to witness.

Charlie had always been drawn to science, although his grades in school never reflected it, and the thought of extra-terrestrial beings visiting our world made his heartbeat faster. Even though it was said to be a meteor crater, Charlie never believed it. He was with the Navajo, and to him, there was no other explanation than extra-terrestrials.

Ever since he was a kid, he was obsessed with Star Trek, and always watched as many Sci-Fi movies as he could get his hands on. It was for this reason Charlie wanted to live in this part of Arizona. He wanted the crater in his back yard and wanted to be able to come here any time he chose. This was why he was determined to purchase the closest property available to the crater, no matter what the cost.

When Charlie was determined, watch out. He had friends in high places and pulling strings was what Charlie did best. So, there he sat on the platform overlooking the big hole in the ground, withdrawing sweaty quarters from his pants pockets, and inserting one after the other into the viewing machine. He didn't care about the little kids who had lined up behind him, patiently waiting their turns. To hell with the parents who would kindly ask him if he would please hurry so their kids, who had been good-naturedly waiting, could use the viewer. It was all about Charlie, and he was living his dream.

Finally, as the sun started to set on the horizon, the rangers came out and notified Charlie they were getting ready to close for the evening, and he would need to leave the already deserted platform. Charlie snorted off and returned to his Land Rover.

He tried to push the chip off his shoulder as he slowly walked through the exit of the platform and out into the parking lot. As he climbed into the front seat, he realized he was happier than he had been in months. Maybe, he thought, his life was finally turning around. He didn't need his wife and all her honey-do-this and honey-do-that bullshit. He had always been his own man, and he didn't need some flat chested bitch to hold him back from what he knew he needed to do in his life anymore. Good riddance. Yep, life was truly turning around for Charlie, and he thought he would soon fulfill his life-long destiny, whatever that might be. Charlie looked down and was pleasantly surprised to see he had a hard on and smiled.

Chapter 5

The next morning, he awoke early, ate the free continental breakfast in the hotel's lobby, and was the first customer to walk through the doors of the Winslow Desert Realty office on Main Street.

The office was comfortable and bright, with a round coffee table covered in magazines placed in fancy twirled stacks on its top. So fancy, in fact, Charlie didn't want to choose one for fear of messing up the display. He knew it took patience to arrange and appreciated the fact someone took the time to go the extra mile and create such a nice presentation.

Within a few moments of sitting down in the reception area, a young girl, fresh out of high school, was Charlie's best guess, walked up to greet him and pleasantly asked him if he cared for any coffee or hot tea. He was immediately impressed with her genuine smile but declined either beverage. He asked to speak with the broker and let her know, matter-of-factly, that just a licensed real estate agent wouldn't do. "I want to speak with someone who really knows the area, not someone who pretends they do."

She smiled and said, "I will see if the broker is available. Please make yourself comfortable and I will be right back."

Within a few minutes, a tall, dark-haired Native American woman dressed in a simple white suit, classic pearls, stockings, and clean, well-buffed black pumps entered the reception area. Charlie was immediately impressed with her professional yet elegant appearance, as these days, women no longer often wore stockings. In Charlie's opinion, panty hose was the epitome of professionalism and should be mandatory in any career woman's wardrobe. It showed competence, and above all else, utmost class, not to mention those four-inch pumps. Those heels gave her another ten points. Yes, indeed, stockings separated the executive woman from the rest of the bunch that were sadly destined to be renters and wives of truck drivers for the rest of their lives.

"Hello, Mr. McKenney. I'm Shirlita Dewey. I'm the broker of this office. How may we help you today? Did Roz ask you if you cared for anything to drink?"

"Yes, she did. Thank you. I am interested in purchasing land close to the meteor crater site. Can you help me with that?" Charlie asked.

Shirlita Dewey smiled and said, "Well, that depends on what you plan on using the land for. Residential? Commercial? The surrounding land is Indian Reservation mainly, and there is limited acreage for governmental access. Residential property is, for the most part, impossible."

"My interest is diverse. I am affiliated with the U.S. Government, but also want to reside where I need to complete my research. My work is confidential, but I wanted to approach you first to see what is available, if anything. I would rather choose my own residence than have the government choose it for me, you see." Charlie smiled warmly.

"I totally understand. I will have to get some information from you if you decide to pursue property on government land, which may be possible since you have those affiliations. But first off, will this be temporary or long term, Mr. McKenney?"

"I am hoping to become a permanent resident, but that may change—and please, it's Charlie."

Charlie was asked to furnish documents proving his affiliation with the government and clearance levels, along with a million pages of past background investigations, and other miscellaneous paperwork to comply with both the Navajo reservation, as well as the U.S. Government agencies, to begin his property search.

In the end, after pulling strings and exhausting every avenue he could, he felt confident that something—some parcel of land near the crater would open up for him. Now he just had to wait and see what options where available.

Shirlita Dewey was unable to offer him anything on government land but was able to offer Charlie a few options. She printed out the multiple listing sheets, highlighted the most pertinent areas of interest, and handed them to Charlie. After his review, he chose three properties he felt would most suit him. They made the arrangements to view the listings the next day.

Charlie arrived back at Winslow Desert Realty promptly at 9:00, and by 9:15, they were in Shirlita's tan Chevy and headed toward the crater.

The first property they stopped to view was a dirty little single-wide, which looked to be about one-hundred years old, in a neighborhood ten miles from the crater. Charlie waved his hand in a gesture of disgust, and Shirlita kept driving. The picture on the listing must have been taken years and years ago because it looked nothing like it did now.

The second property was an actual house. It was a nice size, had a garage, and sat on two acres. The best part was that it had been vacant for quite a while and was listed as a rent to purchase. This property was strategically located between government land that held the crater inside its fences, and the Res.

Charlie knew this property was going to be as close as he could ever get to living near the crater. The house needed a lot of work, but it was perfect. They put in a full price offer that afternoon and it was accepted without any counter offers, two hours later.

Charlie bypassed all the home inspections, and since he was going to pay the seller cash at closing, he was moved in in less than a month. Charlie hired a contractor to oversee all repairs and upgrades that were necessary and to install air conditioning, a new heat pump, and to take care of some remodeling including paint and flooring throughout, new appliances, roof, you name it. When the moving van showed up with all of Charlie's belongings, the house looked brand new. He even had a large hot tub installed in the back of the house with a complete sound system and barbeque area. The final touch was an imaginative landscape design which included a huge water feature and gazebo scheduled to be completed later that month. It was a jewel in a cat box and Charlie couldn't have been happier.

CHAPTER 6

Charlie had everything organized within the first couple of weeks and he felt like he had lived there for years. He bought a black and red Maverick CAN-AM 4x4 to ride through the desert and even found a place in the government fence line that he breached with little effort at all. Due to the location, it was hidden from view by the hilly terrain and large boulders that dotted the area. The only way anyone would notice the broken fence was if they walked the property, and Charlie knew no one ever did that. The entire facility looked as if it had been locked up good and tight for months, maybe even years.

The creepiest thing that Charlie noticed were all the signs. It wasn't just a few that warned people to KEEP OUT. There were many of them. Signs that read, DANGEROUS, THIS IS A GOVERNMENT FACILITY, ENTER AND FACE FINES AND PRISON, POLLUTED AREA TURN BACK NOW, and others. "A tad overkill wouldn't you think?" Charlie said to himself.

That evening after a few drinks and the Tonight Show, Charlie passed out in his big brown Easy Boy like a little kid who had spent too much time at the fair. He was so tired that night he never heard the scuffling noises coming from outside the living room window.

Charlie's new routine consisted of breakfast around 8:00 A.M. then immediately dirt doggin' it as close to the meteor crater as he could get without risking anyone seeing him. He would sit in the desert looking in the crater's direction and reflect. He wouldn't think about anything in particular, but he always seemed content to just go out there and sit. Sometimes, he was back home by lunch. Other times, he would get home in the late afternoon and wonder where all the time had gone. After a couple months he found himself going home to eat dinner, then going back out after the sun went down.

He loved it even more at dusk because he could get closer to the crater knowing the tourist personnel had left for the day. Sometimes he would bring a lawn chair and sit right on the crater's rim.

There really wasn't much to see when you got right down to it. If you've ever been to that part of Arizona, you will remember that it's just dirt and rocks. It's always hot as Hades in the summer, and windy and cold in the winter. There is no vegetation to speak of and the topography is mostly flat and unromantic. Although to Charlie, the land was mesmerizing.

If he looked hard enough into the crater, he could see it moving, as if it were alive and breathing. Sometimes he would hold a handful of dirt and slowly pass it from one palm to the other. Sometimes the dirt itself would move and he would marvel at how the granules would tickle his hand and fingers. The first time this happened it scared Charlie, but after a while he grew used to it and learned that if he spoke to the dirt, it would move a little quicker. If he sang to the dirt, there was a slight vibration as if it was singing back to him.

One night as he dangled his feet over the edge, staring into the steep downward slopes of the crater, he thought he noticed little marks in the dirt. It was then that he realized there was a pattern to the marks. Animal tracks. It had to be. The thought of it being anything else was crazy. Hell, the Feds had this place locked up tight. Nobody got in there. Nobody but him.

CHAPTER 7

A few days later Charlie stood in the kitchen in his Fruit of the Looms, nuking a can of Chef Boyardee beef ravioli and cranking off the lid to a can of tuna for some sandwiches. "Nothin' better than some thick and almost hard ravioli and a tuna fish sandwich, with gobs and gobs of Miracle Whip." Charlie had said this often to those he worked with, and those who knew him well. "Better than heaven." He wouldn't just microwave it a little, he would microwave it a lot. So much that sometimes the squares would be hard to chew. That's when it was the best.

He heard someone knock on the front door.

"Just a minute!" he shouted as he walked toward the bathroom to grab a pair of flannel pajama bottoms. He had gotten used to being by himself. At first, he thought he would be lonely, but found he wasn't. Being alone was wonderfully quiet.

He opened the door to find Shirlita Dewey standing on the stoop. "Hello, Charlie! Am I catching you at a bad time?" she asked, eyeing his casual attire.

"Not at all." He quickly grabbed a t-shirt from the arm of the couch and started to throw it on, suddenly aware of his extra love handles. "Come on in."

"Thanks. Wow, I hardly recognized the place! You've made a lot of improvements. It really looks fantastic." She smiled as she looked around. "It's a whole new house!"

"Yep. That was my plan. The contractor did a good job. I couldn't have done it." Charlie lowered his head. Why did he admit that to her? All men can build stuff. All but him, that is. He never got that gene. Defeated, he looked up at her.

"I just wanted to stop in and see how you were doing. Make sure you're still happy with the house, and to follow-up," she said.

"Well, I appreciate that. You know these days a lot of realtors can't run fast enough once the deal closes. That makes you above most, I'm happy to say." He was surprised at how honest he sounded, but also knew it was true and he meant every word.

They chatted for a few minutes, and he offered her some home brewed iced tea. There was something about her he couldn't put his finger on. He found he could be himself around her. Charlie was never good at saying what he meant in a way that didn't emphasize what a dickhead he was. Somehow, she brought out the best in him, in a way that caught him off guard, but delighted him as well.

"There is another reason why I'm here," she said, looking directly at him.

"Should I be worried? My checks cleared, right?" he grinned.

She smiled. Then her smiled faded and she became unusually serious. "There has been some recent trouble."

"Like what?" he asked as he reached for his glass of tea, unconsciously realizing she was becoming more of a friend than just his realtor.

"There have been a large number of animal deaths on the Res. Not like coyotes. They haven't been eaten; these animals have been gutted and their innards strewn about. People are getting scared. The last time this happened was before the fence line went up around the crater before the government purchased the land. The Navajo Elders have been talking and telling the stories of long ago."

"I don't see how any of this can be blamed on the crater, Shirlita. After all, it's just a big dent in the ground. Is that what they think?" He looked at her slightly amused.

"I don't know what they think. But the number is up to fifteen, now, and people are frightened. The Res has issued a nightly curfew, and those with dogs are being asked to keep them inside at night. It's really getting creepy, Charlie." Shirlita took a sip of her iced tea, and Charlie couldn't help but notice her hands trembling.

"Have you noticed anything weird going on around here? I mean, you are so close to the crater, and you're alone out here. I was almost afraid to get out of my car and knock on the door."

"I haven't noticed anything weird, but I've also only been here . . . what, a couple months? I suppose everything could be weird as hell around here, but I wouldn't know it." He took a breath. "I'll tell ya what. I will be on my toes and report anything I see as soon as I see it. How will that do?" Charlie asked.

"That would be great. One last thing, Charlie."

He looked at her and waited.

"Some of the Navajo have seen weird patterns on the ground near the dead animals and around some of the homes. They think it might be a clue of some kind. No one can place the patterns as being a type of footprint, but no one can explain why they are around the carcasses," Shirlita said.

Charlie could suddenly hear himself breathing and wondered if his breath sounded as loud to Shirlita as it did in his own ears. He remembered sitting on the edge of the crater just days before and seeing a pattern in the dirt. He wondered if it was the same. Surely if something was dangerous around that crater it would have already taken him. After all, he'd been sitting out there for hours every day. "This is nuts" he thought and made himself stop thinking.

"If I see something, I'll be sure and let you know."

Shirlita smiled and stood up. "Well, I'm going to head home, I have a few things I need to do before tomorrow."

As they both walked to the front door, neither noticed a wet spot on the front stoop. It looked like a giant slug trail.

Charlie held the door open for her, and as she walked past him, and over the threshold, he smelled her perfume. Later that evening he fell asleep remembering how nice it was.

She pushed the door button on the fob and her car doors clicked in response. Charlie reached for the driver's door handle and pulled the door open. As Shirlita glided onto the seat, she thanked him and reminded him to lock his doors.

Charlie stood in the driveway and waited until her headlights had disappeared from his view. "Headlights? How long had she been here?" It was only lunch time when she arrived.

He had planned to go out to the crater after he ate, but now, he thought he'd respond to a few important emails and make a couple calls instead.

Chapter 8

The next day, he spent all morning at the crater. This time he took his camara and, as usual, stayed back in the safety of the terrain so no one could see him. He was on the edge of a quick cat nap, when he heard a noise next to him. As he quickly turned, he saw nothing out of the ordinary, accept a big, wet line of slime that went from about an inch from his foot to some rocks and dirt leading in the direction of the crater. As he stared at it, he could almost see it disappearing beneath the sun high in the sky and the heat of the ground. He felt a stab of fear as he wondered what the hell could have left that moisture on the ground? Then it was gone. He gathered his things and headed for the house.

Before heading into town to the grocery store, he decided to stop by Desert Realty and see Shirlita. He had told her he would be in touch, so he was only doing what he said he was going to do. No one would read anything into it more than that. They were on a first name basis now, which was nice, but Charlie had no delusions that they were anything but friends. They had never discussed age, but he guessed he had to be at least ten years older than her, and his traditions were old school. Besides, he enjoyed his selfish ways. He enjoyed living life for himself, he always had. He knew in his heart that would never change. He was only a past client of hers and they kept in touch due to professional reasons only.

"Come in, come in—let me finish this call. Don't make me laugh, okay?" She made a "you better be quiet" face as Charlie sat down on the couch in her office. This made him feel happy inside. It was as if he was privy to a special secret only the two of them shared.

Charlie made a kid-like "cross my heart" movement across his chest with his finger, took his cell out of his pocket, and began playing on his phone.

She finished the call and gave him her one hundred percent attention. "So, what's going on?" she asked. "I see you're still alive and well."

"Yep. I am. The Lord has seen fit for me to remain in this world, so I wanted to swing by and tell you. I don't watch the news, and rarely get out much, so I wanted to see if things were spiraling out of control here in Winslow or if it's still safe to plan dinner this Friday night?" Charlie asked.

"Are you asking me out on a date?" Shirlita questioned as she slowly leaned forward across the desk toward him.

"Nope. I don't want to set myself up for a let-down, so I figured I'll just see if you want dinner, and if you don't, I will still be able to hold on to what little dignity I have if you say no."

"Well," she laughed. "I would enjoy dinner very much, and I must say I've never heard that line before."

"Okay, then. Dinner it is. And since I'm the new kid on the block, why don't you pick the place. I'll wait and let my controlling self out of the box in a week or so," Charlie mused.

"Sounds good. Since we're open on Friday until 7:00, I won't be able to see you before 7:30, or so, and that's only if we don't have any contracts to write. Sorry, but that's the price to pay when you're the broker."

"No worries. I get it." He winked at her. "Business before pleasure. It's a good rule of thumb."

He was amazed, again, at how easy it was to talk to Shirlita. He had never been the type of guy who was good at manufacturing creative banter at will with anyone. He, in fact, had always been an asshole in most social interactions and anyone who knew him would agree. When it came to business, however, Charlie hadn't changed a bit. He could still be the most intimidating fellow around and that made him feel good. Maybe his new environment and lifestyle was changing him? Maybe, he was finally in his element, feeling he now had more patience with others than he ever had before. His thoughts were interrupted and without knowing what triggered it, he realized he wanted to get back to the crater, so he said goodbye and left the office.

CHAPTER 9

That night Charlie sat in his chair on the edge of the crater and drifted off to sleep. It was before midnight and Charlie had never fallen asleep out there before. He was always too afraid of someone catching him; a policeman or military guy doing rounds, checking the fencing, or looking for suspicious activity. He couldn't take the chance of getting caught while this place held his sanity. It was why he had come in the first place.

There was a gentle breeze blowing and the stars were brighter than he had ever seen them before. Those stars, the enveloping black sky, the vast desert. It was amazing how in this place the daylight could drain the life out of someone, while the nights gave you peace and life. It was cool, now, and although he was asleep, he was somehow aware of things one wouldn't normally be aware of in dreams. Charlie was glad he'd brought a blanket to take the night's chill off his bones. He was more content at that moment than he had ever been in his life. That is, until the dreams started.

He dreamed of intruders. These intruders held him down and did "things" to him. He didn't find himself fighting back and he wasn't in any pain. But he was unable to move. Their touch was cold, and their eyes were large and black as pitch. They also had no facial hair of any kind.

During his dream, the ones holding him down looked like they were cutting into him, although he didn't feel any pain at all. They made eye contact with him throughout, and when their eyes met, Charlie became full of ideas and hope. The memories of his life came back to him as though he were watching a movie. His birth, his family, the birthday parties, and even his first horseback ride when he was only ten years old came back like a wonderful memory. Although Charlie was unable to physically move, he found he could easily smile and that is exactly what he did. He knew in his heart this wasn't a dream. The amazing part was that even though he knew this, he wasn't scared. He had more of a feeling of happiness than anything else. Being able to relive all these memories was the greatest joy he could have ever experienced.

In the morning he awoke in his bedroom and found that he was dressed in his favorite pajamas. The prior day's dirt was gone, and he realized he was washed and clean. As he climbed out of bed and went into the bathroom to pee, he stood in front of the mirror. As he looked down, he saw a smooth pink line going from his diaphragm to his groin. The weird thing was that it was almost completely healed. No stitches, no sensitivity . . . nothing.

Charlie wasn't scared or surprised. He knew what that pink line was; it was obviously new scar tissue. His dream wasn't a dream at all.

After Charlie had time to think and get his thoughts together, he realized why the government took the land away from the Indians. They knew. They have always known what was going on out here. Just like Area 51, probably. The government had been hiding all this information since the fifties.

Charlie had been drunk with his new life and failed to see the reality until now. Now he had to ask himself if the alien life form was aware of his new mental position and if they could be monitoring his thoughts somehow. He suddenly got scared; really scared for the first time in his life.

CHAPTER 10

He met Shirlita for dinner that Friday and the topics they discussed were many.

At the end of the evening, as he pulled into her driveway, he looked into her large, dark eyes and told her he needed to tell her something. He was nervous and not sure how she would react, but he told her everything that had happened to him in the past recent days.

After he was finished with his story, he slowly leaned back into the driver's seat, gripped the steering wheel and without looking at her, waited for her response.

She looked at him carefully, smiled, and repositioned herself so that she was looking directly in his eyes. Then she invited him inside. "I think we need to talk, and I'd like to talk right now," she whispered in a serious manner, a manner he had never seen before.

Charlie wasn't sure if Shirlita had further information on the crater, or if she had plans of seduction. He was hoping for the latter.

"I'd like to begin with saying that you are a very intelligent man. Your aptitude and strength in pursuing both your fears and your dreams are a highly individualized trait of your species. I am proud of you and acknowledge your adaptability to the harsh climates of this part of your world."

He stood, took a few moments to think, and suddenly feeling like he'd been hit by a freight train, he calmly asked, "Who are you and how long have you been on Earth? What are your plans, and why am I involved?

"I must tell you that you and your questions are relative to your way of life but unfortunately do not hold any consideration to ours."

Charlie's mind was in disbelief. Was she bullshitting him? Surely, she had to be. Any moment now she would grin and roll her eyes upward and start giggling at him. Unfortunately, those moments came and went, and she stood completely straight and stared at him. He wasn't sure if he was going to fall down or throw up. He thought both options looked pretty good.

"This town is ours, now. It has been for a long time. You are being allowed to live for one reason and one reason only. We need you," she added.

Now it was his turn to stare at her.

"What the FUCK makes you think I would help you? Now it's my turn to ask questions or you won't get jack shit from me, understand?" Charlie was surprised at the power he had in his voice, considering he was questioning to himself if he was going to puke or pass out moments earlier. He held his ground.

Her expression hadn't changed, nor had her composure. "You see, Charlie, or considering these recent changes of events, would you prefer Mr. McKenney?" She continued, not waiting for a retort. "This world of yours is perfect for us. Our world is too populated to withstand our numbers, so we had to find other accommodations to survive. The planet Earth was closest in location, and held the most natural atmospheric conditions to ours. So, to be perfectly honest, Charlie, your big green ball won by a landslide. And there is more . . ."

Her demeanor became less threatening, and Charlie realized his breathing had slowed, although he never dropped his guard.

She must have sensed his thirst, and as Charlie watched, a glass of water drifted out of the kitchen and hovered within two feet from his chest. Her gaze never left the glass.

"Take it, Charlie. I know you want it."

He did.

"Do you have little chrome antennas that come out of the top of your head, too?" he asked sarcastically, remembering the My Favorite Martian sitcom from the 60s.

She looked confused for a moment but said nothing.

"So, you've explained why you're here, and it's not hard to figure out how you got here. Why do you need my help?"

"First, I'd like to ask you to relax. As much as you can, anyway. I have a lot to tell you, and this may be difficult for you to understand. After you hear me out, I think you will feel a lot better," she told him.

"Start talking." Charlie settled down in the recliner next to the couch with his glass of water. "Make me feel better."

"There is a reason why you came here, but it isn't the reason you think. It's not that you love the desert or want to be out of the city. You came here because you were drawn here. You sit at the crater for hours every day and every night. We know because we watch you. The crater makes you feel good. It makes you feel strong. When you are near it you need nothing to survive. It feeds you and it takes care of you. Am I right?"

Charlie said nothing, only looked at her, waiting for her to continue.

"Your life has been a series of incomplete tasks, boredom and frustration. You have a drive for winning and you self-educate yourself in many ways; you always have. Ways that you cannot explain and in ways that no one has ever understood. Your life has led to your coming here. To your joining us," Shirlita said slowly.

"Joining you? Why the hell am I being singled out like this? What is so special about me that I would feel the need, or—putting it another way—YOU would feel the need to have me join you?" Charlie asked, glaring at her.

Shirlita smiled and knelt beside him. He leaned back, unsure of her intentions.

"Because Charlie . . . You are one of us."

He felt all his breath drain out of him.

"We needed to make sure you were *whole* with us. That is why we needed to *look into* you the other night. We made it painless, yet we do apologize. I know that it frightened you." Shirlita looked him in the eyes. "You see, your body is different than a human body. You are impenetrable when it comes to disease and common illness that affects a normal human physique. Haven't you noticed that you are rarely, if ever, sick? You are never very tired, and you always seem to be one step above everyone you know? This is because, although you look and think you are human, in reality, Charlie, you are not."

He didn't know how to react. He stared at his hands as if he had never seen them before. In this way, he supposed he hadn't. He stood up and walked across the living room, and into the kitchen. He slowly dipped his head into the kitchen sink and patted cool water out of the tap onto his face. After drying his face and hands with a dish towel, he put his face into his palms. Although he wanted to cry, he did not. He gathered himself up as best he could, and slowly returned to the living room and sat down.

As he looked at her, still waiting for her to laugh and tell him that she was only fucking with him, but also knowing that she was telling the truth, he said, "But, I have parents. I have a normal life. I always have."

"I know. Charlie, you were taken from us as a child. A resident of Winslow found out about us and thought they were doing you a favor. They were in denial and thought you were human. They thought they were saving you."

"For Christ's sake, they never told me. They never said anything," he blurted out.

"Of course, they didn't. We never thought they would try to tell. Think about it. Who would have believed them? They would have just been another case of "crazy" and they knew it. But we monitored you and we knew that in time you'd come back to us."

"Shirlita . . ." He wanted to say more. He wanted to ask questions and learn more. He had a history . . . they had a history. Where did they come from? Was he being gullible if he chose to believe this nonsense? He stared at her and couldn't speak.

She smiled, and before he could gather his words, she reached for his hand. "I'm so glad you have returned to us and I'm so glad to be finally able to tell you the truth about yourself. I know you have questions, and they will all be answered. This will take time."

She waited to see if he would speak, but they were both quiet. She continued to hold his hand and he continued to let her.

"Rome wasn't built in a day," Charlie said.

"No, it wasn't." She smiled. "I'll walk you to your car."

Charlie had so many emotions running through him as he drove home, and he knew he'd never get to sleep. So many questions he still needed answers to. But he was also relieved in many ways. He always felt at home here, and now he supposed he knew why.

CHAPTER II

The next day, he got in the Maverick and drove to the fence line, mainly out of habit, but also because it felt good. It felt right, and the best thing now was knowing why. Shirlita was right about that. He sat in the desert and began to think. Suddenly, he began to laugh. All this time he had been sitting in the desert during the day and realized he had never needed any sunscreen. His skin never burned. Imagine that.

After dinner, he went out on the porch and noticed the same prints in the dirt he had seen at the crater. How long had they been there? How could he have overlooked them? They were everywhere. He got up and walked around the house. They were under every window and around every doorway. Somehow, he felt violated. Nothing is what it seems, he thought. He didn't like how this made him feel and got bad vibes from it.

He decided he wanted to pull up a chair, sit, and have a strong cocktail. For fun he tried to telekinetically move the chair. He couldn't do it. He concentrated very hard and tried again. He still couldn't do it. "I guess I should be able to do this. What the . . . There must be a knack to it I just haven't figured out yet." Frustration took over and he decided to go to bed. He would talk to Shirlita tomorrow, he thought.

As he lay in bed, he kept wondering how they needed his help. Isn't that what she had said? After telling him about his history, why didn't she ever tell him what help he could offer? Strange.

Yes, he had lots of unanswered questions. In the morning when he woke up, he would grab some breakfast and go down to Shirlita's office and confront her.

CHAPTER 12

The next morning was delightfully cool and refreshing. The sun was bright, as usual, but there was a fair amount of cloud coverage, so the temperature was comfortable.

As he entered the realty office, he was greeted warmly. Roz, (wasn't that her name?) handed him a cup of coffee and he was surprised that it had a splash of vanilla flavoring in it. Another ten points.

Shirlita had a client in her office and as she glanced up and saw Charlie, he saw the look of surprise on her face. As she looked at him, he felt his forehead warming. The only way he could describe the sensation was that his eyes filled with heat and his vision was changing. His eyesight had always been good. He never needed glasses, but now his vision was becoming so clear that he saw things he never noticed before. Dust particles, light filtering from the light bulbs, and window glares. He didn't understand what was happening, but he liked it. He liked it a lot.

He suddenly knew she was trying to communicate with him telepathically. He could read her mind! It was as if she was whispering to him and he knew, without a shadow of a doubt, she was talking to him. He heard every word and felt every emotion she sent to him. It was the most amazing thing he had every experienced in his life. "I will be with this guy for a bit. Can we meet for lunch at Percy's, say noon?"

Charlie nodded to her and felt as though he were from another planet. He smiled and remembered that evidently, he was.

It seemed in an instant his life had transformed into an amazing dream. Charlie had always been happy. Well, at least happy knowing he could always accomplish what he wanted to. He worked hard and was continually able to provide for himself and those he was supposed to care about. What more to life was there?

He knew he was egotistical. Now he knew why.

Charlie stopped. He wasn't egotistical, he was simply out of this Earth.

Although he could feel the change in himself, he could also feel the changing of the Earth. Instead of thinking of the way the Earth's politics were changing the world, he saw how the politics had changed him. Things were happening too fast, although in a strange way, he was happy they were.

Charlie decided he would walk around town and do a little window shopping before heading over to Percy's early to grab a table so they wouldn't have to wait since it was almost the lunch-time rush.

Shirlita arrived on time and gracefully slid into the booth's seat across from Charlie. Her eyes were huge and dark, and he felt like she could see right through him. For all he knew, maybe she could.

"You said you've been watching me since I've been here. What's with the small tracks around the house? Are those from your little snoops? I don't have to tell you I don't like being spied on. Besides being an invasion of privacy, it's also not a good way to make friends," he said.

"Yes, I agree, it's not. You need to be aware that this isn't all about you, Charlie. It's about all of us. We will do anything to protect our way of life here and no one is expendable. Like I told you last night, we needed to know you were intact both mentally and physically. The last thing we need is a loose cannon."

"And if I didn't measure up, then what?" he asked.

"Then we wouldn't have approached you, and that house you're living in right now would not have become available. We have high hopes that you will be a huge asset to us."

"Yes. Very high hopes," Maria Schafer-Longo interjected as she placed two water glasses on the table in front of them. "We meet again, Mr. McKenny."

"Evidently, we do. Although I believe you know me a little better than I know you," Charlie said and thanked her for the water.

"I recommend the meatloaf today. Percy made it fresh, and the sides are green beans and mashed potatoes."

"That's fine by me," Charlie said, looking at Shirlita. She nodded in agreement. "Make it two, Maria. Thank you. Oh, and a couple ice teas would hit the spot."

"Sure thing!" She eyeballed Shirlita as if they shared a secret and disappeared into the kitchen. Shirlita winked and looked at Charlie.

"I must be the town celebrity," he whispered to Shirlita.

"Yes, you are. More than you know. In fact, the elders are having a get-together this Friday night, and those of us that haven't met you yet are looking forward to being formally introduced. Please say you will come. About eight o'clock?"

"Love to. I guess I might as well jump in with both feet." He stared at his water glass. "Wait. I need to know how you need me to help you. That is what you said the other night, right? I need to know why you need my help and decide if I can and want to give it."

She looked far away. He wasn't sure if this was a good thing or a bad thing.

"Shirlita? Talk to me." He looked at her patiently.

"You see, Charlie. We are dying. We have been here for millennia. We thought this planet would sustain us forever, but something is going wrong. Whatever is in this part of the world has turned sour. If we don't leave, we will all die."

"I see. Well, how much time have you got?"

"We aren't quite sure. Maybe another ten or twenty years. I can't say. Our DNA is destabilizing. Reproduction is drastically dropping, and although we are long lived and very healthy, if we cannot reproduce, we will cease to exist. Charlie, we can't let this happen. This is why you are so important to us."

Charlie looked confused.

She stared at him then found his hand. He realized he needed her. He wanted her. At that moment he would have done anything for her— anything to keep her safe. "Your blood is still healthy, undamaged. We need it. We believe your blood can cure us."

"You want my blood?"

"Yes."

"How will my blood help you? If your DNA is weakening to the point of your destruction, wouldn't that be like putting a Band-Aid on a wound that won't heal? It would only be a quick fix, temporary at best," Charlie said.

"True. It would bide us time. But that is exactly what we need for us to leave Earth. We are already searching for another place. It is only a matter of time. There are so many other places. Oh, Charlie, there are so many other worlds, you have no idea."

"Shirlita . . ." He fell silent. Once again, his forehead was filled with warmth and his vision acutely doubled, tripled. In his mind, he asked, "Will this kill me?"

"I don't know."

CHAPTER 13

I n the days following their talk, Charlie tried to carry on as usual. He went to the grocery store, he cleaned his house, and of course, visited the crater. He tried to keep his thoughts private since current events proved mental privacy was evidently a thing of the past.

After contemplating long and hard, he decided he wanted to help. He actually felt privileged and somewhat honored he could save an entire race of a species that up until now, he never knew existed. Plus, he supposed the added bonus was that he was one of them. He really didn't owe humanity anything, and the upside was that he wouldn't harm the human race at all. How many people can say they are able to save an entire species?

He looked at all of this very candidly. He weighed all his options and was determined to base his decision on the most human and most compassionate values he knew.

Friday night came quickly, and as he arrived at the event, he was caught off guard by the numerous decorations. There was a dance floor with many lights illuminating the surrounding area and tables decorated with flowers. He was delighted to see someone even hired a band to play.

He met many people. People? If Charlie had ever been prejudiced, he certainly wasn't anymore. The folks he met that night were amazing in every way. They seemed sincere, educated, and in every way polite and compassionate towards each other regarding issues concerning the world. Human or not, they deserved to live just as much as the native souls on Earth did. They never harmed anyone, threatened anyone, or attempted to steal or destroy any of Earth's many natural resources. The night was a wonderfully enlightening experience Charlie enjoyed wholeheartedly.

He had decided he wanted to help these people survive.

After the party, he and Shirlita drove to her place for a night-cap. He had no expectations about what might happen, but he knew that whatever did happen he would be satisfied. Even if it was only to see her home safely.

As he pulled his Land Rover into the driveway, she asked, "Would you like to stay?"

"I've made my decision. I want to help. I will do whatever I can. Therefore, if you are trying to seduce me to influence my decision, don't bother."

Shirlita leaned across the front seat and kissed him. Her opened mouth slowly parted his lips, and as her tongue gently moved over his tongue, he submitted to her. For the second time that day, he realized he had fallen in love with her.

That night they lay together. Their sex was amazing. It in-toxicated them and they felt alive for the first time in their lives. They looked at one another as if they never had before had such a wonderful involvement with another soul prior to now. Time didn't matter. Nothing mattered. They had each other. That was all they needed. Forever.

Charlie saw that Shirlita was in love with him, just by the way she looked at him. He could genuinely feel she didn't want anything to jeopardize the existence of the man she wanted to devote her life to. Would she want him to put his life on the line even if it meant the survival of her species? He didn't think she did. The new powers of his mind were grasping feelings and emotions he never could as a human being.

Charlie awoke the next morning feeling more alive than he ever had in his life. He had accepted the plan for his blood trans-feral and was scared, although he was not hesitant to go through with it at all. He knew it was the right thing to do. No one knew if it would kill him, but he didn't even consider death as an op-tion. He was simply identifying with the purpose ahead. That purpose being to save his new-found family and species that he was so happy to call his own.

CHAPTER 14

The day was set for the initial blood transferal. Charlie arrived and was taken into a very comfortably decorated room with goose down pillows and thick, homemade comforters.

As he lay there preparing himself for the inevitable, Shirlita held his hand. They didn't speak. There was nothing to be said.

He looked at her and told her that he loved her. If it was meant for them to be together then they would be, in time. He told her it was the right decision for him to make and that she should be strong and remember him always, but never be sad if things didn't work out. The important thing was their race staying alive and he wasn't frightened.

She put her head on his shoulder and cried.

The doctor came into the room and asked if they were ready to begin.

They both agreed they were.

"Charlie, I want to thank you for your decision to help us. We all do. I am confident this will end happily, and you will be joining us in a way of life that will far exceed any of your hopes, dreams, and expectations you'd ever have achieved with the human race," the doctor said.

"Let's get going," Charlie finally said. "I have a girl I promised to take to dinner tonight."

Shirlita tightened the grip on his hand and looked into his eyes. He knew she would have to leave the room and within minutes, she kissed him and left. Their eyes never turning away from one another until the door closed separating their gaze.

"Okay, Charlie, we are going to inject you with a sleep agent, and you will drift off in a few minutes."

"Do you want me to count down from a hundred? I always wondered how far I could count down. I've never had any surgeries, so humor me, will ya?" Charlie said.

"I sure will, Charlie. Now let's do this thing," the doctor said.

Charlie felt himself going from the light of life into the semi-consciousness haze of the "almost asleep" almost instantaneously. He quickly lost the feeling of his body. As he looked down, he could no longer see the rise and fall of his chest, yet he was still breathing. He wondered why he could see anything at all. Shouldn't his eyes have closed, and shouldn't he have by now been in a deep slumber?

He found himself able to look around the room, able to continue to hear what was happening around him, yet he couldn't offer any voice or movement.

Charlie knew he couldn't have been totally under the gas yet. This was just the beginning of the operation. He continued to lay back and relax. He couldn't feel anything and didn't want to. He only hoped his grip on reality would leave and he would glide into the darkness of unconsciousness quickly.

CHAPTER 15

After a few minutes, he saw that Shirlita had re-entered the room and after her, followed all the people he had met in the diner, and at the party. The room turned into a huge number of people he had met while in Winslow and his heart began to beat faster. He only wished he could feel it. He felt naked. Exposed.

"Did he suspect anything?" the doctor asked.

"Not a thing," Shirlita replied. "They never do. They are always so gullible and self-absorbed. This one was more gullible than most, in fact. I gave him suggestions and his brain sucked them in like butter on bread. He wanted to be one of us so badly it was easy to make him believe he was. I told him what he wanted to hear, and he was so lonely, he fell for it. When I read his mind the other day, he was thinking about how he never sunburned since he's been outside and near the crater so often, and that it must have been proof that he wasn't human. Funnier than a rubber crutch if you ask me. Poor soul."

"What the fuck . . ." Charlie became confused, ". . . is she talking about?"

His words were only thoughts at this point, and no one heard him because he could not speak. His pulse pounded in his ears and panic began to set in.

The doctor leaned over Charlie and their eyes met. "Their bodies are exactly like sturgeon fish when you want to catch one for caviar. They secrete a chemical that taints the eggs unless they are completely immobilized first. In case you are aware enough to listen, Charlie, we are speaking about you. You are ripe and ready for us now and we believe you have been worth the wait. In fact, Charlie, we had our first taste the other night as you slept.

We did a similar surgery to make sure you were . . . well, let's be frank, shall we? We needed to make sure you were of the correct "taste" for us. Not all humans are you know. Sort of a first run you could say. Oh, and in case you haven't stood on a scale lately, Charlie, you are about eight pounds lighter than you were last week. Had you noticed? We took everything out of you that we could, that would allow you to remain alive. In fact, we almost got too carried away. You are a rare individual Charlie. We have been searching for someone just like you for a long time."

"As I had mentioned weeks earlier, people who come around Winslow tend to disappear. So will you." Shirlita said looking down at Charlie.

As Charlie was secured with straps and immobile, the fancy linens taken away, he now lay on the cold, metal surgical room table and knew he was helpless to escape. He was unsure if he was imagining things but thought he felt warmth between his legs and under his buttocks, as if he may have urinated in fear. Although feverishly whimpering in his mind like a child, he finally began to realize he could no longer deny his fate. He knew he was on their dinner table, and he was on the menu. He saw everyone coming closer to him.

His breath came quickly now as he noticed them shuffling in and shouldering one another, as if each were trying to get as close to the show as they possibly could. Perhaps they were individually lining up to get as close to their favorite pieces of flesh. Charlie heard murmuring as some exclaimed how delicious "this one" looked.

It was at this point he first began to scream in his mind.

One of them picked up his upper thigh and thumped it as if they were at the grocery store selecting a melon.

His life didn't matter to them. He was only food. He could do nothing to stop them. Charlie tried to struggle, but his body didn't move. It was true, he was nothing but a sturgeon fish about to get disemboweled.

The crowd leaned closer to him. He could see them smelling him. It was then that he noticed their teeth. They weren't the same; they had changed. Now they had small pointy tusks. Each one dripping with a greenish fluid. They were all drooling over him.

They began touching him. Running their fingers over him, although he felt nothing. It was as if they were deciding which piece of him to try first. Now they were drooling a thicker more mucous textured liquid. It smelled horrible. He remembered he had smelled that same odor before—on the platform at the meteor crater his second day in town.

Charlie saw the table slightly moving. They had begun to tug on him. He heard a snapping noise and knew it was a bone and they laughed as the table became red with his blood.

More tugging, followed by the slapping sounds of open mouths chewing.

He could only silently cry when they dove into his torso, face first, and tore apart his body with those large tusks. Their eyes lolling upward in ecstasy, faces covered in crimson red.

After time, he finally entered the darkness he had been waiting for.

Mississippi Shadows

People are haunted by their past every day. I am haunted by a memory of the dark that has terrified me for the last fifteen years. Wherever I am, whenever I am in the dark, I feel as though I am never alone. Not anymore.

In my heart I know how lucky I am to have made it out of that gravel lot with my life that night so many years ago. I've never told this story to anyone other than my wife, but as the years pass, I think I am meant to tell it.

My name is Kenny Lee, and I've driven big trucks for most of my adult life. Out of all the jobs I've taken on, trucking was one of those brilliant career ideas I wished I had never thought of. It seemed like a good idea at the time, and I must admit that it paid the bills and got me out of trouble in more ways than one. The job caught me up on finances and made me feel like a real member of my community. Trucking gave me the opportunity to think. It gave me the opportunity to prioritize things in my life that needed prioritizing with every passing mile marker.

There is always a schedule in trucking. I'm not sure who exactly creates the schedule, if it's God or just the random dispatcher. But there is always a shadow just behind your field of vision that seems to watch you, call your name, and does all it can to remind you where you are supposed to be and exactly which road you need to take to get there. I have often wondered, but the question remains, if our lives are destiny or is life just made up of random happenings? When it comes to the scheduled and daily routine at hand, which consists of picking up and delivering the load on time, there is no room for creativity whatsoever and there is absolutely no room for much personal thought. The job is all about maintaining the schedule. Holding on to what it takes to get the load where it needs to be, on time and legal under the many watchful eyes of the law along the highways and byways - no matter what kind of drama you may run into along the way.

Keeping this in mind, and living "the life" for, at that time, over eight years, I had come to a reckoning with my own personal spirit. In other words, I had the reckoning to distinguish the essential and overriding need to put a gun to my forehead to stop the inner monologue of voices. God, those voices. I have often wondered if this was a thought other drivers had, or if this was the journey I alone was lucky enough to experience.

On the other side of the job, after the run was done and you, once again, could think clearly as God intended without the pressure of deadlines and Motor Carrier constraints, the wide skies opened up to you and you realized how lucky you were to have the time, although short with the clock ticking and counting down until the next load, to think and dream in places most people only visited in movies. It is then that you always found yourself realizing how lucky you really were.

It's easy for life to get out of hand and it's easy to get carried away, and as far as I can verify or even look back and begin to remember with any true conviction, I have always been determined to follow life's path in my own way. Trucking has served me well in many ways until that dark, foggy night when I was going through Mississippi on Interstate 20.

I had to stop to investigate a light on the dashboard. I had never seen it before, and it concerned me because it had to do with the air pressure in the rear suspension of the trailer. I had just gotten a new company truck, a Kenworth T680, and I didn't want to take any unnecessary chances with this load. I was hauling a HazMat load of toxic air pollutants that could be potentially dangerous to anyone, including myself, if there were to be a mishap.

I was coming out of Atlanta and, as usual, I was under the gun to have the load delivered in Mira Loma, California, in a ridiculously short amount of time. I knew I needed to make a quick safety check.

My team partner, and trusted friend, for lack of a better phrase, was a Heinz 57 mutt I found dumped on I-10 in Phoenix. He was scared and shaking along a Jersey wall during rush hour in extremely heavy traffic. He was very small, and I actually mistook him for a desert dog. After a moment of contemplation, I took a second look back and realized it was a puppy. At first glance I saw him looking at the traffic and suddenly he was on his rear legs standing upright, his mouth open. I knew he was crying out. I immediately stopped the truck, engaged the air brakes and hit the hazard lights. I was out of the cab in seconds and took off running between the lanes of traffic until I reached him. He almost ran, but then he stopped and cowered onto the hot pavement. I couldn't believe that some scumbag left a puppy on the interstate. The Vet said he was 6-7 weeks old at most. This little guy, Bunter, is what I called him, was a reddish-tan variety of a mix between a large chihuahua and some other poor, short-haired mongrel. Maybe a terrier or a pit-bull type. I've never been what you would call a dog person, and I know that my description probably covers a million and one dogs, but I can honestly say this little guy brought me many a smile over the years. I suppose I couldn't name anyone on this planet, who has ever known me better besides that damn Bunter. In fact, he had a way of always knowing exactly how I felt when I felt it. It was as if we had a common bond, unlike any I had ever known with anyone else. I don't think I've ever quite gotten over him, nor do I think I ever will.

Getting back to that awful night, I had pulled over on an exit ramp when I realized there wasn't a wide enough shoulder to stop legally as HazMat loads require another five feet distance between the side of the trailer and the road. It had been raining that day off and on and it was still spittin'. I knew with the weight of the truck and trailer I would sink axle deep in that Mississippi mud if my tandems went off the gravel and I didn't need to add a $1500 tow bill to my ever-growing mountain of debt. I felt uneasy enough having to pull over so close to the swamp's edge along that stretch of highway. No telling what could come creeping out of those woods in the middle of the night and try to eat me or slit my throat. I envisioned myself lying on my back looking at the air bags while an alligator or some other night creature came slithering up to say hello.

I continued to drive down the ramp and when I came to the cross street, I decided to take a right turn and check things out, rather than pull onto the entrance ramp on the other side and hope for the best. If the exit ramp wasn't wide enough, why would I think the entrance ramp would be any better?

I saw a dim light that could have been a closed gas station and it looked like there was a gravel lot next to it. Plenty of room for the rig and trailer, and the ground looked hard enough to support the weight. Best choice. Only choice.

I addressed the issue of the suspension, which, at best guess, turned out to be nothing but a bad sensor on the rig's computer. I would know more at the next stop. At least I felt confident knowing I wouldn't screw up anything else by continuing to drive with that light on. Damn, those dash lights are annoying. Everything is computer related nowadays. I started gathering up my tools and put them back in the truck.

Bunter was in need of a bathroom break, so I let him out for a stretch while I finished up doing what I had to do. He was a trustworthy dog, and I knew he wouldn't stray far, if at all. He'd had many chances over the years to take off towards greener pastures, but he'd always stayed with me and ignored the urge to cut and run when he had the opportunity. It didn't take long for me to realize I could use a bathroom break as well.

As he and I were checking the bushes out along the edge of the gravel lot, I noticed how eerily quiet it was. There was a layer of fog settling on the ground and the one light, old and dirty, barely hanging onto the pole by the old gas station, looked as if it wouldn't take much more than a breeze to send it flying off into the night. It didn't illuminate much, but it did offer a little piece of reassurance in the middle of all the darkness.

I lit a cigarette and stood watching the trees and listening to the night creatures. As I blew out the smoke, I watched as it drifted upward and slowly merged with the thickening fog that had slowly consumed the space around me. Suddenly I was hit by a slight stab of uneasiness in all the gloom, as if I were a child caught in the school coat closet when someone turned the lights out. A child who can't stop imagining something awful underneath the coats causing them to move.

I looked back at my truck and could barely see the running lights along the trailer. The fog was coming in fast, and it seemed as if it were purposely blocking my return to the rig. In hindsight, maybe it was.

Swamp sounds at night are full of urgency yet can quiet almost immediately upon the sound of something irregular to the occupant's world. Maybe I was that irregular distraction. After all, I had no business in their world. Maybe they had all stopped their singing to whisper to one another about how to deal with the human intrusion. About how to make me go away.

The moon was in the waning phase. In a few nights, it would become as small as ever. A fingernail moon at best. Rather romantic, actually. Unfortunately, romanticism can get a loner cowboy like me into trouble on the highways late at night. Better to have your thoughts on the job at hand instead of your hand doing a job, if you know what I mean.

We were getting ready to turn back to the truck when I heard a soft noise behind me. It wasn't particularly startling, but it had the unnerving quality of something dragging. It stopped as soon as I turned around. I would have given anything to have had a flashlight. The one I had used to tend to the truck was rapidly dying and the one on my cell phone was a joke. The flashlight now was no brighter than my cell phone at best. It was useless at this point. Damn, I had been meaning to get some extra batteries for weeks, just for a time like this. Sometimes I could kick myself for always putting things off.

At first, I was going to let it go and then I heard it again. The noise was slower this time, but I had no doubt that I had heard it and it was getting closer.

Bunter heard it, too. He stood firm. His tail, which always wagged, was down and stiff, the hair raising on his withers. His ears were alert and I thought, with nothing else that could be anything but respect, that his little heart was doing his best to protect me. He made a guttural, growling noise that ended in a soft exhale. He did not make any attempt to get closer to it, and for the first time, I found myself wishing we were back in the cab behind locked doors.

I noticed the fog again. It was thicker and seemed to move in currents, yet there was no wind. It was July, hot and muggy as ever.

Now, I've never been a guy to jump to premature conclusions, and a wimp ass I am not. I mean, back in the day I had the pleasure of holding my own to a few bouts of assholes that got too close for comfort, but those days were over and my strength sure wasn't what it used to be.

I started walking back to the truck, not realizing I was almost running. Bunter was at my heels, and it was at that moment

I realized that my breath was gasping in my lungs. I knew if we didn't get out of there soon, we probably never would. Though the light was dim, I could tell a shadow was overpowering us, coming quickly up from behind, and if I couldn't get my old legs moving faster, it would be on us for sure, whatever it was.

It was all happening so fast. I couldn't believe this was real. The dragging sounds were changing into what seemed like wet slapping noises. I knew Bunter was just in front of me and I was becoming so scared that I wasn't sure I would have had the nerve to go back and get him if he turned to face our aggressor. I kept thinking how impossible this all was. After all, I was a grown man, perfectly capable of fighting off most anyone who came to confront me, but this was different. This wasn't human. I knew in my soul that we had to get out of there and waste no time doing it.

As I ran across the parking lot, I realized I could not hear breathing behind me. Surely whatever it was had to breathe! But all I heard was a slapping like someone was back there dropping soaking wet towels on the ground.

Then there was a smell. Like rancid puke. That first whiff in your nose as you take a breath after that first awful heave. What the hell was happening? I just stopped for a safety check for Christ's sake.

My first thought was that it may have been an alligator. We sure were in the right place in the country. I have seen many of them along the highway over the years hit by cars or trucks. Some of them so big, I'm sure the drivers had to get their front-end alignment checked out at their favorite service station the next day.

As I ran for the cab of the truck, I felt a moist, hot tendril of something slither around my ankle. As it began to tighten, I had to kick at it frantically with my other foot. Thank God I was able to knock it off. If I would have fallen, I knew it would have been all over for me. I didn't look back as I broke into an all-out run. Just a few more yards to the truck now. I was in total terror when I heard a thick, howling scream from the darkness. It was right behind me but seemed to have slowed down again as the dragging sounds drifted farther away. But in my heart, I knew this couldn't be true. I couldn't be so lucky. Suddenly my hands were tingling and my lower back stung. This feeling wasn't normal. I feared I was having a heart attack.

Was it gaining speed? I couldn't tell. I hadn't run this fast since my days at Gaithersburg High when I headed for the goal with the ball. My one and only touch-down. That was over twenty-five years ago. Back on the field, in those days, I only had a crowd of oversexed teenage boys chasing after me, ready to throw me down and shove my head in the mud. That was nothing compared to this nightmare.

As I cleared the trailer, and with only a few steps to go, I reached for the door. I threw it open, and Bunter flew inside without a moment's pause. I was amazed that his agile, little body had the speed and strength to leap inside, easily clearing the height of the steps; using the entry landing to push upwards, sending him over the driver's seat and into the cab.

I climbed in almost as quickly as he did and slammed the door. I locked it as fast as I could although I felt I was fumbling— my fingers weren't moving like they should, and I could barely feel the palms of my hands. Then there was a loud pounding on the door of the truck. The truck began to rock from side to side, followed by the sound of something sliding along its sides. For a moment, I thought the truck was going to tip over. Things were falling out of the storage compartments above the windshield.

With all that was happening around me, how could we have escaped something so strong to rock the truck in such a way? It could have easily broken a window. Maybe it was prehistoric or blind.

I kept waiting for the door handles to jiggle, but it never happened. I knew whatever it was wasn't human. A human would know to grab the door handles.

My arms felt like lead and my feet were numb. When that thing wrapped itself around my ankle did it poison me somehow? My tongue felt swollen, and I was having a hard time swallowing. It was then that I must have blacked out.

I awoke to find Bunter panting heavily and laying across my chest. I was on the floor of the cab with little memory of what happened after I locked the doors. The truck was hot, and the air was thick and wet. I cranked up the A.C., and immediate relief filled the cab and sleeper.

A dull throbbing and burning sensation caused me to look down and notice my ankle had very red, well-defined marks that looked like four fingers had tightened around it, or at the very least, slid across it with an intense pressure. There was a strange film that had dried on my skin and sock, reminding me of thick mucus. I smelled that odor again. It was the worse smell ever, like pure infection. I began to dry heave uncontrollably.

I must have passed out again because two hours had gone by when I looked at the clock on the dash. Whatever that thing infected me with was still in my system. I didn't have the strength to drive, and I doubted my coordination had improved much either.

Bunter stared at me with both fear and vulnerability. I knew I needed to get out and walk around the truck. I had to check the load to see if there was any damage. However, being responsible just wasn't going to happen. Not that night. I just wanted to get the fuck out of there, and by the way his dark eyes kept staring at me, so did Bunter.

It was nearly dawn. Had I been out of it all night?

Whatever we met up with that night was more powerful than we were. By late the following morning, as we had entered Texas, I began to think it was all a dream. My memory had grown fuzzy. I was relieved I had almost a full tank of diesel and plenty of miles between us and that gravel lot.

Yes. It had to be a dream.

I thought of how funny life was. I almost smiled as I got out of my truck later that afternoon half-way wondering why my legs felt so unnaturally weak and shaky. It was time to eat, and Lord knows I could use something heavy and fattening to fill the void in my stomach. Maybe a stack of pancakes, or at the very least, some biscuits and gravy. I parked the truck and promised Bunter I'd be back with something to eat for him, too. I barely gave a second thought about where'd we'd been the night before and how frightened we were.

As I locked the door to the truck and slid the key into the pocket of my dirty jeans, I noticed dents and marks on the driver's door and along the sleeper compartment. The paint was missing as though it had melted off the metal. The driver's steer tire was gouged and rubbed down to the cords. It was amazing the tire could even hold air. The lenses over the headlight and turn signals were melted down to a misshapen, irregular mess.

My breath caught in my throat as I remembered. Last night really happened. It wasn't a dream.

It's been years later and even now, I can't roll through Mississippi without a chill filling my bones, knowing I was lucky to have gotten out of that parking lot alive.

People say monsters don't really exist in the dark. But I know the people who say that have never been on I-20 in a foggy gravel lot on a late summer's night in Mississippi.

THE COLORADO ESCAPE

CHAPTER 1

Marty sat down at his desk with a frosty glass of Blue Moon and a paper plate covered with Saltines and Cheez Whiz and stared into the growing pile of mail that he had been putting off opening for over three weeks. It wasn't that he hated opening the mail, it was just that sometimes – most times, the reality of it was a bummer. No other way to put it really, just a bummer, plain and simple. Among the bills, credit card offers and other junk mail that he began to separate into their appropriate stacks, he noticed a forest-green envelope with red, fancy script glaring at him between the electric bill and a past-due medical bill. It was a medical bill from two years ago, that he somehow always found himself overlooking. He pulled out the envelope and studied it as anyone would when they see something unusual and a little different. Marty could tell that whoever wrote his address had done so methodically and with great care, taking every precaution to make no mistakes as if it were a wedding invitation instead of a random card. "Marty Lee Montren" Well, they had his name right. Probably a real estate advertisement, he thought.

Marty decided to open the rest of the mail first and save that one for last.

A half-hour later, and after shredding all the evidence of unneeded mail in his $69.95 Walmart shredder, Marty took the last swallow of his now, not so frosty Blue Moon and padded off to the kitchen to get a new one. As he shut the icebox door, his cell alerted him to an incoming call, and he quickened his pace towards the living room where he had last seen his phone and hit the green circle.

"Hello."

"Hey dude what's happening? Do you recognize my voice?"

"I don't know – keep talkin. Maybe it'll come to me." He said, wanting to get this part of the conversation over with.

"Okay. Here's a hint. The last time we were in your mom's Oldsmobile, we rolled it down the embankment in front of Redland Jr. High."

"Holy shit! Shlaypo, is that you? Oh, man! What a fucking trip!" Marty said, laughing.

"Yeah, tell me about it; you didn't have to wear a plaster cast on your fuckin' arm for six weeks in the middle of summer! I couldn't go swimmin' or nothin' that year!"

"Well, you shouldn't have had it hanging out the window! So, what are you doing – how'd you find me? I'm across the country now." He said.

"Well, as it turns out, it's pretty easy to find dudes that are famous these days. All I had to do was Google you, and about a million sites with your name on them popped up." Shlaypo said. "The only bitch was getting your phone number. So then I decided to try your parents' house, and your dad answered and gave it to me." He added, laughing.

"Yeah, they'll never leave that town. They've been there forever. Man, it is so great to talk to you – so what have you been doing? Where are you living?"

"I'm in Georgia. I got a place right on the beach. It's pretty awesome. I own a little bar on the pier. Best beer in town." Shlaypo said.

"I'll bet, and if I remember correctly, you always had the best pot in town, too."

"Still do, man. Gotta get out this way and check it out!"

They both laughed.

"Hey, the reason why I'm calling – Debbie sent you a letter, and she hasn't heard back from you. Did you get it?" He asked.

"Debbie Callow . . ." Marty said. It wasn't a question, really, but more like a sudden rush of warm memories he thought he'd forgotten that came flooding back all at once. Hearing her name after all these years was an unexpected jolt from the good ole' days. Unexpected and highly well delivered.

"Yeah. She's planning a thing, and she wants you to show up; we all do. Did you get it?"

Marty thought about it, then remembered the green envelope on his desk.

"Hang on a minute I might have, let me look. I'm going over to my desk right now" he said running through the house. Marty grabbed the envelope and ripped it open. It was from Debbie. "I got it, I got it. I'm reading it now. I can't believe I didn't open it – I thought it was some weird real estate advertisement, and I came about two seconds from tossing it in the trashcan. I'm not very good at opening the mail." Marty confessed.

"Yeah, me neither. She reserved a few rooms in a hotel up on Copper Mountain at the end of the month. Do you still ski?"

"Colorado? Hell yeah. I haven't been in a long time, but it's gotta be like ridin' a bicycle, right? I will totally be there. Who all did she invite?" He asked.

"I think she invited everybody, 'course not everyone will come, I'm sure. I haven't heard the latest headcount, but you, me, Debbie, Chapman, Bonnie, Franky are all coming. I'm guessing a few more, maybe. I think she put it on a bulletin board on Facebook or somewhere. I'm not sure. Not everybody can pick up and take off work at the drop of a hat though, so no tellin' who will turn up."

"Yeah, I get it. Well, I'm in. I'm gonna call her right now if it's not too late. Did she put her phone number in the letter? Wait, let me look . . . yeah, she did. I'm gonna call her right now." Marty said.

"Okay then – do that, and I'll call ya in a few days or so."

They talked for another couple of minutes and hung up.

He hasn't changed a bit. What a good guy. Marty thought to himself.

Marty's cell said it was 10:00 PM. That meant it was after midnight back east, where Debbie lived. He planned to call her the next day, no sense in waking her up on a Tuesday night when she probably had to get up early for work. Not to mention the fact that he was nervous as hell to call her after all these years. Although all grown up, Marty knew he needed to get his shit together before he called her, and he wasn't too manly to admit it – a spur of the moment guy he wasn't.

Chapter 2

It had been over ten years, and Marty was amazed they all were finally getting together again. By "they" Marty meant the nut sacks that he hung out with in school and who basically dragged him through his youth and helped to cultivate him on the foreign turf of adulthood. These ladies and gentlemen went back to childhood and the memories went far and wide.

As we all know, living sanely through adolescence is no easy task, but having these people to lean on helped get him through times of fear, doubt, and the drama of helping him locate his car on the occasional Saturday night when he had gotten so drunk, he couldn't remember where he parked it.

As far as he knew, they each just drifted apart and started new phases in their own lives. Isn't that, after all, what they were supposed to do?

After graduation and with the insistence of his parents, Marty applied to a college a few states away. He didn't do well, and in fact, dropped out after the second semester, but he could honestly say he tried his best. At the time he just wasn't cut out for having to apply himself towards goals that were set for him, goals he didn't have a say in, and goals he wasn't sure he even wanted to reach.

Marty needed more time. He needed time to make his own decisions and not devote his life to something that, well, for one, cost a fortune to obtain, and second to dedicate all his hard work in a direction that his parents pushed him towards and not one that he desired for his own life.

Marty had always been a smart guy, and his grades proved it. He had no doubt that he would accomplish good things. Not wanting to waste his families' money until he was sure of a direction was a good thing. Unfortunately, his parents felt differently. All Marty wanted was a year or two to get away, experience new places and decide where he wanted to be. This certainly didn't mean he was going to turn out as a fuck-up and in some scumbag job or worse. He had goals; he just didn't know at the time what they were.

In case you're wondering, two years after that experience, Marty went on to Dartmouth in New Hampshire and graduated with flying colors. He became a writer and since college had written four stand-alone novels, one of which was made into a movie, and two months ago, was approached by some bigwig at Paramount wanting him to write a sequel and offering another movie gig. Life has been a blur, and he still pinches himself when he wakes up in the morning. His parents weren't particularly jazzed about the idea of him becoming a writer, but they sure as hell aren't complaining now.

Marty promptly phoned Debbie the following evening when he knew she'd be home from work. Hearing the tears in her voice as they reminisced made him remember how much he had always cared for her. She was a genuine person and always thought of others before thinking about herself. She was all about integrity, even when people weren't watching.

As soon as they hung up, he phoned his literary agent and cleared his calendar for the last three weeks in February. His agent wasn't happy about it, but Marty stood firm. He wasn't going to let anything interfere with this reunion. Besides, he hadn't taken a real vacation since he'd finished his second book, and that was about four years ago. He felt he deserved this, and he was right.

Marty's next phone call was to his travel agent. He had her book a flight to Denver on February tenth, and to confirm and pay for a room that was reserved for him under the name Debbie Callow at the Copper Mountain Inn in Colorado. He planned to arrive two days early so he could relax and perhaps work a little on the next book in the peace and quiet of the mountain setting.

Normally when Marty began a new writing project, he didn't take breaks and preferred to hunker down and let his creativity drive him until the project was finished, but not this month. He was perfectly willing to drop his current life on a dime and head out for this reunion with his old friends. Damn, had it really been almost twelve years? So much had changed – they had all changed. They were spread out and basically all over the country now. They are all grown up, haired over and leading totally separate and different lifestyles. Will they even connect anymore? Marty thought. Will they still find the same things amusing? Well, he didn't know about anyone else, but if someone cuts a fart, he was sure he'd laugh at it. Who wouldn't? The rule of thumb should be that no matter how old one gets, you still gotta laugh at a fart, especially if its unexpectedly loud and in a public place.

As the days passed, Marty became more and more excited to see everyone. He worked but didn't make much progress as his mind kept drifting off to that new Colorado adventure that lay just days ahead.

Marty had everyone's phone number and thought about calling someone but decided to wait and see them at the hotel. He was assuming the gang felt the same because his phone didn't ring once, and that was fine. The grand total of people scheduled to attend was six - lucky six.

CHAPTER 3

The night before Marty's flight, he felt like a woman in the sense that he had no idea what to pack. After a while, he decided he was being ridiculous and would just be himself. That was what he was best at anyway. Why was he feeling so nervous? He wondered if knowing he was going to see Debbie again was what was making him anxious. She and Marty never even dated or went out as a couple. In fact, he wasn't even sure if either of them even thought of each other "that way". He was shy, which is an understatement, and in his eyes, she was always out of his reach. She was a lot more popular than Marty was, and he always felt that he couldn't compete with the other dudes that were always hanging around her. One thing he could say for certain now is that if he had it all to do over again – He sure as fuck would have asked her out.

Marty awakened at 5:00 AM, showered, dressed and called for an Uber driver who arrived within fifteen minutes. LA traffic was always heavy and unpredictable, but that morning traffic was unusually light, and he was at LAX within twenty minutes. An hour and a half later, he was in the air and Colorado bound.

As Marty grabbed the small hard pillow from the overhead compartment and squirmed back to his window seat, he made himself as comfortable as possible and prepared to take a power nap. With any luck, he'd wake up over Denver. As he sat with his eyes closed, he couldn't help thinking about Debbie. She didn't mention having a husband or family. Marty should have asked but didn't want to seem too hungry. Perhaps he wanted to put off bad news as long as he could.

Marty slept soundly all the way to Colorado. The seatbelt sign blinked, and the captain made his little announcement about what was below the aircraft and that they were beginning to descend.

They landed without any drama, thank God, and Marty thought to himself how he was never good at flying. He couldn't imagine having chosen a career where he had to fly often. He tried to keep both feet on the ground whenever possible. He liked life much better that way.

After Marty retrieved his luggage from Baggage Claim, he walked over to the Hertz rental counter. He was happy he had reserved one because they were swamped, even considering it was the middle of the week. He knew this time of year was popular for all car rental companies since skiing and winter sports were so popular in the mountains. He didn't want to take any chances on bad weather or not having a 4x4 if it decided to snow going across I-70. Those mountain roads are brutal in the winter, and you can't get any more winter than February in Colorado.

CHAPTER 4

The hotel wasn't particularly fancy, but it was rustic and very comfortable. It was exactly as Marty always pictured a Colorado ski resort to look like. Both the main lobby area and lounge had massive fireplaces surrounded by reclining lounge chairs; sofas and large pillows were also available if you wanted to sit on the thick, shag-carpeted floor. The beams that ran across the ceiling were dark and rich in color and looked as if they were ancient, but very strong. Windows that went from knee height to the ceiling overlooked the ski slopes and mountainside and ran along the wall without any separation. The slopes outside were dotted with decorative colored lights that glistened off the snow throwing creamy patterns onto the paths and the views they offered were breathtaking. Debbie had either gotten lucky or had one hell of a travel agent. Good hotel choice, girlfriend.

The flatscreen in the concierge area had been announcing heavy snowfall, and winter storm conditions were due to arrive within the next forty-eight hours. Area residents were told to prepare their supplies accordingly. The staff didn't seem very concerned as bad winter weather was a common fact of life in the Colorado passes. Marty felt that as long as he didn't have to board an airplane, he was fine with hazardous conditions. In fact, bring it on. Even though he was out of his personal element, he knew that the hotel management was completely comfortable in theirs and knowing that comforted him greatly.

Marty enjoyed a little skiing after he went up to the room and put his things away. In fact, he was glad he could get a little practice in before the gang showed up. It turned out he needed more practice than he thought, and he was glad no one else had arrived early to watch him sliding down the slopes on his ass as often as he did.

Marty had dinner that night in the lounge with his laptop and a bottle of fine Chateau Bordeaux that a sad, almost lost-looking waitress brought him. He wondered why her eyes were so pallid and empty when she looked at him. He wanted to talk to her but knew it would seem strange as he looked so much older, and didn't want to seem inappropriate.

He was very much surprised at the flow of his writing that night. Coming to Colorado was a perfect way to relax and get a lot of work accomplished. Again, another ten points for Debbie.

Sometime during the night, Marty briefly awakened and noticed the drapes were open and a chair that held his suitcase had been dragged from the den to the windows. He didn't remember doing that, but maybe the wine he had consumed clouded his memory. He got up, shut the drapes and lumbered off into the bathroom to urinate. He didn't think twice about this and blamed it on the alcohol.

Chapter 5

Marty slept like a baby and didn't wake up until after 10:00. He felt like he had been drugged. He couldn't remember ever sleeping that late in a long time, and it felt great to stretch out under the cool sheets. When he got out of bed, he noticed his room looked like a cyclone had gone off in it and thought he must have been looking for something during the night and the wine must have made it unable for him to find.

Room service brought a late breakfast, and he enthusiastically ate everything on the plate.

After a hot shower, he took a walk outside around the hotel grounds and checked out the different slopes available for skiing. Yesterday Marty had stayed on the beginner slopes until he got his sea legs back, but today thought he would brave one of the next toughest slopes and hope for the best.

The weather was a lot windier and colder than it had been the day before. Marty noticed it right away and had to button his coat all the way up past his neck. He had to remember to check the weather station to see if that storm was still on its way. He hoped it wouldn't interfere with his friends' arrival. He'd hate to be stuck here without them.

During Marty's walk back to the hotel, he heard something hit the ground just behind him, and as he turned around, he noticed a turkey vulture. It was staring at him with its wings spread wide as if it was trying to sneak up on him. The vulture didn't seem the slightest bit afraid of him, and for a moment Marty thought it was going to charge. Instead, it hopped into the air and flew off, never once breaking eye contact. Marty didn't know much about birds, but he was glad it took off. He had no idea they were so big. The wingspan had to be four or five feet wide at least. In Colorado, he knew people worried about bears or elk, but a bird was the last thing he felt he needed to worry about. Live and learn.

As he returned to the lobby, there was a crowd that had gathered in front of the flatscreen TV by the concierge desk. Evidently, the storm that was expected had turned into a full-blown blizzard with winds due to peak at forty miles per hour by the following evening, and snowfall expected over twenty-four inches. The kid in him thought this was going to be excellent, and the good thing was that his friends were due to arrive the following morning, so they should easily beat the storm by at least six or eight hours. He wasn't worried, yet.

Marty spoke with Shlaypo on the phone, and he, Chapman and Franky were able to get earlier flights that would put them at the hotel no later than 9:00 AM. He told Marty that Bonnie and Debbie had met up three days earlier in D.C. and decided to make it a road trip in Bonnie's SUV. Even if they got hotel rooms along the way, they should already be nearing the Colorado state line and just a few hours away. Marty was hoping they were aware of the approaching storm and were driving hard to beat it. He just prayed they had thought to bring emergency gear in case of a breakdown or worse.

Marty tried to call Debbie, but there was no answer. He knew cell reception in these mountains was hit or miss, and he told himself they were fine and knew he had to be patient.

Walking to his room, he saw a shadow hit the wall behind him. He slowly turned his head to say hello to whoever was there, but not a soul was anywhere in the hallway except Marty. Strange. He even smelled the pungent aroma of a perfume his mother used to wear long ago. He could never forget that fragrance. Like the shadow, it snuck up on Marty. It was by Avon and probably the cheapest scent ever sold to the masses, but popular as hell. He could even remember it came in a red bottle with a top that looked like a crown. His mother used to collect those damn little bottles – keeping them on her dresser like little trophies. Who in the hell would want to squirt that stuff on themselves these days? At any rate, it made for a nice memory.

That night Marty had a horrible nightmare. Debbie and Bonnie had slid off the road just after the Eisenhower Tunnel. It is an incredibly steep grade at that location and that road has been known for taking a lot of truckers over the years. In his dream, Bonnie spun out of control and couldn't recover the vehicle. It lost its path and hit the guardrail and flipped off the road into the forest. Within minutes the snow had covered the skid marks, and there was no evidence of the SUV. Marty's eyes opened as he imagined hearing the screams of his two friends, helpless and freezing with a blizzard on its way.

He couldn't shake it. Now he had begun to worry.

Marty jumped in the shower, hoping to calm his nerves and knowing there was no way he could get back to sleep. He stood in the comfortably hot water and tried to relax. Then, out of the corner of Marty's left eye he saw the shadow of a person walking past the bed and towards the den. He called out, thinking it may have been a maid or someone who came to gather his breakfast dishes, possibly unaware he was in the shower, and deciding instead to hurry out. There was no reply, and after he dried off and came out into the bedroom, he noticed the tray and dishes were still in the room. Marty immediately phoned the kitchen and was told that no one had come to clear his dishware.

It was at this moment Marty began to question his sanity. He was starting to count up the weird things he had noticed since arriving at the Copper Mountain Inn, and seriously started wishing he was a horror writer instead of a historical fiction writer. He officially couldn't wait for his friends to arrive as he now had begun to look over his shoulder wherever he went.

Marty grabbed his voice recorder and camera, which he took pride in knowing was better than his cell phone's camera and headed down to the lobby to hopefully get a few interviews with some of the hotel's personnel. People are usually very willing to be interviewed unless they have a reason not to talk. He figured a minimum wage employee would jump at the chance no matter what the company policy, especially if someone is willing to throw twenty bucks at them. As it turned out, he was right.

The hotel had a lot of history. The men who built it fought off Indian outbreaks as well as fires that were purposely set to slow down its construction. It seems a lot of people were killed, and the property itself was considered by some to be cursed as its completion was inevitable.

Marty also learned that as the hotel was being built, it was said that families of the workers were threatened and often maimed in cases, to the point where some of the construction workers refused to complete the jobs that they were hired for.

He realized this was not what he signed up for, and although he was excited to see his friends, he seriously thought of getting out of Dodge while he still could. Then, on the other hand, Marty thought this might also be an omen and his creative side urged him on to finish the new writing project that he didn't even realize he had started.

That night Marty slept with the bathroom light on and one foot on the floor. He knew he was walking on creepy, as the saying goes, but now his only thought was about Debbie and where she and Bonnie were. Marty wished she would answer her phone.

Chapter 6

Marty's feet hit the floor at the crack of dawn and went down to the lobby. It was empty of people at that hour, and Marty was alone.

He sat by the window and watched the sunrise spill onto the slopes, and it was one of the most beautiful and timely visions he would surely remember for years to come. The storm was on its way as the sunlight wavered through clouds of dark blue and grey. The wind was blowing through the trees in staggering gusts, and he had to catch his breath as he saw small animals running as if they were searching for safe hiding places to escape the coming storm.

It was now 9:00 AM and Marty found himself staring at the front entrance. Shlaypo, Chapman and Franky should be walking in anytime, and he was waiting for them as a father would wait - anticipate the birth of his child.

At 10:39 they walked into the hotel lounge. At that very moment, Marty was holding a mimosa in one hand, his laptop balanced on his legs, while he checked the weather on his cell phone with his free hand. He heard Chapman's voice holler "What the FUCK are you doing here?"

His cell hit the floor, the laptop almost hit the floor, but thankfully he was able to catch it, and with great regard, he managed to hold onto the mimosa, without so much as spilling a single drop. When he finally managed to stand up, and after a few choice words, they embraced in what must have looked like extreme emotional exhibitionism. They all cracked up and looked at one another in disbelief as they sat down together for the first time in twelve years.

They spoke nonstop for hours. They started in the lobby, then moved over to the lounge, then drifted over to the restaurant, and it was there that they addressed the fact that the storm was coming, and Debbie and Bonnie hadn't yet arrived.

They called Debbie's cell and she picked up on the third ring.

"Hey! What's happening! We are on the way! Who all is there?"

"We are all here – just waiting for you girls! Did you hear about the storm? Where are you?" Shlaypo asked.

"We know about the storm, and we are almost there. We passed the tunnels and should arrive within an hour or so. No worries - is the hotel nice? I hope I picked a good one!"

"Everything is great – just get here." Shlaypo said.

"10-4, we will get there soon! Sorry, we're a little behind schedule, we should have called you guys. Bonnie and I wanted to stop in Georgetown. We found a little diner and decided to get some food. That little town is so cool, we just had to check it out. If you guys are hungry, go ahead and eat. Don't wait for us – we're stuffed." Debbie said.

"That's fine. We're just in the lounge catchin' up." Shlaypo said.

There was talking in the background, then Debbie continued, "Hope nobody plans on going to bed too early because these two gals wanna party, and you boys are buying the drinks."

Shlaypo laughed. "We wouldn't have it any other way, so drive safe and get here before the snow does."

"Okay we will – it's already coming down here, but it's not too bad yet, and Bonnie's SUV has four-wheel drive. Besides, we drive a lot better than we did in high school! Can't wait to see you . . ."

At that point, the connection was abruptly lost.

Shlaypo hung up with a weird look in his eye. Chapman, Franky and Marty looked at one another and back at him again.

"What's happening? Why are you looking that way?" Franky asked.

"It was weird we were just disconnected. We were going to hang up anyway, but I think the call was lost. I'm sure it's all good – they are past the Roosevelt Tunnel and should arrive within an hour or so."

"Hell, let's get another round – I'm buyin!" Chapman said.

They looked out the windows and realized the snow had already started coming down at the hotel, too. It wasn't falling heavy yet, but they knew it was going to start dumping on them soon enough. Sunset wasn't far away, and they were all hoping the girls wouldn't have any unexpected problems on the road.

CHAPTER 7

D ebbie was fidgeting in her seat and looking down. Bonnie, who had taken over driving in Georgetown, asked her if she was alright.

"Oh, I'm fine. You know."

"No, I really don't. I know something is on your mind and has been ever since we hooked up back east. I just didn't want to pry." Bonnie said.

"You've always been such a good friend. How could we have let so much time go by without reconnecting? It's been so long, but I swear it feels like only weeks since we spoke last." Debbie said sincerely, looking at Bonnie.

"I know! Isn't it great? I guess it's true what they say, real friends stay close no matter how long they spend apart."

"I guess so." Debbie breathed out slowly.

"So, what's going on? Want me to pull over? Fuck the snow." Bonnie said.

"HaHa – NO! Please don't; another couple inches of this shit on the ground, and I may start getting nervous. The hills are too steep in these mountains, and this snow isn't going to stop anytime soon.

"True, dat." Bonnie said. "Now spill it, sistaah."

"Do you remember that guy in band that was always bugging me? He used to follow me around and try to get me to go out with him?"

"Do I? Oh my god, what was his name . . . give me a sec . . . Brad Wesley, right?"

"Yep."

"So, what about him? You can't tell me he's still following you around after all these years. I mean, that would make him officially psycho." Bonnie said.

"No, he's not. Well, he wasn't." Debbie breathed. "I don't know. Recently I was having my tires rotated and balanced on my truck, and while I was in the waiting room, I looked over and there he was, sitting in a chair right across from me, reading a magazine. His hair was longer, and he was a little heavier, but it was him."

"What did you do? Did you say anything to him?"

"No, are you kidding? I'm not a snob, and I totally would have said hello if he had been a normal guy in high school, and not a stalker for Christ's sake. But thankfully, he didn't notice me."

"So, what happened, Debbie?"

"Well, I sat there and turned sideways in my chair. I was on the end of the row, so it didn't seem strange. I got out my cell, looked down and let my hair slide over the side of my face. It all went fine until the counter guy hollered out my name when my truck was done. I got up and went to the register, but I could feel his eyes on me the moment the guy yelled my name."

"Did he try to talk to you or anything?" Bonnie asked.

"No. He didn't. But, ever since then, I can't help looking over my shoulder and feeling like he always knows where I am. I know I'm probably over-reacting but, when someone creeps you out once, you never forget it and you always wonder what they are capable of, ya know?"

"Yeah, I guess. Well, just stay cautious and keep your eyes open. I'm sure he's not gonna bother you anymore. I mean, it's been twelve years, right? We've all grown up; he's grown up, Besides, we are at Copper Mountain, and we're gonna do some fantastic skiing and reuniting with our best bros. Let's leave him in the past. I'm sure that is where he is anyway."

"Yes, we are. BonBon, I'm sorry I brought it up. I won't mention him again."

"No problem. You can tell me anything. If psycho dude shows up, it's six against one. Can you remember that?"

"Yep. I can." Debbie sighed with relief.

"Now let's roll. We got four handsome guys a few miles down the road, that are willing to buy us drinks. We shan't be late."

CHAPTER 8

An hour later, Bonnie and Debbie slowly rolled into the lobby parking area of the Copper Mountain Inn precisely on schedule. The old-world balconies hanging off the sides of the hotel were huge. Each one overlooked the breathtaking mountains that were covered with snow. The main entry of the resort held lots of old, rustic charm with its stunning trim work along its edges. Gargoyles sat on either side of the roof, protecting or conversely menacing all who entered, depending on the individual's point of view on such things. The valet took care of their luggage as well as tucking Bonnie's SUV into a safe spot for the night.

The snow hadn't made their drive too difficult, after all. By the time they arrived, there was only about five or six inches on the ground, which wasn't much for the SUV. Considering they were from Maryland, and plenty used to driving in the white stuff, the trip had been a good time had by both. The only annoyance was that some bitch in a Pathfinder kept following them way too close. When Bonnie pulled off onto the shoulder so that the girl could pass them, she would then slow down to a crawl, thus forcing Bonnie to go around her once again. Finally, the girl turned off, and they were rid of her, but what a way to start a vacation!

The girls checked in at the lobby, then quickly visited their rooms and were delighted to find they were as lovely as the website had advertised. Bonnie's room had plush sapphire blue carpeting with powder blue walls and white trim. It was stunning, and the off-white couch in the waiting room, along with the country-style white linens were beautiful. Debbie's room was comparable, except instead of blue, a deep garnet carpet greeted her with a room filled with beautiful tans and creamy hues of darker green. Her room was more rustic and old-fashioned. The rooms were so cozy and homey it was hard to believe they were in a hotel.

They both freshened up, changed their clothes and hurried downstairs to find the rest of their group. Both were so nervous and excited to finally be in Colorado that they had completely forgotten all about their hard day traveling. Neither was tired, however, they both knew that sleep would catch up with them tomorrow, but neither cared. They were going to enjoy every moment of this trip no matter what their bodies told them.

The two women stepped out of the elevator and found their way into the lounge. The guys were sitting in a booth, boisterously laughing and talking about old times. Franky spotted them first and immediately jabbed Marty in the ribs. The conversation came to a hush, and Franky waved his hands to let the girls know where they were sitting.

The large booth was against the immense windows, and with the colored spotlights outside on the ground already covered with snow, the illumination was magnificent. Fires roared in the fireplaces, and the lights flickered off the mounted elk, big horned sheep, and other animals that had fallen prey to mankind and were now adorning the walls in this magnificent space.

As the men stood, Bonnie and Debbie walked over to them, and everyone embraced each other, full of love and flashbacks of memories of special times with one another. They all had tears in their eyes, especially Debbie, as Marty held her in his arms. Neither wanted to let go of the other.

They laughed and reminisced until after 1:00 AM. They took many pictures that night, and no one would notice, not until much later, that in the background of many of their photographs was a person hunkered low in their seat in a corner booth. Someone who didn't want to be noticed. Someone who was discretely watching them.

They enthusiastically discussed all of the usual high school stuff. Who's doing what for a living, who lives where, who married who, and most importantly, who's been cheating on who.

Franky blatantly admitted, "I think the whole marriage thing is bullshit. I've never felt the need to walk that plank and most likely never will."

"Why would you say such a thing? Don't you believe in love?" Bonnie asked.

"Sure, I do – I do. But there's just too many variables."

"Variables? How do you mean, bud?" Shlaypo asked.

"Well, first off, people change. We are in our thirties right now. I don't know about you, but I am nowhere near the person I used to be when I was in my twenties. Everybody changes. The number of people who change in the same exact ways is extremely low. Hence, the divorce rate. It's appalling. Plus, people don't take marriage seriously like they did in the 40s and 50s."

"Oh paleez" Chapman chimed in, "The reason people married so young, and there were so few divorces back then was because there was no birth control. Plus, divorce laws were much stricter. Everyone knows that. If you wanted to get laid, you got married, and nobody got divorced because then you couldn't get laid. It was a vicious cycle – Waitress! Another round for my friends, and that guy is buying!" He pointed at Marty.

At that very moment the lights suddenly went out. The music stopped. If it hadn't been for the candles on the tables, they would have been in total darkness.

"I could get used to this." Debbie said happily and giggled.

The waitress quickly approached them. "I'm sure it was the storm, but don't worry, we have generators, and they should kick in pretty soon. We are used to power outages around here. Unfortunately, it's going to have to be cash from here on out unless you want to charge your room." She said. "Oh, and for safety's sake, you'll have to take the stairs when you return to your rooms. Sorry, but management doesn't want to risk anyone using the elevators while the generators are being used."

Due to the impending snowstorm, the hotel had a lot of cancellations, and even though it was their most popular season, the hotel was less than twenty percent booked.

They all had another round on Marty and decided to call it a night. The girls were whooped as they had been driving for the last two days with little sleep. The drinks had caught up with them, and Debbie had been leaning heavily on her right elbow with her hand holding her head up straight for the past half hour. Marty thought she looked more beautiful than ever.

No one noticed the waitress stop and put her tray, which was full of beers, down at the end of the bar to quickly tally up the bar tab. As she walked to the register, again, no one noticed the person who had been sitting at the booth walk over and drop something into one of the glasses and quickly sit back down again.

CHAPTER 9

They decided to meet for breakfast at 9:00 AM, and then they would hit the slopes. Hopefully, the storm would have stopped by then.

As they left the lounge, practically holding each other up, Marty held Debbie's left elbow, and along with Bonnie, made sure Debbie arrived back to her room safely. Everyone else trudged off in the direction of their own rooms. Marty was not sure if over the years his old friends had become pros at arriving home drunk, and out of their minds or if everyone was just hoping for the best. Figuring it was a short way to go, Debbie was top on Marty's list, and he wanted to make sure she and Bonnie got to their rooms in one piece.

Upon trying to open the door to enter Debbie's room, Marty realized it was blocked by a chair lying on the floor. He pushed and finally finding the light switch, the three of them entered the room. It was in a total state of disarray. He immediately notified the hotel staff, and within minutes two security employees arrived.

Security did what they could, which was basically nothing, and since no personal property had been stolen or destroyed, pictures were taken, and Debbie was told that the event would be noted, and the police notified. She was visibly shaken by the ordeal and decided she would sleep in Bonnie's room that night. Marty agreed, and without delay, Debbie grabbed a few toiletries and something to sleep in and together, they walked to Bonnie's room where they hunkered in. Debbie swiftly crashed onto the extra bed. The hotel offered another room, but Debbie didn't want to be alone, nor should she be.

The next morning, everyone met for breakfast. Everyone, that is, but Chapman. They waited for him, but finally decided he'd probably ignored the wake-up call and needed to sleep off his last few beers, so they went ahead and ate. Everyone was thankful that all of the utilities were up and running, and each of them was as hungry as ever. The buffet was excellent. They all enjoyed a large and hearty meal except for Debbie, who coveted her coffee and a small bowl of fruit. Her face was only slightly green, but she quickly acclimated herself for the new day.

After the meal, Franky went up to Chapman's room to check on him and see if he was going to join them on the slopes.

He banged on the door three times, and finally, the door slowly opened.

"Man, you must have tied one on – we just finished eating. We thought we should leave you alone to recuperate for a while. You look like shit, dude."

"I appreciate that. What time is it?" Chapman asked.

"It's almost eleven and we're getting ready to hit the slopes. Are you alive, or do you want to stay in bed for a while?"

"To tell you the truth, I've been sick as shit. I thought for a while I was going to have to call a doctor. I've got room service bringing up something carbonated for my stomach."

"Are you serious? You didn't drink any more than anyone else – "

"I know, and I was well within my limit. I've been up all night, puking. It comes in waves. I feel like I was poisoned. I gotta lay down." Chapman motioned to Franky to come inside as he turned and walked back to bed. "It's coming out of both ends if you catch my drift. I'm not in any shape to ski today. Will you tell everybody?"

"Sure, man. No problem. Do you want somebody to sit with you?"

"No way – I want y'all to have fun. I'll be up and running tonight, though, no worries." Chapman said as he rolled over and drew the covers up to his neck.

"Okay. I'll let you sleep. Do you need anything?"

"Nope. Just more sleep."

"Okay. Don't get up. I'll let myself out, you miserable bastard."

"Fuck you, Franky."

"Yeah man. I love you, too."

CHAPTER 10

As unpredictable as the weather always is in higher elevations during this time of year, the hotel staff was not surprised to see that another storm was on its way. This new one was expected in about fifteen hours, and it looked like it was going to be a doozy. Weather blows in fast in the Colorado mountains and when it comes, predicting its exact course is oftentimes impossible.

CHAPTER 11

On the slopes, the group was glad the storm hadn't yet arrived with its expected intensity and were happy so many people canceled their reservations. This had provided them with no lift lines and greater service. They had no idea a new storm front was on its way.

Skiing was exactly what the doctor ordered, and everyone had an excellent time. As it turned out, no one in their happy little assembly had been on the slopes since high school, so during the entire day, they basically fell all over each other laughing and piling up in mounds of arms and legs, often at various intervals throughout the ski route. Marty kept it to himself that he arrived early and was able to get his "ski legs" back and just enjoyed the reunion and the good times.

However, the big problem that Debbie hadn't been able to shake or share with the group was her "almost" encounter with the slimeball, Brad.

Debbie kept reliving the day at Big O' Tires. Brad had always been such a psycho, and his behavior used to bug the crap out of her, but it had never really scared her until then. She couldn't help but think about him, and even though they didn't actually speak that day, maybe he had noticed her after all, and had begun following her around again. She kept telling herself that after so many years had gone by, Brad surely had to have outgrown his infatuation with her. By now he had probably found a wife, and maybe even had kids. Surely, he wouldn't still be the same old creepster that practically terrorized her so long ago. Would he?

She had been blowing off these thoughts for days, but now that her room and privacy had been invaded, maybe she should tell the others. Perhaps she should bring it all out in the open. After all, if it was Brad, it would be unfair for her not to tell everyone. After thinking about it, Debbie decided to let them know. Besides, she knew it would make her feel better to get it off her chest.

CHAPTER 12

That night Chapman never showed up for dinner. Franky told everyone that Chapman was really hungover and just needed to sleep. When he didn't show up that night, no one wanted to bother him. They'd all been there and knew what it was to feel like shit. So, they thought it was best to leave him alone and let him sleep it off.

Bonnie told everybody that she had slipped a note under his door just before she came downstairs to meet them for dinner. She said she knocked first, but he didn't reply. She didn't want to bother him by knocking again, so she left the note.

After they ate and moved over into the lounge, Debbie spilled the beans about Brad. No one seemed overly concerned, except Marty.

"I don't like it. I don't like it at all." He said. "That guy was a whack job, right?"

"Yeah, he was but that was over ten years ago. He's bound to have outgrown that shit by now." Shlaypo said.

"I don't think whack jobs ever outgrow being whack jobs. But I doubt it was him who broke into Debbie's room. For one thing, how would he even know she was here? Besides stalkers are just a pain in the ass – they don't break into people's hotel rooms, right?" Bonnie said.

"I don't know. Maybe they don't, but maybe they do." Franky said. "Who the fuck knows. Where's the waitress?"

"Who knows?" Debbie asked. "Do you think we should go check on Chapman? It's been all day – he's had plenty of time to sleep it off. I say let's all go up there and see how he is. Then we can come back down here. What do y'all say?"

"I'm in. Let's go." Marty agreed.

They paid the bill and started towards Chapman's room.

When they got there, they knocked on the door, but Chapman didn't answer. They called the front desk and had them ring the room. Still no answer. Finally, Mr. Hundley, the hotel manager, met them at Chapman's room after a brief conversation regarding the recent issues and fears for Chapman's safety.

Mr. Hundley knocked and waited. Then knocked again and loudly said "This is the hotel manager. Is anyone in there? If so, please respond immediately, or I will be opening the door." Again, there was no response.

CHAPTER 13

Marty stood behind him and watched as he slowly turned the master key and carefully pushed the door open. It was very dark inside, and as they entered; Debbie was the first to notice the faint odor of alcohol. Not the type of alcohol you drink but rubbing alcohol. The deeper they went into the room, the more intensely they all smelled it.

The manager flipped the light switch, but nothing happened. As they walked deeper into the room, the motion sensor in the bathroom kicked on and illuminated the area with enough light to enable them to see that the place was a mess. It looked like someone had gone through it with a chainsaw. A good portion of the furniture had been destroyed, and it was amazing that no one had tripped over the debris on the floor. Chapman lay on the bed with his hands and feet tied to the bedposts. The next sound they heard was a heavy thud as Debbie passed out and fell onto the floor.

After many hours of intense investigation, an emergency vehicle came, and the first responders unceremoniously loaded Chapman's sheet covered corpse onto a gurney. They wheeled him out in an eerily silent exit from the resort and into the coroner's wagon; then they departed the resort. The police also interviewed numerous other hotel patrons. None of which were helpful in the investigation of Chapman's death. Unfortunately for them, the one person who could have offered information chose to remain in the woods from a safe distance for most of that night. A distance that luckily for this individual, was far, yet not so far away that they could not keep good visibility on what was going on. It also helped that they had acquired online a very expensive night vision scope specifically intended for this particular night.

The room was taped off as the skies remained dark and heavy with clouds filled with impending snow.

CHAPTER 14

As everyone met in Marty's room later that night, discussing what they should do next, no one wanted to leave the resort. No one wanted to leave Colorado. The bond they had always felt with one another since high school continued to tie them together. Each was determined to stay and take care of the others, and each one of them knew they couldn't find out what had happened to their friend if they were to leave for home.

Chapter 15

The next morning, they awoke and met in the restaurant. No one was particularly hungry, and as they picked at their food, words of conversation were hard to find. Under the circumstances, talking didn't seem needed, and it felt good just to have the fellowship of one another as they thought about Chapman and his death.

Marty could see Debbie tearing up and quickly moved closer to her. He put his arm around her as she melted into him and began sobbing. He held her close and rocked her in his arms. Her warm breath on his neck made him feel much needed, and he once again realized how heartbroken they all were.

"What's happening?" Debbie asked. "Do you think this is all my fault? What if – well, you know."

"Hey quit that." Shlaypo said. "First of all, if it were Brad Wesley, one of us would have run into him by now in the halls or someplace, right? This hotel is big, but it sure isn't that big. Plus, there just isn't anywhere to hide."

"He's right. I don't think it's him either. But maybe we should go down to see if anyone by that name has checked in. It can't hurt." Franky said.

"I think that's a good idea," said Bonnie.

"Me, too, but he'd be nuts to register in his own name. I wouldn't." Marty added.

Suddenly there was a loud crash in the kitchen that sounded like someone had dropped an enormous tray of dishes. It was perfect timing because they all stared at each other and began laughing. It was exactly the break they needed to feel, at least, a little normal again – even if it was only temporary.

"I guess whoever did that won't be working here much longer!" Shlaypo said. "Hey – if you can't pay your bill and have to wash dishes to pay the tab, I wonder what management expects you to do if you work in the kitchen and drop a bunch of people's meals?"

"That's fucked up, Shlaypo. You're a dick!" Franky said.

Bonnie added, "What's fucked up is that you are thirty-two years old, and you're laughing at some sad mistake a poor employee made who's here just trying to feed his family."

Marty said quietly, "I'm just glad we didn't order dessert."

With that, Debbie broke her stare out the window and began smiling in amusement as she slowly shook her head. The way she looked into Marty's eyes told everyone how much she cared for him. The moment was very touching for Marty, and it would have been for everyone else, too, if they hadn't been thinking about Chapman.

Chapter 16

At that moment, a man of great height walked into the restaurant and began speaking to the waitress, who was busily adding up their check. With her head tilted upward as if studying the heavy oak beams high above her head, she slightly turned and pointed in the group's direction. Soon the man arrived at their table.

He introduced himself as Detective Fairbanks with the Copper Hill Police Department and asked if they had a few minutes to speak with him.

Shlaypo held out a hand toward an empty chair and asked him to have a seat. Tension suddenly filled the air as each of them waited to hear what the detective had to say.

"Would you like something to drink – coffee, maybe?" Marty asked.

"No, thanks. I'm good." He replied as he pulled the chair out and made himself comfortable at the table.

Fairbanks began by offering his sincere condolences for the loss of their friend. He further stated that test results had proven that Chapman had been poisoned by an "undetermined" drug, and although this drug didn't kill him, it could have made it possible for the killer to have the upper hand in the execution of Chapman's murder. He said their lab would soon know exactly what they were up against. They knew it wasn't a street drug and could only speculate at this point what it was and where it came from.

As they looked at one another, Debbie spoke first. She told the detective all about Brad Wesley. She was honest when she said she didn't think he was really capable of being that evil. But she also admitted that she couldn't know for sure.

They decided being together was the safest for all of them. Separating at this point would only make it easier for the murderer to pick each of them off one by one. If, in fact, they were all on the murderer's agenda. Going home wasn't an option, and everyone felt safer knowing they were together.

Marty suggested they should all stay at the hotel another week, and everyone agreed. Their employers would have to understand. If they didn't, it was worth the risk of losing their jobs versus losing each other.

They spoke generally about Chapman and his murder. Fairbanks asked questions, but no one could offer any substantial information that would help with the investigation. It had been so many years since they had any contact with him, and no one could comment much on his life or those he shared it with. Although each wished they could offer help, it was evident to Fairbanks that they could not.

After giving each of them his business card, the detective left, requesting that if any of them needed him for any reason, or thought of anything that may help the investigation, to contact him immediately. They all agreed.

As the waitress brought them their check, she apologized for the noise in the kitchen earlier and hoped it hadn't disturbed their conversation.

"The new girl we hired a couple of days ago, sort of lost it. She didn't have much experience when we hired her, but these days good help is hard to find, and she really needed the job. I think she'll do well but she needs a little practice." The waitress said.

"No worries. Everyone needs to start somewhere, and it's good she's giving it a go. We'll add a little extra tip to give her some encouragement. Tell her to keep her head up." Bonnie said.

"Thanks. I'll let her know what you said, I know it will make her feel better, and thanks for understanding." The waitress collected the payment and was off towards the register, never skipping a beat.

CHAPTER 17

The rest of their breakfast consisted of reminiscent conversations, mainly including Chapman and the old days. So many fond recollections of youth and Chapman brought pangs of sadness to their hearts. However, soon the topics turned to Detective Fairbanks and back to ill feelings and how they were going to deal with the recent turn of events.

They decided their number one priority should be Brad Wesley. They knew the Detective would be following up on him as well, but also knew that time was short, and they couldn't just sit and wait to hear back from Fairbanks. They would start a little investigating on their own.

Early afternoon back in her room, Bonnie ran an internet search and found out Brad was still living in their hometown of Potomac, Maryland. She found his address, close relative's information and for fifty bucks, she also got his police record. She was amazed at how easily one could obtain so much knowledge about someone just by googling their name. It actually kind of freaked her out. This whole thing was getting creepier and creepier as her search continued.

Bonnie discovered an article in the Washington Post about how someone had purposefully waited outside his place of employment one night, and as he was leaving for home after working late, plowed into him as he was getting into his vehicle. He was pinned between his car and the offending vehicle. The driver backed up and hit him a second time before speeding off down the street. Luckily for Brad, his door was open, and although he was mashed between both cars when the driver backed up to have another go, Brad was pushed inside. He had been at Suburban Hospital in Bethesda ever since and was still in critical condition. The investigation was continuing, and people were being interviewed, but as of yet, there were no suspects listed in the article.

They met in the lounge to decide their next move later that afternoon. The atmosphere was troubling, and there wasn't much activity at the hotel. They supposed with all the drama some of the hotel's valued customers had left for greener pastures.

Bonnie shared the information about Brad Wesley, and everyone was speechless.

Now they were back at zero. So, who else would have killed their friend and would now be trying to harm them?

CHAPTER 18

The person hunkering in the booth that first night, silently observing the group, and trying to be unseen, was now sitting in another booth, deep in thought. Happy at the sadness and terror they'd inflicted on that bitch, Debbie and her little group. How dare those little goodie-goodies all have the perfect lives and gather back together after all these years despite the shit they've done to others? The destruction of others' lives and dreams that they've caused? The sad part was that they hadn't a clue. They were all so self-absorbed. That's why they were going to get what they deserved. The plan was set. There was no turning back now.

CHAPTER 19

It was still early as they each left for their rooms, Debbie destined for a power nap and Marty wanting to chill for a couple of hours to try and catch up on a bit of writing. Marty walked Debbie to her room. He almost asked her if he could come in, and she almost asked if he wanted to, but neither spoke. Instead, they held each other and looked into each other's eyes and kissed. Debbie thought that one, single kiss was perfect. What was the old cliché? Good things come to those who wait. She was betting on it.

The gang would meet back up around 8:00 or so for drinks. Hopefully, everyone would be refreshed and have some new thoughts.

Franky and Bonnie decided to run into town for some odds and ends from the CVS and local grocery. Bonnie also needed a new phone charger, so they would try to find a nearby Verizon store. Truth be told, they mainly wanted to get the hell out of there and breathe a little normal air for a change. Neither had signed up for all this drama, and they wanted a break. The icing on the cake was that the weather stations were predicting yet another storm front coming in, and it was due to hit any time. No one had been keeping up on the weather or anything else of any importance. Instead, each of them was immersed in their own sad little world - mostly dealing with Chapman's death on their private terms. Franky and Bonnie would be back within an hour. No harm, no foul.

They flipped to see who would drive, and although Franky won the toss, Bonnie suggested they take her SUV since it had four-wheel drive. As Franky shut the passenger door and was already fiddling with the GPS on his phone, Bonnie mentioned something about how they should probably go ahead and leave the hotel or at least switch hotels just to give them a little peace of mind. It was then she turned the key, and the fire was so brilliant and intense the last thing they saw before they died was the look on each other's faces and the sound of their screams.

CHAPTER 20

Detective Fairbanks had been up all night, devoting all the time he could to determining what exactly had happened regarding Chapman's death and was only minutes from arriving back at the hotel when he heard the explosion in the parking lot.

CHAPTER 21

Debbie pressed her earbuds firmly into her ears and closed her eyes when LeAnn Rimes' beautiful voice began singing "How Do I Live". The music filled her head, along with the help of the hotel room's vodka. She only wanted to drift into sleep and forget everything bad that had happened during the last forty-eight hours. She thought of Marty and his sweet smile. She felt selfish that after the harm that had befallen Chapman, she had the audacity to think such good things about Marty. Before she knew it, she was unable to think of anything else and seemed to drift into a state she had never found herself in before. Debbie was not afraid, she was not asleep, and she certainly wasn't dead – not yet. There was a knock on her door, and she barely heard it.

Chapter 22

Detective Fairbanks found himself, once again, in chaos at the Copper Mountain Inn. He immediately read the tags of the flaming SUV to the station dispatcher. It came back Bonnie Grant of New Melborn, Connecticut. All he could do was sigh as he lit a cigarette and stood in the densely falling snow. The second body was identified as Frank Hazelton of Memphis, Tennessee. Fairbanks knew they had a killer on their hands. It wasn't rocket science.

Chapter 23

Shlaypo, Marty, and Detective Fairbanks entered the lounge. Anywhere alcohol was served always proved to be the first choice in meeting locations these days, and some things never change no matter how old you get. The view never got old. They discussed how to break the news to Debbie. Since she and Bonnie had reconnected, their friendship was on an all-time high, and they each knew Bonnie's death would hit her extremely hard. Marty had told them she had gone to bed and knew she wouldn't have heard the commotion outside. Her room was in the back of the hotel, and the extra distance assured them that she was still unaware of the incident.

The hotel's new waitress had come around to take their orders, and it was apparent that she still hadn't quite caught on to the whole waitress "thing" yet. Everyone was patient, however, as she did her best. They would tip her well and be as forgiving as possible. Besides, no one was particularly hungry. How could they be? Luckily the hotel wasn't busy, so they didn't feel guilty about using the table space for their discussion. They ordered drinks and minimal food, with only Detective Fairbanks ordering coffee.

She took the order into the kitchen, then returned to a nearby table and began to wipe it clean. Although she wasn't a very good waitress, she sure was trying hard, Marty had to give her that. Eavesdropping never occurred to them.

Detective Fairbanks told them about Brad Wesley and his unfortunate accident and hospital stay, which they already knew from Bonnie's recent internet search. What they didn't know, however, was that not only did Brad Wesley have a horrific accident, but he had also been scheduled to be married two weeks before. It seems he'd canceled the wedding without much explanation to the bride, and she was now the main suspect in his murder attempt.

"Does anyone have any idea why he canceled the wedding? Marty asked.

At this question, Detective Fairbanks put down his coffee and looked at both of them. He said, "The only explanation that Wesley gave was that someone came back into his life, and he knew that marriage wasn't the right avenue for him at this point in time. There is one more thing." Fairbanks said. "Wesley died four days ago when someone cut his oxygen line in the ICU. I'd like to gather you two and Debbie and move you to another location. It seems if the EX has, in fact, lost it – I'd like to get you all out of here as quickly as we can. There is no telling where she is, and I don't want to take any chances."

"Okay, let's get out of here. I'll go upstairs and get Debbie and meet you in the lobby in what, half an hour? How does that sound? It's gonna take her a few minutes to get her shit together." Marty said.

They heard a loud crash that sounded like dishes falling in the kitchen. Probably that poor waitress, Shlaypo mused to himself. "Some people need to know when it's time to quit and get a new career."

Detective Fairbanks looked at him not understanding the sentiment but smiling just the same.

When the waitress didn't bring the check out, Marty asked one of the busboys to get her. A few moments later, another waitress came over and politely gave them their bill. She asked Marty and the Detective to kindly review it to make sure it was correct. She told them the hotel had been having issues with the server who had been waiting on them, and it seems she'd had to leave the restaurant quickly. She leaned a little closer to the table and said she had been having personal problems and couldn't quite get a handle on things.

"Poor dear." The waitress added. "She was left practically standing at the altar a little while back. Good riddance, I say. Bastard didn't even tell her proper. Anyway, sorry for the drama."

The three men looked at one another.

"You don't think . . .?" Shlaypo whispered. "It couldn't be her – could it?"

"I don't know, but I'm not waiting around to find out."

Detective Fairbanks looked at her and stood up. "Where is your manager, please?"

"He's over there," pointing to the bar, "the guy in the red shirt. Is everything alright?"

"I'm not quite sure yet" Fairbanks said as he wiped his mouth with a napkin and walked to the bar.

Marty threw his share of the bill on the table and stood up. "I'm going to get Debbie. I'll meet you in the lobby in a few. Things are rapidly falling apart around here, and we need to get out of this hotel."

"I'm right behind you," Shlaypo said.

CHAPTER 24

Shlaypo left the dining room and hurried along the corridor to the elevators. He made a quick stop at the lobby desk and told them they would be checking out in the next few minutes and to get their paperwork ready.

Although he was moving fast, it seemed as if he were walking in cement shoes, and his feet weren't moving as quickly as his mind was.

He punched the fancy green up arrow and stood waiting for the elevator to arrive.

Shlaypo's heart was beating furiously, and he had to lean against the wall. He knew he was upset, and with all the recent turn of events that had taken place, he had every right to be shaken up. All he wanted was to be out of that hotel and back home with the memories of this place far behind him.

Moments later, the elevator arrived, and he practically fell into it.

His head was spinning, and the last thing he remembered before he hit the elevator floor was grabbing for the floor selection button. He managed to hit one of them, not sure which one, but didn't care. Shlaypo blacked out just as the doors began to slowly close, and the new waitress glided in.

Chapter 25

Most of the guests, who weren't many, had checked out of the hotel and were headed for other destinations. It was early in the week and between the inclement weather, the klutzy waitress, the guy who was found dead in his room, and now the explosion, most decided the fun was over at the Copper Mountain Inn.

Marty wasted no time and, within minutes, was knocking on Debbie's door. Once he knew she was safe, he would help her gather her things and together, they would go to his room and collect his stuff. No way he was going to leave her again. Not even for a second.

At first, he thought she wasn't going to answer, but soon he heard footsteps slowly making their way towards the door.

"Who is it?" Debbie asked.

Marty could faintly hear her breathing and knew she had her face pressed to the door, trying to look through the little peephole.

"It's me – you need to open the door, Debbie. We need to talk."

"Okie-dokie-hokie-pokie" She sounded very drunk and began laughing. As she turned the knob and pulled back the door, her smile went wide as soon as she saw Marty.

"Hey, baby – I was just thinkin about you! Come on in! I swear I only had one of these things, and I feel like I did when we went to that Bad Company concert in high school! Remember that night? Oh, my GAAWD! Didn't somebody wreck their parent's car that night? Hey, who was drivin' anyway? Do you remember? Man, I'd like to see them again, wouldn't you?"

Marty entered the room, quickly closed the door and locked it.

"You said you only had one? Had one of what Debbie?"

"I'm not sure what you call it, but that nice waitress brought it by a little while ago. I told her I didn't order any room service, but she said she wanted to apologize for her lousy waitressing the other day. Wasn't that sweet of her? She brought some candy, too. Want some?"

"No darlin', not right now. Tell you what, we're gonna call Fairbanks and head down to the lobby, okay? Can you help me a little bit? Maybe sit right there and talk to me a little. Where's your suitcase?"

She pointed a finger at the closet door.

Marty quickly opened the door, pulled it out and threw it on the bed. Then he reached for his cell phone and rifled through his pockets until he withdrew Detective Fairbank's business card.

Fairbanks answered on the first ring, and a minute later, he was at Debbie's hotel room. Marty had just finished shoving all of Debbie's clothes and toiletries into the suitcase and clicked it shut.

Marty let him in at once.

"An ambulance is on its way, and if Debbie can, maybe we should get her to the lobby as quickly as we can. Every second may count." Fairbanks said in a powerful, authoritative voice.

"What the heck are you guys talking about? Marty, where are we going? I don't need an ambulance – You both need to lighten up a little bit!" Debbie's voice started to drop in tone, and her speech became noticeably slower with every sentence.

"Marty, I'm feeling pretty tired all of a sudden. Will you hold me for a minute until I fall asleep. I'm so glad you're here . . . oh Marty. Promise me you won't leave . . . me . . . again."

Ten minutes later, an ambulance pulled into the front entrance, and Marty got in the back to ride with Debbie. He held her hand all the way to the hospital.

Detective Fairbanks, along with other police, searched for Shlaypo. Marty had told Fairbanks that he and Debbie were supposed to meet him in the lobby in minutes, and that was almost an hour ago now. Marty couldn't imagine why he hadn't shown up and thought something must have happened. They both feared the worse.

CHAPTER 26

The new waitress was Veronica-Ann "Ronnie" Bruce. If everything had gone according to plan, she would now have been Mrs. Brad Wesley and would be sitting on a fancy lawn chair in the Cayman Islands having the time of her life with her new husband. But, unfortunately, her plans hadn't turned out quite the way she had hoped.

Brad had arrived at Ronnie's house one night only a couple of weeks before the wedding, which was also the night after he ran into – well, almost ran into, Debbie at the tire shop. He had told Ronnie that as soon as he saw Debbie, he had immediately and hopelessly fallen back in love with her. Brad said it was then he realized he knew he had always loved her, and was sorry he had never mentioned her before. Brad repeated how sorry he was and that he hoped she could forgive him.

No matter what Ronnie said or how much she cried, Brad didn't change his mind. He only looked down at his feet and finally turned and walked away. He refused to take her calls or talk to her again. She had been dumped at the altar like a bad joke, and she wasn't happy about it.

Ronnie had attended the same high school as Debbie and Brad. She graduated two years after they did and still spoke with lots of the same old friends. She was also on classmates.com, so she received a lot of the same notifications and posts. To Ronnie's surprise, she saw Debbie's notice about the reunion at Copper Mountain. Without a moment's hesitation, she had decided to crash the party and began preparing almost at once.

She was quite pleased with herself as she realized how easy this would all be. She would have her revenge with them, just as she had with Brad. Easy-peasy.

CHAPTER 27

Two hours later, the police found Shlaypo's body in the basement of the hotel under old Christmas decorations and other seasonal items. He had been gutted with his intestines wrapped around his neck, hands and feet like some kind of sick, Halloween-style, calf-roping prank at a rodeo event.

Luckily for him, the drug that Ronnie slipped in his drink during lunch was in an amount that was almost immediately lethal. Shlaypo never knew what hit him, and that was a good thing because next to his body, they found a very dull envelope opener that was bloodied and bent.

Later at the hospital, Marty and Fairbanks sat in a waiting room discussing poor Shlaypo's recent demise and the steps that were currently being taken to catch Ronnie before she could harm anyone else. Marty knew without question that the "any-one else" was he and Debbie.

Debbie was in and out of consciousness for two days, and the Drs said she was very fortunate to have lived through the ordeal. Finally, on the afternoon of the third day, she opened her eyes and slowly smiled when she saw Marty sitting next to her bed, holding her hand. She said she felt pretty good, just sleepy, and the Dr. said that was normal. He said they wanted to keep her overnight just to make sure she was completely out of the woods, and that was fine with her.

The next day Marty told her about what had happened. They both cried tears of sadness until they could not weep any-more. Marty never left her side for a moment, and he held her tightly as she slept.

When the nurse was wheeling Debbie out of the hospital and as Marty helped her into the rental car, he mentioned that he had made her flight arrangements. He held both of her hands in his and told her there was a slight change in plans. She looked up confused, and he asked her if she would mind an extreme-ly lengthy stay in Los Angeles. She smiled, kissed him long and slowly and as they looked into each other's eyes, she said she wouldn't mind one bit.

Chapter 28

Ronnie seemed to have disappeared. The police couldn't find her anywhere. The manhunt was fierce and spread throughout Colorado, Wyoming, Kansas, and New Mexico. Within two weeks, it was on the national wire, and her picture was on the nightly news for weeks. She had done the impossible by slipping through many fingers without a trace. It was as if she never existed at all. How she accomplished this was anyone's guess.

Six months after Debbie and Marty were married, they took a little trip to the Caribbean. First to Antiqua, then to St. Barts, then lastly to the Cayman Islands. It was a belated honeymoon as the demands of Marty's new book were too great, and he couldn't get away for an extended getaway at the time they tied the knot. Debbie didn't mind at all and was just happy to have him finally in her life for as long as the good Lord would allow it. She felt blessed, and so did he.

They made quite a few friends while they were traveling and knew they would be back often. In fact, they were already making plans to return to Grand Cayman.

The pool bar's backup bartender who was on vacation during their stay, happened to come in to pick up her paycheck and was very surprised to see Marty and Debbie in the lobby. It had been a long time, but she immediately knew who they were.

Debbie had been digging for something in her purse when Ronnie walked right past her. Debbie looked up and saw the pretty figure of a girl walking away and towards the manager's office. For some weird reason, a chill seemed to settle in her lower back, but it disappeared entirely as Marty came up behind her and put his arms around her.

No one ever saw the wicked eyes or the evil smile on the young woman's face as she kept walking.

ALLISON'S EYES

CHAPTER 1

Graham Coughlin had stared out his bedroom window for about seventeen years. The town folk thought he was crazy, but his family and loved ones knew better. His life had been destroyed by the very thing that made him once so happy and proud.

This particular window faced the eastern side of the river and had a perfect view of the Old House. He was now living in what used to be his parents' house and the Old House was his and Janel's first home, which had been vacant since the disappearance of his daughter and the murders of almost his entire family.

This small town has always been a happy one. The only tragedy most anyone remembers, other than the one at the Old House, was when they found four neighborhood dogs drowned and floating in Jeff Teeter's algae covered pond in 1946. Poor dogs. The dog's owner swore up and down that it was ole Jeff Teeter who'd drowned them and left them in his pond as a result of his numerous calls to the local police that the dogs barked all night, and no one could get a moment's sleep, and nothing had been done about it since the owner proved the dogs weren't outside at night. It turned out it was a jealous woman whom the dog's owner used to date and dumped a few months before. Nothin' like a woman scorned, they say. Sad, but true.

Graham had been sixteen years old then, and he and Janel met at the last summer barn dance before school resumed in August of the same year. That had been in '47, the year of the big blow. The strongest hurricane the East Coast had felt in over fifty years, so they said.

As soon as Graham looked into Janel's dark green eyes, he knew she was all he was ever going to want out of life, and she him. It wasn't that she was beautiful, with her long legs and dark auburn hair that cascaded down her back and brushed gracefully across the roundness of her bottom as she walked. In fact, he hadn't noticed those things at all, not at first. It was the honesty and innocent aura she had about her. Her soft voice and piercing eyes simply mesmerized him.

When she looked at Graham, he couldn't think straight. He lost all poise and strength and seemed to become a different person. No girl had ever done that to him before and he knew no other girl ever could.

He had dreams of college and leaving town. Going someplace warm; some place where he could maybe have a farm and be near the water. A few hundred acres and some cattle. To him that would have been a life in heaven. But, as he learned very quickly, any kind of life with Janel would have been heaven.

His family was fully supportive of him; they always had been. They loved him very much and he had been a very good student. His parents were proud at the way he was growing into a trustworthy and hardworking young man. He even had the approval of the town seniors and the church.

Earlier that year, he earned the award of the Key, which was a large wooden key the pastor would give out to one lucky teenager every year. It went to the most promising teenager that showed aptitude and desire of becoming a reverend. Along with the big wooden key, the award entrusted him with privileges of co-pastoring during certain church services and helping plan and oversee fieldtrips and such. It was considered an honor by the other young adults, and he accepted it with pride and gratitude.

Graham and Janel danced and stared into each other's eyes almost the entire first night. They were inseparable every day thereafter.

At that point in time, the Old House was the quarters where the farm hands lived. Those who took care of the daily chores that went along with all the aspects of a working farm back in the day.

Farm hands came and went, don'tcha know. Mostly travelin' people or people runnin' from something or other. The Coughlin's always hired the best of the lot, though. Only trustworthy, honest folks worked at the Coughlin's farm. Still, not many ever stayed much longer than a season or two. Silvia and John Newton stayed the longest. A darky family out of Charleston heading north with two youngins' in tow. They worked the farm for about five years and only left when Silvia caught her man beddin' down with the fertilizer salesman's wife. That surely gave everyone something to talk about. Small towns have their share of gossip just like big towns, maybe more.

But that was a long time ago and Graham was old now. People thought he had lost his marbles back when he was still relatively young. But the truth is, he had always known exactly where his marbles where—he just had priorities. Priorities that were very important.

CHAPTER 2

As the years, or should I be honest and say months, went by, it was evident by the "glow" in Janel's eyes that she and Graham found themselves in the family way, so to speak, which back in 1947, wasn't a good position to be in at all if you were young and unmarried. If you didn't have family or money to get you out of that tough spot, your goose was cooked in the community, and respect, especially for the girl, was gone forever.

Graham's parents decided to build another house for the farm hands, and due to the closeness of the existing house, they allowed Graham and his soon-to-be wife to move into what is now referred to as the Old House. It was just the right thing to do.

Soon it was the day of their wedding, which took place by the river on the farm. It was a beautiful sunny day with just the right amount of breeze as to not mess up the decorations or, heaven forbid, the bridal party's hair, and the whole town was invited. Things couldn't have gone off any better.

Back in the day, the Old House was remarkably comfortable for a farm's hand to reside in. Now that the owner's son and new wife were living in it, updates and additions were made that would make anyone feel honored to live there. All in all, Graham and Janel were very lucky to be able to live in such a beautiful and well-maintained home, and they knew it and were thankful.

Although Graham's life's plans and aspirations had changed for the time being, he always felt happy, and being with Janel and starting a family was the best blessing he could ever had imagined or hoped for. He was determined to be the best father and husband he could be.

Janel was also happy and in love, and although very young, they both had a strong determination to be together forever. With Graham's parents to help them get started, they knew they had good things ahead of them.

Chapter 3

Unfortunately, Janel's family was not quite as well off as Graham's was during this time. Her family was from the "other side of the tracks", which was the expression for those who lived in what was referred to as "Poor Town".

Janel was one of six children born to Jeb Albright and Nina Kamfer. Times were tough back then, especially with six children to feed and clothe, but Jeb did the best he could for as long as he could.

You see, he worked odd jobs, and on one occasion he was working a plow in a corn field when the horse was spooked by a snake and reared back and fell on Jeb, trapping his leg between it and the plow. As the horse panicked and struggled to get on its feet, poor Jeb was caught underneath the weight and suffered numerous injuries.

He walked with a horrible limp after that incident and the doctors commented on how amazed they were that he was even able to walk at all. They said they had never seen a man's pelvis shattered in such a way and he was very lucky he wasn't paralyzed.

It took Jeb close to a year before he was out and about, and he used a cane from that day forward. Some of the town's older citizens swore that Jeb made a deal with the Devil when he realized he couldn't properly provide for his family any longer.

He wasn't a man to accept charity and it was said that over time, Jeb was seen hitting the town's only bar, the Dust Bucket, over on McDermott Street every now and again. The Dust Bucket was the perfect name for the place because it really wasn't much fancier than most people's barns. It was the local watering hole where the men folk used to visit mostly on payday. Local boys played music there on the weekends and it was a favorite of people passing through town for a quick drink and maybe a burger. Food wasn't their finest point of interest, the bourbon was, and where Jeb got the money to drink with was anybody's guess. But if any man needed an excuse to down a couple of shots every now and then, Jeb did.

One day, he lucked into some money, evidently a good amount of it. My guess was that a family member must have passed and left Jeb a pretty hefty inheritance. But, like I said, it was just my guess. How else could he have lucked into that kind of dough? Exactly how much dough, no one really ever knew, but it sure was enough to get the family caught up on things. He was even able to get a new car and pay off the mortgage he took on that dump of a house he owned and fix it up real nice, too. Yeah, it was good to see how his luck finally changed. It was just too bad all that money didn't change his drinking habit much.

Shortly after the money rolled in, Jeb began frequenting the Dust Bucket more often than he should have. Every now and then turned into every night and sometimes afternoons, too.

He was oftentimes seen falling-down drunk and weeping for God to forgive him. Something about a trade with the Devil and he wished he could take it back. He didn't make sense when he was in such a state of mind, but everyone knew he just wasn't the same man as he was before his accident.

When Janel and Graham were married and Jeb saw how happy his daughter was, and that things were both prosperous and joyful for the newlyweds, it was as if he became a new man.

He suddenly stopped his drinking and seemed to have mentally overcome whatever it was that had been destroying him for so many years. It was as if he finally cheated his way back to the good graces of the church. A man finally unchained and free again.

Some people commented that after so long, God must have finally forgiven Jeb for whatever it was he must have done—whatever deal he made must have turned around.

God surely works in strange ways. Can anyone say Hallelujah!

CHAPTER 4

Finally, the blessed day arrived, and their baby greeted the world with hardly any drama. They called her Allison Marie, and she was born healthy and a full eight pounds and two ounces. She didn't even cry when the doctor swatted her bottom at birth. She only seemed to grin a little and looked at them with what seemed to be hungry eyes.

The baby was born in a room full of excited grandparents waiting to greet her. Her skin had no blemishes, like most babies almost always have. It was smooth and pink and absolutely perfect. Her feet were long and perfectly formed and all ten fingers and toes were accounted for as well.

The only oddity the baby seemed to have at her birth was that her eyes were very dark. Allison's eyes were so dark there wasn't even a hint of color in the iris. In fact, you could barely see where the dark pupil met the irises at all, and the whites in her eyes were practically nonexistent. The family was concerned that the baby was blind, but as the days went by all the doctors agreed, baby Allison's vision was perfectly normal.

As she grew, it became apparent that her vision was better than normal, in fact she seemed to be able to see in the dark better than anyone else could. As the years went by, friends joked, saying little Allison could find a needle in a haystack if she had to, in no time flat.

They brought Allison home three days later to a room freshly painted with beautiful violet walls and white trim. The floor was a dark hard wood and the windows had wooden blinds that were well built and could be adjusted to let in bright morning sun light, as well as keeping the room dark for easy sleeping.

The nursery furniture was white and there were wall hangings of Daffy Duck and baby cartoon characters in frames on all the walls. The crib was beautifully engraved with tiny cherubs who seemed to look down over the baby and to protect and watch over her. Graham's mother had procured a wood carver from Annapolis, Maryland, which was the next town over, to create these special cherubs as a surprise for Janel, because everyone knew Janel loved cherubs. They spared no expense.

The room turned out perfect in every way. Little Allison was already on her way to being the most spoiled baby in town.

The first few weeks of Allison's life were very joyful for everyone. People came to visit, and everyone cooed over her as if she were the first baby they had ever seen. Some commented on how big and beautiful her eyes were, while others never mentioned them at all.

But it was impossible not to notice those black, saucer-sized eyes that seemed to cut right through you when she looked your way. In fact, some people could not even look at her for fear those eyes would find them and never let them go.

Her eyes were beyond stunning, and to some people those eyes were so intensely creepy, they felt when she looked at you a bird could fall dead from the sky and the phantoms that flew by night could drop dead.

It wasn't long before friends and visitors stopped dropping by for visits entirely, and as the baby grew up, Janel and Graham had difficulty having guests over for the smallest of parties or celebrations. It was as though the very atmosphere in a room would change when Allison entered, and if she stayed for longer than a few minutes, some people became nauseous and had to quickly leave their home.

CHAPTER 5

Graham knew that Allison was different. He knew she made people uncomfortable, and on one occasion, a woman who was standing next to them in line at the grocery store had to run out of the store and vomit on the sidewalk. There was no way she could make it to the rear of the store where the public facilities were located. She barely made it outside. A fat man with a long, tangled beard and white tennis shoes happened to be standing nearby, saw the woman failing and leaning to the point of no return. He grabbed her and helped her to the closest exit.

Graham told himself that she had probably been ill with the flu, but he knew in his heart that somehow it had been Allison.

This type of thing seemed to happen more and more regularly as Allison grew older. It seemed she had that effect on people wherever they went. These people were not frail or especially feeble in any way, but normal, healthy people who simply succumbed to Allison's energy. Allison's dark and petrifying energy.

Janel was in complete denial. She loved her daughter and was determined to do right by her, and even mentioned that she wanted to conceive another child as soon as possible.

Janel's father seemed to relapse back to the bottle whenever he visited their home. Nina had confided in Graham that her husband would drink to the point of passing out and mumble about how he thought the debt had been paid and why did the Devil hurt innocent children. His mutterings never made any sense to her, but then neither did his drinking.

Graham loved Janel, and also wanted another child. Surely, these horrible feelings concerning Allison must be over dramatized and in his own mind. His whole family came together so fast and was so unplanned, yet . . . they loved each other, and he knew he would do anything to make Janel happy. Having another baby would be wonderful and loving her made his life complete.

Love and new life were always a blessing. They were young and he knew in his heart that he and Janel were going to have many wonderful blessings coming their way.

Chapter 6

One day when Allison was about four years old, Max, the Collie Graham had grown up with since childhood, was killed as he lay in the driveway. Runover by a tractor. Ole Max was getting up in years and his hearing had been getting worse. By the time of Max's accident, his hearing was gone altogether, and he just didn't hear the tractor coming. Graham felt awful, but at least he was relieved that it was quick.

In the following weeks they had brought home a Great Pyrenes puppy for Allison. Her first dog! How excited Graham and Janel were. The breed was known for being good livestock guardians and they thought it would fit in perfectly on the farm. The breed's temperament was perfect for a family pet, as well.

When Graham came home that night and introduced the puppy to Allison, she looked at it and made no attempt to hug or show any kind of affection at all to the puppy. It was as if the dog held no cuteness or kinship at all to her. The dog also did not move toward her in any way.

Janel's kind words of enthusiasm and passion towards the puppy did not seem to bring a response from Allison, and she did not seem to be happy in any way about her parent's gift and receiving her new companion. In fact, the puppy backed up and quickly leaped into Janel's waiting arms as if it were terrified. No words were spoken, and the dog stayed in the main house with Graham's parents after that.

Allison looked at the puppy as if it was a threat, as if she was telling the dog that it was the enemy and had to go. If looks could kill, that puppy would have been dead in an instant. That poor puppy must have sensed it and ran away to the only solace it could find. It went as far away as it could.

There had never been talk of buying another animal and Janel had only looked at Graham with sadness in her eyes. He knew what she was thinking. He was thinking the same thing— all children love animals.

CHAPTER 7

The following months were a whirlwind. They welcomed their son, Elijah Dean, whom they nicknamed "Eli", who came on board a month premature, but healthy and vibrant with all the gusto and exuberance a little boy could bring!

He had bright blue eyes and the most beautiful blond hair that seemed to pale three shades lighter when the sunlight hit it.

Graham and Janel had never been happier.

Allison proved to be the perfect older sister, always wanting to help Mom with changing the dirty diapers and feeding her new brother when he needed feeding.

Graham and Janel thought the baby was the perfect answer to their prayers. Maybe the new addition to their family was the exact thing Allison needed to help her with the socialization and communicative skills she seemed to lack.

Graham and Janel never knew when they would leave the nursery, Allison would quietly go back in and stare at the baby. She would touch his face and run her fingers around his neck, and she especially enjoyed gently pushing the soft spot in the top portion of her brother's head. Allison sometimes thought to herself it seemed she could push her thumb so far into that little soft spot her fingertip would almost disappear.

Chapter 8

School started the following year and Allison was in kindergarten. She would walk out to the end of the lane every morning and get on the school bus and return home, never having happy stories about her day and never asking if she could bring a friend over to play. When Janel would ask her if she had made any friends at school, Allison would always reply that she didn't need any friends and she was happiest alone.

They both had been worried about Allison for quite some time, and as she was now getting older, the worry they felt was quickly amounting to fear. It just wasn't healthy for a child to not want any friends.

As Graham laid in bed that night, he had many thoughts dancing in his head. Odd thoughts, but the first one he had was actually a memory. A memory of his Collie, Max. Max who never left his side while he was growing up and who would wait at the door until he returned home from school.

He remembered how Max never came to the house once Allison was born. Not once did he recall Max ever coming close to the Old House. Max was his best friend, and over hell and high water that dog was always there for him. Why did he stop coming to see him?

CHAPTER 9

Allison was amazed that her baby brother was already a year old! Still so small and weak, she thought, still so helpless. In fact, him being so helpless was the best part about him. He couldn't run from her or tattle on her when she would pinch his toes or stick the sewing needle deep in the bottom of his feet.

Her latest rave was inserting the baby aspirator down deep into his nose and quickly squeezing the bulb closed over and over again. Watching his eyes bulge outward and hearing him choke and gag was the funniest thing ever!

Chapter 10

As Allison entered grade school, she seemed to have stopped getting taller. She was always comparable to other children her age in height and upon entering the first grade, her growth slowed down to a point that the other children all shot up past her. Within months, she was the shortest girl in her class.

As time passed, Allison went from having no friends at all, to no one willing to even sit at the same table for lunch with her or walk next to her in the hallways. Even the teachers would avoid contact with her. She gave everyone around her a bone chilling, lost, and undeniably sick feeling whenever they were around her.

Family members, neighbors, and even people whom she had met from church kept their distance as if they never knew her at all.

There were no more invitations to family reunions. There were no more birthday party invitations from kids in the neighborhood.

If Janel and Graham decided to attend a town Barn Dance or spend the day at the local carnival, they would feel a coldness from everyone. Glaring eyes and accusing attitudes. Hateful jeers. Hiring a babysitter for her was impossible.

They were no longer welcome at Sunday church services. No longer were they included in any event or potluck. No words were spoken, it was just the way it was.

At the end of worship services one winter day, as Janel, Graham, and Allison walked up to thank Pastor Joe Gavin for his fine sermon and powerful message, Pastor Joe became suddenly ill as he turned to speak with them and vomited. It would have gone all over Graham if he hadn't been quick enough to jump back out of the path of the spewing bile. Pastor Joe could not take his eyes off Allison. It was as if when their eyes met, she held him against his will. He began to shake and sweat beaded up on his cheeks and forehead.

His lips slowly parted, and he softly started moaning. It was so quiet that Graham thought no one had noticed, but the sound Pastor Joe emitted quickly grew until it became more of a whimpering, high-pitched cry. It was at that moment they noticed a puddle forming at his feet. In addition to vomiting, he had uncontrollably urinated.

When Janel looked at Allison, she had a daunting, amused smile on her face that gave her and Graham both bone shattering chills.

That was the last Sunday Graham and his family ever attended the New Hope Baptist Church.

Chapter 11

Allison, who had always been kind to her family in the past, although incredibly distant, was now growing colder and more and more agitated with each passing day.

Her eyes seemed to be getting darker and rounder, and whenever she spoke, it was with growing evil intent that made a normal family life completely impossible. She had even started hurting bugs and eating flies as if they were candy.

One day, soon after their worship services had been abruptly cancelled at the New Hope Baptist Church, Janel found Allison in the back field with a baby goat. She had a shovel, and thank God Janel was there to stop the attack. Who knew what Allison would have been capable of doing to that poor kid had she not interceded at that perfect moment?

Graham and Janel had to stop leaving Eli unattended even for a moment whenever Allison was nearby. They started noticing bruise marks on various parts of his body and the boy had begun going into crying fits whenever Allison was close to him. It was evident the boy had been suffering at the hands of his sister. When they confronted Allison about the bruises, she only laughed in the most sinister way.

They spoke with counselors and clergymen about the situation with Allison and how things had gotten so out of control, they just didn't know which direction to turn to next. No one had been able to offer any help or words of advice.

It was during this timeframe Jeb refused to visit their home and had almost completely regressed into the sad, drunken character the town used to know those few years ago.

Graham decided the only thing they could do was to take Allison to the State Hospital for some thorough tests and psychological examinations. Maybe the doctors in Baltimore would be able to help her, but it was obvious no one in town was able to come to their rescue, and the situation grew worse as each day went by. The decision was made to take Allison that Monday morning.

CHAPTER 12

O n Sunday afternoon, they had decided to go to town for a shopping spree. Mostly to get away from the house for a while as tensions were building and they thought it would be a nice idea to treat Allison to a nice buffet lunch at her favorite restaurant before the big drive to the hospital the next morning.

After a few miles, Graham noticed that Eli had begun choking. His car seat was in the center of the backseat, with Allison sitting behind the driver's seat. He immediately pulled the car over in order to help him.

Eli had turned blue and could not breathe.

Janel's eyes widened with fear as she realized what was happening to her son. Without hesitating she darted out of the front passenger seat, flew open the back door and grabbed him attempting to clear his throat.

Graham put the car in park, jumped out and opened Allison's door. She jumped out so her dad could climb in and help her mother with Eli.

While they tended to their son, Allison had closed the rear doors of the car and climbed into the front seat to watch the show with a sick, yet amusing sneer.

In the drama of trying to save Eli, no one had noticed that Allison turned on the safety door lock feature which kept kids from accidently opening the doors when the car was moving.

Before either of her parents realized what was happening, the car suddenly jerked forward at an outrageous speed and drove itself right off the shoulder and down the highway embankment.

Alison had leaped from the car and stood along the road watching as the vehicle rolled three times and landed upside down in a retention pond.

After the initial surge of speed, Graham later recollected the rear wheels losing traction as they slid off the gravel shoulder and caught in the moist dirt, which seemed to pull the car sideways and down the embankment. As the car's rear end slid down the hill, the front right wheel must have hit a big rock or something to cause the car to start rolling. It was like slow motion.

He remembered hearing Janel scream at him to help hold on to the baby. Those were the last words he ever heard her say.

Since the windows were down and no one was buckled up, Eli was the first to fly out of the car, then Janel followed him. The car was upside down when it stopped rolling and submerged in about three feet of water. Janel never stood a chance to swim clear as her right leg was caught between the roof and the bottom of the pond.

By the time Eli landed in the water and quickly sunk to the bottom, he was already dead. It took rescue services over an hour to locate his body. His face had gone from blue to a pasty, dark grey, and his eyes seemed to be almost as big as plates.

No one ever knew Alison placed a large rock on the gas pedal. If they noticed the rock inside the vehicle at all, it was assumed it got inside the car from rolling through the weeds and muck.

During the autopsy, the doctors at the hospital found a candy bar wrapper in Eli's throat, which had caused him to choke. The doctors commented in their report that it wasn't just in his mouth but jammed way down deep. Too deep for the child to have accidentally choked on it. It was jammed down into his throat as if someone inserted it on purpose.

Graham escaped drowning, but he had multiple internal injuries, as well as a fractured tibia, four broken ribs, a broken arm, and facial lacerations. He woke up two weeks later in intensive care calling Janel's name.

The first thing he asked was where was his daughter, Allison.

CHAPTER 13

The series of events following the accident were about as unbelievable and tragic as anyone had ever heard.

Allison was taken to Janel's parents' home. Nina was very excited to have her granddaughter and took on the responsibility without hesitation. After losing their precious Janel in the accident, she felt it would be wonderful to have Allison come stay with them. Jeb, however, was silent but knew it was his responsibility. In fact, he knew he was responsible for all of this.

Neither Graham nor Janel had mentioned to anyone about their plans to take Allison to the State Hospital. It was no one's business, and until the doctors could examine her and determine exactly what her behavioral disorder was, no one needed to know. It was family business. They certainly had no way of knowing Janel would be dead soon and Graham would be unable to convey any kind of plans like this to anyone. Allison should not have been allowed to live in a normal environment at all, let alone go to her grandparents' house without them knowing her situation. Oh, why had they agreed to keep Allison's instability so hush hush?

There was a house fire during the second week of Allison's stay with Jeb and Nina. Authorities said it started in the kitchen when a dish cloth was left too close to the burners on the gas stove. Somehow it ignited, and within minutes, the fire had grown out of control.

Jeb and Nina both died in their beds, along with Janel's two youngest siblings, who were still minors and living at home.

It had happened so fast that no one could have done anything to stop it. The house was old; there were lots of papers and books lying about, and on top of everything, the laundry room was right next to the kitchen where cans of lighter fluid and cleaning supplies exploded like bombs when the fire hit them.

The only one lucky enough to make it out of the house that night alive was Allison. She didn't even have a scratch on her.

Allison was taken back home to Graham's family, whom upon hearing of all the recent tragedies, also welcomed Allison into their home.

Quickly they noticed Allison's queer attitude and evil intentions. They knew she had always been a strange child, one who enjoyed her privacy, and remembered how she didn't interact with them much at all over the years. But since the last time they saw Allison, they were amazed at how much she had changed. They feared her and began questioning the fire and the car accident. After so many red flags were being waved, it didn't take long for them to realize Allison needed professional help.

After discussing her questionable personality traits with the hospital's social worker and explaining the series of events that had unfolded, it was advised they bring her to have immediate psychological tests done. She was relocated to Stormhaven Psychiatric Institute in Upper Marlboro, Maryland, which specialized in treating young adults and children with mental disorders.

CHAPTER 14

As Graham began his rehabilitation process, he was relieved to learn Allison was being taken care of and was at last in an appropriate environment to best care for her needs.

He grieved Janel and Eli deeply and tried to heal as best he could. He missed them and knew it would be a long road. But right now, he needed to concentrate on Allison.

He had many conferences and meetings with doctors over the next two years. It was determined that Allison would never be let out of Stormhaven. She was simply too dangerous and a threat to society. They determined it was Allison who caused the car accident which killed her mother, and murdered her brother, as well as the house fire that ended her grandparents' and cousins' lives. There was no way she would be let out and her next placement, upon turning eighteen years of age, would be Pinehurst Home for the Criminally Insane, located in Baltimore, Maryland.

Graham couldn't help but dwell on the memory of his little girl, the memories of a daughter he once tucked into bed every night and loved so much and would have done anything to protect. He finally realized she was gone forever. She had turned into a monster.

The last thing Allison said to Graham, that made any sense, was that she would come back for him and the rest of her family. She told him she would get even with him for allowing her to be put in the institute and she was just beginning to grow.

He thought she was crazy and didn't take it seriously. After all, she belonged to the system now and her days of returning home were over, most likely forever.

Chapter 15

I t had been twelve years, and Allison was ready to be transferred to Pinehurst. Had it been so many years since Graham
had lost his family? He couldn't remember. He didn't really
want to remember.

He visited Allison often in the beginning, but as the years
went by, he knew it didn't matter. She only stared at him with
contempt and showed no enthusiasm or happiness to see him
anymore. He did not know who she was, if he ever did, and she
had turned into pure evil. She only wanted to hurt others and
destroy things.

The stories the doctors and nurses told him were horrific.
She now needed to be strapped into bed at night, and during
the day she had to be cuffed and forced to wear a face mask to
prevent her from biting others. She loved to bite.

The morning of her transfer was as any other morning. The
routine hadn't changed, and she was awakened by 7:00, led to
the bathroom, bathed, and taken to the dining area for breakfast.
She was strapped, of course, and fed by hand. No chances were
ever given to her to feed herself as she could not be trusted not to
stab someone with an eating utensil. She never attempted to hurt
herself, only others, and she was good at it.

After breakfast she was led to her room to gather her things.
She didn't care about belongings. She didn't have a use for them.
All she wanted was to see blood and pain. They were the only
things that made her smile.

The transport vehicle arrived promptly at 11:00. She was
discharged, and with two guards at each side, they walked her to
the van. The men were told not to look her in the eyes. Her eyes
were very suggestive and even the strongest and most seasoned of

officers were swayed by her gaze. First, you lost your coordination, then your concentration, and before you knew it, you were in a bad situation you couldn't control. The joke on her block was that she could make you do anything if you looked at her long enough.

Two guards were in the back of the van with her and the other two took turns observing her through the window between the cab and the back cell. The driver was armed, and once the doors were closed, they could not be opened until they arrived at their destination.

At eighteen years old, Allison had surely grown into a lovely young woman. Although still very small and childlike, Allison had the ability to be whatever she needed to be and the men transporting her were amazed at her beauty. She looked at them and did not drop her eyes. She began talking softly, erotically. Not in a rude or disgusting manner, but in a luring and innocent way.

The men in back had fallen prey to those eyes and she was now in control. She knew it and liked it. She didn't try to harm them. She didn't need to even speak.

When the guard in front looked through the window, he, too, fell under her ominous spell. She trapped him like a fly stuck in a drop of buttermilk. He was hers. After all, she was magic now.

Just before the truck rolled onto the property of Pinehurst, it abruptly stopped. The driver was told by the guard in the window that something was wrong.

The driver got out and reached for the back doors, which he shouldn't have done, but there was a cage that was locked and even if the back doors were opened, the vehicle was still secure and no one inside the cage could get out.

The instant he opened the doors, Allison threw open the cage door. She leaped toward him and thrusted her face onto the man's neck and instantly began chewing on the soft flesh of his throat. He was down in five seconds and the other men hauled him into the truck. The man in the window got into the driver's seat, started the van, and drove out of town.

Chapter 16

Graham heard the news almost at once.

When the phone rang, he was asked to come to the Institute immediately. He was told there had been some updates in the transport of Allison to Pinehurst and he needed to be made aware of them. His gut heaved and he knew something must have gone incredibly wrong.

After being told of her escape, he knew he had to prepare himself and his family for Allison's return to the farm. He didn't know when it would happen and he couldn't foresee the extent of her revenge, but he knew she was going to come back. Eventually she would come home.

He prepared his family as well as he could.

Graham's parents loved him very much and although sympathetic to all he had been through and fully aware of Allison's vengeful agenda, they were older now and their life plan was to leave the farm to Graham and head to warmer climates and sit on a beach. They were determined not to let intimidation alter their plans for retirement and threaten their senior years happiness.

Graham's parents had invested well and planned for retirement in a manner that would have made anyone proud. Unfortunately, they didn't expect Graham to have become so preoccupied with what they considered to be an unnecessary worry. Years had passed. If Allison wanted to come home, she would have arrived by now.

Graham's parents moved to Florida and started a new life. They hired a general manager to work the farm while they were gone, knowing Graham could no longer handle the demands of tending to it properly.

The general manager, Nap Burley, did a great job and earned every penny, while Graham waited for Allison's return.

As the years went by, and the farm flourished, thanks to the help of Nap, Graham progressively became more and more despondent. He could no longer maintain any structure in his life as he waited endlessly for his daughter's return. Slowly, he grew old, and his strength left him. His only resolve came through both drink and lack of mental clarity, as far as the township was concerned. Graham resigned himself to the upstairs window of his parents' home watching and waiting.

After a few years, Graham's parents hired a live-in nurse to keep an eye on their son and make sure he was eating properly and taking care of himself. He stopped keeping in touch with them, and it was cheaper for him to stay at home rather than a nursing home or an adult care facility.

Although Graham did have mental clarity, at least for the most part, the town was compelled to keep their distance from him, and as long as there was no trouble, they were content to let Graham remain on the farm with only the supervision of the hired nurse.

Since Allison left, there had been no reason for alarm or further action from the authorities.

Chapter 17

It happened one night, shortly after midnight. The moon had been so full and bright Graham could see the corn blowing in the breeze as he stared out his window. He watched each individual leaf flutter, and the moon was so high there were no shadows from the tall oaks that served as the perimeter of the field separating the corn from the Border Leicester sheep who called the farm their home.

Adjacent to the sheep pasture there was the river that ran through the farm, and many times, the local kayak enthusiasts would be seen paddling past as they enjoyed the swift currents and winding trails the river offered.

This particular night, as Graham looked across the water, he thought he saw a slender figure of a child standing at the water line looking up at his window. The same location where he and Janel took their vows as man and wife so many years before. At first, he thought it was a couple of kids about to do a little skinny dipping, but as he continued to observe, he realized it was a female and she was alone. Even though he was somewhat far away, he could see that her eyes were enormous. He was positive it was Allison.

As she stood, looking up at his window—at him—he saw two other figures emerge from the corn and walk through the clearing to join her. Moments later, the three turned into four, then eight. All persons had her build, her short height, and large black eyes that stared at him without the slightest blink or wisp of personality. Soon, a crowd of identical girls that looked like children stood together and began to hold hands.

Graham had never been so afraid in his life. What was going on? How could this have ever been his daughter, whom he had loved and given every wholesome and moral value in his heart to? What horrible, sadistic entity had she become, and why?

He had often heard stories about black-eyed children. Most often they were talked about in ghost stories told on camping trips in front of roaring fires while marshmallows were being strung on long twigs found on the forest floor, to be roasted and happily eaten by hungry youngsters as they listened in fear to the stories.

Graham's heart stopped.

Some people completely believe in ghosts and the paranormal. Some people believe in aliens and Big Foot. Black-eyed children never crossed his mind, but why couldn't they exist, too?

He noticed, as he was mulling over these thoughts, the small crowd of "children" were coming toward the house. As they followed the river, they continued to walk, but as they got to the water's edge it was as though they walked right over it without sinking at all. He thought he was going out of his mind. This couldn't be real!

As they walked, he noticed their lips didn't move, and even though they knew he had spotted them, the children did not walk any faster or hurry in any way. It was as if they knew they were indestructible.

Graham knew Allison had the ability to sway people's consciousness if anyone looked into her eyes. Maybe this was the gift they all shared and used to enter the minds of their victims to do their magic.

Black-eyed children were always known for knocking on doors and requesting entry into homes. It's been said that anyone who ever encounters a black-eyed child wants to help, in fact feels compelled to, because, after all, they are children. But at the same time feels an immediate and impending fear for their lives. The gruesome and heavy feeling of doom is so overpowering the only cure is to lock them out. An invitation would surely be a death sentence.

As he continued to watch Allison's approach, Graham suddenly remembered years earlier in a solemn state of serious drunkenness when Jeb had approached him. Jeb said he needed to tell him a story that utterly changed his life and would no doubt change his as well. Jeb was shaking and distraught to a point of almost panic. He began by saying his story was about how a fallen man had a gun to his own head one night in a bar parking lot and found himself on his knees pleading to God for an alternative to his troubles instead of the bullet he was about to eat. He told Graham that a traveler in black wearing dusty wingtip shoes appeared in front of him. He held a bottle of whiskey in one hand and an envelope with red writing inscribed just below the flap on the back in the other. Jeb told him he thought the writing was in blood and it said, Last Chance. Jeb didn't think it was a man at all, but something from beyond the grave—something that had no business in this world.

The man looked as if he hadn't cleaned himself in a long time and the lines on his tanned face were deep and long. Jeb said he knew he was evil, but even so, he couldn't look away. The man was captivating and haunting. Deep in Jeb's bones, he knew the man wanted his soul. He offered him the envelope and promised Jeb that if he opened it, he would have money, a new home, and his family would be able to live comfortably for many years to come. He only had to promise one soul to him in return. The man then looked deep into Jeb's eyes and told him he had until sunrise to choose the intended soul. If he didn't then the man would choose for himself.

All Jeb wanted out of life was for his family to have what they needed. He had just had the accident in the field and his recovery was very slow. He clearly couldn't support his family. His life was falling apart around him. After great thought, Jeb agreed.

He took the envelope and the man disappeared. Jeb began to cry. As he looked down, he opened the envelope and read its contents, which was a contract written in an old language in blood, but Jeb knew what it said. A tear rolled down his cheek and fell upon the page. In an instant the envelope and its contents vanished. At that very moment he knew his fate was sealed.

As Jeb returned to the bar contemplating whose soul to pick, and halfway thinking he was just drunk and imagined the whole thing, his evening turned into more drinks than he could count, and he eventually passed out. Two of the waiters carried Jeb to his car to sleep it off.

Upon waking Jeb realized he never chose the soul and the sun had already breached the horizon. He wondered if it was all a bad dream, but that very next day was when the money started rolling in. What had he done?

Jeb begged Graham's forgiveness because he knew the man had made his own choice. He had chosen his first grandchild. He chose Allison.

Why did Graham think of this story? For god's sake it must have been true.

Although Graham was scared and physically sick at knowing Allison had returned, he also had a sense of peace. It was as though fate was finally going to end the nightmare.

So many wasted nights and tortured thoughts of the future would finally end.

Graham prayed for mercy from whatever God would listen, and met his fate with dignity as he watched the black-eyed children walk into the yard towards the front door.

Chapter 18

The nurse found Graham dead on the morning of March 9, 2007.

His throat was cut and there was a message pinned to his forehead by a thumb tack that read, "Dad, now I have many friends."

FOREST CREATURES

CHAPTER 1

Pour me another drink and I'll tell ya anything you wanna hear," the obese man said at the end of the bar with an inebriated smile. Obviously, he was at his limit and beginning to make a spectacle of himself. The other patrons nearby slowly started fidgeting in their seats, and one by one inched away from him. Soon, they would ask for their checks and leave to find another bar without a sloppy drunk intruding in their space and ruining their good time.

The bartender was not about to let that happen. Not on his watch. He had five more payments on his F250 and had already called the bank twice to beg forgiveness on late payments and try to arrange an extension on the loan. It was 2008 and times were tough, especially in Prescott Valley, Arizona, formally and proudly known as Jackass Flats, Arizona.

The name Jackass Flats, was chosen due to the wild burros that used to run through the town and flourish. In recent decades, the town's population had grown incredibly and the powers that be had decided Jackass Flats was not a name that would attract most people. It was all about politics. What would this world be like without politics? Prescott Valley, once a blossoming little pocket in the high desert countryside, was just a little stop before Prescott on the one lane dirt road. Now, the burros are gone, and the old times have faded into the past. Out of sight, out of mind. That's the way this forever changing world is.

It was a busy night at the local tavern and tips were good. The bartender was on top of his game, and for a Friday night, which was the best night of the week for making money, he was in no mood to deal with some obnoxious guy on the verge of scaring off paying customers, no matter how good his credit had been in the past.

The obese man was named Ralph McClendon. He worked as a Juvenile Detention Officer over in Cottonwood, which was a short drive from Prescott Valley over I-17. Ralph was unfortunately a better drunk than he was a detention officer. He was a kind soul and bore a resemblance to Baby Huey in the old cartoons back in the 50s. You know, the super big kid with the diapers, whom everyone made fun of?

Ralph never meant any harm to anyone and was unfortunately about as gullible as the Democrats are these days. He'd had his fair share of tragic events in his life, which wore him down, and he was a super nice guy who had to deal with hard patches in life with basically few people to talk to. This can make for an intolerable drunk. At the very least, a lonely and bitter drunk. You couldn't help but feel bad for the guy either way you sliced it.

"Hey dude, I think it's about time to hit the road. You're starting to freak out my customers," the bartender said. "Would you like me to call you a cab?"

"Naah man—I'll walk it. The last time you called me a cab it took forever, and I could have walked home and back before the guy showed up."

"10-4, I hear ya. Have a good night then. Finish your drink and be safe." The bartender was a nice guy and had mastered the art of kicking people out of his establishment without offending them. Some still left substantial tips as they were nicely shooed out the door.

CHAPTER 2

Along Ralph's walk home, which began uneventful and certainly typical in the residential area he lived in, he noticed the usual nightly happenings. People taking their dogs out for nappy-time wee wees and the big screen T.V.'s that glowed from every picture window were very comforting to him. He found himself thinking how lucky he was to live in a place where people were still half-way normal.

Ralph had always kept up on watching the nightly news and was aware of how things have been changing in recent years. It scared him very much.

Sometimes he wondered if the world ever changed to the point when someone would initiate another Civil War, how would he manage? How would he live and prosper if he was barely prospering now? Some things were best to not dwell on and he left those thoughts on the back burner tonight.

Ralph arrived home at about 11:00 PM and immediately threw a pizza in the oven. Those frozen jobs from Pizza Wizz, down the street were amazing. Pizza was always a good choice no matter what time of day, especially after you added a little more sauce from a can and some fresh mozzarella. A good drunk could always grate a little cheese before bedtime with minimal knuckle scrapes. A little cooked ham from the lunch meat container was always a nice addition as well. The frozen pie was just step one. The real home run was the added toppings you could find in the fridge. Nope. You just couldn't go wrong with a midnight pizza.

Ralph decided it was time to turn in as soon as he finished the last slice. It was later than he thought, and it had been a hard day. He was also pissed off because those boxes the pizzas were packaged in were always a lot bigger than the pizzas actually were.

How could those companies sell pizzas not represented correctly? What a rip off, he thought. "Just a smart way to sell them at a higher cost. It was all about marketing." He mumbled to himself as he flicked off the kitchen light and stumbled to the bedroom wishing there was just one more slice.

He was asleep before his head hit the pillow. Thank God he didn't have to work the next day.

About an hour later, Ralph was awakened by the sound of the screen door banging shut. Had he forgotten to close it?

He got up slowly, careful not to jam his foot into the dresser that was too close to the foot of the bed. God knows he'd tripped into that thing more times than he could count. It was a wonder his toes weren't crooked.

He rounded the dresser and walked down the hallway, passing the spare room that served as his gym, a room he entered as infrequently as possible these days. Beyond was the only bathroom in the house, and onward into the living room. His home was very small and modest, but all he needed.

He caught an overpowering odor of something organic. It smelled like someone's dirty hot tub or an old, rotting tree wafting in from the front porch. A candle was burning on the small table just to the right of the front door. He didn't remember lighting a candle.

"Who's there?" he asked in a tired voice, and he hesitantly walked outside.

There was no sign of anyone. He knew he hadn't imagined that awful odor, but he thought perhaps the wind had blown just right and it could have been from a neighbor's yard, or even someone walking past the house with some bad take-out. After checking around the porch, he decided to go back to bed without thinking twice. His buzz was turning into a hangover and sleep was all he wanted.

Once again, sleep enclosed him quickly, and he didn't wake until the next morning.

During the night, he hadn't dreamed, but upon waking, he noticed it must have rained when he'd gone outside to check the porch. Dirty footprints stretched across the floor from the front door to the hallway into his room.

Ralph grabbed a dirty hand towel in the pile of laundry to be washed, moistened it, and threw it on the floor. With his foot he wiped up the marks as best he could and jumped into the shower.

Had he been a little more sober and alert, Ralph would have noticed that the marks on the floor did not go all the way to his bed, and they didn't look like footprints at all.

CHAPTER 3

Ralph had a nice day off. He hit the grocery store and drove into Prescott to visit a friend, whom he hadn't seen for a couple weeks. They had gone to grade school together and had always kept in touch. Ralph didn't make friends easily, and Kevin Andrews was the only person in this world who stood by him when times were tough, and in Ralph's life, he always had more tough times than easy ones.

They regularly got together to shoot pool and hit the bars on Whiskey Row in Prescott, which was a favorite of both tourists and hometown folks alike.

Kevin was the quiet type. Very handsome and very humble. You couldn't help but like him and although the women always tried to gain his favor, no one ever really won it. He was a quiet man with many secrets. Ralph was always there for him and to-gether they lived their lives in peace.

Neither Kevin nor Ralph were homosexuals. Their lives were fulfilled, or so they thought, just being individuals and living day-to-day trying to make ends meet doing the best they could, which seemed to be what everyone else on the planet was trying to do. The fact that both men were alcoholics and teetering on the edge of sanity wasn't a point of notice that either of them perceived.

What no one knew, and what they no longer ever talked about between themselves, was what had happened on the full moon of October 14, 1989. It was as if that night was forgotten.

It was a blessed thing because neither of them wanted to remember.

Ralph and Kevin had borrowed Kevin's parents' old Ford Tradesman Van. They were driving to a Blues concert at an out-door amphitheater in Flagstaff. They had waited all summer for that show and tickets weren't cheap. B.B. King, John Lee Hooker, and Willie Dixson were on the bill. Talk about an excellent line-up. They scrounged the cash and bought four tickets.

Kevin had a fight with his girlfriend the night before the concert, which ended badly. Needless to say, she didn't go along, and Ralph's date had come down with a high fever and sore throat at the last minute. It all ended on a happy note because they sold the extra two tickets in the parking lot and got double what they had paid for them.

After the concert, they headed back home through Oak Creek Canyon in Sedona, testing their driving skills after they both drank more booze than they should have. It didn't help that Oak Creek had plenty of switchbacks and dark places which could be considered a task for any seasoned driver. However, the dark places were rather nice since it seemed they had to stop every five seconds to take a leak.

After another twenty minutes or so, they decided to pull over yet again. As they stood alongside the van, they heard bushes moving and soft cries coming from within the darkness. Moments later, a young woman stumbled out of the trees holding her lower abdomen. As soon as she saw them, she began waiving her arms. Her clothes were ripped, and she was obviously pregnant. In fact, she was absolutely huge. They guessed she was most likely past her due date, and by the looks of her, she had to be very uncomfortable.

She quickly waddled up to the van, holding her enormous belly, and pleaded with them to give her a ride into town.

Her face was bruised, and it looked as if someone had really done a number on her. Her clothes were muddy, and her hair hung limp across her blackened face in dirty ropes.

When she climbed into the van, she smelled of urine. Ralph and Kevin looked at each other and both rolled down the windows in synchronicity.

"I am Laura Taylor. I was taken away and I have been gone a long time. Oh, please start the engine and let's get going!" she said breathlessly, "I've been raped and . . . oh my God . . . they were monsters!" She started moaning like a tortured animal. "They told me I had to breed. They told me I was never going to be found alive. Oh, get me out of here!"

"You might just want to try and relax," Kevin said. "You are ok now—we will get you some help, just try and . . ."

She screamed, "You don't understand—I said they were monsters!" Her belly moved as if it heard her and didn't like what she was saying. The skin pulled and stretched as if there were two hands inside tugging on her womb, trying to cause her intense pain to make her stop talking.

She screamed again. "It's trying to kill me! For the love of God, it's trying to kill me!" Her breath was coming in short bursts.

Saliva dripped from her mouth and saturated the neckline of her shirt. It was as if her entire body was completely out of control.

She started writhing and bucking wildly. Her pants began to turn dark red at the crotch and the carpet on the floor of the van soon became saturated with blood.

"It hurrrrts!" Laura's eyes rolled backwards in their sockets and her hands clenched. She started scratching and digging at her stomach, drawing blood as she did. "I have to get this thing out of my body! I have to kill it! It isn't human, I'm telling you! If only you saw what put this inside of me! OH MY GOD HELP ME PLEASE HELP ME!!"

Kevin and Ralph didn't know what to do. There was nothing they could do, only watch in horror, and came over to kneel beside the woman like statues.

They assumed she was tripping on some bad drugs or was just plain insane. Obviously, this baby was coming and nothing anyone could do would stop that. They needed to get to a hospital. Neither Kevin nor Ralph had any idea how to help her. Their guess was that no one could at this point.

"We need to get out of here right now! They will be following me! GO! GO! GO!!" she screamed.

Kevin climbed back into the driver's seat and was getting ready to throw the transmission into reverse when something at the edge of the woods caught his eye.

He looked out of the windshield and noticed six figures standing at the tree line, staring at them. They didn't look like human figures, but instead some kind of creature bent out of shape. They didn't have legs, only three very thick trunk-like roots coming out of a middle section. This middle section had tenebrous weavings throughout its outer layers, as though it had thin wire or hair growing from it. This "hair" seemed to move like it had its own thought process, reaching or stretching outwards toward the van, or maybe to the woman inside it.

The figures came closer in a sluggish movement. Suddenly they reached out, and Ralph saw, in what could only be their hands, long fleshy pieces of gore dripping with some kind of fluid.

Their heads did not look like heads at all, but pulsing mounds of flesh with eyes. Red eyes. Eyes, that if you looked into them, it would surely drive you mad. Is this what this woman had to endure? Did these things impregnate her? Could these things have pulled her to them and put themselves inside of her?

Ralph wondered how she got away from them. She must have waited for a perfect moment and somehow slipped away.

But now they'd found her. Now they were coming for her.

Ralph dropped the tranny into drive, but they stood in front of the van and made no attempt to get out of his way.

"There are other girls—lots of them," she whimpered as she lay on the floor of the van. "Most are all insane now. They make us lie on the ground and won't let us sit or even get up. The monsters just rape us over and over. They throw some kind of meat at us so we will eat, and then violate us more. If we try to move, they hurt us. They make us lay down and they never let us up."

With panic in her eyes, Laura attempted to pull herself up so she could look out the window. "I thought I could escape, but I can't. They told me I belong to them now. If any of us try to leave, they'll take our legs off just below our crotch. They tell us we don't need our legs. When that happens there is no fighting. That is what they will do to me when they catch me. I've seen it."

Laura screamed and pointed. The figures were now at the sliding door of the van. The door slid open, seemingly on its own accord. Kevin and Ralph looked at one another, powerless to move while Laura kicked and screeched at the tops of her lungs.

The voice coming from one of the creatures stilled their blood. "We have been on this planet since its creation. Your women are our women. It has always been that way, and it will always remain that way. We will let you live. You cannot find us, and you cannot stop us. Now go," the creatures advised.

Kevin gripped the steering wheel and Ralph knelt beside the woman, eyes wild and wide.

Laura continued to scream, but this time out of pain.

One of the creatures leaned into the van and casually lifted her dress. Laura tried to pull back, but suddenly stopped, as if relaxing and unable to do anything else but obey their touch. The horrific expression on her face did not change.

The creature put a wet stump of an extremity, dripping with that strange and thick fluid, on the woman's stomach and wiped it from just below her red and swollen breasts to between her legs, and then slowly pushed deep inside of her and then out of her, again and again. She flew her head back in a violent rush and opened her mouth silently and shook.

At that moment her belly stretched and opened. The sound of tendons and muscle tissue tearing filled the van.

What lay inside was a throbbing sack of membranes, pus, and black hair. Her tears stopped and the look on her face was something neither Kevin nor Ralph would ever see again in their entire lifetimes. Unbelievably, Laura was still alive and looked up at them with total despair. Her naked and abnormally wide, splayed legs twitched and shivered in the night air.

As the monster child was pulled from Laura's womb, and as blood and afterbirth drained from between her legs, one of the aliens touched her protruding and distorted belly. Slowly they witnessed her abdomen move as if it were trying to heal itself. It began to close, and the ripped portions of skin melded itself back together.

Laura's grip on Ralph's hand loosened as the creatures pulled her out of the van and carried her towards the woods. They could only hope that she would be released from this misery by drifting into complete and forever insanity.

Ralph wanted to say something to these creatures, to stop them, but he couldn't find his voice. Both fear and shock kept him from being able to utter even a single word.

"She will live and bear us many young. Her time is only beginning. This is why your kind is on this planet. You human men breed them for us."

Kevin sat motionless and quiet as he watched with astonishment as Laura and her infant monster were carried away.

What Laura Taylor said was true. Her life belonged to the creatures now and was no longer her own. As she was carried into the darkness, she looked back at Kevin and Ralph, and with one outstretched hand, tried to reach for them.

In moments the creatures and Laura Taylor were enveloped in the darkness and shadows of the forest.

Kevin and Ralph sat weak and unable to comprehend what they had just witnessed. They got settled in the van as best they could and drove straight home in silence.

They never spoke of the event that took place that night until almost two decades later.

CHAPTER 4

Ralph and Kevin sat peacefully on a bench eating lunch as they watched traffic go by in the town square. It was a beautiful Sunday afternoon and the sunshine felt good on their hands and faces. It was already going to be a good day.

They were deciding to go back to the saloon and get Ralph's car which he had left in the parking lot the night before. Management always went easy on customers who had too much to drink and chose to leave their vehicles behind after getting loaded, as long as they picked them up before the next day's happy hour and their tab was paid in full.

A very pregnant woman walked by with a tiny Pomeranian wearing a diamond studded pink collar. It was tugging on its matching leash and wanted to stop and greet them. The woman smiled, giggled, and hurried along, seemingly without a care in the world.

The two men looked at one another.

Finally, Ralph broke the silence. "Do you think we could have imagined it?"

Kevin looked down and considered what he was about to say. He knew exactly what Ralph was referring to and paused in what looked like deep thought. He sighed heavily and replied, "I've asked myself that question every day for the past nineteen years."

"I believe it happened," Ralph replied. "I also believe they told us the truth." He turned to face Kevin on the bench. "When I stop and think what that poor woman had to go through . . . and what she must continue to go through . . . Hell, what she and those other women she spoke about have to constantly endure, well, it's caused me to drink for the most part of my life now. Shit, I've been looking over my shoulder in case those things decide we know too much. I was never afraid until that night and now I'm afraid all the time."

"Do you ever feel like someone is watching you, Ralph? Like someone is always checking on you to make sure you remain quiet? I just can't shake the feeling. I've felt that way since the night it happened. Do you ever think they might come back for us?"

Ralph abruptly broke into a cold sweat. He remembered the other evening when the screen door slammed shut in the middle of the night and that weird organic smell permeated his home. No matter how drunk he got, or how much of a hurry he was in, he never forgot to lock his doors. He also suddenly remembered all the other unexplained things that have happened to him at the oddest of moments since that night in 1989. Ralph knew with the amount of alcohol he consumes, it certainly made things easy for him to deny or completely disregard many things that have happened since that night. "Yes, I do," he said. "I think they are always nearby."

Maybe what happened that night, long ago, was why neither of them had ever married, or for that matter, never even have let themselves get emotionally close to a woman. Maybe the horrific ordeal affected both of them on a subconscious level. It was surely possible.

Ralph and Kevin stared at each other, while on the other side of the square they heard a woman scream.

The Indian

Chapter 1

Life in Prescott, Arizona was everything Maureen-Ann and Bobby Butler had hoped it would be. Big blue skies, rolling hills, and the heavy scent of pine that hung in the air made them want to throw down a blanket, grab a good book, and get lost in the moment.

The couple had recently transitioned from northern Maryland where they had been taking care of Maureen's mother, Adeline, who had been dying of brain cancer. She fought it bravely for two long years, but as with any debilitating disease, it finally had its way.

Maureen had never been around someone dying before and although it was extremely hard emotionally, when the end finally came, it seemed to be swift and nothing like the horror stories her friends and hospice nurses had been preparing her for. Her mother simply closed her eyes, breathed deeply, and they watched as her chest slowly fell, and remained still. There were no sudden jerks or harsh cries of pain. Her mother never sat up and blindly reached for some imaginary entity who had finally come to take her into the next world. She simply died. No tears or drama. During her moment of death, Maureen and Bobby looked stupefied at one another. They both knew what the other was thinking and looked into each other's eyes with the same inquisitive expression. "That's it?"

The nurses gave Maureen and Bobby plenty of time to sit with Adeline alone. Then they came back into the room to perform their final duties for the deceased. Maureen thought to herself if she heard the horrible term "expired" one more time she would hit someone.

Originally, the family had decided to put off a memorial service for Adeline until a future date, most likely in the spring of the following year to give out of town friends and family time to make their travel arrangements. They were thankful times had changed, since funerals were traditionally scheduled within only days following someone's death. Maureen felt having this option relieved the emotional pressure of not having to think about funeral services and all the hotel decisions for friends and relatives so soon after losing a loved one when the family only wanted some personal time to heal.

Her mother had thought about cremation, but in the end, Adeline and her family had decided that a traditional burial in the family plot would be the best thing. She was to be laid to rest next to her husband, Maureen's father, who had passed after a quick and massive brain stem stroke ten years prior. The plots had been purchased jointly thirty years before and everyone decided it was best not to change the plan this late in the game.

Maureen finally agreed and was amazed at how quickly all the details were tended to, wrapping her mind around the fact that her poor mom was gone and soon to be interred in a dark box under the cold ground made her both very sad and very angry. She quietly sat in the funeral director's office long enough for Bobby to write the check for the services and then, as soon as their good-byes were whispered, they left the facility hand in hand. Maureen kept her dignity intact without a display of tears.

As they exited the building and walked to their SUV, Maureen thought how proud her mother would have been of her for handling all the details so well. She smiled as Bobby closed the passenger door for her while she got settled, happy in thought that this whole ordeal was finally over.

Now that Adeline's house was up for sale, it was time for Maureen and Bobby to get on with their lives. They both wanted to get away from the east coast and find a little place where the pace was slower, and the winters were more forgiving. Prescott, Arizona was the answer, and they would soon head west before the snow started falling.

CHAPTER 2

The house was built back in 1864 when the town was founded as the Territorial Capital of Arizona. It was one of the first homes ever built by the settlers and, therefore, had seen many changes. The land originally belonged to the Yavapai Indians and said to have had many battles fought in the surrounding mountains over the years.

As both soldiers and Indian warriors fell, cemeteries were established to hold the dead. Eventually, pits were dug for burning and disposing of the bodies that were either so badly decomposed or torn up beyond recognition for proper distribution to family members. In fact, one of the "Death Pits", as the settlers began to refer to them, was located on the southwest corner of the property they had purchased. There had been some stigma pertaining to building a home so close to the Pit due to accusations of disrespect for the dead, but as time went on, and since the house had been situated so far out in the woods, the issue was eventually forgotten, and it never resurfaced in later years.

The house had been renovated a few years before Maureen and Bobby bought it and as far as they were concerned, it was the perfect retreat and a great place to raise a family. Quiet, clean, and remote. It was exactly the home they had been searching for.

They celebrated their first night with a roaring fire and a couple bottles of wine, and without a care in the world they spoke of their hopes and dreams and future plans, as any young couple in love would in their new home.

The place smelled of old wood and aged, organic sweetness.

The electricity hadn't been turned on yet. An oversight by Bobby, but one that would make the night more memorable in every way possible. Candles and lanterns were on the menu that night and it was perfect.

The fireplace was so large you could almost stand in it and there were rails in the stonework for hanging pots for cooking. The place was magic, and they had everything they needed.

About 10:00 that night Bobby went out to the side yard where the grass ended, and the woods began and watered the ground. He stood looking up into the night. They'd had a big day, and he was looking forward to laying down soon.

As Bobby stood there, he felt what he thought was a spider web brush his arm. He looked down to brush it away as it somewhat tickled him. He was surprised to see a very thin, very old, piece of silk on the ground by his right foot. He assumed it was something that belonged to Maureen that must have fallen out of a packing box during the move. Picking it up, Bobby put it in his pocket to return to her once he got back in the house.

That night they made love for hours. Neither of them ever knew they could be so happy. They were finally living their lives for themselves in their own little world.

CHAPTER 3

The next morning, they awoke fully rested and ready to begin the job of unpacking everything.

When they entered the living room, they noticed one of the boxes. The one with pictures and knick-knacks had been opened and its contents lay neatly on the floor around the box, as if purposely and thoughtfully arranged. Neither asked about it, assuming the other had woken earlier to begin going through its contents.

As Maureen looked around the clutter she said, "This is going to be one hell of a job. You know that don't you?"

Bobby came back with, "I sure do, but don't worry, I won't rush you."

"Ha ha ha, you are a nut bag! I'm still not sure why I married you," Maureen responded with a grin.

"I'm fairly confident it was because of my nut bags, honey."

"Oh gaaawd!" She threw him somewhat of an embarrassed glare as she covered her face.

Maureen began breakfast and an hour later they were outside on the porch with hot coffee, orange juice, sausage, fried eggs, toast, and home fries.

"Yep. Kill me slow, baby. I love it," Bobby said. It was going to be a good day.

The first item on their agenda was to jump in Bobby's old Chevelle and head into town. He wanted to see about getting information on applying for a building permit for a garage he was planning to build to store the car, which had been his pride and joy for better than ten years now. Then they'd head to the grocery store to get some meat for the barbeque. Maureen was also dying to visit the nearest hardware store to pick up a few things for a garden she had been wanting to hoe ever since they first decided to buy a home. Maybe if they didn't purchase any frozen items, they'd let the Chevelle steer them around town a bit so they could take in a few sites. She and Bobby both were dying to get acquainted with their new little western town. But then it was their first day, after all, and they could always plan to sightsee another time.

Maureen hit the shops, while Bobby went to the Planning and Zoning office for the building permit. The friendly man behind the counter asked Bobby if they were enjoying Prescott so far and asked about their property. The conversation that followed was a bit strange and Bobby felt the hairs on his neck begin to stand up.

"I know you've heard all the history about the property," the man told him. "It's something the town folk and, to be honest, myself included, have often spoken about. In fact, your property and that house have been kind of a town legend so to speak." The man looked into Bobby's eyes as he spoke as if he were trying to gain insight into his personal thoughts and uncertainties. Bobby didn't like it. He didn't like it one bit.

Bobby looked at him thoughtfully, grinned, and said, "Why don't you just go ahead and ask me whatever it is you want to ask me." He was congenial and friendly, not wanting to put the man at unease. He was, after all, too new to the small town to want to burn any bridges on the first day.

"I'm sorry. I guess I've just always had a passion for this town and the old ways," he said. "My name's Sylvester Hampton. People call me Hamp; I prefer it that way. The other sounds too much like that asshole in the movies," he smiled.

Bobby couldn't help but laugh at the guy's honesty. On second thought, Bobby immediately knew they could become friends.

"Ya know, there are a lot of stories about that place where you are—people talk. I've always considered it mostly bullshit and I, for one, never believe anything I don't see first-hand. The land up there is beautiful, and I know you and your family have only been there . . . what? One night?"

"Yep. So far," Bobby threw back.

"Well, I'll tell ya what, once you get settled, and if you ever want to cook up some burgers or hit the famous Prescott night life on Whiskey Row, give me a holler. My wife makes the best brisket in town and her martinis aren't bad either. You know where I am during the day, and it'd be a pleasure to get to know you and meet the Mrs."

"Well, shit," Bobby responded. "So far, you're the first person I've met in this town, and I must admit you've got me curious. How can I refuse?"

They both had a laugh. Bobby paid for the building permit and got the regs and headed to the town square to meet Maureen for lunch.

"So, how'd it go? Did you get what you needed?"

"Yep. If we keep it no taller than 12 feet high and no bigger than 400 square feet, we can get away with just a permit and no inspections."

"Is that big enough for your manly ambitions?" Maureen asked.

"Barely, but we can always add to it later if my testosterone kicks in." They laughed. He loved her sense of humor. It was the first thing that attracted him to her when they met.

Chapter 4

I t's so beautiful. I'm so glad we came here. I've never felt more at home anywhere in my life," Maureen said as she stared up at the stars and held Bobby close. He agreed as they re-entered the house and locked the front door for the night.

Later, as they lay in bed, they heard a noise outside. It wasn't particularly loud or threatening, it was more of a sound as if someone was simply walking through the leaves by the house. In fact, they never would have heard it if the windows weren't up. Bobby thought it may have been a bear or a deer. They both got up and went out on the front stoop. The night was cool, but comfortable, and the sky was crystal clear.

Maureen's gaze immediately left the sky and she gasped as she saw what was approaching through the trees. She thought she was hallucinating when she saw what looked like an Indian standing by a tree. He looked as if he was hiding, yet his shadow seemed to be getting closer.

Bobby saw the Indian at the same time and immediately grabbed Maureen and pulled her behind him to protect her. In that same moment, the Indian disappeared.

"Oh my God, did you see that? I can't be crazy; I know I saw that. Did you . . ." Maureen's breath caught in her throat as she could barely finish the question.

"Let's get in the house, baby. It's late and we need to get some sleep," he said, trying to keep his voice sounding natural.

Once inside, Maureen ran to the window. She couldn't see anything outside with the light reflecting off the panes, so she hollered to Bobby to turn the living room light off.

No one was out there.

They both knew they hadn't imagined it. It was as if an Indian was walking straight toward them but didn't notice them at all. If he really was there, he had to have seen them. He had to have seen the lights from the house, hear the TV, and for Christ's sake, he had to have heard them talking. Bobby didn't want to add any more drama to the situation. In hindsight, he was trying to protect Maureen, but he realized he was more worried about how he was going to deal with this. Weird happenings weren't exactly his thing.

In an instant Bobby remembered what Hamp had said about the old town stories regarding their property and made a mental note to give him a call. This was something he knew he couldn't let go of. He and Maureen were going to get to know Hamp and his wife a lot sooner than he had originally intended.

Chapter 5

The next few days were peaceful, and they managed to accomplish a lot of homeowner tasks that most people tend to put off. Things were coming along nicely and both Bobby and Maureen were happy about their progress.

Just after sun-down, as Bobby was throwing some trash into the back of his old pickup truck for a run to the dump the next day, he saw a shadow of someone quickly coming up behind him. He spun around and the Indian was almost right on top of him. The Indian looked at him and made no attempt to walk away this time.

Bobby held his ground, although later, he couldn't believe he didn't run like a baby into the house.

The Indian was dressed in skins and wore makeshift sandals with red feathers attached to them. Bobby saw black paint on his face and feathers in his long dark hair. He was silent, and as he moved, he made no noise at all. If it hadn't been for the porch light being thrown onto his truck, Bobby would never have seen the shadow he cast. It was clear the Indian was only an apparition and didn't hold any real form. He was no more alive or physical than the faces one can see inside a campfire flame if you look close enough, yet he did cast a shadow.

Bobby spoke to him in a frightened, but strong whisper. "Who are you?"

No reply.

"Why are you here?"

Again, no reply. The Indian just stared at Bobby with eyes as deep as the ocean and black as midnight. His expression was that of confusion and deep concern.

After what seemed like forever, the Indian turned his head and began walking away. He looked back at Bobby once then disappeared.

At that moment Maureen walked outside and asked if he planned on staying out there all night.

He forced a laugh and told her he was coming and to keep her pants on.

He decided to keep this incident to himself until he had time to think. Until he could figure out the Indian's intent, he didn't want to alarm Maureen. After all, if there had been any violent purpose, the Indian had the perfect opportunity to carry out whatever he wanted but did nothing.

As he walked back to the house he happened to look down and notice there was another piece of that thin cloth he had found on their first night at the house when he was outside taking a piss. It was old and worn and had a smell to it. As Bobby held it up to his face, he noticed it was the smell of campfire and gun powder.

CHAPTER 6

The following day was warm and breezy, and after Bobby went to the dump, he drove over to the Planning and Zoning Commission to pick up another copy of the building permit. While he was there, he asked Hamp if he felt like going to lunch. They met at noon at a local burger joint right off the Town Square.

After trying to figure out just how to bring the subject up about the stories Hamp had mentioned during their first meeting, Hamp saved him the trouble and brought them up himself.

Hamp simply asked, "So tell me, have you or Maureen seen or heard anything kinda weird after sundown yet?"

Bobby felt the hairs on his wrists stand up but recovered quickly and didn't know how to respond. He could have been honest and mentioned the Indian, which would have led to Hamp immediately thinking he was nuts, or he could have lied and laughed it off. Instead, he tried to reach a happy medium.

"Oh yeah, the old stories. Are you trying to find out if they are true?"

"Well, I suppose I am. You know, I grew up in Prescott and I've heard a shitload of things about those woods. I've always kinda thought they must be somewhat true, considering the history of the place. Plus, when you hear a thing or two, it's easy to forget, but when you hear considerably more, you tend to believe it. When I was a young kid, my friends and I used to dare each other to go into your woods. How's that for a head trip?"

Bobby thought before he spoke and said, "I can't deny that you've got my curiosity up at about a hundred percent. You've also gotta know that Maureen and I really want to hear some of these stories. In fact, she wanted me to see if you and . . . sorry, I've forgotten your wife's name . . ."

"Erica."

"Erica," Bobby said with a smile. "Would yawl like to come up the hill for dinner? We can grill some burgers outside over a fire. Maybe you guys can provide the entertainment, we can provide the cocktails and with a little luck, those old ghosts may show up to say hello. But, the real entertainment, of course, being those freaking stories I keep hearing about."

"Oh, that would be great, we'd love to."

"What's your favorite poison?"

"Erica is a Bloody Mary person and I'm happy with just about anything. Just don't try to give me any beer with the word Lite in front of it," Hamp offered.

"10-4, I hear that shit."

They went on to talk about town stuff and, of course, the most popular subject of where exactly in town did Billy-Jack kick the sheriff on the right side of his face with his left foot, and where the ice cream store was located from the old 60s movie "Billy Jack" that was so popular. It was funny as they both admitted that their parents signed them up for Karate almost immediately after leaving the movie theatre. They supposed all teenagers could admit to the same. What a great movie. Both agreed.

Bobby and Hamp would not have denied, if anyone asked them, if there was a kinship between them right from the start. It was as if they had known each other their whole lives. Talk came easy and honest, and Bobby felt more comfortable talking with Hamp than anyone else he could remember in years. In fact, he had forgotten about the Indian. Almost

CHAPTER 7

I t was about 7:00 PM, three days after their lunch on that Friday evening, and there was a light knock on the front door. The voice from inside the house yelled, "I hope somebody's thirsty because I don't know what the hell to do with all this Lite Beer."

There was immediate laughter as Bobby threw open the door and Hamp and Erica came inside.

"You said you were gonna cook burgers and you never said if we should bring anything so here's a bag of buns and beans! If you can't use them tonight, I don't know, make barbeque tomorrow!" Hamp roared enthusiastically. "Oh, and I'd like you to meet my other half, Erica. She's been dying to meet you both. Spin around darlin. You know, I think she went through about five outfits before she walked out the door."

"Shut up!" Erica whispered. "Oh my god, I can't believe he said that!" She quickly composed herself. "Hi, I am so happy to meet you! Hamp's said so many great things about you—and for the record, it was three outfits, and that's what girls do!"

"Hell, if it were me, I would have gone with the five outfits. I'm not proud! And that's EXACTLY what girls do! Come on in here. Men just don't get it sometimes," Maureen said smiling, and they hugged each other as if they were old friends.

Maureen and Erica almost immediately retreated to another room. Soon there was laughing, and it was obvious that they hit it off just as quickly as their men did.

Bobby felt great love for his wife at seeing the happiness in her eyes upon their meeting. He felt, once again, as if they had found home and moving across the country was a good decision.

The meal was fantastic, and the conversation even better.

Around the fire pit, Bobby had arranged four hammocks suspended in a large circle between large pine trees, with wooden tables to hold drinks, cell phones, or whatever was needed to be easily reachable by the hammock's inhabitants. It was all about comfort and the fire was warm and cozy. Bobby also threw in one of those logs that threw out colors as it burned to add to the fire's ambiance. It was also his way of keeping their guests in a good place, so they didn't feel they needed to drive home if they were too intoxicated.

Earlier that day, Maureen had made a trip to Home Depot and bought a small, outside bar that they placed on the south end of the circle so everything they needed was close and convenient. She had also bought a Dura-Log, actually a few of them, as they didn't pop or spark like natural wood. They were both very cautious and knew of the fire hazards that existed in Prescott's dry climate, so they took every precaution necessary for a safe evening. Maureen was a born hostess, and her parties were always a great success. She was balls out intent on this one being one for the memory books.

Soon the conversation turned to stories.

Soon after, the stories turned into ghost stories.

Hamp began with the tale he had heard most often as a young boy on camping trips. He looked off into the woods as he told it, as if he were looking for someone or something to drift out and kill them all at any moment. Bobby wasn't sure if Hamp was truly a little scared or if he was just giving a good performance for the girls' sake.

As the night drew on, Erica mentioned how interested they both were in the history of Prescott and commented on the devastation that occurred in establishing territory in this region of Arizona. At that point, she looked down into her wine as if she didn't want to have any direct eye contact with anyone.

Maureen asked Hamp about the history of the Yavapai Indians and the unjust killings of the wives and children of the warriors she had heard about from some women she had spoken with in the town's library recently. She wanted to know if it was true, and if anything had actually happened on this particular parcel of land.

Hamp's mood seemed to turn inward, and Bobby caught it immediately. "These warriors were defending their way of life and their families and were in no way being aggressive towards the white men until they realized they had to fight or be killed," Hamp stated matter-of-factly. "They simply didn't have enough time to prepare for a battle, as history proved that the tribes were caught off guard. It was kill or be killed. Life's a bitch when you don't have any warning." Hamp looked up and stared at Bobby.

Bobby knew Hamp wanted to proceed, but he appeared as if he wasn't sure how, or if he should continue.

Bobby thought to himself, "Ok, this is what I've been waiting for. Let's do this."

Suddenly, as they all seemed to sit in silence for a moment, there was a movement of light on the south end of the circle. It caught them off guard and happened so quickly that no one had time to respond until the moment had passed.

An Indian dressed in full war paint ran toward them and stopped abruptly in the center of the circle. He stood by the fire, completely unaffected by its heat. He was, as the night before, only an apparition. He had no real physical form. Yet, that didn't matter as everyone was still scared out of their minds.

The Indian pointed at the woods. He held up a large cutting tool in his left hand that resembled a knife and a small axe in the other. He walked over towards Maureen and stopped within only a few feet from her.

She whimpered and recoiled into the fabric of the hammock as best she could.

Bobby stood and began to move in her direction, but as he did, the Indian continued to hold up the axe and glare at him as if he dared him to come any further. He stood pointing a finger at the woods with a look of lost abandonment.

Bobby yelled at the Indian, "What do you want?"

At that instant, the Indian picked up Maureen and ran into the woods.

Maureen screamed, looked over the Indian's shoulder as he carried her quickly away. Everyone immediately tried to follow.

Bobby ran as fast as he could for as long as he could, but the effects of the alcohol he had been drinking and the fact that he did not have any shoes on, slowed his progress immensely.

No one had any strength or endurance compared to the Indian or the willingness to enter the dark woods, except for Bobby, so they watched with fear and hopelessness as Maureen was carried out of sight and into the night.

Hamp followed briefly, but he was worried about Erica and couldn't leave her behind, alone.

CHAPTER 8

Bobby had been crawling and trying desperately to find Maureen.

As he lay on a hillside, out of breath and panicking at the thought of never seeing his wife again, the Indian appeared.

Again, the Indian pointed at the hillside, and again the Indian's efforts of communication were useless.

A hint of pink touched the sky and Bobby realized that Maureen had been in the woods, alone, all night. These woods stretched forever, the ground was rutty and unstable in a lot of areas, as the terrain was hilly and there were many washes made by monsoons most common in late summer. Despite these issues, Bobby knew Maureen was safe. Somehow, he knew wherever she was she was alive. He didn't know how he knew, but he did, and he trusted his gut.

Hamp and Erica had phoned the police immediately. They quickly realized if they told the police how Maureen was taken away, they would be thought of as crazy. No one would believe that an apparition came and carried her away. Instead, their story was she had gone into the woods looking for wood and never returned.

A few officers had started looking for her and now that morning had arrived, they decided to head back to the station and wait out the day. If she didn't come back on her own, they would return with more men and begin a search after twenty-four hours.

Finally, Bobby wandered back to the house, and without a word, he fell on the couch and stared at Hamp. "What the fuck is going on? This is insane! I'm going back out there to look for her."

"The cops just left, but they were looking for her 'til just about sun-up. They'll be back, but they want to talk to you."

"Yeah," Bobby nodded. "I bet they fucking do."

The three of them didn't know what to say. Erica made a little breakfast, which no one ate, only picked at, and then they went back in the woods to search for Maureen.

Bobby finally broke the silence that had been lingering. "I know you saw that Indian. I know you saw it and I did, too. Shit, he could have grabbed Erica."

Hamp stopped walking and turned around and met Bobby's eyes with his own. "Yes, I did. Now I have a question for you."

Bobby said nothing and let Hamp continue.

"Have you ever seen him before?"

"I have. Three times in fact. Our first night in the house I went out to take a wiz at the edge of the woods. Something brushed my arm. When I turned around there was an old thin cloth on the ground at my feet. I didn't think anything of it—I thought it came out of one of the packing boxes or something. Looking back, I had a feeling, just a strange feeling, like I wasn't alone anymore."

"Keep talkin'" Hamp said.

"Maureen and I were outside, and he walked right past us. He looked at us for a minute, turned away, and just disappeared. Maureen pretty much freaked out at first. But once we got inside, she calmed down."

Hamp shook his head, held his hands up by his ears and bent over a little feeling both amazement and shock, never realizing this could really be happening.

"The third time I was in the driveway. He walked right up to me. I asked him what he wanted. He only looked at me and pointed to the woods. I didn't feel threatened. It was as if he was trying to tell me something. I didn't tell Maureen about that. I was afraid it would really upset her. It was then I decided to get you over here and listen to your stories and try to get some more history about this place. I was hoping your stories might help me make some sense out of all this."

"So, getting Erica and I coming here was planned."

"Yep, it was." Bobby softly chuckled. "I figured it was inevitable anyway, I thought we hit it off the first time we met. I knew we'd all become friends in time. To be honest, I didn't want you to think I was completely nuts, right off the bat. Otherwise, I would have told it all to you straight."

"I thought so, too," Hamp said. "So now we've got this fucking Indian and no Maureen. Come on, let's keep walking."

CHAPTER 9

The sky was slowly darkening, and the air had taken on a dank, organic smell they imagined was similar to when the past battles were fought here.

Erica stayed at the house in case Maureen showed up. Neither Hamp nor Bobby wanted her traipsing through the woods.

As Maureen slowly opened her eyes after her long sleep, she realized she was lying in an indented area of dirt with pine needles underneath her. She knew she was lost, yet she was not afraid. The Indian would be back. He had not hurt her, and when he had looked at her, it was as if he wanted to tell her something. His eyes were full of a story that he had not been able to express. On some strange level, Maureen was looking forward to the Indian's return. She knew she should be scared, but instead felt sorry for him. If he wanted to hurt her, he would have already done so. Instead of trying to run, she wanted to stay. The Indian needed her for some reason, and she had decided she wanted to help him. She felt that it was the right thing to do.

The sky was full dark now and there was no moon. The night was full of the sounds of crickets and small creatures scurrying along the forest floor and the wind was blowing at a good rate. The hair on Maureen's arms stood up as the air chilled.

As she drifted in and out of a light sleep, she knew the Indian was nearby. She could feel him. Slowly, he moved out of the shadows, and they stared at each other. He motioned for her to follow him and she did not hesitate.

They passed a brook where he waited as she bent down and drank some water. She was dying of thirst as she had remained in her little bed of pine needles all day not wanting to risk going further into the woods. Maureen knew if anyone was looking for her, she should stay where she was.

Finally, the Indian stopped walking and pointed to a section of the forest floor. The ground looked as if it was somewhat sunken compared to the surrounding ground and Maureen thought it looked as if it could have been a grave.

Her breath caught in her throat. He wanted her to dig. She was close to tears as she pushed back years of old pine needles and brush. The ground was soft, and it wasn't difficult to scoop the dirt up with her hands and move it away.

Within minutes, her hands touched something that was not rock. She looked up at the Indian who had been standing next to her. His face was somber, and she felt herself starting to breathe in short gasps. She heard herself saying "No. No. I can't." The Indian nodded reassuringly and knelt beside her, as if trying to comfort her.

Maureen kept digging. Soon there was a small doll in her hands. She looked up at the Indian and began to weep. She finally understood why the Indian had brought her to this place and knew what lay beneath this ground.

Chapter 10

Bobby and Hamp had been walking south. Finally, they saw movement in the forest and their worst fear changed to hope as they saw Maureen on the ground. They called to her, and she cried back and waved. She made no attempt to get up and run toward them, however, Bobby and Hamp picked up speed in their effort to get to her.

Upon running up to her and seeing her filthy dirty, they noticed the Indian. On the ground between them were the skeletal remains of a small child in the arms of what they knew must be the child's mother. Maureen held a small doll in her own arms and gently rocked it with great care and cried.

Bobby dropped down on his knees and wrapped Maureen in a blanket he'd brought and held her tight.

The following morning the police and investigators came for the bodies and took them to the morgue for autopsies to be completed.

It was confirmed that the two bodies were Indian and that they had been part of the massacre that took place many years ago as the town was established.

Maureen and Bobby submitted requests to the court for the little girl and her mother to remain on the property and properly buried. This was granted, and they built a small and beautiful resting place for them, surrounded by a white picket fence and two tombstones. A bench was set up and they often placed flowers on the graves.

One year after the burial, Bobby and Maureen visited the graves. It was midnight and the moon was full. It was a beautiful walk, and the night was alive with the soothing sounds of the breeze through the pine trees and the humming of the surrounding wildlife. They placed flowers in the vases at the base of the tombstones and thought of the Indian. They had not seen him at all after his family had been found and hoped that wherever he was, he was now comforted.

As they sat on the bench and spoke of the sad ending of this family, they saw movement in the trees. As they shifted their gaze, they saw them.

The Indian stood, no longer in war paint or holding his weapons, but instead, holding his small daughter in his arms with his wife at his side.

The Indians looked at them and smiled. The woman walked towards Maureen and held out a hand in thanks. Maureen reached out to feel nothing except the comforting breeze. As she brought her hand toward her face, she looked at Bobby who had tears in his eyes. Together they realized how lucky they were to have each other, and they watched as the Indians turned and as a family disappeared into the night.

The Gambril House

Chapter 1

The big house at the edge of town was the scariest place on the face of the Earth. That's what the kids used to say, and I agreed wholeheartedly. In fact, I still do. I ought to know because my house was right next to it—well, it was the closest house next to it, anyway.

The Gambril House looked like a barn or mill house with its large tower-like chamber jetting up from its western corner, and it was rumored that the few windows it had were boarded over to keep whatever evil inside contained. The gravel drive was rutted and deeply sunken in many areas. When it rained, the potholes would fill up with water and hold the moon's reflection. From a distance it looked like lanterns welcoming visitors inside to a party no one would ever leave.

The house still stands, barely. It's been boarded up for years, and I can't remember anyone ever living in it. After all, who'd want to? That place has had so many bad stories surrounding it, anyone would have to be out of their minds to want to live there.

As kids we used to dare each other to go in it. At that time, it wasn't boarded up yet, it just had big white signs on the property with big red capital letters that read NO TRESPASSING and KEEP OUT! Us kids thought it was a big joke. I mean, how many kids do you know who would obey signs that said to keep out? For kids, signs like that are nothing but a big invitation to do the exact opposite.

I guess every town has a property that is abandoned. Every town has a haunted house. The Gambril House was ours.

Back in its day it was beautiful. The town's Historical Society still has pictures of it in their office on Main Street right next to the Town Hall. In fact, the Gambril House was first built and used as a Catholic church in 1883, when the town was new and becoming popular for its mining. There was a large cemetery on the property, and it is still there today. The town was first established and named Val Verde after its founder who built the first smelter used to mine ore. In 1904 the smelter changed hands and then in 1905 it burned down. As a lot of townsfolk left the area and the attendance of church services dropped to a catastrophically low number, the church was closed. Later, in 1906, the new owner of the property built a 1,000 ton per day smelter, which in turn, brought more people to the area for the abundance of copper and lead. Once again, the town thrived. Since Val Verde was no longer mining this part of Arizona, a new name was chosen for the town, and hence, the name Humboldt, after the German naturalist, explorer, and traveler Baron Friedrich Heinrich von Humboldt won the toss.

It was during this time an investor and entrepreneur bought the church and had hopes of turning it into a high-end hotel due to its large square footage, elaborate floor plan, and scenic beauty. It flourished for years until the smelter closed in 1968, at which time it sat vacant in a developing and still prosperous community where it still stands today.

When the Gambril House was a hotel, it was noted for entertaining lots of mining tycoons, as well as international socialites and dignitaries. Between being able to allure travelers with the mild climate, and being able to offer all four seasons, the hotel attracted people of all ages and those with varying outdoor interests.

The graves on the property used to be maintained, but not anymore. Now, as I think back, I remember being amazed at how even as the years went by, the engraving on the tombstones seemed to appear clearer and deeper as time went on. If I had been wiser, maybe I would have seen this as an omen, or at the very least, a sign that would have helped me warn others to stay away. But life is what it is and I'm no psychic.

CHAPTER 2

I loved looking at the place. It had an enticing quality to it. But it scared me shitless.

I would lay in bed on warm summer nights with my bedroom window open and hear strange noises from a close distance. Sounds like chainsaws, rappings and strange howlings that I assumed were coyotes. I knew the noises weren't coming from my yard or my house. They weren't inside my head or coming from the television my parents constantly had on all night, every night. The noises came from the Gambril House. Sometimes subtle, sometimes not.

My mom, dad, and my sister, Ripley, and I had lived on Cemetery Circle in Humboldt since I was born. We had a bright yellow mailbox with our last name, Fallen, printed in huge black letters on one side with the street number right below it. We were "3" and the Gambril House was "4", although its mailbox was long since bashed to the ground, probably by bored teenagers and their baseball bats.

On my twelfth birthday my parents said I could have a slumber party and invite all my closest friends. I was so psyched.

Mom took me to the mall, and we bought invitations, a few decorations for the front door of our house, balloons for the mailbox, and tons of food like hotdogs, frozen pizzas, candy bars, and various flavors of soda. My mom even bought me a new sleeping bag and sewed a patch on the front with my name on it: Travis.

That afternoon my dad drove me around the neighborhood so we could pass the invitations out. The party was set for the upcoming Friday night, which was three days later. It was early June, so it wouldn't be too hot, and it was weeks before the monsoons would come so we were pretty much guaranteed to have good weather.

Everyone I invited showed up at 7:00 and they all brought their own sleeping bags, pillows, and most importantly—presents.

My dad made a fire pit in a back portion of our yard and since we didn't have any neighboring houses behind us, we had plenty of space to roam if we wanted and do the usual twelve-year-old stuff in the middle of the night.

After the hotdogs were gone, along with Mom's award-winning potato salad, we sat around the campfire and Dad told a bunch of ghost stories while we made smores. It was the most perfect twelve-year-old's birthday ever.

We had eight tents set up, but as the night progressed, everyone dragged their sleeping bags outside and laid them around the fire. The bags of Doritos and containers of onion dip accumulated freely in the yard. We were all without a doubt, fat and happy.

After selling us the "Do not put another log on the fire" speech, Mom and Dad officially said goodnight around 11:30, but I could still see them peering at us from time to time through their bedroom window. The bedroom curtains were religiously closed all the time, but that night they were open. Looking back, I would have done the same thing. I mean, what kind of parents would leave a bunch of twelve-year-olds alone, outside at night on the edge of the desert?

CHAPTER 3

B ack in those days my best friend was Jon Hunt. He was a wild guy that would do anything on a dare, and that night wasn't any different. He always had a huge desire for adventure, and nothing seemed to scare him.

The fire was dwindling, and Jon broke out a pack of Marlboros he had taken from his dad earlier that day. His dad bought them by the carton and stashed them in their hall closet, so it was easy for Jon to snag a pack when he felt like it. Plus, he knew his dad never kept count of them so getting caught wasn't an issue.

As we all sat around the fire smoking and talking about girls and sex (which was every boy's favorite topic at that age and every age past puberty), somebody mentioned the Gambril House, and wouldn't it be fun to cruise the cemetery and read the tombstones.

I knew somebody would suggest doing that, so I wasn't shocked at all, and in fact, I was totally into it. Within a few minutes we were walking down the rutty, dirt road, flashlights in hand, and laughing about dumb stuff all the way.

As we entered the yard of the Gambril House, there was a mist covering the grounds that wasn't particularly thick, but still very pronounced, and it had a kind of a glow to it in the moonlight. It was very eerie and very cool, considering we were all experiencing what would turn out to be our first right of passage into manhood. Therefore, any ground fog would totally boost the drama of the night. Guaranteed.

The gates to the cemetery were, of course, padlocked, but at our age it was easy to climb over the fence with little to no effort.

We read each tombstone and were amazed at the dates of death that were around us. Some of the people died back in the 1800s, some died as late as 1980.

The tombstone along the far back wall of the cemetery was tilting in a drastic way, so naturally we all seemed to drift right toward it. It looked as if it would fall over at any moment, and I couldn't believe the weight of it hadn't caused it to fall already. As we approached the headstone, we noticed the ground dipping and it looked as if the ground itself had given way beneath the grave.

As we all stood in the back of the cemetery and stared at the grave, Jon decided to perform his own little impromptu act as he hopped onto the stone. While he used it as sort of a stage, he began telling his own ghost story. He passed out more cigarettes and we all hunkered at the base of the stone in the concavity and formed a tight circle to light them. His dad's Bic was getting low on juice so we tried our best not to let the wind blow out the flame before we could get them all lit.

As Jon preached, we all kicked back and listened. You could have heard a pin drop. It was the perfect night. A little mist on the ground, a faint, but chill wind blowing the air currents along the memorials. The waft of our campfire in the breeze. It was total freedom. A bunch of boys exploring an old graveyard in the middle of the night, alone. Who could ask for anything better?

We all were starting to get a little spooked when we heard a cat over by the Gambril House. It must have been trying to get inside the basement because we heard scratching noises as if it were trying to pry the coal hatch open or trying some other way to get inside.

When Sunny Curtis commented on how it wasn't really a cat by the house, it was instead the undead trying to escape their coffins beneath our feet, we all looked at one another and cracked up. What perfect timing that was. Sunny was always pretty sharp and had a quick wit when necessary.

At that moment, the ground shifted below our bodies and suddenly dropped about three feet. The tombstone fell the rest of the way over and rolled onto Johnny Mae's right foot. He gasped in pain and surprise as he realized he was caught beneath it.

Our first instinct was to run, but we discovered we were all trapped to a certain extent and the only way out was to climb. Not only had the ground given way, but it had dropped to where we were inside it up to our shoulders in the new hole that had just appeared.

Even as a team, we could not budge the tombstone that had imprisoned Johnny's foot. But, as we took turns digging the dirt out below his foot, he was finally able to slide it out. His foot was a little bloody, but he could put weight on it, so we were all relieved.

"If that thing fell a little more to one side it could have squashed me. I want to get the fuck out of here, right now!" Johnny said.

No one disagreed.

"You guys, check this out!" Jon said as he pointed his flashlight into an opening created from the cave in. "It looks like a hallway or something in there! Are there underground walkways or paths below this graveyard? Does anybody know?"

"I have no clue and right now I couldn't give a shit." Brady chimed in. "I'm leaving; there is no way I'm going in there."

"Well, wait a minute, man," Jon said. "This place used to be a Catholic church, right? There's probably all kinds of neat shit down there."

"Yeah, old shit—shit that's like two hundred years old. Any wood framework, if there is any, is way rotted and just waiting to fall on us," Brady said.

Rusty Newman was a new kid in town. He had just moved in the beginning of the previous school year from LA. I didn't know him well, but he seemed to be a nice guy and he had gotten close with some of my other friends, so I invited him. Mostly so he wouldn't feel left out. Humboldt is a small town, and I didn't want to hurt anyone's feelings by not including them.

Rusty's dad was the new Chief of Police, so he was practically a celebrity. He and his family mostly kept to themselves and were quiet, but they seemed like good people. Their house was always dark, and it looked like no one was ever home. They always kept the shades pulled over the windows and after they moved in, my parents would comment on how weird it was that they let all the shrubs and flowers die. In the desert, you have to water your yard. Everyone knows that. He lived on the other side of the Gambril House and was closer to the cemetery, which was almost directly behind Rusty's house, if you didn't count a couple of vacant lots.

"If anyone wants to go in, I'll go with you. The rest of you all just stay here and wait for us to come back. If something happens, we'll yell, and you guys will be right here to go get help. Plus, this is hard ground. Plenty of granite. I bet a cave in would be the least of our problems," Rusty said.

"You mean like the cave in that just happened?" James asked in between smoke-rings.

"What the heck does that mean? What other problems are you thinking about?" I asked.

"Well, this is a graveyard. Could be all kinds of creepy dead shit down there." Rusty laughed. "So, who's in?"

"I'm totally in," Jon blurted.

"I guess I'm in, too. We each have flashlights, right?" James asked. "I'll give it twenty paces and if something doesn't grab my leg, I may go twenty more."

"You're so fucking manly it's amazing," I said. Everyone laughed.

"Okay—I'll go in, too, but if I start smelling anything rank, I'm leaving," Sunny said in a low voice. Sunny was the class clown. Everyone liked him and he was cool to anyone that was cool to him.

"Trav, if your parent's find out about this they are going to be pissed as shit. Are you prepared for that?" Johnny asked me.

"Yeah, I know. But they won't find out unless someone tells them, right?"

"Or unless there's another cave in." Sunny said.

"How's your foot, Johnny?" I asked.

"It hurts and I can't walk very good . . . so I guess I'm gonna wait here," Johnny said, looking down. "I'll be your look-out." I could tell he thought everyone was going to tease him, but no one did. I think we were all relieved he would be there, just in case . . .

Brady decided to stay behind with Johnny, and it was all settled.

CHAPTER 4

To get into the entrance of the tunnel we each had to get on our hands and knees, and with our flashlights in our mouths, we crawled the first four feet or so. The ground was hard and Rusty had been right, there were a lot of rocks. But I had no idea if they were granite or not.

Once we had all gotten under the ground, we were surprised that it really was a tunnel. It was about six feet tall and about the same in width. Just wide enough, Jon thought, to carry a casket with a row of pallbearers on each side.

There was a strong musky odor. Evidently, it didn't fall under the category of "rank" because Sunny was still present and accounted for and he hadn't seemed to want to turn back yet.

Inside the tunnel, red brick lined one side of the passageway. Remembering we were at the far end of the graveyard, we knew that beyond the sections of brick were other coffins laid at rest. Back prior to 1880 and until recent times, the people who built cemeteries laid brick right in the graves to encase the coffin. They hadn't invented cement vaults yet.

We continued to walk with the help of our flashlights leading the way. Should the beams of light turn off, we would be in complete blackness with no hope of our eyes adjusting to the darkness.

The smell of dank earth was overpowering and the ground beneath our feet was unstable due to rocks.

Before long, Johnny's voice hollered from above to ask if we were okay.

"We're fine, Dude," Jon yelled back.

"What's it like down there?"

"It's dark!"

"Smartass—just be careful. I don't like this, you guys," Brady yelled next.

I was amazed at how far away their voices sounded. The echoes they made in the tunnel were eerie and frightening. We kept walking.

After another fifty feet, the tunnel branched off toward the right and we knew it was heading in the direction of the church. Soon there was another tunnel, and then another. Now there was a noticeable downgrade to the passage. "Okay, you guys," I said.

"I'm afraid if we keep going, we are going to get lost down here. We have no idea how many tunnels there are and—"

There was a sound from behind.

"Hey Johnny, is that you? Brady? Are you down here?" Rusty asked.

No answer from above.

The sound had returned and soon turned into shuffle. It sped up and headed our way.

"I think we ought to keep walking. These tunnels have to end somewhere, right?" Rusty asked.

"Relax," Jon said with a little frustration in his voice. "It's just Brady and Johnny trying to freak us out."

Suddenly, there was a reflection in the tunnel from where we had come from. A set of eyes, coming closer now and coming faster. The eyes were a pale yellow, but they were offset too far to be a small animal.

Without thinking, we took off along the tunnel, and without warning, met a stairway. We flew down it. All we could do was pile up at the base of the stairs and huddle, lost and scared in the blackness. Sunny's flashlight went out. "It must have banged on something when I fell." He tapped it lightly into the palm of his hand and the light came back on. "Oh, thank God!" he said.

We waited for those awful eyes to appear at the top of the stairs, but nothing happened. As we got to our feet the only sound was our rapid breathing.

We found ourselves in a large chamber. There were six doors, each made of heavy wood with elaborate cast iron doorknobs and dead bolts. It was both mysterious and frightening. The hard ground had changed to a tiled floor of dramatic beauty. It was very dark in color and the tiles were laid in a circular pattern, with letters on each corner in a large font that looked more Latin than English. Not that my friends and I would know what Latin looked like, but we knew it was definitely a foreign language.

I reached for the first door handle and the knob turned without resistance and slowly swung inward into a large, very dim chamber. The only furniture was antique tables with old, dried leather bindings on each side. "These aren't tables, these are gurneys," Jon whispered.

"What are all these things?" Sunny asked as he pointed to rows of shelving.

There was a variety of items on the shelves. One looked like a hat with gears attached to it and knobs with screws. Another item was a large triangle, about three feet tall and made of wood with a strap over the top, as if it were some kind of incredibly uncomfortable seat. There were also hammers and things that looked like ice picks and a variety of other weird tools.

The worst thing of all was what we found in the third room. In the corner of the dark space was a chair. There was no actual seat, but only an open space like a toilet seat. Below was a wide groove in the tiles where liquid would have flowed into a hole in the floor. Hanging from a metal stand were various sized knives, and other puncturing gadgets. The armrests had nails protruding upwards like maybe at one time there was padding on them. These armrests had straps hanging from them and beneath them there were old, very dark stains on the floor.

We all looked at one another, dumbstruck, as we realized where we were at the same moment.

"We are in a torture chamber," Jon said in a hushed voice.

"But this was a Catholic church and then a fancy hotel!" I exclaimed.

"Maybe this place was somehow sealed off and no one ever knew about it?" Jon whispered back, trying to make sense of it. "Churches are always getting caught for doing fucked up things, don't you watch the news?"

"I just can't believe after all these years this stuff is still in here. We need to get out of here right now," I said.

"Trav, do you think we should go back the way we came or try to get up through the church? There has to be a way, plus it'd be a lot faster than running all that way through the tunnel again," James said. He had been so quiet I had forgotten he was even down here with us. As I looked at him, I realized he had a big dark spot on the side of his shirt. It wasn't dirt.

"What's on your shirt James? Is that blood?" I asked.

"Yeah, I fell on something at the bottom of the stairs. I'll be okay. I just don't want to pull it out."

"You mean there is something stuck in you, and you haven't said anything?" Rusty asked, staring at him with wide eyes.

"Let's just get out of here. Those eyes might come back, and I think we should just move forward. What's through that last door?" James said as he pointed further down the corridor.

James was stronger than all of us that night. I never would have thought.

CHAPTER 5

As we all ran over to the last door, we grabbed the handle, but it would not open.

Rusty found a piece of wood and a piece of metal that looked like one of those things you see next to your fireplace, although we knew no one in this place used it for that, and together we tried to pry the door open. Finally, it gave way releasing a sick rush of a smell that was so bad, it was all we could do not to vomit. We all covered our faces as best as we could, but it was too late.

We shined the lights inside to find what looked like a dead woman. Blood dripped from her fingertips as they hung loosely over the side of the gurney she was draped over.

As we walked up upon her, she gasped with fright and her head shook violently against the metal head rest. "NO! NO! DON'T TOUCH ME—NOT AGAIN! FOR GOD'S SAKE PLEASE DON'T HURT ME ANYMORE!" She wailed and sobbed, and we all surrounded the table without any idea of what to do next.

We noticed that her arms and legs were strapped down to the table, so we started to quickly undo the buckles. We could tell she was very weak, and she had lots of bruises beneath her torn, dirty clothing. Blood streaked her hair and she looked to be on the very edge of sanity.

When she realized we weren't a threat to her, she pleaded for us to get her out of there, but not before crying, "Oh thank you! How did you find me? I have been here for so long!"

Jon asked her if she had any idea how to get out of here. She did not.

As soon as we got her off the table, we each helped her as best as we could by getting on either side of her and supporting her weight. Her legs seemed useless as we all left the room.

The corridor we took went up a flight of stairs and opened into an old kitchen. Not the kind of kitchen any of us had ever been in before, but a kitchen all the same. The walls were made of stone and there was a spit for cooking large slabs of meat, like a pig or something equally big. There were old kettles and cooking utensils, but the place didn't smell like anything good had been prepared there for quite some time.

A large kettle of water boiled over a fire on one side of the kitchen. It was huge, in fact, big enough for a small bear, at least. Whomever had planned on using it would surely be returning soon.

We searched for a way out, but found none, other than the one we had entered through.

The place was massive. We assumed we were in the oldest part of the church. A part that was hidden somehow within its huge expanse of square footage. Over the years it must have been completely overlooked by everyone, including contractors and any hotel staff. There had to be a way out!

We were being as quiet as possible, but cautious, as if someone would be waiting around every corner.

The girl said her name was Katherine Wilson. She wasn't making much sense, but from what we gathered she had been on a kayak trip running down the Verde River. She was grabbed in the woods when she had pulled her boat over to pee. She had told her friends to go on and she would meet them at the next turn of the river. She wanted her privacy, and we couldn't blame her for that. This is when she said that someone had snuck up behind her and hit her on the back of the head. She had woken up in this place.

She had deep cuts on the bottoms of her feet. Probably to keep her from trying to run away. She had been held against her will for days.

We prayed that Johnny and Brady got tired of yelling for us and went to get help.

CHAPTER 6

Johnny and Brady never left the tombstone that had fallen over, where they were told to wait. It seemed a long time had passed, and they had started wondering if they should go back to the house and get my parents.

As Johnny stood up with a little help from Brady, they noticed a lantern being carried by someone entering the graveyard near the rear of the Gambril House.

"Hey, you kids!" the person with the lantern hollered. "You stay right there." As the man approached them, he seemed a little out of breath. "What the heck are you boys doing out here in the middle of the night? Where are your parents? I want names and phone numbers."

Brady told the man, who introduced himself as the caretaker, exactly what he wanted to know, and also told him about their friends who were investigating the tunnel they had just discovered. He didn't stop to think how weird it was that someone had a job as a caretaker in a place that obviously wasn't taken care of, or the fact that it was the middle of the night. After all, what kind of caretaker works in the middle of the night and carries an old lantern and not a modern flashlight?

As they were being distracted, the boys were grabbed from behind and covered with what they thought were old, smelly burlap sacks. The sacks were thrown over their heads, and as they fought as hard as they could, their struggles were useless. Whomever had snuck up behind them was a lot bigger than they were.

As Brady and Johnny's heads were covered, their hands were tied along with their feet, and they both were hit with something big and hard. They fell to the ground and felt themselves being dragged toward the Gambril House. Anyone who happened to be outside that night would have heard their sobs of fear and their pleas for life. Unfortunately for them, no one was outside.

Chapter 7

I thought I heard someone coming and motioned for the other boys to be silent. Katherine stood on bloody feet shaking with fear and tried her best to keep her mouth shut.

James found a closet next to other kettles of various sizes in the corner of the kitchen. We all went quickly inside and closed the door. Luckily, the door had cracks in the old wood and each of us were able to have a good view of the room.

Something was wrong.

"We are one short," James whispered. "Where is Rusty? He's not here!"

"Oh, my fucking God," I thought. We all stared at each other in the small space of the closet. I could hear Sunny crying.

As we heard footsteps entering the kitchen, we saw three men carrying two large sacks. The light was very dim, and we couldn't see who the men were through the cracks in the door, but their voices were incredibly familiar. One man heaved a sack onto the butcher block counter as the other sack lay motionless on the floor.

As they shook it upside down a body, curled into a fetal position slapped onto the butcher block. It was Johnny!

The men quickly stripped him of his clothing and began wiping his body with a steaming rag. He whimpered with every swipe.

The men grabbed him, and Johnny kicked and screamed and as they lifted him off the butcher block and began walking toward the kettle. Johnny made the saddest and most heart wrenching sobs imaginable. Within seconds he was being pushed deep down into the boiling water. After only a couple weak upward thrusts of his arms, his lifeless body began floating with one arm hanging limp over the kettle's rim. His skin turned red, and his hair floated to the top of the water, the only proof that a person was inside. One of the men nonchalantly picked up Johnny's wrist with a meat thong and plopped it back in the pot, backing up a little so he wouldn't be splashed with the scalding water.

Katherine passed out and slowly dropped to the floor of the closet.

The men seemed calm, and it was obvious they had no idea Katherine was no longer strapped to the table. As soon as they realized she was gone, they would search for her and find all of us. What would happen to us then?

After finding Brady and Johnny they had to know about us—they had to know we were around here somewhere in the cavity of their dungeon.

And where was Rusty?

Chapter 8

After a few moments, two of the men left the room and the other was left to tend to the boiling pot with our friend inside. He kept looking inside and stirring it when necessary, adjusting the flame beneath the pot as he smoked a cigarette. He looked like he was heating up a can of tomato soup.

We knew this was going to be our only chance for escape. If the other men returned, we would be greatly overpowered.

Jon slowly opened the closet door and, luckily, still had the iron rod in his hand that he had earlier used to pry open the door.

None of us breathed. He crept up behind the man and slammed him over the head with the rod. His head jerked downward. Caught off guard, we all jumped on him with knives and forks we had found on the counters.

He went down easily, and we were amazed that we had been able to kill him so swiftly and quietly. As he lay on the floor, his foot ticked back and forth as though he was listening to a song no one else heard. Then it stopped.

We dragged him into the closet and closed the door. Finding a towel, we mopped up the blood that had splattered on the floor and tossed it into the dark space with him in hopes that when the other men came back, it wouldn't bring any attention to the fact that he was gone.

Brady was in the sack, and together we opened it and pulled him out. He was moaning and crying, and had a large gash above his right eyebrow, but otherwise seemed okay. Although scared to death, he was happy to see us and able to walk.

We found a small door that opened into a hallway and followed it to another corridor.

We heard nearby voices. One of the voices was Rusty. He was telling the men where we were hiding. He told them everything and laughed about how we had no idea he was a part of this—about how easily he'd fooled us.

It was then we remembered how familiar the voices were. One of the men was his father! How could the chief of police be in on this?

We all realized the tunnel beneath the tombstone had led us to the Gambril House and the only exit we knew was back the way we came. We were comforted having our flashlights and the weapons we stole from the kitchen, and we wasted no time.

As we climbed to the top of the stairs that led to the tunnel, we heard the shuffling noises again. The sounds came closer. A raspy breath, and finally those horrific eyes once again. We had no choice, but to wait until it came upon us. There was nowhere to run. It was coming toward us fast now. As we braced for the unthinkable, we saw that it was Rusty's German Shepherd dog. Fully police trained and skilled with attack maneuvers only a service dog could master, he jumped toward us without hesitation. His teeth bared and fixed on Jon since he was the first of our procession. He lunged, but Jon was able to cover his face with his arms and then we all jumped on the dog. We stabbed him to death almost as easily as the man who had thrown Johnny into the pot of boiling water.

Jon took the brunt of the attack with numerous flesh wounds to his face and chest, but after time he healed with minimal scaring.

All together, we ran—no, we flew toward the opening of the tunnel, practically dragging Katherine as we went.

Jon was in front, I was second for most of the way, then Sunny, Katherine, James, and Brady fell in last.

Within minutes Brady started to yell, "Someone is coming! They're following us!"

It was Rusty. "You guys! Slow down—why are you running?"

Rusty had no idea we had heard him speaking with his dad and that we knew who had tortured Katherine and was now trying to kill us. He also had no idea we knew Johnny was dead . . . or did he?

Brady screamed as Rusty caught him. We all stopped. There was no way we would leave Brady.

As we turned around and faced them, I noticed Rusty was holding onto Brady's shirt with the clenched fingers of someone not about to let go. I looked Rusty in the eyes. His fingers relaxed and he asked, "Where have you guys been? I lost you back there."

"Yeah, you sure did you whack job," Jon said. "You'd better back the fuck off right now or you're gonna look just like your dog."

There was a slight wince in Rusty's expression.

Without hesitation, Katherine stepped out of the darkness and into the beam of the flashlights from behind James and sprinted towards Rusty. Her movements were quick and unexpected by everyone. She had a two-foot Zombie Killer in her hand and stuck Rusty directly in the center of his abdomen. She sunk it in all the way to the handle and started twisting. Rusty dropped to his knees and as he tried to speak the only thing that came out of his mouth was blood. Deep dark and red.

She kicked him in the face and spit on him. He toppled over like a sack of concrete.

"Time to go!" she said as she ran past all of us obviously ignoring the pain in her feet.

We fell in right behind her. No doubt that girl had guts. Where she grabbed the knife was anyone's guess, but no one was surprised to find out it was laying around.

We got to the fallen tombstone and looked around as we began crawling to the surface. At last, we were out, and before we knew it, we made it to my house.

The sunrise was just beginning to glow pink along the eastern horizon.

Chapter 9

My parents, full of shock and rage, called the police in Prescott, then Cottonwood, then Sedona. The FBI even became involved. There were so many lights and sirens at the Gambril House there was no way for those involved to escape.

As it turned out, there were many miles of tunnels underneath Humboldt. Most went directly to the home of the police chief, and all went to the Gambril House. The torture chambers were discovered, and all the graves in the cemetery were exhumed. They found that each crypt held numerous body parts from missing children from all over the country.

The man posing as the caretaker turned out to be the town judge. The Honorable Milton Rutledge. He had been appointed eight months after Chief Newman started with the department. When the authorities visited his house, they found him hanging in his basement. He was naked and had a large upside-down crucifix tattooed on his back.

As the years went by, and as we all tried to forget what happened that night, the boys and I seemed to lose track of each other. Jon married early to some gal right after high school and has a couple of kids. I believe he is working as a Ford mechanic somewhere in Arizona. Sunny's family moved away that same summer. His parents never said where; they just sold the house and disappeared. James is an attorney down in Camp Verde and doing very well for himself from what I hear, and Katherine lived in the next town over, so no one ever knew what happened to her. I hope she is well and is happy and was able to move on with her life. I still see Brady from time to time. We both went to college at ASU. It's been a few years since we have spoken. I joined the

Forest Service here in Prescott and married a local gal and have a baby on the way. Brady wound up working at a radio station down in Tempe and is doing very well. My parents are still in Humboldt. I'm sure they will never leave.

We all went through a lot that night. It's hard to put depraved events behind you when you keep in touch with those that remind you of what you're trying to forget.

A week after my party, we attended Johnny's funeral. It was the largest funeral in the history of our town. It was also televised. What was found of his body was cremated and his family moved to Maryland six months later. We never heard from them again.

When they arrested Rusty's father, I was told he was eating a large, meaty bowl of soup and laughing.

A Good Trip Gone Bad

The night of the party I began feeling restless—in a happy way, but I also felt anxiety taking hold of my emotions. I had never taken acid before that night, so I was pretty excited to see what it was going to do to me. I'd been told it affects people in different ways, and I had always steered clear of it for different reasons, until now.

My name is Nick Kochukas. In a former life I was a motorcycle mechanic in an out of the way place in Maryland called Point of Rocks. We got visitors, mostly from local areas, who want to slow their pace down a little, relive history, and play in our water. It's an old train town that sits at the merging of the Potomac and the Shenandoah Rivers with Harpers Ferry, West Virginia across the bridge. I grew up there and had never been anywhere else. This town and the surrounding fields were all I'd known; all I wanted to know. I had no idea that night was going to be the first time I would ever leave it.

A few friends decided to have a party just off the C&O Canal at Violets Lock and it seemed like a hell of a good time . . . at the time. A lot of people showed up that night, and as the Lock is pretty much off the beaten path, we each decided to bring a few things to get us through the night and most of the morning. No one wanted to risk driving home high on that shit so camping seemed like the safest plan. I brought a change of clothes, a couple bottles of water, and a couple cans of tuna fish. I was only going to be gone a day or so and that would be plenty of food for that length of time. I always tried to think of the unexpected when going outside of the norm and I knew considering the drugs I was planning on eating, that night would definitely be outside of the norm for me.

As things turned out, I had no sooner set up my tent that night when a dude I knew offered to sell me a couple hits of purple microdot. After a brief moment of contemplation, I agreed to buy it. I held one on my tongue, allowed it to dissolve, then wanted to spit out the little square of paper it was on, but I didn't. Instead, I downed it with a large mouthful of cheap beer and waited.

I hadn't mentioned to anyone that I took any acid except for Ron Patchet. Ron was a good friend of mine, and I didn't really want anyone else to know. I was afraid if people knew I was tripping they might start fucking with me and try to freak me out. I didn't want to be the butt end of any jokes later if I couldn't handle it well. He told me he wouldn't say anything to anyone, and I believed him.

A couple hours had gone by, and I still felt relatively normal. The beer kicked in and I was being careful not to overdo that. I drank about four, and on my fifth one I thought it was best to slow down and wait for the acid to catch up.

About a half hour later, I figured what the hell, and ate the second hit. I've always been a big guy and figured my size probably warranted a double hit. Not long after that I felt the power rush and enjoyed every minute of it.

The sun had gone down, and the moon was big and bright. The reflection it cast across the Potomac River was breathtaking, and the swaying of the trees and the sounds of the nocturnal animals were amazing. The acid magnified all these senses, and it was a good time. What a ride.

I felt myself become the life of the party. I had never spoken so freely and honestly. I have always been a tad on the shy side and kept mainly to myself in public situations, or with a few chosen individuals at most. I was not the kind of person who felt comfortable with everyone. But that night I felt as comfortable as a kid on a ferris wheel. It was fan-fucking-tastic.

I laughed with the guys and had quite a few witty conversations with a few of the ladies, too, that night. Why had I waited so long to try this shit? The night was going well, and it was turning into a hell of a party.

The music came from a big boom box someone had brought and Lynyrd Skynyrd, Peter Frampton, and Kansas drifted out on currents of air so sweet, I couldn't take my eyes away. I don't remember how long I stood there swaying back and forth just staring at the music, but it was the best time of the whole night.

Everything just kind of rocked and I could feel the blood pulsing through my veins with every beat. After a while I started thinking about the music controlling my very heartbeat. What if the music stopped? Would my heart also stop? The bass was so intense, I felt my heart hammering with every beat. I found myself getting closer to the boom box as if I were protecting it. I realized I was being ridiculous, so I wandered over to a bunch of friends standing by the canal's edge to try and take my mind off the music.

As I listened to the conversations, I didn't join in, but instead found myself lured to the water. It was murky during the day, but now it was nighttime, and it was absolutely black. The canal had no current, but as I watched the dark water, I saw a slow rise in its surface. Not quite a ripple, but definitely movement. Could someone be under the water drowning? Perhaps caught on a log or entangled in fishing line? No one else noticed it, and when I pointed it out to Tommy Felton, the guy beside me, he just grinned at me and shook his head. Why did he do that? Someone could be drowning! I was concerned about it, and this clown just grinned at me.

When Tommy grinned at me it looked like he hadn't brushed his teeth in months, and I could make out the white crust between each tooth. I couldn't believe it. He even had dried spit stuck in the corners of his lips. The spit caked up and got thicker with every word he spoke. It was revolting. It was one of those things that once you saw it, it could never be unseen in your mind. I must have made him feel uneasy with the intent way my eyes wouldn't leave his mouth or the horrible expression of disgust I had when looking at him in general. Soon after, he left the group and found another cluster of people not too far away. I remember praying he wouldn't open his mouth any more for the rest of the night. I should have told him to brush his teeth, and wished I had. Perhaps I would later if I saw him again. Had his mouth always looked like that? Christ, I couldn't keep thinking about those teeth all night, what a buzz killer.

Realizing I had to take a leak, I walked just off the path, or so I thought, and into the woods separating the canal from the river. Alone at last. I unzipped and let it go. Relief overtook me. I must have waited too long because it seemed as though the stream of urine wouldn't quit. My God, how much liquid could the human body maintain? What if my bladder had burst and I didn't realize it because of the drugs I took? I began to feel extremely uncomfortable, almost as if I had started to cramp up. It could have burst because the front of my groin was hot and felt like it had been over stretched. What if thousands of deadly bacteria were floating around in my body right now infecting my organs? It was so dark, and I couldn't see, what if I was urinating blood? I would never know. My kidneys could have shut down and I would never know it until it was too late.

As I observed the urine trickle to a stop, I felt so relieved. I would go back to the party and ask Ron to look at my eyes. If the irises were yellow or green, I would know that my bladder ruptured and was exuding dangerous microorganisms throughout my system, and I had jaundice. I would have someone take me to the hospital. Good plan. Geez. How long had I stood there thinking about THAT? Minutes? Hours?

I didn't know what time it was. There used to be a lot of voices and music, but I couldn't hear anything except the croaking of bullfrogs and crickets in the woods.

How long had I been peeing?

Had everyone left? Surely not everyone would have left, and my friends wouldn't have gone without finding me, right?

I thought we were camping! Did I say something to offend them? Did I piss everyone off and now they hated me and want to get even with me by leaving me in the woods? I bet they were all waiting for me to leave to take a leak so they could run off as soon as my guard was down . . . Okay—I knew I was getting paranoid. It was the drug. It was just the drug. Stop being paranoid.

Only I couldn't.

I quickly walked back to the towpath that followed the canal and looked around for my friends—for anyone.

The music had stopped.

I only peed for a short time; how could everyone be gone? It was still early, wasn't it? The last time I checked it was about 10:30. For Christ's sake, it was late, but not that late. They probably thought I left ahead of them. Fuck!

I started staring down the towpath and into the woods were everyone had parked their cars. I thought for sure I would see some type of reflection from all the chrome, but I saw nothing.

My head started to pound, and I guessed that my blood pressure was off the charts due to the fear of being alone. I knew I shouldn't have taken that other hit. I would probably have been fine if I hadn't eaten the second one. I needed to calm down. I needed to think. The thought of being out there by myself was the most frightening thing I could imagine right then.

Everything was loud. The mosquitos buzzing, the crickets. Even the river took on a wild rushing sound like the water could be rising—maybe rising over the banks. I hoped I was far enough away. I need to get further inland. Maybe a dam broke upstream or it was raining hard, causing the river to flood and I was in danger and didn't even know it yet? Maybe someone came while I was taking a piss and told everyone they had to leave right away because there was going to be a flash flood. I didn't hear the warning and now I was going to get caught in rising waters and die with no way out.

"Ron!" I yelled into the night. "Ron!" There was no reply. I was all alone.

I walked to the area where I'd stashed my backpack with my camping items. At that moment, I thought of them as my survival gear. I picked up my backpack and opened the flap. Everything except a flashlight. That figures.

My hands shook badly. I felt like I needed to hide. I had to so the beasts in the woods watching me would go away.

As the tree branches moved in the wind, the light from the moon danced in and out of their shadows in erratic patterns. The forest turned into a haunted, scary place and my tortured mind imagined the worst horrors from every nightmare I'd ever had as a child.

Every sound penetrated my head like it was being hit by a rock. A little click of a branch sounded like an axe plunging toward me. The smallest animal's voice sounded like one hundred demons screaming.

Mosquitos flew around my head. They landed on my arms and face biting me. They made me itch. I felt my skin swell into lumps and fill with mosquito venom and pus. This wasn't good. I needed to calm down.

I had to sit down, but I was too afraid. If I had to run, I knew I wouldn't be able to get up fast enough to escape whatever might chase me. My eyes darted back and forth trying to see everything at once. I knew something was out there. Something was waiting for me. My heart was pounding so hard, and I knew I would fall down if I didn't sit and try to calm myself. I think I began to whimper.

For a moment I thought I should wade out into the river. If anything were to come at me, while in the water, I could at least see more clearly. But the Potomac River is one that changes often. It is calm in some areas and drastically unforgiving in others. It would be a death sentence for anyone to wander in, especially without a PFD, and some asshole on acid wouldn't stand a chance against the possible currents out there. Even as fucked up as I was, I knew better than to do that.

I stood and teetered as long as I could. If I had to, I'd stand all night. But I was wired and tired and I knew sitting was my only choice.

Somehow, I had gotten wet. Somehow, I found myself in a dark forest with living, hungry things. They had to be insects around me. If I could just make it until morning, I thought. The light of day would be life. I was still incredibly fucked up and probably imagining things, but I knew that even if I was perfectly straight, I'd still be scared shitless.

I was imagining things because of the acid and overpowered with fright. The smartest thing I could do was to talk myself down and try to relax a little, so I did.

As time went by, the forest seemed to get darker. The light from the moon was barely visible and darkness was everywhere. I shuddered.

I had been leaning against a tree but found myself sliding down its trunk and in an instant my butt landed on wet ground.

I sat shivering, scared and alone.

I looked down and saw leeches. There were many of them slowly slithering on both my legs and a couple were on my arms.

I managed to brush a few off, but others had already latched on to my skin. I knew I had to be imagining them. I wasn't in the water. That's where leeches lived, right? I ignored them.

Moments later, I felt things crawling in my hair, down my neck, and into my shirt. I felt covered in crawling things. The pain was intense. I was tripping. It was the drug. I ignored them.

I had been living here since birth. I've camped here. I've made love in the grass here. There was nothing that could harm me. I ignored it. It was just the drug.

Hours slowly came and went.

I saw the grass move. It looked to me as though a wind was blowing directly towards me as the grass parted and leaned in my direction. The harder I looked at it I could have sworn insects were coming at me like an army. I told myself I would never eat acid again and ignored them.

I looked at my body and thought I saw blood on my shirt and felt intense pain that wouldn't stop. Time played tricks on me. I found that the sky had grown darker still. I couldn't see myself, but knew I was fine. I told myself there was nothing in these woods that would hurt me. I was tripping on acid, and I took too much. The second hit was a mistake, I knew that now. I was having a bad trip and imagining being eaten alive by bugs and that was it. Get over it. Suck it up. Keep ignoring it.

I heard Ron's voice. It was far away and very faint. He called my name. I smiled. I tried to answer, but something crawled over my mouth, and I couldn't respond.

I heard footsteps. Slowly at first, then they sped up as they got closer to me. I think I may have been laughing.

The next thing I remember was hearing Ron's voice almost screaming and telling me to get up. I couldn't. I tried, but my legs had gone weak, and my strength had left me hours ago.

I remember looking down and seeing red. Red shorts. Red shirt. Had I been wearing red that day? Why would I do that?

I remember a kid in my neighborhood came to school one day wearing a red outfit. The boys all made fun of him. I never forgot that, and I refused to wear anything red after that.

I heard a loud noise that had to be music. I saw strobe lights. Finally. I guessed everyone left to get more beer or something and now they had returned. They were back!

But it wasn't music. I wanted it to be Frampton trying to "Show me the way . . ." However, in hindsight it had to be the siren of an ambulance.

Two weeks later I woke up with a feeding tube inserted in my throat and a large black woman wiping what was left of my ass. Oh my God, what had happened? Where was I?

My skin was wrapped in gauze. I had tubes sticking out of me and every movement I made felt like someone was touching me with a red, hot poker.

The party. Something happened at the party. I remember everything now. How could I forget? I lay there and began to scream. I screamed and couldn't stop.

Life as I knew it had slipped away.

These last four months have been a series of skin grafts, oral and reconstructive maxillofacial surgeries, and leg muscle reconstruction.

I thought I was being eaten alive and as it turned out, I was. The mental focus of my denial due to the hallucinogenic drugs I ate was, as it turned out, overthought, and inappropriate. Who knew?

My neck and face had been stripped of most of the muscle tissue needed for expression and support of the weight of my head. That being said, I will now always wear a brace to hold my head erect.

I will never walk again. My penis is now in the stomachs of insects and the nerves in my legs are gone. I will be forever bound to a wheelchair and my bowels are infested with killer microbes that harvested my intestinal tract, forever limiting normal kidney functions.

As I have been educated, since this monumental affliction has happened to me, it turns out that the Fire Ant, which lives in huge numbers in China, Australia, the United States, and other countries, are an extremely aggressive type of ant. In fact, they rank in the top four most dangerous types of ant species in the world. Another type of ant, which ranks number one in being the most aggressive and destructive, is the Bulldog Ant. These ants, according to scientists, have devastating venom and are believed to have evolved from wasp-like beings, which explains their appearance as looking like wingless wasps. It seems that I had unknowingly discovered an ant mound of a cross between these two species.

As I had leaned against the tree, and sat so near to the mound, I was considered an immediate threat and attacked. I never stood a chance.

I will always remember ice skating on the neighborhood pond and running away from the bad kids in the neighborhood. Nights catching lightning bugs and sticking them in jars, chasing the girls and making them scream. Secretly hoping Debbie Sheftell would let me take her to the homecoming dance my senior year. Admiring her beautiful long hair and that smile that never quit. Oh, the memories I have of her. She had always been my first crush and to this day I think of her fondly. If only Debbie could see me now! How horrible it is to realize I have so many wonderful memories and now they're all I will ever have. Forever. And ever.

My working days are over as I am now on Social Security and Disability. No more motorcycle riding or going swimming at the quarry. No more hopes of a family or enjoying vacations in wonderful places.

From now on I will have bowel movements and urinary releases through a bag on the side of my torso until the day I die.

Drugs. Yeah. I'll buy, you fly.

That Deluxe Shine

Chapter 1

My name is Lindsey Everest, and for the last month of my life I have been staying at a mental health facility in Cottonwood, Arizona called Windhaven. It is not a world renown facility, nothing in Arizona is, but it specializes in traumatic disorders of the mind. Specifically, Psychiatry, Necrophilia, Bestiality, among other sexual disorders of the rarest kinds. Fortunately for me, I wasn't a patient there due to any strange or deviant, carnal behaviors, but only the traumas that affected my mind. Due to the facility being so close to my home, the courts felt Windhaven was the best fit.

Windhaven wasn't an awful place, and I must be honest in saying that although the patients I met were incredibly psychotic and disturbed in the worst ways imaginable, they were also, for the most part, happy, interesting, and able to make my time at Windhaven much more bearable.

I think I should begin by telling you I am not crazy. What happened to me could have happened to anyone. I was just in the wrong place at the right time and unable to know what I was getting myself into.

It all started in the fall of 2019 when I decided to purchase the most beautiful motorcycle I had ever seen. You see, I was drawn to it. Plain and simple. It was as if it knocked me over with the energy that surrounded it. I couldn't even ride a motorcycle when I bought it and, honestly, prior to that day, I had no intention of ever learning. I was almost twenty-four years old and scared to even ride on the back of a bike much less operate one myself. It was a 2018 Harley Davidson Softail Deluxe and it was the most beautiful shade of blue. It looked more brilliant than any crystal, pansy, or gas light you could imagine. You see, I believe it knew if a person looked at it long enough, they would be unable to deny it anything—even a life. I know that sounds kind of crazy, but as this story turns out, that was exactly what happened.

Chapter 2

The day I first saw it I had entered a bike shop in Phoenix. My boyfriend, Henry Sawyer, needed to pick up a few items from the parts department for his own bike and while he was speaking with the guy at the counter, I found myself looking at the t-shirts and jewelry under the glass case by the cash register. Although they had some wonderful things, they were also Harley, which meant everything was drastically overpriced. Since I wasn't made of money, I was strictly in the window-shopping mode and planned to stay that way.

Although I had always enjoyed going with Henry to run his errands, on that particular day, I was tired and wanted to hurry home. It seemed every time we left one place, he wanted to go to another. It was all fine and good, but like I said, I was tired and just wanted to go home, smoke a joint, and put my feet up. My patience was almost at an end, and I was quickly losing my sunny personality with every passing minute.

I left the counter and started wandering around the sales department. They had a lot of bikes, and since I wasn't particularly a motorcycle enthusiast, each one looked like the other and I began to feel like I was drowning in a sea of chrome and wheels.

As I walked through the rows, a glint of sunlight stabbed my eyes. It was intensely bright, and I had to turn away. For a reason I still cannot explain, I felt the need to turn back and look to see where that glare was coming from.

In the back of the show room where the used bikes were kept, I saw a shiny, blue fender barely sticking out from between two bikes. It wasn't just blue, it had a weird, sapphire brilliance I knew I had to see up close. Truth be told, I didn't just want to see it up close, I was drawn to it, as if there was an urgency pulling me toward it. It sounds funny, but that is the only way I can honestly describe it. I was compelled.

As I turned around and approached the bike, a feeling of sheer desire swept over me. I loved the shade of blue. I loved the white wall tires. The bike seemed to call to me. I really can't explain it other than that, and I've tried a million times to doctors drilling me for information.

As I said, I had never in my life ridden a motorcycle and I could barely ride the Schwinn ten-speed my parents had bought me when I was fourteen. But, for some reason I was really interested in it and couldn't stop thinking about it.

My mind kept going over the likelihood of learning how to ride, even though I wasn't very coordinated. Just crossing the street and chewing gum was a chore at times for me.

The whole idea was ridiculous. When I'd entered the store with Henry, I only thought of getting out of there and going home. Suddenly, now all I could think of was buying a bike, not just any bike—that bike, and wondered if there was enough space in the garage for it. I had heard of impulse purchases, but this was nuts.

A moment later a salesman walked up to me and asked if I had any questions about any of the motorcycles on display and if he could help me. Without thinking, I told him, "Yes, I think you can." I was rather shocked at my rapid response.

He proceeded to tell me all about the bike I pointed out, and the salesman even had information on its past service history. The bike was barely a year old and only had 4,880 miles on it. He said the previous owner came into the store and seemed as though he was in a huge hurry to sell it. Actually "unload it" was more of an exact description. He said he had gotten tired of it and wanted it gone. The salesman said he was in such a rush to sign over the title that the guy even left his driver's license behind at the end of their transaction. When the salesman called him back, he continued to flee (for lack of a better description) through the parking lot, got in his car, and drove away. He said the guy never returned to get it, so the dealership had to mail it back to him. "Weird, right?" he said looking at me.

As I sat in the salesman's office, I made my decision to purchase the Deluxe and didn't even consider Henry's opinion. Looking back that seems unfair, but at the time it was my business and my business alone. I had become so excited about it I couldn't think straight. I convinced myself I could learn to ride it, after all, tons of girls rode bikes nowadays, why couldn't I? I was small, but I had remembered talking with a friend of Henry's who also rode, and she had told me even she couldn't pick up her bike if it went over. She said the trick was to learn well, practice, and just don't drop the damn thing. I remember laughing at that, but as I stood standing in the showroom that day, it resonated like church bells on Sunday. I convinced myself it would be easy. It would be a learning experience and I couldn't wait to get started.

I filled out the loan application as I waited for Henry to walk up behind me, but he didn't. After I completed the form and handed it to the salesman, he told me the credit check would be approved in a few minutes and he'd let me know the outcome. I made great money working from home on the internet and my credit was flawless, so I knew I wouldn't have any problem getting the loan. I wasn't sweating that at all. What I was sweating, however, was how to break the happy news to Henry. I knew he would be ticked off that I'd made such an important decision without even discussing it with him. Oh well. But that alone shows the power the bike had over me already, right?

I left the sales office and returned to Henry at the parts counter. I must have been fidgeting and he must have started to feel as though I was getting anxious to leave.

"I'm sorry this is taking so long. What I need is back-ordered and the guy is trying to find it at another store. Are you pissed?" Henry asked.

"Not at all," I said. "In fact, you may want to brace yourself for a little surprise."

"Okay, consider me braced. What have you done now?" Henry said with bright eyes.

"I think I'm buying a bike."

"What? You can't even ride. What do you want to buy?"

"The salesman called it a Softail Deluxe. I don't know, but it was pretty, and I thought it would be fun."

Henry laughed and said, "A Deluxe? You've got to be freaking kidding me! A Deluxe is a big bike and you can barely ride a bicycle!" He grinned. "What brought this on all of a sudden?" Then he quickly whispered as if he were a little kid, "Let's go look at it!"

"Well, I filled out a loan app, and the guy is running my credit now. He said it should take a few minutes."

"You already did the paperwork? They're already running your credit? How could you have made that decision without telling me? I can't believe you would do that!"

"Well, let's call it an impulse purchase. I just really liked it. Are you angry?" I asked.

"I guess not, but it would have been nice if you would have consulted with me first. I mean, we are going out and living together. Shouldn't we consult each other regarding big purchases?" he said. "Pardon me if I feel like you don't give a crap what I think about all of this. Besides, a pack of gum is an impulse purchase, a $25,000 vehicle is not."

"You're right. I'm sorry. Let me show it to you and tell me what you think I should do. I just thought it would be fun to ride together," I said, trying to smooth things over. "It's beautiful, Henry, and I really want it."

He looked at it and agreed it was very clean and seemed to be well maintained. He considered the mileage and the extra chrome on it and told me he thought it was a good buy at a good price.

Moments later the salesman came back out and said the loan was mine if I wanted to buy the bike. There wasn't much dickering about price, however Henry suggested they throw in a helmet and $100.00 worth of credit towards the first service, and of course, the T-shirt of my choice. The salesman agreed happily, and Henry and I looked at each other in disbelief.

Delighted, I signed on the dotted line and that afternoon I drove back to the house in Henry's pick-up while he followed me on my new Deluxe.

CHAPTER 3

The next month was filled with many lessons of dos and don'ts relating to safe motorcycle riding practices and Henry had signed me up for a beginner's riding class that was offered at Yavapai Regional College. For $250.00 the school provided a little 250 cc enduro, a few classroom hours, and a big parking lot with lots of bright orange cones that showed the abuse of many other students before me. The school was a third-party test site, so they were able to provide the DMV driving test without my having to deal with the DMV directly. The bonus to the deal was that my insurance provider offered me a twenty percent discount for taking the class. It was a total win-win situation and Henry was happy I was getting professional instruction. He was an experienced rider, but also knew he didn't have the coaching techniques and background he felt I really needed to learn properly.

The day finally came, and I took my driving test and passed with flying colors. I was so happy. Henry took us out that evening for a congratulatory seafood dinner in Prescott with all the trimmings, and that night as we lay in bed, he held me and told me how much he loved us being together and he was proud of me. He had known how difficult it was for me to achieve this accomplishment.

In the past, I'd always had a fear of riding and I know he felt I only did it for him. For some reason, he must have felt I had to make this drastic leap of faith in other to keep him. I never let on that it wasn't him, it was the bike I really needed.

We made love and within minutes we were both asleep.

The next morning was Friday and we both took off work to explore a few historic towns and scenic highways. A long weekend was on the menu, and we were excited to hit the open road together for the first time on motorcycles.

As we rode up 89A towards Jerome, Az., and as the Mingus Mountains began their beautifully scenic journey through the high, slanted switchbacks, I was totally in my glory. The wind blowing through my hair and the sound of the Deluxe's motor combined with the unbaffled drag pipes was the biggest high I could have ever imagined. "Why have I always been so afraid to live my dreams?" I thought to myself. I felt so terribly sorry for those friends I've known in my life, who instead of making their own journey, chose, instead, the easy way out, which was to pick a man who had the knowhow and marry them, rather than do the hard work for themselves. I wondered why most women didn't take their own chances to build their own life, instead choosing to flip a coin in hopes some guy would fulfil their dreams for them. I felt so sorry for their weakness. In the end, I thought, it was so much better to know you'd lived your life your way, making your own rules, rather than just riding behind a man, and helping him to achieve his.

At the rest area near the end of town, we stopped for a coke and to stretch our legs. Henry suggested switching motorcycles for a few miles so he could get a feel of the Deluxe. He wanted to see how it handled and I considered that a huge compliment as I was such a new rider, yet he was willing to trust me with his bike.

As we merged back onto the highway, I felt uneasy even though his bike was basically the same. It had the same frame, front end, the only difference was the saddlebags and tour pack on the rear. Why did everything seem so huge and unstable? It felt as though I had forgotten what I had learned from the riding school. When I was on my bike it felt incredibly natural. It was as though I didn't have to think. As if the bike actually drove itself.

At the same time, Henry, while riding my Deluxe, felt he had barely any control. The bike passed with flying colors on the test drive and DMV inspection, and I had been riding effortlessly with no problems or concerns at all, in fact, it seemed as though I had been riding for years with total control and accuracy in every move and turn. However, when Henry rode the Deluxe, he said later that the bike wouldn't handle at all for him. In fact, it scared him to death. The throttle was extremely touchy, the bike rode top heavy to the point of overbalancing, and he had to hit the brakes often just to make sure they would respond. To Henry it felt like the bike had a mind of its own. Also, when entering turns he commented on how the tires would suddenly feel flat, so that turning was almost dangerous.

About five miles after the rest area, we hit a slow down along the highway. Thinking back, I basically freaked out when downshifting and locked up the rear wheel when, confused, I tried to shift from fourth gear to second gear in a patch of sandy material. The bike slid a little and I took off onto the shoulder and nearly into the field beyond. This is typical for a new rider, although very strange considering I had been doing so well, so often on my own bike.

As I stopped the bike, I put the kickstand down, climbed off, and told Henry I had had enough. I didn't want to ride his bike anymore and wanted mine back. I was obviously very frightened.

Henry was wary of letting me ride it again, considering how difficult it was for him, but I remember persisting and refusing to ride his anymore. Finally, he agreed with the stipulation that I would stay right in front of him and wouldn't go over thirty mph. We would run our hazard lights and go slow until he could get a chance to look over the Deluxe. I agreed.

He watched me the rest of the way home. The bike seemed to handle perfectly, it sounded normal, and I had no problem navigating, stopping, or controlling the bike in any way. Why had he had such a difficult time, yet I rode the Deluxe with ease?

In hindsight, he said he wished he would have made me sell it right then and there. But who knew the chain of events that would soon follow that day's experience?

Upon arriving at home, Henry had adjusted the clutch on the Deluxe and checked it over. He found absolutely nothing wrong. Even the oil looked as clean as tea.

At the same time, I had become mesmerized with the Deluxe. I washed it every day, polished it, and even spoke to it as if it was an old friend. On our usual Friday night outing with our friends, I had told Henry I wanted to cancel and stay at home so that I could polish "Old Blue". That was what I had started calling it. He reminded me I had just washed it the day before, but he remembered me telling him I wasn't happy with the job I had done and wanted to do it again.

Henry started to realize things were beginning to get a little out of hand but wasn't sure what to do about this sudden obsession I had with the Deluxe.

A week later Henry took Old Blue out on a test run after doing some general maintenance and while rounding a turn, the throttle twisted back and stuck wide open. As the bike seemed to make the turns on its own, and as Henry realized he had no control at all, he said he made his peace with God and had no choice but to ride it out. He said it was at that moment he knew why I was riding so well, and why I had been able to ride like a pro with so little experience. The bike was doing the driving for me. I was simply hanging on and enjoying the ride.

He told me his first thought was to sell it and sell it fast. At first, I wouldn't even discuss it. In fact, I told him that if he didn't want me to ride it, he could move the fuck out.

He said he knew at that moment the relationship was doomed, or I was.

CHAPTER 4

A few nights had passed, and Henry had been continually trying to overlook the constant intensity of motorcycle mania growing by leaps and bounds in our once quiet and easygoing household.

As we lay sleeping, no longer holding each other in our arms, but each of us settled uncomfortably at opposite ends of the bed, Henry heard what sounded like the garage door moving. He couldn't tell if it was going up or down, but it was definitely moving.

He quickly climbed out of bed, put his slippers on, and grabbed the Barretta 380 semi-auto which he diligently kept loaded in the bedside table beside him. I heard him get up and followed him like a lost puppy.

As we carefully slipped out the back door and came around to the side of the garage, he noticed that the door was down, locked, and all was dark and quiet. Exactly as it should be. We quietly entered through the side door and turned on the light. Ready for anything, we waited for something to happen. Nothing did. He walked through the garage looking for anything out of the ordinary but found nothing. I stayed low by the doorway. "Well, I guess this is a good thing," he said, somewhat relieved, and began to turn back to the door to go back to bed. Then he noticed a ticking sound. The sound of a hot motor cooling off. The sound he knew all too well.

He walked over to the bikes and looked at his own Fat Boy and touched the rear tire. Cold. He tapped the pipes. Cold.

Then he walked over to Old Blue. It was ticking like a bomb. He knew it was hot. The heat off the pipes and jugs were practically burning his fingers before he even touched them.

Henry knew I kept the keys inside the house. One on my keyring on the hook in the kitchen and the spare in my jewelry box on the dresser. I had been with him in bed all night. He was a light sleeper and there was no way I could have left the house without him waking up. "What just happened here?" he whispered slowly.

As we left the garage he turned back to Old Blue and looked down at the cement floor. He pointed out a wet tire mark leading from outside to where it was now parked inside the garage.

Suddenly, we both felt a chill run up our backs.

We didn't talk much that night.

The light of day brought a certain peaceful feeling that only cool air and flannel pajamas can bring. I made hot coffee and waffles as Henry laid in bed wondering how to deal with the recent discovery in the garage the night before.

After he reminded me what had happened, I remember looking at him strangely and queerly tilting my head as I smiled with a faint and somewhat uplifting expression. "Isn't it amazing?" Somehow, I got the impression that Henry wasn't comforted by my response.

I must admit I was in absolute fascination at the thought of my bike being—well, for lack of a better word, magic. Henry also pointed out the fact that I was a brand-new rider, who somehow, can ride better than any guy he'd ever met in what, a month? Realizing he was right, and the bike saved my bacon numerous times and had basically taken over the entire process of shifting, balancing, braking, accelerating, well, you get my drift. No wonder I couldn't ride Henry's Fat Boy. I hadn't really ridden since I was in that riding course and my skills and attitude had grown completely idealistic. However, knowing all of this, I still loved the bike more than ever. The best and scariest part was I felt it loved me back.

CHAPTER 5

As the days followed, Henry and I decided to stay up at night and wait for Old Blue to leave the garage again. We had decided to follow it and see where it went. Only then would we have a clearer picture about what might be happening here.

Henry had also made it clear he didn't want me riding it anymore. That hit a nerve in me and although I knew he was right, and I knew he was trying to protect me, it was something I couldn't agree to. I often took the bike out for lengthy jaunts along country roads while he was at work or out with friends. At first, I worried about him finding out, thinking he would certainly glance at the odometer and grasp the fact there were a lot more miles on it than there used to be. Maybe he did and thought the new miles was due to Old Blue herself and her secret midnight runs. Worrying had been unnecessary because one day after I washed it, I looked at the odometer and to my surprise, every mile I had put on it, was taken off. I guess the bike could do that, too.

The most exciting moment we had was while lying in bed one night and hearing the garage door open. We had recently gotten used to going to sleep in our clothes and we immediately flew out of bed and headed for the pickup truck as soon as Old Blue rolled out of the driveway. The bike went down our dirt road and took a left onto Muncaster Mill Road, which was paved, but narrow and dark. It seemed to only take roads that were less traveled and very remote. Obviously, a bike with no rider would be incredibly suspicious.

We followed Old Blue for about an hour and finally it slowed to a stop at a cemetery. It went through the entranceway and as we watched, it finally stopped at a large headstone. The motor quit, and it leaned over to the left as some invisible rider carefully put the kickstand down.

We waited for something else to happen, but nothing did. The bike just sat there next to someone's grave.

Henry and I looked at each other. We didn't know whether to be afraid, or incredibly sad. It was as though the bike was visiting a loved one who had passed. Maybe that was exactly what it was doing. I can't speak for Henry, but my heart became very heavy.

We sat there for hours. At 4:00 AM the motor started; the bike righted itself as the kickstand was put up. We heard the transmission clunk into first, and slowly the bike continued down and around the one lane gravel road that went through the graveyard and exited on the main drag.

In the next four days Old Blue left the house three times and each time it went to that cemetery, and each time it left at midnight.

On the morning of the fifth day, I drove my car out to the cemetery and took a few pictures of the tombstone. It read:

Andrew Jackson Underwood
June 14, 1979 – June 14, 2018

He had died on his birthday.

I went straight to the Office of Vital Records to find out more about this person. I was determined to find out how this man and my motorcycle shared a strange bond that crossed the boundaries of life and death.

It seems Andrew Underwood was the prior owner of Old Blue, and his death was tragically due to his confrontation of a would-be motorcycle thief.

When I was purchasing the bike from the dealership, I remember the salesman telling me the story of the frightened man who had brought the bike in to "unload" it. He said the man was so scared he left his driver's license in his office. Now I know why the man was so scared, knowing the bike's personality. However, I had assumed he was the owner. Perhaps he was Andrew's brother or close friend. I wanted—no needed—to contact him. I had to know everything about Old Blue's past, and I needed to know immediately.

I drove to the dealership, but they told me it was against their policy to divulge any personal information on their clients. I understood. We all have our rights and confidentiality is important to everyone. I would find the information on my own.

The prior owner's name and address was on the title so that was the easy part. But when I drove out to the house, there was no one home. I left a business card with a little note in an envelope and slid it into the frame just above the doorknob. It was the perfect place and right in plain view, yet secure in case a breeze came by unannounced.

Within forty-eight hours, I received a telephone call from Mrs. Andrew Underwood.

She was very cordial. Not too nice, not too despondent. It was obvious she had loved her husband very much and was still in shock from his death. She agreed to meet me the following day for lunch at a local hot spot close to both of our homes. I had suggested we talk about the issues I was inquiring about in my note, and she wasn't hesitant at all to visit with me.

I was finally getting somewhere.

I woke up at the crack of dawn and the morning was eerily dark. The clouds hung low and intimidating and I knew rain was imminent. I got Henry off to work and began mentally preparing for my encounter with the Mrs. I hadn't mentioned to Henry that I was going to meet her. I knew he'd want to come or at the very least have suggestions or talking points I may or may not have found necessary to deal with. Besides, this was my game and I wanted to play it my way.

I showered, dressed, and climbed in my car, giving myself ample time in case of any unforeseen delays with traffic, and arrived promptly at 11:45 and got a table.

As I sat, not quite knowing how to feel or what to expect, I looked up and saw a woman walking toward me. She wasn't young and glamorous, nor middle-aged and greying. She was classy and carried herself in a confident manner that was neither intimidating nor judgmentally offensive. She had a warm smile as she walked up to me and asked, "Lindsey?"

"Yes, I'm Lindsey. Thank you so much for meeting with me today." I waved my hand towards her chair, and she sat without hesitation.

"I'm Andy's wife, Edith Maxine." She hesitated and added "I'm sorry. I still can't quite get used to the word widow."

I immediately liked her. I'm not sure why, but she had a genuine personality. No pretension, no airs, or false fronts. People like that are hard to come by these days.

"Please call me Max. Everyone does." She smiled.

At first, I was worried about how to begin. I didn't want her to think I was some nut bag with her beloved husband's motorcycle by jumping into the whole "the bike drives itself and has a mind of its own" thing. I surely didn't want to lose my chance to speak with her and instead see her running out of the restaurant in a panic. I had to take my time and choose my words wisely to keep her attention and respect.

To my surprise she began first.

"I believe I know why you contacted me."

I didn't know what to say, so I quietly sat and let her continue.

"In fact, I was wondering how long it would take before I heard from you." Her eyes fixed on me, not waiting for a response, but I could see her sadness and need to get something off her chest.

I was honest with her and said, "I bought the bike on a whim. I saw it, and felt I just had to have it. I've never even ridden a bike before; I've always been afraid of motorcycles. I only went into the dealership with my boyfriend because he needed a part for his."

Max said, "My husband never rode either. Harleys are addictive to a lot of folks, but this bike controlled him. It was as though he couldn't think straight. He was absorbed by it, fascinated by it. I couldn't stop him from talking about it." She added, "If you own it now then you have to know what I'm talking about."

"I do. But there's more," I said, uneasily folding my napkin.

She looked at me and reached for my hand. "Lindsay." Now it looked as though she was the one choosing her words wisely. "Whatever is happening with that motorcycle, and I assume something is, because otherwise you wouldn't have contacted me, you should take my advice and sell it. Sell it today, right now. No good can come of it. I know." She took a deep breath. "I honestly believe I lost my husband because of that damn thing."

Words started flowing out of my mouth and I couldn't stop them. I told her everything that had happened up until this point, and she listened to every word with sincere interest.

Then I asked the question I needed to know most.

"What were the circumstances surrounding his death? How did Andy die?"

"He was out on it one night. It was late. The moon was full, and it was a perfect night for riding. Well, that's what he had told me. I believed him. He never cheated on me, I know that. In fact, our relationship was perfect—until that bike came between us.

Anyway, he was on Haynesville Road. He loved that road because there were switchbacks and wonderful views. He used to say he could really "open it up" out there."

She began drifting a little and slowing down as she spoke.

"Not quite sure what that was about, but you know men and their machines." Her eyes rolled in a sad, but amused way.

I nodded in reassurance.

"The police think he must have stopped to either smoke a cigarette or pee or something. They found him about twenty feet away from the bike at a scenic pullover that overlooked the valley. We used to picnic there before we got married."

"I know the spot. It's lovely," I added.

"It seems a couple teenagers saw him out there alone and must have tried to rob him or steal the bike, who knows. A couple that was in their car a short distance away saw the whole thing. Andy tried to defend himself and they overtook him. The couple started to honk their horn and they ran away. They just ran away. The couple identified the thieves in a line up, but it was dark, and they had been drinking. The attorney for the boys was a good one and created so much doubt that the case was dismissed, and they walked free. Nothing could be done."

She took a sip of her tea and began again, "I'm not at all surprised that the bike goes to the cemetery. It sounds like something from a horror novel, doesn't it? This can't be happening, Lindsay, it's against nature and everything we know that's possible. But I still believe it."

Chapter 6

After dinner that night I told Henry I had met with Max earlier in the afternoon for lunch. He got up, grabbed a beer, and wanted all the details.

"So now what are you gonna do, Linds?" he asked.

"I'm going to go to the courthouse and find out who those boys were. Its public record and can't be that difficult. I'm sure the case was in the newspaper."

"Then what? Are you gonna hunt them down and try to get them to admit to the murder? Why would you possibly want to get involved? It's over, Linds. Let it go. Plus, it's none of your business."

"I just want to know who they are. I want to see for myself."

"See for yourself, what exactly? You're gonna open a can of worms that might explode in your face."

"I won't do that. I just need to know more." I got up and began doing the dishes. Henry didn't say any more about it.

The next day I washed Old Blue and rode her up to Auto Zone and got some more chrome and wheel polish. Funny how quickly that stuff seems to disappear at our house.

As I was riding through town, I stopped at the courthouse without even thinking about it. I sat on Old Blue, my right foot slowly tapping the running board as if I was listening to a good song and stared up at the big, white stone building in the center of the square.

By the end of the afternoon, I had all the information about Andy's murder case I felt I needed. I also visited the Prescott Courier and cried when I read through the past editions. So many stories were printed during the trial. I believe I was almost as obsessed with the trial as I was with Old Blue. I had to go home and think. I needed to decide what I wanted to do with all the information.

A week or so later, Henry told me he needed to go to California for a business conference and wouldn't be able to get out of it. He asked if I wanted to tag along and said I'd have the days to myself, but the nights I'd share with him. I graciously passed on the offer but told him I'd make it up to him when he got back. He was fine with it, but as he left two days later, he told me to promise to stay off the bike while he was gone and no more meddling in business that didn't concern me. Crossing my fingers, I told him I'd "be good". I felt guilty telling him that, but I knew he'd worry and deep in my heart I knew Old Blue wouldn't hurt me. I had the feeling he was getting fed up with the whole mess and was tired of hearing about it. He was chewing on his last straw. Looking back, his trip to California was exactly what the doctor ordered for him.

He left the following afternoon. As I leaned through the driver's window we kissed. I stood in the driveway and waved until he was out of sight.

Chapter 7

The next night, at midnight, the garage door went up and Old Blue rolled out onto the driveway. I was ready and waiting and as soon as her headlights hit the road, I was already climbing in my car.

As predicted the bike parked right in front of Andy Underwood's grave.

Although the night was starless and very dark, I wasn't afraid. The trees were swaying in the light wind and somehow, I was comforted and did not feel alone.

I left the car along the road and walked into the cemetery.

I wasn't sure what to expect when I walked up to the tombstone. I carried a flashlight, a small blanket, and a bunch of flowers that I laid over the grave.

I didn't say anything as I put the blanket on the ground and sat down.

I looked at Old Blue.

"I know you miss him. What can I do?" I said into the night air.

Not a moment later I felt a weird, lost energy surround me. It was as if the oxygen had been taken away and I couldn't catch my breath. I was covered in it.

I felt warm hands penetrating my mind as if massaging the thoughts out of me—my information. Old Blue knew where I had been and what I obtained for it! Now it wanted to know everything I knew. It was gentle and knew I was trying to help. I still had no fear.

My eyes felt heavy and as I opened them, I realized I was laying down, unharmed. Had I fallen asleep? No. I think I was put to sleep. I gathered my composure and stood up collecting my blanket and flashlight.

Old Blue had gone. I hadn't even heard the motor.

I walked to the car and drove home as quickly as I could.

I arrived in just over an hour and my bedside clock read 3:00 AM. I wanted to check the garage but was terrified at the thought of looking in and finding Old Blue not there. I changed into my pajamas to get back in my normal routine, but it didn't help. I couldn't stop the thoughts of where the bike was and what it could be doing. Yes. I knew the garage would be empty.

Every sound hammered in my head as my thoughts kept hitting me. What had I done? What did I start? Are those boys in harm's way? Of course, they were. What was I thinking? I felt like such a fool.

I knew then that the bike owned me. It had climbed into my soul. I should have listened to Max, to Henry.

Although with great difficulty, I finally drifted off to sleep.

I must have slept hard because I awoke to knocking on my front door. It was two in the afternoon. I looked out the window and saw three police officers on the stoop.

I opened the door slowly and they asked if I was Lindsay Everest. I told them I was and in moments they were reading me my rights, cuffing me, and walking me to the patrol car.

It seems the two boys who were tried for Andy Underwood's murder had themselves, been murdered hours earlier. Witnesses told the police my 2018 Softail Deluxe was seen at the crime scene.

Each boy had been run down in the street. In fact, one of the boys was hit once then the vehicle circled around and ran over him again. They had been out partying and when each arrived home that night they were taken off guard before they could enter their homes.

I was taken to the Sheriff's office and held overnight on two counts of first-degree murder. The prosecuting attorney found out that shortly before the murders I had gone to the courthouse and the newspaper asking questions about Andy Underwood's murder, and that put me in the perfect position to be the first suspected. Especially since I was now the owner of Andy's motorcycle.

The police found no witnesses to say I was riding the bike at the time of the boys' deaths. That was my good fortune. In fact, the witnesses said it looked as if there was no rider at all on the bike during the time of the murders. The police were baffled.

After the arraignment, when I stated the bike was able to drive itself and explained the chain of events that led to the boys' death, the court decided Windhaven was the best place for me to stay until the murders were sorted out. I was ordered to complete tests for a psychiatric evaluation. That was over a month ago.

I have been taken out of my life, thrown in a cell, held in a mental hospital, and now, by some miracle, am allowed to be set free. The circumstances of which still confuse me. But they are letting me go, and I'm grateful.

When I arrived back at home, Henry's things were gone, and I have not spoken with him since the day he left for California. He left no note, no words of grief, no good-byes. I was devastated. But soon became very angry knowing that he could have left me during such a traumatic time. I went from being crazy distraught to having total disbelief that he could abandon me the way he did. How could he be so mean and cruel? How could anyone do that to someone they love? I would have done anything to get even with him for hurting me so badly when I needed him the most.

After a short time to reflect and gather myself, I became dreadfully frightened as I realized the energy behind Old Blue, the magnitude of power it held, and what it was capable of. I thought about how I felt regarding Henry and how openly I was expressing my anger towards him for leaving me so abruptly. I then wondered if Old Blue was powerful enough to read my mind on some level.

I began telling myself Henry had decided the whole ordeal was just too much for him to deal with. I told myself I would have done the same if I were in his position.

I hold no grudge or ill will toward him. I find myself saying that out loud every day.

I am afraid to even breathe resentment or sadness over his departure from my life. There must be no revenge.

The police have told me Old Blue was never found. It never came back to my garage, and to my knowledge it has disappeared forever. I hope so.

Chapter 8

The noises have started again. I hear them as I lay in bed. I don't sleep well because I keep waiting to hear the garage door rise.

She's back.

THE CABIN

CHAPTER 1

Kellie's husband ran out to grab more beer and said he'd be right back. That was over a half-hour ago and now it was starting to get dark. Kellie wasn't worrying yet, although she hated the thought of him out there on that damn motorcycle. They were quite a ways from town, but those country roads were dark and not very well maintained.

Jerry was a seasoned rider, so she really had no call to be worried, it was just the fact that the bike was old as the hills. Built in 1945 to be exact, but in great shape. It was simply the mother hen in her surfacing again. Jerry was practically born on a motorcycle. He raced the flat track circuit and won many titles back in the day. The bike was running fine now, they had just picked it up from the shop, but you never know when that old knucklehead was going to quit, and she didn't feel like going out on that dirt road to find him. She had just put her pajamas on, after all, and didn't particularly want to change back into her street clothes.

A few months ago, Jerry found a cabin located about two hours out of the city, and Kellie loved the idea of a weekend get-away so close to their home in Gaithersburg, which was a little po-dunk town in Maryland about two and a half hours from the eastern shore. The deal was phenomenal, and they would have been crazy to pass it up, so they bought it on a whim and were very happy about their decision to purchase it. This weekend was the first chance they had to get away and enjoy it.

Jerry threw the bike in the back of the pickup and off they went. In the excitement of deciding to go, neither had told anyone they were leaving for the weekend. It wasn't that it was a big secret, it was just that the decision to go was made quickly and neither had time nor thought about mentioning it to anyone.

Kellie remembered to bring all the important stuff: bed linens, a couple days' worth of clothes, a loaded cooler with tons of food, her "bag of fun", which consisted of word search puzzles, adult coloring books, connect the dot books, a harmonica, crochet hooks, yarn, and some candles. Her Bag of Fun went with her everywhere. "One never knows when one will need items of such importance," she often said.

She even remembered the Glock 21 .45 ACP.

Kellie and Jerry had each been long time gun enthusiasts. In fact, they met at a handgun tournament given by a local shooting range that was close to both of their homes. "Love at first sight," Kellie often said to friends. Laughing, Jerry would correct her and say, "It was really lust at first sight, but don't tell her parents."

She sat on the living room couch as she waited for Jerry to return and noticed how comfortable it was as she ran her fingers over the soft, dark fabric. The cabin was sold furnished, which was nice, and she thought the prior owners had impeccable taste. Plush area rugs, an L-shaped couch with rustic end tables on each of its sides and mounted above the fireplace hung a huge elk head dressed in its long hair, ready for the cold winter days that were stolen from him with one shot. She thought the head was kind of creepy, but Jerry loved it, so it stayed. The curtains were thick and very heavy. She knew no one could see in through them from the outside. Even the sun had a hard time peeking in.

As she looked around the room, she noticed the locks on the doors. There were three on every door plus each had a wooden arm that came down and secured. "No unwanted visitors were getting in here," she said to herself. The doors reminded her of the homes in the old western movies she used to watch as a kid. "Why would anyone need so many locks way out here in the woods?" Maybe the prior owners were paranoid, as well as having good taste in furniture.

She padded to the cooler in her new, furry house slippers and lifted the lid. She threw some ice in her favorite glass and looked around for the Jack Daniels. A little coke for good measure and she was set.

"Where's Jerry?" she thought again to herself.

She realized another hour had gone by. Now she was getting worried.

An owl hooted its long, melancholy tone from somewhere outside. The sound was eerie, but beautiful and she wondered if the owl was also sitting alone, patiently waiting for its mate to come home.

Her cell phone rang. It was Jerry asking her if she needed anything else from the store. She told him that she didn't and to hurry back.

As they hung up, she realized the battery in her cell phone was about to die so she grabbed her sweater and walked out to the pickup to plug it in the charger. It would have been so convenient if they had turned on the electricity in the house, but since they were only going to be there for the weekend, they decided they'd rough it.

It was full dark now and the wind had been blowing since late afternoon. It seemed to be blowing harder now and the old hard woods surrounding the property creaked as their ancient limbs bent and swayed. She thought how awful it would be if one came down on the house. As she looked up at them, she glimpsed a movement just beyond her range of vision.

"Was that a face? Impossible. Something dark and huge bending out of the trees and . . . Stop it," she thought. "There is no way I'm going to let a little wind get to me like this. Jerry will be back in a little while so I'm just going to make another cocktail and relax."

She didn't want to leave her cell in the car in case something did go wrong. If Jerry called, she knew she'd never hear it. On the other hand, it wouldn't be any good to her with a dead battery. She left it and started back toward the house.

Kellie almost laughed to herself as she realized the combination of darkness and forest sounds made her feel scared. In fact, so scared she was on the verge of being freaked out. She felt everything around her changing. The trees switched from feeling reassuring and comforting to haunting and dangerous. She wanted to get inside, fast. It was as if the atmosphere was becoming unusually heavy.

As she spun around, looking at the woods behind her, her mind grasped the fact that what she felt was not her imagination. There was a horrid and evil presence out there, everywhere, and she NEEDED to get in the house.

Kellie couldn't remember the last time she felt this frightened.

The owl hooted again. She looked up, and as she did, the owl's beak opened and revealed what looked like teeth. Large teeth. Rows of them. Its wings started to spread as it fell forward off the tree limb and started gliding toward her. Swooping low, Kellie could feel the wind from its wings blow past her head as she quickly ducked out of its way.

Her walk turned into a sprint. Every footfall was uneasily placed on the soil as she couldn't see in the darkness. Had it suddenly become darker?

The ground slowly undulated beneath her as if it was breathing. Afraid she would lose her balance and stumble, her steps became shorter, faster. As if running over thousands of bugs. With every step she heard a crunch and realized they really were bugs—huge, winged ones and seconds later, she realized they had begun to crawl inside her slippers. She felt them latching onto her skin and imagined them trying to burrow deep inside to lay eggs in the juicy meat of her feet.

The trees were watching her. She sensed each of them coming closer as she tried to run between them. Their giant boughs covered in insects with eyes huge and hungry. They dropped from the limbs, landing on her shoulders, and tangling themselves in her hair. She desperately tried brushing them off, but they stuck to her as if they had been dipped in honey, or worse, her own blood.

Forest creatures of all sizes emerged from the darkness.

Something that looked like a large bat with hands and spikes on its head flew toward her. As Kellie ducked to avoid it, she noticed its large, hairy fingers and saw its nails were like razors. Its small black eyes glared into Kellie's with a face she had seen in a hundred horror movies.

Bears that weren't bears as we know them spoke to her from the forest's edge, and she understood them. In their deep, scratchy voices they began chanting "You better run. If we catch you, you're going to die!"

She bolted for the front door. Thank God, she had shut it behind her when she walked outside, or there would be no telling what could be lurking inside by now. They wanted to eat her. She knew they would not let her survive this night.

As she reached the doorway, she whipped the door closed behind her and the crashing noise it made as it slammed shut was a wonderful relief.

Now she knew why the prior owners had so many locks on the doors and window shutters.

Kellie had to fight to catch her breath as she ran through the house frantically making sure all the windows and doors were secure, while shaking bugs off her clothing and out of her hair. Then she remembered Jerry would soon be home. He wouldn't stand a chance against the creatures outside. He would be caught completely off guard and on that freaking motorcycle! There was nothing she could do except wait until she heard him coming.

She was crying as she lit candles in the darkness and tried her best to think straight. She would light a fire, knowing that those things outside would try to come in through any opening they could find. Luckily, there was plenty of logs stacked along the wall, so she threw a few pieces onto the grate. As she did, she remembered that she would have to open the flue. Her vision blurred and she began to get light-headed. She would have to stick her hand up into the cold darkness and feel around for the handle.

"Something is in there, I know it."

She wrapped her hand in a dish towel and kneeled in front of the hearth. She tried to see as much as she could with the flashlight and held her breath. Her voice ebbed a dry squeak that sounded like a child's cry, and she reached inside.

The air was much cooler in there than in the rest of the house.

Something fell on her hand. "It's just soot," she reassured herself.

At last, her fingers felt the cold metal arm of the flue, and she tried to move it. She wasn't sure which way to pull it or push it, but finally it gave way and opened freely. As it did, she heard herself cry with a guttural stab of relief. Nothing had grabbed her hand and she felt no pain.

As she pulled her hand out there were small beetles crawling over the dishcloth. For a moment she thought she could hear them whispering her name. She tossed the cloth onto the wood.

She found the lighter she had packed and quickly began ripping pages out of the book she had been reading and wadded them up to jam around the wood. After flicking the lighter once, twice, three times, it finally caught, and she thrust it under the paper. It lit quickly and soon she had a wonderfully warm and comforting fire ablaze.

Something pounded on the doors. "Jerry?" she yelled, hoping, but knowing it couldn't be him because she hadn't heard the motorcycle approach. Whatever it was it sounded like they would break it down. Thank God for the locks. There was no response.

The heat of the fire was heartening, and the flames were high.

Sounds from the surrounding woods had shifted and now they were right outside the doors and windows. Things banged on the sides of the cabin and scratched the surfaces around the door frame, relentless and lurid.

As Kellie rocked back and forth, she cradled the .45 in her arms and waited for Jerry to return.

How would she warn him? She couldn't risk opening a window or door, and she couldn't call him on her cell. There had to be a way!

It seemed like hours had passed.

The wind still howled furiously, and she hoped it wouldn't overpower the sound of the bike's engine as it approached. It sounded like a tornado out there.

The rain came, torrents from the sound of it. All Kellie could do was pray that Jerry would have to return to town due to the high winds and rain.

Without her cell, she had no idea what time it was, but knew it was getting late. It had to be.

As she sat on the couch in a state of both shock and desperation, she finally heard the rumble of a motorcycle coming up the driveway. At last, he was back.

It wasn't raining as hard now, although it was still steady. She ran to the door and unlocked two of the locks and threw the bolt. From inside, Kellie yelled, "Run Jerry! There are things in the woods! For Christ's sake, run inside!"

She stood with her hand on the last lock, ready to throw open the front door as soon as she heard his footfalls on the porch. But they never came.

Suddenly, the RPMs of the bike's engine accelerated, and it sounded like the motor was redlining.

She was sure he was being attacked or chased by something. And then there was silence.

The next sound was Jerry's screams as he was dragged away from the house and into the woods.

It was over. She knew he was dead.

As she lay on the couch, she held onto the bottle of Jack and stared at the fire. The bottle was almost empty, but it felt good in her hands; the way a nice fat burrito would feel in the hands of a starving man.

Her eyes were heavy as she waited for sunrise, hoping the horrors of the night would be gone upon seeing the sun's first light on the horizon.

She slowly pushed her hair off her face and added another log to the fire.

Kellie was alone now. How could all of this be explained? She wanted answers that she knew would never come.

She and Jerry met late in life and there were no children or family reunions scheduled in the future. Now that he was gone, she had nothing and no one and she laughed when she realized all she had was a quiet little getaway—her only visitors being monsters after sundown.

If only she could make the whispers stop. She felt as though something were beside her pushing her mind into lunacy. It was hard to think. She tried to remember, but her mind was fuzzy. What was happening to her?

She stared at the .45.

The flames from the fire reflected off the gun's blue metal slide with such clarity.

When she picked up the Glock, she was amazed at how good it felt in her hands. How soothing the cool metal felt and how smooth it was. She held it along side of her face, and it seemed to rock her into a freedom that took away her fears and disappointments. It calmed her as she massaged her temples with the side of its barrel.

The glint of light of a new morning was beginning to peek through the clouds of the stormy night.

CHAPTER 2

Friends and co-workers had phoned the local police to let them know Jerry and Kellie had not been seen in days. They told them their pickup was not at their home and neither had been answering their cell phones. It simply was not in either of their characters to not show up to work, and everyone was very concerned.

Officers Harry Stillwell and Eve Dodd arrived at Kellie and Jerry's cabin the following day. The area outside was pristine and very well maintained. No sign of wind damage or foul play.

"What a fantastic little get-away," Officer Dodd commented as they pulled in the driveway.

They saw Jerry's pickup and found the motorcycle in a large ditch about fifty feet from the cabin. "This ain't good," Officer Stillwell hollered over to Dodd as she looked around the truck.

Dodd wandered over to Stillwell and they both saw scratch marks on the paint and noticed the seat was torn on the bike. "Probably happened when he crashed," Stillwell commented. "Nobody lays down a sweet bike like this and doesn't pick it up. Let's check out the house."

As they knocked on the door, they noticed deep scratches had been painted over and fresh ones all over the entryway. No one answered, and after some creative ingenuity they finally got inside the house through an old coal hatch in the back of the cabin.

They caught a sickening stench immediately upon entering and knew exactly what it was. With their weapons unholstered, they slowly continued into the living room.

They found Kellie on the couch with the .45 on the floor by her right foot. Brain matter and blood had hardened on the wall and window behind where her head used to be. Officer Dodd had to fight the urge to puke.

"If houses have bad luck, this one sure does," Stillwell mentioned. "The past three owners died in this place."

"Are you serious?" Dodd questioned.

"Yeah. Check it out for yourself. They either disappeared or committed suicide. The history of this place is pretty fucked up."

Rescue services were dispatched, and Kellie's death was determined a suicide, while Jerry's body was never found. Investigators still aren't sure if he is dead or alive, but they assume dead.

The investigation is still underway, as are the others that have taken place in the cabin over the years.

A month following Kellie's suicide and Jerry's disappearance, Realtor, Mary Ehrlich, put up the For Sale sign on her new listing.

She thought to herself how beautifully decorated the cabin was and knew she'd be able to sell it quickly. After all, it was an easy listing and this property always sold fast.

CAUTION

Cliffs & uneven, slippery terrain

KEEP BACK FROM EDGE

Sweet Revenge

Chapter 1

Most people, when asked, remember how everyone in school used to tease Marta Linwood. The kids who grew up with her could be brutal and it seemed as if they could sense poor Marta coming from a mile away. Even though she rode the same school bus with the other students every day, no one in her class ever took the time to get to know her very well. The cool kids always sat in the back of the bus with friends while she sat as close to the bus driver as she could. Anyone would have, after all, it was the safest place.

Marta was a mousy looking kid. When she walked, she always held her head low, and her back was bent over as if she was carrying something very heavy. Over each ear, she wore pigtails, which always seemed to be very dirty. Some kids felt sorry for her, and Marta often saw children throw pitiful glances her way. In fact, it was rumored that the principal had called Marta into his office and told her she needed to 'be more conscious about her personal hygiene.' It was gossiped that he even sent her home for the day and warned her not to come back until she washed her clothes and took a bath.

It was both easy and hard to dislike her. On one hand you felt sorry for Marta because she was so quiet and never stood up for herself. Kids would push her around during recess, and in the hallways, people would knock her books out of her arms and steal her lunch. She never fought back or said a word. On the other hand, if anyone would try to help her or talk to her, she would immediately wither like a dying flower. She never looked directly at anyone or even attempted conversation. That frustrated the hell out of other kids at times. I mean, why help someone who wouldn't try to help themselves?

It wasn't until her final year in high school that things really started to change.

It was the first day of school and the students were getting seated as the bell rang. The teacher had just walked in and started to close the door behind her when a long, slender hand stopped the door mid-swing.

What happened next left everyone breathless.

A tall, auburn-haired girl walked into the room. But walking wasn't the correct word—it was more like gliding. Her long legs graciously carried her as if she was a foot off the ground. She was silent and moved with such ease and grace that once you saw her you could hardly look away. Her posture was perfect and her long, thick hair fell past her shoulders and swept against the small of her back. The silkiness of it glimmered in the sunlight streaming in through the classroom windows.

Her skin was smooth and creamy white, and her bright green eyes scanned the room as she looked around and into the eyes of the other students. It was obvious the boys were fascinated. The girls however, seemed to plot their devious intentions as they knew they stood no chance of winning a boy's favor if having to compete against her.

Tim Hellborn, a fellow classmate, jammed the end of his pencil in the middle of his best friend's back, who was sitting a row ahead, and said, "HELL YES! I got dibs on that one, my man. It'll be like takin' candy from a baby!"

So, the next question was, who the fuck was this chick? Obviously new to the school, and no one had yet found out who she was.

"Fresh meat," another boy chimed.

She took her seat at the back of the class and gently crossed her legs, resting one hand on her knee as her other arm laid loosely over the top of her desk. She was confident and knew she had everyone's attention.

The school was very small compared to most high schools. The entire graduating class only numbered about 645. Everyone knew everyone. That's the way it was in small towns and Derwood wasn't any different. Before the end of the day, we would all know who she was and where she lived. It was that simple.

Ten minutes after the bell rang and attendance was taken, the class learned who she was. She was Marta Linwood. When the teacher called her name, and she responded with a firm, "Here", everyone just about crapped their drawers. Total silence. The guys' jaws dropped, and the girls suddenly realized they had a new force to reckon with. Rivalry at its finest. Girls can be bitches. One can imagine those that had always been so mean to Marta over the years instantly regretted it.

CHAPTER 2

As the days followed, Marta displayed her amazing transformation from a sickly, non-sociable reject into a remarkably social butterfly. She had sincere qualities of thoughtfulness, helpfulness, and a self-assured nature of wittiness and clever conversation her fellow classmates had never seen. She was the up and coming, hands down, most popular girl in school. Always willing to come to someone's aid with a smile and a creative way to make people feel happy and secure.

Although Marta was friendly and seemed sincere, there was also a side to her that no one had noticed.

When Marta was alone, she would daydream. Her daydreams weren't just drifting off in deep thought about random happenings. Marta's daydreams were frightening. They were filled with horror and painful wishes towards people who had hurt her both physically and emotionally. She hadn't forgotten all the mean and evil things her new "friends" had done to her in the past. She hadn't forgotten all the hurtful words and ass-kickings she'd received on a regular basis. No comfort from her family, no comfort from those that were supposed to be her allies, no comfort from anyone. Ever. Marta's world was one of darkness. It always had been. Now that she had bloomed into a beautiful and alluring young woman at her best, in her heart she knew she was still alone. No one understood her, no one ever had.

Marta had never known true kindness from a family. She had never known the understanding and helpful guidance others experience from a loving household. She had never learned tenderness or trust. She was instead a warrior, always defending her right to life and peaceful solitude in her dark room. Her home was murky with sadness and unfulfilled promises.

When Marta awoke one morning a few weeks before the end of the last semester, she decided it was about time for things to change. She was going to make things right and she was going to start fresh. She would feel good about herself for the first time in her life. If this feeling happened to come into opposite emotions with those that had hurt her in her earlier years, then so be it. After all, Marta was not above crushing those that fucked her over. Not at all. In fact, she felt the fun was just getting started.

CHAPTER 3

Marta lived by keeping her friends close and her ene-
mies closer, therefore, most of the girls in school practically begged for her friendship. Equally, every boy
in school fawned over her, hoping to get in her pants, which was
never going to happen. She would flirt one-on-one but would
never give in to their desires. Keeping them at bay and on the
cuff of winning her was her strongest talent. She could keep them
there forever and she knew it. They were all chunks of butter in a
pan, and she controlled the heat. She liked it.

She decided to organize a party the night after fall break at a
nearby lake. Marta was on one of the senior organizational com-
mittees and when she suggested the idea, it took off like a flash
and the weather would still be comfortable.

As the special night approached, Marta and the committee
hired a fantastic band and a light orchestrator to create amazing
effects over the beach. They were able to put quite a lot of money
towards making the night perfect due to the bake sales and car
washes the students had organized over the past few weeks. The
party was set on a nearby lake which had a long pier with stable
railings along its sides. The pier was so wide in fact, they could
use it as a dance floor.

What no one seemed to remember, or care about, was the
quarry, which was located about one hundred yards west of the
party site. It had once been a site for mining copper, but the miners struck water and it filled up most of the way. It was rumored
that the water filled in so quickly that a group of mineworkers
was unable to get out. They drowned and their bodies were never
found. Pieces of unrecovered equipment are rumored to litter the
quarry floor, but that's just the talk of the town. They say when

the moon is full the ghosts of the miners can be seen wandering around the lip of the quarry. It is also said that if a miner sees you, he will grab you and throw you off the side into the water. The sheer cliffs and steep angles made escaping the water's bite impossible to overcome. Anyone unlucky enough to fall into the dark waters would surely die. This was precisely Marta's plan.

As the days went by, everyone grew excited about the event and hoped the weather would hold out. The girls frequented the many dress shops in town to find the perfect formal gown and the boys also searched for the right tuxes to match their date's colors. Many students on the party committee had put a lot of hard work into the preparations and it would be awful if things were spoiled due to inclement weather. Also, bad weather would interfere with Marta's plans. She, too, had been planning for the party. In fact, she had been planning a lot.

Marta bought a beautiful dress. Stunning was the word for it. It was incredibly sexy, yet she could easily run in it. In fact, she bought four of them. The woman at the cash register looked at her as if she were crazy, but Marta only smiled and said they were going to be used as Bridesmaid's dresses. The cashier returned her smile and said that she was sure the wedding would be beautiful.

The day before the party, Marta went to the quarry and left three of the dresses at the foot of a tree in separate bags, along with stockings in case she ruined the ones she would be wearing, and baby wipes. She also hid three knives along the lip of the quarry. The knives were Dietmar Pohl Force MK-9's. They cost a fortune, but they were worth it, each with a 9-inch blade and the exact model Sylvester Stallone used in his Rambo movies. Marta always had a thing for the Rambo character. She considered him very much like herself. Unloved, strictly at odds with the world, and at heart, very wise and misunderstood. She considered him a brother and a fellow warrior.

Chapter 4

The day of the party came, and Marta had been flirting her best. All the boys who had embarrassed and harassed her over the years, those who'd made her feel terrible about herself, were now at her beck and call. The girls who never helped her and turned their backs were also singled out. Marta also had something special planned for *them*. Things were progressing nicely, and everything was in place.

As people arrived at the party, Marta helped everyone find their tables and complimented them all accordingly.

When she knew no one was paying attention, she walked over to Don Bernie. Don was the worst. He had spit on Marta and pushed her down at times in earlier years. He humiliated Marta every chance he got, and it was hard to watch. Peer pressure is a hard thing to conquer in school.

Marta seductively brushed against Don and whispered that she would like to get to know him better. She asked if he would meet her in ten minutes at the south end of the quarry and to please be discreet and not say anything to anyone. Don obliged and said he would be there in five. They separately left the party, yet Marta held back to make sure he didn't talk to anyone before he left. He didn't.

As Don met her by the quarry, she greeted him with a warm embrace. She looked into his eyes and whispered she was happy he had come and that she had been thinking about how wonderful it would be to connect with him on a new level. They stood near the edge, and she offered a warm smile as she began to pull the straps of her dress slowly off her shoulders. Her dress dropped onto the ground, and she stood naked in the light of the moon. Don kissed her gently and reached for her breasts. As he undid his belt and lowered his pants, he balanced himself with one foot in the air, sliding his foot out of his pants.

Marta slowly reached for her knife that she had hidden at the foot of the tree they were leaning on and was prepared. As he was balancing and vulnerable, she whipped out the knife and slit his throat with one swift movement and pushed him over the quarry's edge. It was a running push as he was standing about four feet from the rim. Marta's attack had been spot-on, and she was able to catch him off guard. Thus, he was easily forced over the edge. Mission accomplished.

It had been so easy that she didn't even need to change her dress.

Now Marta just needed to hurry back to the party to entice her next victim.

CHAPTER 5

When she returned to the festivities, Marta looked at her watch. Only twenty-five minutes had gone by. Ed Zacka was next. Again, she flirted and again she watched as they left the party unobserved. This was easier than she thought it would be. She marveled over how calm she was.

Only a few minutes later she stood at the same spot along the edge of the quarry.

Taking off her dress slowly and feeling Ed's hardness as he pulled her to him, she danced her tongue along his lips and un-buckled his belt. Ed unzipped and slid his pants down, and once more, as he lifted his leg off the ground and bent over, she drew the knife back and buried it into the back of his head. It slid in quickly and all the way to the grip. Ed dropped to the ground.

This time she had to physically drag him to the edge and push him over. That done, she kicked some surface ground dirt over the edge, to get rid of any possible blood splatter and began to redress. She noticed that this time her dress was covered in blood due to the force of it squirting from the wound and her stockings had ripped across her right knee. Good thing she bought the extra dresses and baby wipes. She quickly pulled a new dress and stockings from the bag she had hidden at the quarry the day before.

She followed the path along the quarries rim and promptly arrived back at the party.

By the end of the evening, as the clock struck 11:00, Marta had finished off all six of her foulest male tormenters. She felt good. Lingering after the final kill to remove the dresses, knife, and baby wipes, she was confident any evidence found would not directly incriminate her; she was satisfied and returned to the party once again.

She reached for the ladle to pour herself a glass of punch just prior to the parties' end. Marta wanted to mingle and knew it was important for people to see her and notice that she was perfectly clean and fresh. Looking marvelous, she worked the crowd.

People had begun to ask where Ed and Don were. Marta heard someone say they probably just left to go to a bar. People always came and went at parties, so no one made their disappearances an issue and everyone knew they had fake I.D.'s. Neither Ed nor Don had dates, but Ed had given his sister, Caitlyn a ride to the dance with her boyfriend. They also assumed Ed had gone off to party with the others. No chivalry for the cold hearted in Derwood.

Someone in the crowd commented, "Hey, wouldn't it be fun to go do some night swimming over at the quarry?"

Marta's breath stopped in her throat. She knew the bodies would be found, and she knew there would be ongoing investigations. Everyone would be questioned and requestioned, and it would be a nightmare for months. She was prepared for that. But she just wasn't expecting the bodies to be found so soon. She wanted them to decompose for a while and the water to get rid of any possible evidence that might lead back to her.

She relaxed when someone else quickly responded, "Why don't we hit the shopping center instead and see if IHOP is open? Let's get some food. The water is probably too cold anyway."

The girls in the crowd liked that idea much better as everyone was dressed so fancy. No one wanted to get their beautiful gowns wet or dirty.

As everyone got in their vehicles and headed out, Marta offered to drive a few in her car since it was an SUV and had plenty of seating in the back. Since no one could find Ed, Caitlin and her date caught a ride with Marta. They all arrived at IHOP fifteen minutes later.

Chapter 6

The next afternoon, a man jogging with his Old English Sheepdog discovered the floating bodies of the six young men. Evidently the wind had picked up and blew everything to the southwest corner of the quarry. At first the jogger assumed they were logs, but then realized they were human bodies. He immediately called 911.

The parents of the dead boys were overwhelmed with grief. The town had never experienced anything of such horrendous magnitude and the citizens pulled together as small towns always do to comfort one another.

The town was at an utter standstill. All matters of business were put on hold and the town officials and police department were on high alert. The roads in and out of town were immediately blocked and no one came or went without proper identification.

Questions were asked. Answers were demanded. The entire town was on lockdown.

Marta did her part and was extremely helpful offering anything she could to the officers and anyone who needed assistance in the search for the killers. She had them all fooled.

"What a bunch of losers. I should kill them all," she said to herself.

As the days passed, she felt as though she had forgotten something. She wasn't sure what it could be, but the thought hounded her like a bad dream.

She went over and over the events of the evening but came up with nothing. The fourth night after the murders, she awoke in a cold sweat as she began doing an inventory in her mind of things she had purchased to prepare for her plan. Three extra dresses in case the one she wore had ripped or soiled, three knives, baby wipes to clean herself up . . . and extra stockings. She didn't remember getting rid of the torn stockings! Could she had left them along the edge? Could they be floating in the water or left somewhere along the rim of the quarry? They would have her DNA all over them and most likely one of the boy's blood as well! If they were in the water, it would be fine since the DNA would have been rinsed off, but if they were on the ground and someone found them it would open herself up to numerous questions and fingers would be pointed in her direction for sure. This was not good.

Surely after four days someone would have found them if they were there, and if someone had found them, how long would it take for them to be tested for DNA?

She couldn't sleep. She knew she had to go out there and see for herself. She would wait until after 1:00 A.M. By then her dad would be drunk and passed out, and her mom would have been long since asleep, along with the rest of her family.

She also wondered if anyone would be guarding the crime scene, but then she thought, no. Not after four days. She knew she wouldn't be able to rest unless she went out there and looked for herself. A trip to the quarry during the day would be better, but she didn't want to draw any attention to herself if someone happened to see her. Yes. She would leave that night after everyone was asleep.

Chapter 7

It was colder than she had expected, and the night was very dark at times. The moon was full, but its light diminished often as the wind blew clouds across it in random gusts.

Marta parked her parents' car along a forest road about a half mile away from the quarry that was mainly only used by hunters, crack heads, and horny teenagers. It was the middle of the week and not hunting season so she was confident no one would see the car at this time of the night.

She wanted to do this fast and quiet, so she hopped out of the car and sprinted down the forest road and ran between the large poplars to the edge of the quarry. She had brought her father's snow boots and stuffed them with newspaper so they wouldn't fall off her feet, knowing she could make good time without having the fear of losing them. She had watched enough shows on T.V. to know that she didn't want to leave any tracks from her shoes in the dirt. When she arrived home, she would rinse them off with the hose outside for good measure.

As she walked, she started planning the revenge she had on the girls in her class who had also caused her great pain and embarrassment over the years. After all, she was only half done. Her time was truly at hand, and she had just begun.

Marta was delighted that she had so far, slipped under the veil of possible blame.

As she walked and searched for her used and torn stockings, she paused, believing she heard a noise in the surrounding bushes.

No lights. No worries. She kept walking.

Again, she stopped as she felt someone close by. Maybe it was just the wind, or maybe it was just a feeling. She thought she caught the fragrance of a man. Cologne perhaps, old and stale. It had to be the wind. She kept walking.

As she scanned the ground for anything she may have left behind, she found nothing. She had brought a flashlight with her and was careful to keep the beam close to the ground as to not attract any unwanted eyes.

In one last steady motion, Marta whisked the beam of light over the ground where she had stood with the unsuspecting boys just a few nights earlier, and again, saw nothing. Her mind was finally at ease.

As she looked down over the calm, black waters of the quarry she felt the chill of the October wind slipping beneath her jacket and discovered how cold her hands were in the night air. It was time for her to get home. It was time for her to put all the drama behind her and to get on with her life.

It was at that moment Marta finally realized hate was a hopeless feeling and it would only lead to roads paved with despair and sadness. No matter what those boys had done to her in the past, she had no right to end their lives in such a tragic and gruesome way.

Maybe she would rethink her upcoming plans and let the girls who stood by and watched as those mean boys embarrassed her all those years live. Marta smiled as forgiveness filled her heart. Yes, she would put the recent tragedies behind her, help those she could, and dedicate her new life to one of peace and kindness.

Marta sat on the ground and closed her eyes for a moment, and for the first time in her existence, said a prayer. She asked for forgiveness and felt a sensation of warmth overcome her. She was looking forward to moving on with her life and couldn't wait for it to begin

Chapter 8

As she slowly stood up and turned back towards her car, Marta sensed that someone, or something, was out there. She was frightened realizing she was so desperately close to the edge of the quarry.

Remembering the town folklore about the miners who were killed when the quarry had filled with water, how they were left to drown as the water relentlessly filled the mine, came to Marta's mind.

Marta remembered the stories of ghosts who walked the rim of the quarry, pulling in innocent people to die so that they would have revenge for the lies they were told and their lives that were taken from them.

It was then that she noticed that same manly odor again. Now it was old and awful. It smelled like rotten eggs and dirty clothes.

Suddenly, Marta was pushed to the ground. It happened so fast and hard that her arm hit a rock as she collided with the path, and she knew her left elbow had been shattered upon contact. White pain ran up her arm like a shot and her fingers pulsed and tingled with every beat of her heart. She let out a hideous scream that would have chilled the bravest of souls.

In an instant she saw the glowing figures of dead men wearing hard hats and work boots coming toward her. Their clothes were worn and wet, sagging with the weight of years gone by. Their faces held no expression except for eyes that looked lost and haunted and full of contempt. She could see through these apparitions and knew immediately they were the ghosts of the dead workers. The stories were true!

The miners were upon her, and she was seized by her coat collar and dragged closer to the side of the quarry. She would have been completely disoriented, but due to her throbbing arm she was unfortunately very much in control of her thoughts and knew she would be dead in seconds.

Suddenly, Marta felt cold, dead hands around her and she found herself falling into the quarry's dirty waters. She was tossed into the cold water effortlessly and swiftly like someone flicking a cigarette out of their car window. Marta's thoughts of rescue became pointless and all she could do was try to stay afloat. She had been wearing heavy boots and clothing and her struggles were useless.

She felt hands pulling her down. They held tight and would not let her go.

Marta died a swift death as the fall and the cold water took her down into the dark depths of the quarry.

Marta wasn't missed for nearly a week. Her family hardly missed her at all. In fact, they told police they thought she ran away from home. Marta had just turned eighteen, so her family thought she'd left town.

Her body was found floating atop the water in the same location as her classmates when they were found.

It was assumed that her life was taken by the same person who killed the boys of her class weeks earlier.

There hadn't been much of a fuss regarding Marta's death. She didn't have any close friends to speak of, and when she was referred to in conversation it was in a sad, but very general way.

A plaque was erected in the town square naming the boys and honoring their short lives. Marta's name was not on it.

THE VACATION

CHAPTER 1

Today was the first day of Olivia Aragon's vacation and she'd be damned if anyone would fuck it up.

Olivia, "Liv" was a hard woman. Maybe it was due to being the only girl in a family of four boys and growing up on a working ranch in Arizona didn't exactly aid in her feminine growth potential. She had to get up with her brothers and tend to sheep and cows, mend fences, even castrate calves same as they did. Period or no period, cramps or no cramps. Squatting behind junipers and big rocks had been the way of life for her. She was tough and never pretended to be otherwise. In fact, she was proud of her ability to cope with life and fix her own problems. Yes sir, no one would stop 'ole Liv from getting what she wanted.

The alarm went off precisely at the desired time, which was 6:00 AM, as promised by the alarm clock manufacturer, if all instructions were followed properly that is. It was a Sonic Alert SB1000SS, a combination unit with a Super Shaker, and an extra loud alarm that came with a vibrating bed device. She wasn't entirely sure of what all that meant, but it was on the label, and she'd paid a pretty penny for it.

In recent months, Liv hadn't been able to fall asleep as easily as she had in the past and her mornings were always foggy. It seemed as though she kept waking later and later. Once she was late for work, which was something unheard of. She wasn't raised that way. She remembered hearing her mother tell her only losers and inconsiderate people are late for their obligations. "People depend on you! It's all about integrity, Olivia!" God, if she had a dime each time she'd heard that come out of her mother's mouth, she'd be knee deep in . . . well . . . dimes, she supposed.

Now that the day of her long-awaited vacation finally arrived, she sure as hell wouldn't miss her plane.

She packed her suitcase the night before and checked and double checked to make sure everything was in order. She wanted to safeguard against any unwelcome surprises and made sure she hadn't forgotten anything at the last minute. Heaven forbid she get to the airport and forget her plane tickets or passport documents. She wasn't flying internationally, but she spent good money on a passport, and she was determined for someone to see it.

The first stop was Sky Harbor International by 5:00 AM, which was two and a half hours prior to her scheduled flight. She hadn't flown in years and with all the raucous going on in the world, she'd heard about airport delays. Under no circumstances was she about to take any chances on anything going wrong. This was HER time now!

Liv would then arrive in Baltimore, Maryland a few glorious hours later with the dust of Arizona blowing off her boots, and within another couple hours she'd be ankle deep in the cool Atlantic Ocean with a strawberry daiquiri in her hand, forgetting who she was and extremely happy about it!

At Liv's age, which was a delicate thirty-one, most women traveled with their husbands or family, but in her case she was alone. Liv was always alone, in fact, she rather liked it that way.

She always tried to be a friendly person and was very intelligent. She felt that she did her best to do and say all the appropriate things for most situations and yet—somehow always wound up being the third wheel when attending parties or going out to dinner with friends. It used to bother her, but no more. She was confident in herself and the thought of being "over the hill" was just a sad notion by women less self-assured.

The airport was packed, as she knew it would be. She sailed through each line and was relieved that no one asked her to open her luggage during check in. She was proud that she had planned her arrival at the time she did, and once she saw things seemed to be running smoothly, she relaxed a little and her fear of being delayed faded away.

Upon boarding the plane and finding her seat, which happened to be a window seat two rows before the wing, she was happy and felt fortunate that the drama of embarking was over. Liv proceeded to turn off her phone and read the safety documents located behind the seat in front of her. She always hated watching the stewardesses, who she thought now were called Flight Attendants, demonstrate the plane's safety features.

She found herself forcing a smile at a little boy who stared blankly at her from the row just ahead. Hopefully, the parents would keep the little fucker quiet during the flight, and she wouldn't have to deal with him or his noise.

The plane touched down on time and as she proceeded to baggage claim, and then to the Hertz Rental Car booth. She was glad to have all the airport drama behind her. She never enjoyed flying and this was the part of the trip she had dreaded the most.

They gave her a burgundy Camry, which she had read was rated the #1 mid-sized vehicle in Consumer Reports for about seven years running, or something like that. As long as it started and the air conditioner worked, that was all she really worried about.

Liv's first stop was at a McDonald's she saw on Rt 50 Eastbound. She ordered a Big Mac Meal and told them to make it a large fry instead of the small ones that they usually threw in the bag. "Something about those fries," she thought as she gave the guy a ten-dollar bill and waited for the change. "They're so stinkin' good."

As she began the 150-mile drive to Ocean City, Maryland, she turned on the radio and cranked up the first soft rock station she could find. Yep, vacations were sweet and hers had just begun.

She passed a guy hitchhiking early in the drive, gave him a dirty look, and didn't stop. He looked as if he hadn't washed his hair in weeks and his jeans were filthy dirty and badly wrinkled. "Probably a crack-head," she said distastefully to herself. She realized he may have seen her lips move but didn't really care. After all, she'd never see him again, and he probably was a crackhead. She giggled at that last sentiment and drove on.

Liv drove another fifty miles or so and realized she needed to put some gas in the Camry. She thought that Hertz would have filled up the tank prior to her renting it, but they must have forgotten, and she kicked herself for not thinking to check the gas gauge. She would make a mental note and be sure to talk to someone upon returning the car. Perhaps they'll give her a little credit when she paid up at the end of her trip.

She pulled up to the first pump and got out of the car. Liv would never think of paying at the pump. She'd heard way too many horror stories of people having their identities stolen from using those machines, so she always walked inside and paid the cashier directly. It was a hassle sometimes, especially when it was raining, but well worth the peace of mind.

As she walked back to the pump, an old pickup truck pulled up directly beside her. She paid no mind and grabbed the gas handle, shoving it into the tank. She chose the cheapest fuel available and set the automatic lever on the handle. As she grabbed the squeegee to clean the windows, her eyes wandered over to the pickup that was fueling next to her. That grubby hitchhiker was in the backseat staring at her. It caught her off guard, and as their eyes met, he gave her a stare that would chill an Eskimo. "Was that him?" she thought. "It had to be," she relented in her mind. His stringy, greasy hair hung partially over one eye and she noticed that his teeth were a dingy yellow, appearing as if he hadn't brushed them in years. She wondered who would have picked a guy like him up and shook her head in disgust.

Now, all she wanted was to get in her car and drive off, but she had to finish cleaning the windshield and filling the tank. She returned his gaze with a stone, expressionless regard. There was no way she was going to give this guy the satisfaction of any look that he could mistake for fear, or even compassion for that matter. People who couldn't get their life in order, and had to, of all things, resort to hitchhiking at his age weren't worth her pity or her time. He sure wasn't going to be her charity case today. She had too many good things on her mind, like the strawberry daiquiri waiting for her at the beach.

The gas handle clicked off, and she topped off the tank a couple times before placing it back in its cradle on the pump. She tapped yes, after the "Would you like a receipt?" blurb and waited for the paper to pop out. She grabbed it a second later, gave it a little yank, and turned to get in the car. As she did, she couldn't help but glance over her shoulder at the hitchhiker in the truck. He was still staring at her! She rolled her eyes a little to let him know she would not be intimidated, flipped her head a tad, and got back in the front seat and drove back onto Rt. 50 eastbound.

Liv was happy she'd booked the earliest flight in the day because she knew it would take some time to find the hotel and didn't want to arrive at night because she wasn't one hundred percent sure where she was going. She knew how to get to Ocean City, of course, she had been there a million times, but not to the condo she had rented.

When she crossed the Bay Bridge, she got an immediate spurt of excitement. It was always such a beautiful view of the Chesapeake Bay off that bridge. She had many memories driving

268 | BJ Lawyer

over it, it was like being home. She remembered hearing stories of all the construction men who had died while building it, falling into the molds as they poured the concrete and were unable to be saved. The ends of the bridge held memorial plaques that held the names of the men who had lost their lives. It was very sad. Although Liv still had one hundred or so miles to go, that bridge always meant BEACH, and she was more than ready to sink her feet in the warm sand and feel the sea air blowing through her hair!

Just before the bridge ended, she noticed the old pickup truck passing her. This time, however, the dirty hitchhiker was driving, and she saw no one else in the truck with him. As he drove past, he looked over at Liv and smiled. It was the creepiest smile she ever saw, yet she could not turn away. It was more like a grimace. A grimace with worn down, crooked teeth. As she continued to watch him, she could swear there was something like gristle hanging out of his mouth that was caught in the saliva covered corner of his lips. Did his teeth have a reddish tint? It must have been the light bouncing off the window. A chill ran through her.

She let him continue to go by and backed off the gas pedal, thinking it better to let him get as many miles ahead of her as she could.

Chapter 2

Liv arrived at Ocean City with plenty of daylight left to enjoy a walk down the coastline after she got settled at the condo. As she drove over the last bridge, which connected the highway to the peninsula, she spun her head around to see if the old sign was still there. Sure enough, it was. She was happy to see "3,000 miles to Sacramento, CA." on the highway sign over the west bound lanes of the inlet bridge. She always loved seeing that sign. Several years ago she had to go on a business trip to Sacramento to fill in for someone in her company who had taken ill and happened to notice a signed just north of Sac on I-5 that read, "Ocean City, Maryland 3,000 miles". How awesome was that? Just a random, but very profound kinship. Only the elite in the Who's Who would ever know it existed.

She made sure her GPS was on and working and was happy to see it was before deciding to head to a grocery store to pick up a few staples that would get her through until morning. Then she would go out again for the rest of the week's groceries. For now, she just wanted the important stuff like Bourbon and coffee, and maybe a frozen pizza and sunscreen.

As she pulled into the ACME Market on Coastal Highway, her heart skipped a beat. No more than one hundred feet in front of her was that old pickup truck, parked up front in a handicapped space. If she were to go in the front entrance, she would have to walk right past it.

She parked the car and took the key from the ignition, forcing herself to think before she got out. It quickly came to her that she didn't want to walk pass the truck. In fact, she knew there was no freaking way she was going to walk past it and put the key back in the ignition. Looking up to exit the lot, she saw that the hitchhiker was about to leave, and as he pulled out, he drove right across her path.

As the truck rolled up directly in front of her, blocking her in, it slowed to a stop. Liv looked up to find his awful face staring at her over his left shoulder with a grimace. She knew she couldn't hide the fear in her face, although she tried to keep it composed. But she had the sense that he could see into her eyes and smell her fear, just like a dog. He held his gaze on her and she remembered later that the right side of his upper lip curled upward to again show those yellow fangs.

"This couldn't have been planned on his part!" she said out loud to herself in the car. "How could he have possibly known that I would be stopping here?" She hoped he wouldn't think she followed him into the grocery. It was then a chill broke out over her arms as she wondered about the people in the truck who had picked him up. What happened to them?

All she knew was that she wanted to get out of there. But until he moved, she couldn't go anywhere. When she looked at him again, he only nodded at her. Then, slowly, he pulled forward, his gaze never shifting from her eyes until the truck exited the lot.

She sat in the car and shivered, trying to gather her thoughts, and concluded that she wasn't about to let this miserable fuck ruin her vacation. Instead of going to the grocery store, she drove to a liquor store and went straight to the condo. Liv rented a second floor, beach front condo on 13th Street, which overlooked the Boardwalk. It was old and it wasn't particularly classy by any stretch, but it had everything she wanted. A place to cook, a place to sleep, and a place to poop. Who needed anything more?

After unpacking, she went out on the deck and watched the people walking up and down on the Boardwalk. If she got hungry later, she would order a pizza like everyone else in the world.

The Boardwalk was the best part of Ocean City, attracting most of its visitors. It was a three-mile long, giant tourist trap from 1st Street to about 27th Street. The streets beyond boasted high rise, fancy hotels that cost a fortune and were far enough away from the Boardwalk that the people staying there didn't have to deal with the real element who also shared the beach. But, as far as Liv was concerned, those folks lost the ambiance of the whole beach experience. Loud, drunk, crazy, single people went to the beach and stayed on the first few streets where the old, yet quaint, run-down mom and pop hotels lined the potholed streets. If you weren't single, you stayed on the higher streets where boring, quiet, book reading, breast feeding, conference calling people belonged.

She decided to hit the beach and waded in the water before lounging on the four-dollar chair she bought at the liquor store, as she tried to relax. She forced herself to forget about the creepy, whack-job on the highway by taking a few selfies and texting them to friends.

She must have fallen asleep because when she woke it was twilight and the sun had just fallen below the hotel roof lines. "How relaxing is this?" she thought as she stretched out trying to decide what to do next.

As she gathered her things together for the quick stroll to the Boardwalk, a tennis ball landed on her blanket. She bent down, picked it up, and spun around to throw it back to its lost owner.

She was horrified to discover it was the hitchhiker standing about twenty-five feet from her. He was wet from the ocean, and his hair stuck to his emaciated, amphetamine-riddled bones. She had the ball in her hands, and as he stood anticipating her throwback, she instead threw it in the ocean with a swift hurling motion.

She immediately turned around to pick up her things and without looking back, she started toward the hotel. She knew she was probably reacting a little more intense than most girls in her situation, but she was in her own world and wasn't about to take this crap from any guy who just wanted to get a rise out of her.

Once arriving at her condo, she showered and threw her beach towel into the washer. Her fears were real at this point, and she knew she wouldn't enjoy her vacation until this guy was gone, or at least out of her space. Liv knew the cops couldn't do anything, there was after all, no threat, or any forcible entry into her space. She would have to wait and hope that no further intimidation would come her way.

Chapter 3

As excited as she was about starting her vacation and mentally reviewing her list of things to do, Liv realized she was also exhausted. Even though she was only in the water a short time, the sun took its toll on her, and she knew it would be an early night. That was ok. She wasn't eighteen anymore and she wasn't going to feel guilty at all about sitting on the balcony with a book while watching people walk up and down the Boardwalk.

She loved her new digs. It was only a one-bedroom condo, but it was all she needed, and it was super close to everything. Plus, it was located right over a popular junk store that sold all the usual tourist stuff like cheap surf boards, sunscreen, and gawdy rocks with faces and stupid sayings painted on them. It got a lot of foot traffic, which assured her that she wouldn't miss any pedestrian tourist drama. After all, what was a vacation without a little drama?

She jumped in the shower, which washed the slimy ocean water and leftover sand she hadn't shaken off yet down the drain and put on an oversized Kim White Band t-shirt that was old, soft, and properly broken in, and some flannel, baggy house pants that she'd owned since the dawn of time. The t-shirt reminded her of good music, good times, and best friends, and of course, great memories of her life before adult responsibilities overtook her. It was also her favorite band, and she knew when it wore out, she'd be pretty upset if she couldn't find another one to replace it. Therefore, she always took care of it more so than any of the other shirts she owned.

Next, she made a bourbon and coke, grabbed her cell phone, and went out on the balcony to enjoy the view. It was about 8:45 PM, and for Ocean City, the night was just beginning.

She no sooner sat down and got comfortable when something flew up from the Boardwalk. At first, she thought it was a giant bee or mutant winged beach thing. Then she realized it was only a tennis ball. She hopped up and saw that it was lodged in a fake potted plant next to the sliding glass doors. As she walked over and picked it up, she noticed it had writing on it. Her heart skipped a beat when she read the words, "You better not tell."

The ball felt like hot lava burning her hands and she suddenly dropped it. It bounced off her foot and under the railing, then fell back onto the Boardwalk.

There he was sitting on a bench that faced her balcony, grinning at her with cold dark eyes. Hateful eyes. Eyes that looked so powerful they could make you hurt your own mother.

Now Liv wasn't just getting scared, she was also getting pissed. This was her vacation, and this wasn't in her plans—oh no, not at all.

The fact that he knew where she was staying—her address, where she parked her rental car, and most importantly, that she was alone, hit her. She suddenly felt vulnerable for the first time in her life.

She looked down, noticing he hadn't shifted an inch on the bench. He was still watching her, and their eyes met. She wouldn't back down. She wouldn't let him know she was scared to death. It wasn't in her nature. She was going to hold her ground. She may be alone, but as far as she knew, he was alone, too. "Can't outrun a bullet, buddy. Back off," her mind hissed at him as she held his gaze. "Better just back off."

She wasn't about to let him intimidate her, but she did, how-ever, check the windows and door to make sure everything in the condo was locked and secured. It was.

Liv returned to the balcony and forced herself to sit down. She stayed out for an hour or so, determined not to let the man know he had scared her. Not knowing exactly why, she secretly placed a kitchen knife on the table beside her while finishing a few chapters in her book and a couple drinks. Knowing the knife was there made her feel safer and more in control of her situation.

Glancing randomly down at the boardwalk and watching the people walk by settled her nerves. For most of the evening Liv avoided looking at the bench where she knew the hitchhiker was probably still sitting. Instead, she tried to focus on him out of the corners of her eyes. Sometime during the evening, most likely while she was reading, she realized he had left. At that moment she would have given anything to know which direction he had gone and exactly what time he had disappeared.

She wasn't sure if there was a chill in the air, but she noticed the hair on her arms and the back of her neck stood upright. Liv told herself she was getting sleepy, so she grabbed the knife and went inside about midnight or so and slept light, but well. When she woke, she was rested, and ready to start her day.

Chapter 4

After a shower and a light breakfast at the café, which was located on the west side of the hotel, Liv rented a bi-cycle and set off for the ferris wheel. She tried to be as nonchalant as possible as she kept gazing behind her, searching for her hitchhiker. She couldn't stop thinking of him now and kept imagining him running up behind her and doing something unspeakable. As she peddled to the ferris wheel, which was just off 1st Street and all the way down at the Boardwalk's beginning, she realized that she could not continue living with the dread of knowing he was out there, waiting for her.

It was early and the heat hadn't become unbearable yet. It was a great ride. Then upon returning to the condo she searched on the internet for close grocery stores and gun shops. "What a combination!" She laughed to herself as she entered the address of the gun shop into her cell phone's GPS.

She knew there was a waiting time for handgun purchases, but she thought the store may have something that would help her feel safer. Perhaps a taser or something would be good. She had heard that there was a gun that discharged bean bags. That would be pretty neat. Something cheap, but effective. Her new mission had just begun.

Leaving the condo and walking to the car, she noticed something was under her windshield wiper. As she got closer, she saw it was a dead fish, sliced down the middle, its organs sliding out and spread all over the glass.

In a frenzy to get out of the parking lot, for fear he was close by and watching her reaction to the fish, she frantically looked for something on the ground to wipe the sickening thing off the windshield but found nothing. She grabbed the fish bare handed and threw it on the ground before quickly jumping into her car and locking the doors. She quickly turned on the wipers and hit the wash button. She covered her face with her hands forgetting they were wet and sticky from the dead fish and began crying as the water sprayed on the glass. Thankfully, she always carried a small, travel size pack of baby wipes in her purse and today she was very happy she did as she used them to clean off her shaking fingers.

Alas, one more stop she would have to make—the Ocean City Police Department. She punched the address into GPS and arrived within minutes.

She explained to the officer at the reception desk the series of events leading up to the "fish" incident, and especially the words written on the ball that landed on her balcony. The officer asked many questions and stated that there had been no information about a pickup truck being stolen or anyone missing. There had been no crimes reported and the only thing they could do was take Liv's report of the hitchhiker and notify the officers in the area to be aware of anyone fitting the man's description and have them keep an eye out for any kind of unusual behavior.

Her information was noted and that was it. Liv understood, but was still pissed. After all, it wasn't their vacation being ruined by this white trash POS. And there was no way she was going to call it quits and go home with her tail between her legs. Not Olivia. If this guy wanted a fight, she was going to give it.

As Liv arrived at the apartment, she realized that she had been at the police station most of the morning and was starving, so she grabbed some famous Boardwalk fries, a soda, and a couple hot dogs and retreated to a bench to eat.

She gazed up to her second-floor balcony and saw that someone . . . HE . . . had taped a sign on the railing that she had no problem reading. "I know where you went today." She almost choked as she realized that for him to have put the sign up, he would have had to enter her apartment or climb on the dangerously slanted roof. Which was it? She called the cops, and they were at the apartment within twenty-five minutes.

Liv felt relieved that the guy was now officially on the cop's radar, and they were going to keep an extra eye on her apartment and the nearby areas surrounding it.

That night she treated herself to a nice crab dinner and an evening swim in the hotel's pool. She was determined to keep her vacation normal and relaxing, even if it killed her.

Around 2:00 AM she heard loud noises coming from the Boardwalk below her balcony. She was slightly hung over, but she awoke quickly and shuffled to the window. Her hitchhiker was standing under a streetlamp just under her balcony watching the disturbance of three drunks trying to ride their bikes.

As she stepped out onto the balcony, the man looked up at her and made the hand gesture of shooting a gun right at her. She looked at him and forced a laugh, determined not to look away. After a few moments she went back inside and called the police. By the time they arrived the man was gone. It was late and she was tired. The police were unable to help her, and she was reaching her limit of patience.

The next morning Liv woke up and hit the beach. It was fantastic. What a great day. The shore was about one hundred feet from her condo, and it was exactly what she needed. She had packed a couple sandwiches and a few water bottles, and thanks to the giant umbrella she brought along to block the sun, and the 50 SPF sunblock, she was a happy camper. Liv had forgotten how wonderful alone time was and soon the thoughts of the scumbag hitchhiker totally disappeared from her mind as she closed her eyes and squirmed her feet in the warm, moist sand.

She was close to falling asleep when the man suddenly resurfaced by parking his yellowed beach towel next to hers. He sat down and began to make innocent conversation.

Lying on her four-dollar beach chair, she pretended to sleep. She didn't know whether to get up and run or stay.

"How dangerous is this guy?" she thought to herself and had absolutely no idea what to do. She hoped there were cops within ear shot, but, as usual, they were never around when you needed them.

He was clearly insane, speaking to her as if he knew her and as if they were old friends. He spoke to her in a voice that was childlike and seemed to speak very candidly about incidences that he felt they had experienced together in the past. She didn't know whether to humor him with general courtesy or tell him to get the fuck away from her.

Liv wanted to be civil and honestly thought that if she regarded him with a little respect that he might just go away and leave her alone.

That was a nice thought, but she quickly discovered that it was only wishful thinking. When she sat up and reached for her beach bag, he firmly grabbed her arm and pulled her close to him. "Do you realize that in forty-eight hours you will be dead?" he asked her. She shook her arm loose, stood up and spit on him as she gathered her things and ran back to the safety of the condo.

As Liv entered her apartment, she knew the only way to get this guy to leave her alone was to do something drastic. The police weren't very helpful, and she had to start thinking of a strategy to save herself.

In a last-ditch effort to remove herself from the current situation, Liv switched hotels. After situating her things into the new hotel room, she sighed with relief and fell onto the bed. All this excitement was becoming too much for her and a power nap was a perfect ending to a tense afternoon. She had continually been looking over her shoulder to make sure he hadn't been outside watching her checking out and she felt confident that she'd pulled it off. Good for her—free at last! Now she could rest easy and give her vacation a new start.

The next few days were relaxing, fun and full of adventure. With the hitchhiker nowhere in sight, she rented a jet ski, took a catamaran class, and even went parasailing for the first time! She was on the other end of the peninsula and although she had always called it the place where all the old people stayed, she had to admit it was still wonderful. She'd be home in two days, and she was happy that the week turned out great despite the earlier drama she was trying to forget.

CHAPTER 5

O n her last night of vacation, she decided to take a walk along the beach. There were no clouds, and the moon was full and bright; its reflection on the waves was magnificent. She hadn't used her camera the whole week, only the one in her cell phone. It had always been good enough, but she still always grabbed her old Nikon whenever she travelled. Some habits were hard to break, and she always wound up happy just knowing she'd brought it along even though it was huge and heavy compared to the new cameras, which were much lighter and more compact. Tonight, she would try and get some nice photos.

She had an excellent seafood dinner and watched the sun go down from an outside table that overlooked the ocean. The patio was decorated with candles on every table and the small white lights that hung from the deck rails and roof edges reminded her of weddings. It would have been very romantic if she had been with someone, anyone, but tonight it was just plain beautiful, and she realized that being alone didn't matter one bit. She was happy with herself and that's what counted. Clouds had started drifting in from the ocean and hung low overhead, promising rain soon and maybe a nice storm.

She washed her meal down with a couple dirty martinis, paid the waitress, and headed for the Camry.

She was leaving early the following morning, hoping to beat the Bay Bridge traffic that was a routine nightmare and wanted to turn in relatively early that night. It was just always so hard to leave the beach!

Retrieving her camera from the back seat of the car, Liv took it out of its dusty case. Thank God she'd remembered to put new batteries in it before she left the house. She kicked off her shoes, rolled up her pant legs to well above her knees, and put her hair in as high a ponytail as she could to keep her hair from blowing in her eyes and the pictures. Five minutes later she was on the beach almost up to her crotch in water. She knew she'd get wet but laughed it off, being very careful not to go in any deeper and keeping an eye on the waves that were threatening to break on her.

The clouds that had blown in were dark and threatening now and it was getting chilly. Liv wondered how long it would take until the rain began. Heat lightning flashed in the distance and with it, a rumble of far-off thunder. But the moon was still visible, and Liv thought the clouds would add a nice effect in the pictures. Menacing clouds were always cool to have hanging among the stars.

It was the last real week of summer, and the beach was mostly empty of people. She liked it that way and felt she had the whole world to herself. She supposed if she were a poet that tonight would be a perfect night to write.

As she stood with her back to the coastline, she began changing the aperture setting on the camera and enjoying her solitude. Suddenly she felt a hand on her right shoulder. She spun around and found herself staring at the man who had threatened her life days before. The sound of the ocean had drowned out his approach. She thought she was rid of him!

She screamed as loudly as she could and almost fell backwards, but he quickly grabbed her and held her up. She felt like a bug caught in flypaper and his strength completely overpowered her. Liv whimpered. She was in shock. It took a moment for her to start thinking straight.

As she struggled against his grip, her camera dropped into the murky water and disappeared into the darkness. He got close to her face and spit on her just as she had done to him on the beach in front of her condo days before. Then a rumbling laughter erupted from him. "How does it feel bitch? How does it feel to know your gonna die?"

Realizing she had the camera's neck strap clenched in her fist, she swung it over her head as best she could, and as the camera resurfaced from the water, Liv whipped it hard. She prayed the strap wouldn't snap as it hit him square on the side of his head and he let out a short groan of unexpected pain.

"You bitch, I should kill you right now!"

As he yelled at her, she stepped closer to him and brought up a knee that landed home. She never in her entire life kneed someone in the balls and he bent over in agony. He went down to his knees just as a wave broke, knocking him over and forcing him under the water.

Liv couldn't run fast in the deep water, but she did the best she could. She was able to get a few feet away, but then she felt a hand grab her leg and pull her back.

The clouds were upon them now and the thunder was much louder. The rain started coming down in sheets and she thought if he didn't kill her, the lightning and rising seas would soon kill them both.

She kicked and tried to hit him, but he was just too strong, and she couldn't break free from his embrace.

He grabbed at her and found her breast. He squeezed it hard and pinched her nipple, the pain so intense, she screamed as loud as she could. To make her stop he pushed her head under the water and then let her back up. Coughing up water, Liv fought to breathe. Her strength was running out. She didn't want to die this way and she used every bit of willpower she had to fight him off.

Then he whipped her head back and with her breast in one hand and ponytail in the other he was at her neck, first kissing her then biting her. She was at her most vulnerable at this moment as she felt her pants being pulled down and her legs parted.

He was all over her, and she was unable to stop him. She felt him slide into her as he lifted her off the ocean floor. His hips pumping at an alarming rate as he pushed himself deeper and deeper inside her. She was unable to fight anymore. She had no choice but to accept his thrusts as her head fell forward and rocked against him. Unbelievably, he supported her neck as he breathed against her throat. She kept waiting for him to bite again.

She tried to yell, but there was no one to hear her. It was full dark now that the moon was covered in storm clouds. The storm was raging, and she knew he was going to kill her.

She hated it and it sickened her, but to keep her head above the churning waves, she had to hold on around his neck to keep her upper body from falling back in the water. He was huge, she could feel him filling her up. He was like a monster. "Oh please, please stop!" She cried again and again.

The storm was raging, and she couldn't believe he was still able to stand. "Please! Please! Please!" She felt him as he grinded himself against her harder.

He grabbed her face and as he came inside her he kissed her in a rough, non-passionate way.

Moments later he pushed her off. As she tried to find her footing on the sandy bottom and gain her balance it all finally sank in, and she looked at him.

They were in a rip tide and being pulled out into the ocean. Then she finally remembered . . .

She had no idea if it would work since it was wet, and she couldn't believe he hadn't found it on her after pulling her pants down, but she knew she only had seconds to reach for it. Her hand went to just under her chest. Under the smooth material strapped tightly around her she pulled out the Barretta 380 that she had purchased two days before just in case he found her again.

She held it up, clicked off the safety, and pulled back the slide. Then before he had time to realize what was happening, she pointed it directly at him.

His eyes blazed with hatred and surprise. He also had to regain his footing as the waves turned violently stronger. "You know you wanted it," he teased.

"You fucker!" she whispered at him. "Why don't you bite this!" and fired three rounds into his chest.

He flew back into the water and before he was out of sight, their eyes met again. This time she was the one smiling.

His last words to her were a warning, "I will come back as someone you love. You will never be free of . . . me . . ."

As the ocean current grew stronger, she let herself float. She knew she couldn't fight the undertow or the thrashing waves and didn't try. She didn't have any fight left in her. If the ocean wanted her it was going to get her. Liv kept waiting for his hand to grab onto her leg once again and pull her down, but it never happened. In fact, she knew he was under the water, and she also knew he wasn't coming back up.

She effortlessly floated for what seemed like forever. She still held the gun and she realized she was finally free of him. Drifting about fifty yards out, Liv knew she needed to start swimming. She was strong and agile and a good swimmer. After about half an hour she was quite a way down the beach, but she was finally on dry land and thanked God for it.

She had been humbled for the first time in her life. The ocean had lured her in but let her go when she thought there was no hope.

The hitchhiker was dead and had been carried out to sea during the storm. She only hoped that the tides would not bring him back. If they did, she was sure no one could tie her to his death, the gun was untraceable. The salt water would get rid of any DNA she would have on him, and she would have to be content believing in that. Besides, he was a drifter and a lowlife. He probably had a sheet a mile long and his death wouldn't be investigated too strenuously.

Liv was leaving the next morning and she walked the beach waiting and watching for something to surface or drift to shore. Nothing appeared.

She went back to her room, showered, and packed for home.

Chapter 6

Liv checked out of the hotel with a smile on her face and exchanged a little innocent conversation with the front desk attendant. Ten minutes later she was on Highway 50, westbound toward the airport.

She was amazed at how peaceful that gun made her feel. The minute she bought it she was immediately comforted knowing that there was a Barretta under the covers with her every night, in the body holster under her shirt every day, and beside her on the couch in the evenings. As form fitting as the holster wrap was, not showing any bulges, she only noticed the weight. The comforting weight that only she would feel. At that time of her life, it was well worth it, but it wasn't a way to have to live and she was glad to be going home.

She had picked up the gun from a guy who was advertising it on Ocean City's Craig's List. She never particularly wanted a gun, not that she was against them, or because of the violence that seemed to always surround them, but she bought it out of good old common sense. Self-preservation was a true motivator. To kill or be killed, that was the question, and she knew the correct answer. Yep, Craig's List bypassed the whole ten-day waiting period, and that was truly a wonderful thing considering her current situation.

She had taken a Firearms 101 class in college because she needed an extra credit, and she was now glad she did. She aced it, and once a week the class met at a local range to shoot. She enjoyed it and thought with a little practice she could be pretty good at it. She just hoped she wouldn't have to start practicing this week. As it turned out, practice did start and she aced that, too.

Life continued normally for Liv, and no one ever knew or suspected that she had been involved in a murder. Her job was going great, and she had even bought a small home with a little backyard. It would be perfect for the new baby she was expecting. The test results came back, and it was a healthy baby boy.

She couldn't wait until the birth and knew she'd be a wonderful mother. They would be together forever, and she would hold him and comfort him and show him the world. Yes, she would love him very much and he would always be with her. Always.

KAY'S NEW CAT

CHAPTER 1

K ay Connelly and I had been best friends since elementary school. We used to spend the night at each other's houses every weekend, and in ninth grade, we used to walk the neighborhood on Friday nights. It was all innocent fun back then, not at all like it is now if two young girls are out at night walking the streets. Nowadays, we would be up to no good, party girls; or worse. Besides, it wasn't just us walking around the neighborhood, it was practically everyone in our age group.

I'd never considered myself anyone special. I'm Heather Mondell, a single gal from Maryland, which is where this story comes out of my memory. It was forgotten for many years, but in the end, things always come back.

For us kids, the main place to go and hang out was Pizza Wheel. It was in a little strip mall on the corner of our one-horse town. Next to Pizza Wheel was a pub that only the people out of high school mostly frequented because of the alcohol that was served. The next in line was Carlo's Video. That left the parking lot for the younger kids.

The high schoolers who had their licenses would all roll into the parking lot and hang out to smoke weed and drink beer in their muscle cars. Back then if a guy didn't have a bad-ass Chevelle, Trans-Am, Nova, or other two-door hot rod with the back jacked up and L-60s on the rear, they weren't shit.

We sported our Peanut pants with pride and embroidered jeans. In case you're wondering, Peanut pants are extremely low cut. So low you had to wear a body suit with them, or your butt would hang out when you sat down! It was about 1976. The popular term "Hippies" had long since expired. In those days school kids were basically divided into three groups. The Freaks, who drank, smoked weed and partied on whatever drug they could get their hands on. The Jocks, who pretended to drink, played sports, and spoke harshly about anyone they were jealous of, and the Nerds who were in the Math and Drama Clubs, and had no life. This included the wrestling cheerleaders who basically had few friends and were mostly overweight. Kay and I leaned toward the Freak group, but also dabbled in a little Jock. We were just plain cool. But wasn't everyone cool when they were in the ninth grade?

One distant memory that always comes to mind happened on a snowy day in January, when Kay and I were walking down the main street of our neighborhood and a car full of losers threw an ice ball out the window at us. They were going about thirty miles an hour and the ball from hell hit me just above my right knee. I thought I was going to die. When I think about it, I still remember it hitting me and I still remember the pain as it dropped me in the street. It felt like I would never walk again. The pain was so intense, I thought I would need an ambulance.

Being so young, I couldn't believe anyone would do that on purpose. To hurt another human being without just cause wasn't comprehensible to me, it was the lowest of the low. I wasn't raised to be mean to anyone, and to make matters worse, I swear I heard them laughing when I fell in the street.

Kay helped me as best she could, and I will always appreciate that. But, in hindsight, no matter how good your best friend is at comforting you in an emergency, you still want to kill somebody.

Shortly after that incident my opinion of human nature changed, yet again, for the worse.

This was around the time when the Bunting family lived down the street from our house. We used to see them outside grilling burgers on their front deck or playing board games. They always used to wave at us when we bicycled past their house, and everyone who knew them thought they were great neighbors and very friendly people.

On a Sunday afternoon about a month before, little Cora and Elizabeth Bunting were both playing down at the creek. It was warm that day, unusually warm for December, so Mrs. Bunting was glad to see them able to go outside and get some fresh air. At 5:00 when they never arrived home for dinner, both parents notified the local police and rounded up some friends and neighbors to begin looking for them.

They had only been gone a short time, but dark came early that time of year and they were so young it didn't take long for everyone to start worrying. Cora was twelve and Elizabeth was seven. They were good kids and always listened to their parents. The kids just went to the creek to skip rocks and were told not to go in the water at all. Cora was tall for her age and was the smartest kid in her class. She was fully capable of looking after her sister.

A short time later, someone found both kids floating face down in the murky water alongside a huge oak that had fallen during the last big storm of the summer. It was determined that someone had held them under the water and killed them. The police offered a reward for any information that would lead to the capture of the killers. As it turned out, the murderers were never found, and our neighborhood was never quite the same after that. As far as I know, the only fact given out by the police surrounding the murders was when they took Elizabeth out of the water, she had cuts on her arms as if she'd been clawed, and she had a wad of fur in her right hand, which was never explained.

There was no more staying out past sunset catching lightning bugs or daring each other to make trips into the woods after dark. Kids went home promptly when the streetlights flicked on, and we all had to get used to it because complaining wasn't an option. We all understood why our parents became so strict with us, but it didn't mean we had to be happy about it.

The Buntings soon moved away. I supposed continuing to live in a neighborhood where such a horrific family tragedy occurred was a daily reminder that made life too painful for them. Therefore, a month or so after the deaths, the house went up for sale and they moved out a short time later.

I remember the day they moved away. Not much was said. What was there to say? There were sad, understanding looks, and short hugs. Everyone knew why they were leaving, and words were hard to find. Deep, penetrating expressions and heartfelt well wishes were given; then they were gone, and the Buntings soon became just another couple who once lived in the neighborhood. Another faded memory, like their poor children, Cora and Elizabeth.

Chapter 2

At the time, the Homeowner's Association had voted to add on to one of the main streets in the neighborhood and about two miles of construction was actively underway. They were putting more houses in, along with a county connecting road that would completely ruin the fields and creek where Kay and I, and the rest of the neighborhood children, always played. They even filled in the pond we all went ice-skating on during the cold months. The pond was big entertainment for families and memories fill my head of all the girls wearing white figure skates with yarn balls tied onto the laces, and all the boys had those black hockey skates. It was so much fun back then.

One day after school just before summer vacation began, Kay and I were hanging out at the creek, as usual. We were trying to make a small section a little deeper so we could swim in it. As it was, we could only wade up to our knees. The thought of being able to at least sit on the bottom with the water up to our necks would have been great and it would also allow us to float. In small towns with little to keep teenagers occupied, creeks were a favorite for all ages. We filled up buckets with mud and rocks that we emptied onto the hillside next to the road. Under the road was a big drainage pipe and lots of kids used to play in it, but not that day. We were all alone.

As we filled the buckets, we heard a noise coming from the direction of the pipe. At first, we thought it was just a rabbit or some other animal rustling through the grass. When it didn't stop, curiosity got the best of us, and we wandered over to take a look.

It turned out to be a small cat, creamy tan in color. It was beautiful. The hair was very long, and it was obvious the poor kitty was homeless because it was matted and desperately needed grooming. It also looked very thin and neither Kay nor I thought it had eaten in quite some time.

We sat down in the grass and called it over to us. It was a miracle because the cat slowly walked right up to us and sat down. Usually, homeless cats are scared to death of people, and they most certainly never walk right up to them. Everyone knows that cats are born with an inherent instinct of knowing human beings suck and usually wanted to grab them by the tail and fling them, especially boys. But this cat must have had a nice home some time in its life to be so trusting.

Almost immediately, Kay and I both tried to agree on which one of us would take it home.

We had two dogs at our house and my mom hated cats, so I knew I wasn't going to be able to keep it. On the other hand, Kay had a cat named Stormy that was old and not very healthy, so we both agreed we would try to con her parents into letting her keep it.

That afternoon the cat never tried to leave us, and it seemed very content to stay by our sides. It even followed us back and forth from the creek to the hillside, watching us with its fantastically large lemon-gold eyes. I remember thinking to myself that I had never in my life, ever seen eyes that color before. It seemed to never take its eyes off us. Looking back, it seemed to be examining us. It was almost as though you could see it trying to look deep inside us with growing inquisitiveness, as if educating itself about each move we made. It turned out that was exactly what it was doing.

As the sun was setting and the streetlights automatically turned on, we started the hike back towards home and tried to shake as much mud and dirt off our clothes as we could.

We had dug a lot of dirt and rocks out of the creek. If we could have stayed a few more hours it would have been better, but so far, it was a job well done. In the next day or so, as the creek ran, it would eventually fill up with more water and the dirt would settle back down to the bottom where it belonged. We were proud of ourselves and thought we'd have quite the swimming hole come summer. It would have been heartbreaking if only we had known Kay would never get the chance to swim in it.

Kay begged me to come with her to her house, so that she wouldn't have to confront her parents alone about the cat. I did as she asked, and it went well. Her mom said it could stay the night. She agreed the poor kitty could use some food and a warm bed.

The general rule of thumb was if your parents said an animal could stay one night, it really meant you'd be picking out names by the following day. This rule proved true and sure enough, the next day Kay had a list of names we were discussing on the bus.

The next afternoon during lunch, Kay said the cat sat on the windowsill in her room and stared at her until she fell asleep. Kay said she woke up to go to the bathroom sometime during the night and the cat was still on the windowsill. She didn't think it moved a single inch. Kay also mentioned that upon waking she thought the eyes had changed color a little, switching from a golden color to a shade of bright green. She wondered if cats' eyes could do that.

School was uneventful that day, and when it was over, Kay was excited to get home to play with her new pet.

Kay and her family had decided to start calling her Nebbie.

I got the flu and stayed home from school the next three days. I spoke with Kay a couple times on the telephone while I was recuperating and she seemed as though things were normal, saying Nebbie was getting along fine at her house. Kay said Stormy, her older cat, kept his distance and acted afraid of Nebbie, but that was normal with cats. Her dad said cats always need extra time to adjust to new things. Kay and her family had also gone to Pet Smart and purchased Nebbie a large, flowered cat bed and food. I was happy she was able to keep her.

In the following days, I noticed that Kay was very short-tempered and seemed nervous. It was as if she wasn't the same girl I had been so close to for so long. We were best friends and always had the same sense of humor. Oftentimes, we could just look at each other and crack up laughing for no reason at all. Now, she wouldn't even look me in the eye and when I asked her if she was mad at me, or if I had done something wrong, she would only stare. Her eyes would just gaze at me blankly like she didn't even know who I was. It was really getting creepy.

A day later she called me and asked me to meet her at the dead end. The dead end was exactly halfway between both of our houses, and it was our favorite meeting spot.

When she showed up, she looked as if something horrible had happened. Her clothes were wrinkled and looked as though they hadn't been washed for days. She had tears in her eyes and said her family had recently begun talking badly behind each other's backs and they were always fighting with one another. The arguments were getting worse every day.

Kay looked deep into my eyes and told me she knew it sounded crazy, but thought it was the cat's fault. It would only sit and stare at them with those forever changing eyes. It wasn't only the color that would change, but the shape of its pupils would change, too. Kay also said she never saw its chest rise and fall and doubted if it even breathed air. The cat was telling them to do bad and hurtful things to each other. In a sudden gasp she said the cat wanted them to kill each other!

Kay wiped her wet eyes and added the cat never wanted to eat, it just sat and glared at them. It never purred and no one saw it sleep. Her parents dismissed the idea of it being unusual and said Nebbie only needed more time to adjust to living in a house, but in time she would get used to her new environment.

Kay quieted for a minute, but the look on her face was strange. I waited for her to speak again, knowing she had more to say. Then she cried, and said her father slapped her mother for no good reason the night before and he had never hit any woman in his entire life! He had big opinions on that issue, in fact. The worse part was he had a look on his face of sincere happiness when he did it. Even more strange, when he hit her, Kay said she saw the cat smile. It was a deranged smile of a psycho, not a cat.

Later, she said the cat walked around the house looking at things in her father's office as though it was planning something. She swore to me she saw it pulling drawers open and looking at file folders. Impossible! It would walk around the house going from room to room looking at tools, papers, everything . . . as if it was learning.

The cat would be in the kitchen watching her mother cook dinner and then it would be gone without a trace. It could disappear. Then she would see it in the den watching her father. It was always watching. It never groomed itself or did things cats normally do, like get into boxes or bags. It never wanted to play at all. If you tried to get it interested in anything it would stare at you like you were an idiot.

Kay said that the cat walked up to their older cat and gazed at it. After a minute or so, Stormy let out a low whining noise and took off running outside. The neighbor lady called shortly after and told Kay's mother that she saw Stormy run into the back wheels of her husband's car as he backed out of the driveway. He was killed immediately. The neighbor also said it looked like Stormy tried to kill himself by running under the wheels on purpose. The neighbor lady was obviously very upset and said she had never seen anything like it before. Kay told me she thought Nebbie told her cat to do it.

When we said goodbye to each other that day at the dead end, I saw something in Kay's eyes that was beyond hope. It was as if she was afraid the cat wasn't a cat at all, but something evil pretending to be one. Kay gave me a frightened look and I had a weird feeling I would never see my friend again alive.

296 | BJ Lawyer

Chapter 3

The next night Kay's dad came home with a box under his arm and put it in the bedroom closet he and his wife shared. When Kay had asked about the box, he simply shrugged and changed the subject.

Family fun had ceased to exist in their house. No more home cooked meals. No more watching sitcoms on the television together with hot, buttery popcorn and homemade hot fudge sundaes.

Kay's mother stopped volunteering at the local Meals on Wheels; her father stopped going to work where he had just been promoted to regional manager at the Frito-Lay Company, and Kay stopped going to school. In fact, Kay's last day at school ended with a permanent suspension due to her attacking another girl in gym class when the girl asked if she could borrow Kay's math book. Kay had a pen in her hand and began stabbing her repeatedly with it. She tried to stab her in the face and neck and would not stop.

Kay didn't have a mean bone in her body and would have normally given anything to anyone without batting an eye. To become so violent and wanting to cause anyone pain was not in her nature. What was happening to my friend and why?

It was very lucky the girl was bigger than Kay and able to ward her off. If it had been anyone smaller, Kay would have killed her easily, or at the very minimum, put out an eye. When the gym teacher pulled Kay away, she simply laughed and smiled at Nebbie, who, for some reason, was in the locker room with her at the time. Kay knew no one else could see Nebbie. It was marvelous how Nebbie was so good at hiding when she needed to.

That same evening, when Kay's father came home from a long walk with Nebs, he was in rare form. He adored the fact that his new cat enjoyed taking walks with him, and while they spent time together, her dad was amazed at how many ideas came to his mind on how easy it would be to solve his problems. It seemed he could correct any difficulties in his life with little effort whenever he was with the cat. He realized he had been afraid his whole life of doing the things he really wanted. Why had he always given up on his happiness before? It seemed to him that he always gave the upper hand to everyone else. It was about time he would take control of his life again and regain his power.

CHAPTER 4

Nebbie was a clever cat. Kay learned she could do many things. She could become invisible when she wanted to, and she could even tell you what she wanted. Not in words, you understand, but by putting pictures in your head. It was easy to figure out what Nebbie wanted, and Nebbie always got her way.

Nebbie even told Kay that when little Elizabeth Bunting saw her pretty, glowing collar down in the water, she thought it was a cat caught on something and was struggling to free itself, so she stepped in the water hoping to save its life. As soon as the little girl grabbed the cat's collar, Nebbie's paw tightened around her wrist and pulled her under. Nebbie pulled her lips back in a perverse smile and told Kay it was all very easy. Sadly, her older sister jumped in to help her and she was taken to her death, too. She added that, for fun, she even let Cora come up for air a few times so she could prolong her death a little longer. Feeling the children kick and fight for their lives as they tried to hold their breath was the most fun part of all. Nebbie loved the thrill of the kill. It was, after all, what she lived for. Not only could Nebbie make herself disappear, but she could also manipulate her body to suit her needs. Hands made it much easier to grab a child and hold them under the water until they stopped breathing.

Kay commented to me how she has recently been able to easily accept things that had always used to frighten her. It was kind of like forgetting to cover the bacon while it was cooking and getting hit by the popping grease, or like burning your leg on the motorcycle's hot exhaust pipes. It hurts, but it's okay. Her new cat taught her many things and gave her new insights about life and managing discomfort.

She was being brainwashed by that damn cat and I was helpless to do anything about it! When I suggested to Kay, they should get rid of it and take it back to the creek, she immediately pulled away from me and told me to mind my own business. She refused to listen, and at that moment, I knew the cat had her in its evil.

Chapter 5

The last day I ever saw Kay was when she was strapped down and carried on a gurney to a women's correctional facility on the east side of town. Even though she was a minor, they considered the crimes she had committed warranted the adult system of justice. Apparently, Kay had done much worse than assault another student with a pen. I believe she was totally insane. I believe the cat drove her mad.

Can evil take the soul of a cat? Can a cat be inherently malevolent? Could aliens steal an animal's personality? What had really happened?

Chapter 6

Kay's father went on a midnight rampage and one by one murdered everyone in his home while the National Anthem played softly on the television in his room.

He silently drowned little Wayne, Kay's first cousin in the bathtub which he had filled with very hot water. Then walking down the hallway to the guest bedroom he entered and proceeded to slit the throat of his own mother as she lay sleeping peacefully. She never saw it coming. His father on the other hand, did. He tried to get up to defend himself, but between the arthritis in his knees, which caused him to move slow and his son's youthful speed and agility, he didn't stand a chance. Old Grandpa was hit square in the mouth with the butt end of his son's twenty-gauge Remington. At first, Kay's dad tried to suffocate him by jamming the stock down his throat, but it was too wide, and he couldn't get it passed his jaws even after smashing all of his teeth. It was then he decided to slit his throat as well. It was a little messier, but hell, he knew he wasn't going to have to clean up the mess.

The next in the lineup was Kay's loving mother. She had heard commotion and was sitting on the side of the bed putting her slippers on. As she began to stand her husband once again brought out the Remington and let her have both barrels point blank in the chest.

Lastly, he turned the gun on himself. He put the barrels in his mouth, but found he had a hard time reaching the trigger. To his amazement Nebbie walked out of the darkness and pulled the trigger for him.

Kay hadn't seen her cousin in nearly two years. Her grandparents thought it would be a nice surprise for Kay to be able to visit with him in the hospital. They had planned to visit her the following day.

Kay managed to live long enough to write down only that she hoped her cat, Nebbie, could be placed in a loving, forever home as quickly as possible. After attempting to slit her own throat with her long, hard fingernails and realizing she could not, Kay then hung herself in her hospital room.

CHAPTER 7

A few miles down the highway, a family of six were picnicking at a rest area. They had stopped for a quick bite as they were anxiously heading to their brand-new home. They had lots of miles to drive before they reached their destination, but hunger seemed to turn into starvation as the kids were getting more and more restless to get out of the car.

To their amusement, a beautiful, small, tan cat with very long fur jumped up on the bench beside the man and looked at him with its brilliant, cobalt-blue eyes. The man thought to himself he had never in his life, ever seen a cat with eyes that color before.

DNA Don't Lie

S top trying to scare the children!" Charlotte told her husband Cory. "Keep it up and we'll never get them to want to come camping again."

Cory turned his head and looked at her, stuck his tongue out, and rolled back his eyes. He made a creepy noise from deep in his throat and growled at her. "Oh, come on Mothaah . . . I believe they are coming for you . . ." He sounded like the guy in Night of The Living Dead. "Look—there they are . . . they are here . . . I told you they were coming foor youuuu!" He bent his fingers as if they were claws.

"Stop it, Daddy, stop it!" Mary yelled in a tone that was not fearful, but more annoyed. "Mommy, come sit next to me!" she pleaded.

"Ok, ok, I'ma comin - move over a little, please, I don't want to trip over you and fall in the fire!"

"Sure, Mommy!" Mary happily replied as she shifted over, being careful not to scoot off the sleeping bag she had laid on the ground. It was a gift from Santa last Christmas and was exactly what she had asked for. It had moons and star designs all over it and even had a secret compartment along the side to store candy, or maybe a flashlight.

Charlotte and Cory were in their mid-thirties, with their forties just around the corner, and had decided to take advantage of a nice long weekend by camping out at a local lake before he started his new job later that week. Cory's career had become very time consuming, and he felt blessed that Charlotte was so forgiving since he had to spend so much time away from her and the kids. This new job was going to be the perfect fit for all of them with more money and more time at home.

Charlotte was a great mom. She came from a huge family, and they were all very close. When Charlotte married Cory, it was like a match made in heaven. They hit it off right away and they both wanted to start a family as soon as they were financially able.

Cory was orphaned at an early age and didn't remember anything about his childhood prior to being adopted by a sweet Baptist family in North Carolina. He had always been a good student and had many aspirations of a promising future.

Cory had started having dreams at night. Awful dreams. Dreams that upon waking he had to stop and think if they were real or just nightmares. Sometimes he couldn't tell. He knew they had to be due to the constant stress and he was so happy to finally have all the recent job drama behind him. A little family fun was just what he needed to chill out and get his head together.

Their oldest, Mary, was in the fifth grade. She had dark auburn hair and beautiful brown eyes. She was very typical for her age and was already determined to be an actress. In fact, she was already planning her move to Hollywood as soon as she was old enough.

Denny was five and a half and had already passed out on the cot Charlotte had placed by the fire. After the marshmallows were eaten and his sticky fingers were wiped clean, his head hit the pillow and sleep came fast. Cory would carry him into their tent as soon as it was time for everyone to go to sleep. It was about 9:30 and Cory was amazed that with all the day's excitement, he'd lasted as long as he had without drifting off to sleep.

Mid-way through the first campfire story, Mary's eyes started to haze over. Cory knew she wouldn't last much longer, and he was right. Ten minutes or so later, her head slopped over to one side and her breathing became slow and deep.

Charlotte had already blown up the air mattresses and laid out the blankets and pillows, so tucking the kids into the tent was quick and easy. Now it was adult time, and they always took advantage of that when they could.

In recent months Cory would sometimes find his mind wandering in directions that were far away from his family. In directions that were not socially acceptable and that scared him. Sometimes he found himself becoming very angry and resenting Charlotte, and he would quickly push these thoughts out of his mind. It was as though he couldn't keep happily ever after separate from the 11 o'clock news. These thoughts and dreams concerned Cory, but he summed it up to the middle-age crisis men his age often spoke about.

When Charlotte had gone into the tent, Cory decided to walk around the campsite to make sure things weren't left out and the trash was picked up properly.

At the Ranger Station, where you pay for your campsite, there were always signs posted about bears and how important it was to pick up after yourselves. He'd always had a fear of bears, among other forest creatures with large teeth, and didn't want his family to be the main course for one, and tonight wasn't any different.

While Cory tended to the campsite, he heard the normal nocturnal sounds that took place under the canopy of large oaks. He heard crickets and the occasional coyote, and other sounds that he had absolutely no idea what animal they were from. He was basically a city boy but wanted his kids to appreciate nature and the good ole' outdoors whenever possible. In all honesty, he enjoyed the family camping trips very much. He was also glad campgrounds were within a relatively short distance to both a police station and a hospital. Knowing this was always a comforting thought for him.

Suddenly, he heard what sounded like a deep moaning—possibly a hurt animal was his first thought. He hoped it wasn't suffering but was also hell bent on not going out there to check it out. He didn't hear it again, so he quickly stopped worrying about it and climbed into the tent, zipped up the door and prepared to sleep.

After a while, he realized he had to pee and sleep would never come until he did, so he threw on an overshirt, slid on his tennis shoes, and ventured to the edge of the campsite by a tree to urinate.

Again, he heard that weird moaning. It was a little closer to the campsite, but like before, it didn't come again, so he didn't think about it any further and started back to the tent.

He had thought about bringing the flashlight with him but didn't think he would need it. Now, he wished he had it so he could have at least scanned the area, maybe see what was making that sad, hurtful sound.

As he lay on the air mattress covered by the extra blankets Charlotte brought along, he began listening to his wife's soft breathing. He loved looking at his children's innocent faces bathed in the moonlight which was spilling though the screen at the top of the tent. Cory was happy and looking forward to the new job and all the new responsibility that went with it. He had been nervous, but now it seemed to be the next step in life. After all, he did have a family to take care of and he loved them very much.

A strange feeling crept into his thoughts, and he thought of his dreams. He pushed those evil thoughts away and again closed his eyes and waited for sleep to take him. He prayed his slumber would be dreamless.

Just as he was drifting off, a sound interrupted him. He heard not just a moan, but also the swishing sound of the bushes alongside their campsite. He didn't hear footsteps, but instead, heard what sounded like something going by at a fast pace. Twigs cracked and limbs stirred. It abruptly stopped right where he knew the picnic table was located.

Cory was afraid to move. He didn't want whatever was out there to hear him. Cory had brought a small caliber handgun, as he often did when they went on camping trips. In case of what, he had no idea, but it always was reassuring to know it was with them, just in case. A lot of good it would do now, especially since he'd left it in the damn car.

He laid there. Paralyzed. Praying the kids wouldn't wake up or that Charlotte wouldn't make a noise. He was scared and discovered that he was completely man enough to admit it.

He heard whatever it was move about. Then, it was gone.

Cory couldn't get back to sleep for a long time. Finally, he drifted off, but awakened soon after and knew sleep was a useless goal.

After laying in his sleeping bag for what seemed like hours, he quietly peeled himself out of his cocoon and exited the tent. As he began to walk to the car to plug in his cell phone, he noticed there were blood stains on the cement picnic table and around the cooler. It must have been the poor animal who had possibly been shot and wandered into the campground for food. Was it hunting season? He had no idea. It seemed that all year long was hunting season for one kind of animal or another. Cory was not a hunter and even fishing grossed him out when it came right down to it.

Cory quickly cleaned the blood so the kids would not have a horrible memory of a fun camping trip turned crazy. He could imagine what a shot and bleeding animal, suffering and dying in their children's minds would do to them for the rest of their lives. He was thankful they had brought a couple gallon jugs of water. When Charlotte needed the water to clean the dishes, he would tell her he accidently kicked them over and would wash the dishes for her when they arrived home. After cleanup he jumped back in the tent and tried to resume sleeping.

When Denny woke up at sunrise, Mary followed him soon after, and they emerged from the tent to find their mommy cooking bacon over a large fire that daddy made a little while before.

"Up and at 'em! Breakfast is almost ready! Hope you guys are hungry!" Charlotte said in a happy voice.

Together they sat and ate pancakes, sausage, bacon, scrambled eggs, and toast. Charlotte always enjoyed cooking big breakfasts for her family and being in the woods didn't change that.

"Hey, how'd you sleep? My god, I must have totally passed out. I didn't even wake up to get a drink of water or anything. That's not like me at all, right?" Charlotte asked Cory as she wiped out the skillet with a paper towel.

"Yep, you were out like a light, for sure. I guess you can't keep up with me after all, ole lady." Cory said as he grinned and kissed her on the cheek. He hoped she wouldn't figure out he had been up all night, scared. That would have done nothing to elevate his manhood.

He didn't want to mention what had happened during the night. He knew it would upset her. He would wait and tell her after they got home.

After a short hike on the trail next to their site, and bicycling around the campground, they packed everything up and left for home.

It had been a few hours since he woke up and as he was driving out of the campground, he was mentally going over that night's surprises. He was trying to remember if it was another dream or if it all really happened. There was so much blood, and he couldn't remember the exact chain of events.

As they passed the campground manager's site, they were stopped by a ranger who greeted them and asked Cory to roll his window down and step out of the car. Cory noticed the ranger was sweating very heavily. It was a nice cool morning, certainly not hot enough for him to be sweating so much. Maybe he was getting sick, Cory thought, and he slowly tried to back further into the car and away from the window. The ranger also asked if Charlotte would get the kids out of the car and have everyone follow him to the office. Evidently, their check for the campsite had gotten wet and the ranger needed her to initial her signature.

It was at that very moment Cory and Charlotte noticed numerous squad cars and SWAT vehicles beginning to surround their vehicle. As soon as they were a safe distance away and after what seemed like forever, the policemen dragged out a man who had tied himself to the under carriage of their car.

The man had a vest on with duct tape all over it and beneath the tape it looked as if he was wired to a homemade bomb of some sort. He was laughing and crying and threatening everyone. It was evident he was very weak and could not put up much of a fight, as he was passing in and out of consciousness. Most likely from loss of blood. Somehow, he had a large cut in his chest area, possibly from fleeing his incarceration, but impossible to know for sure.

This man had escaped from a maximum-security prison about eighty miles north and had been on Death Row for three years after committing horrible crimes involving two elderly women and dismembering their bodies, which were found buried in five large coolers. He had also murdered two small children by putting one in a microwave and the other by leaving him in a cage and starving him slowly.

Cory could not believe what had happened. How could he be so stupid as to think it was an animal at their campsite?

Mary asked her mother, a few weeks after they got home, if it was okay if she opened the present the guy at the campsite had given her. Mary told her mother the man said he would tell her when she could open it, but he never came back.

Charlotte and Cory immediately called the police.

"I went to the bathroom, and he was in there. He was really nice, and said he wanted to be my friend. He said I could call him Uncle."

The chief of police took the small box and opened it.

What was inside changed them forever.

As the police detectives slowly opened the box that was decorated with red ribbon and covered with handwritten pictures of happy faces and hearts, they found inside, laboratory test results, which included the killer's blood DNA. The man had been suffering from a hereditary disease that affected the males in his family. The onset of symptoms from this mental disorder attacked the individual when they entered mid-life at approximately forty years of age. The first symptoms were forgetfulness, nightmares, anger and other personality disorders. Then as the disease progressed the effected individual would become dangerous and eventually lethal to both animals and people. Complete madness was the final prognosis.

There was one other piece of paper included in the box. It was on the letterhead from the Tyrrell County North Carolina Department of Child Records. It was odd this was the same county that Cory was born in. This document indicated that the man had been orphaned at the age of four years and three months, along with a brother that was his junior at the age of one month. Cory's blood ran cold as he read the rest of the document.

The individual's birth name was Mitchell Lambert Dawson.

This man's last name was the same as Cory's.

DUE CAUSE

CHAPTER 1

The wind is whispering to me like I am a child. I wish I could make it stop because the sound is hurting my head. I feel something warm on the side of my neck, and I think it's blood. How much blood have I lost, I wonder, as I lay here in this dark place? I'm getting cold now, which is not a good sign, and I want to sleep.

I have done all I can to keep my thoughts together in hopes of writing it all down. If only I had enough time left to write. In these last few days, everything has come down to time. I'm not scared anymore. Things have progressed way past fear. Sometimes if I close my eyes and try hard enough, I can almost forget the past few weeks and the horror that has been escalating. Then I open my eyes and remember.

The only people who seem unaffected are the children. They wander, apparently healthy, although their faces blank and lost; there are so many of them.

It is still spring, my favorite time of the year. Except this year, the flowers are not in bloom, and the trees are not green with new growth, but maybe I'm imagining it. I hear no birds chirping, nor do I see families of opossums or bantam quails hurrying across these country roads. Could it be that they are all simply dead, or have they all fled this contaminated land? If I am still alive, surely there are others—animal or human. There have been no bombs or chemical warfare. There has been no actual war. Yet even the morning dew seems sticky and unyielding.

Yesterday seems like a lost memory to me. I can't remember much except that I was cold, and my heart knew it was time for me to leave this place, this wonderful place, which I have called home since back in the winter of '91. The house was a pale blue rambler with white trim and a large deck across the front. I put an old-fashioned swing on the south end so I could relax and look at the huge hardwoods that always seemed to give me peace as I watched them sway in the wind. When it comes to comfort and that old time, homey feeling, hardwood trees and swings are immediately on the top of the list, as far as I'm concerned.

I hope my wife found her way home. When people started dying, and the autumn winds came, I sent her to her father's up in Wisconsin. It was her homestead since birth and where I thought she would be the safest. Her family has had a small farm up there since practically the dawn of time. Passed down from generation to generation it had slowly become smaller and smaller; as a few acres at a time needed to be sold for taxes, or just to help make ends meet during those lean years. Their farm is very small compared to the commercial, big boy operations and competing with them had always been impossible. Anyway, it had been a long time since she had seen her father, probably about five years or so. I feel awful now thinking how we kept putting a visit off. When we moved away, we told each other that we would plan a trip out there at least once a year. Why hadn't I kept my word and taken her back for a visit? I guess it doesn't matter now.

Life has a way of getting too busy, I suppose. The job becomes too demanding, and the budget seems to get so stretched that sometimes it's hard to put gas in the ole' truck, let alone try to cram the cost of a couple of airline tickets into our ever-shrinking bank account. I should have sucked it up and put her on a plane myself every year. I'll never forgive myself for not doing just that. She would always smile and say we would get around to a trip soon when the time was right. I should have seen through that understanding smile and not been so selfish. If I get another chance, I am making the promise now that I will get us both on a plane every year for a little family reunion. I know now how important it is to keep in touch. Yeah, if I ever get another chance. Please, God.

Life used to be easy for us. I used to wake up on clean sheets and have a purpose. I would accomplish things that made me happy. Learning was enjoyable. Now my daydreams have turned into nightmares, and I cannot escape them. What has changed? Maybe nothing, maybe everything.

Everyone calls me Kep, but my full name is Harrison Keppler. I grew up in a sleepy, little, naive town located in the foothills of the Bradshaw Mountain range in Arizona. Humboldt, to be exact, which should not be confused with Humboldt, California, where the best marijuana in the country is grown and harvested by mostly poor, but willing participants in the ever-growing CBD business.

During my last year in high school, I remember commenting to my dad about going on to college upon my graduation. He laughed and told me he wasn't dishing out tens of thousands of dollars for me to continue my D grade point average. His point was taken, and I knew he was right. College just wasn't going to be in the cards, and that was fine with me.

I worked the usual jobs guys acquire right out of school, a local motorcycle shop in the parts department, a couple of gas stations, and I was surprised to discover I had a natural talent at welding. This was how I earned my living for the last thirty years or so. It paid well, and I was able to make most of my own hours. If I showed up an hour or two late from time to time, not much was said, as long as I stayed a little later in the evening. I enjoyed the flexibility, and not having to put a tie on or those pansy-assed shiny shoes was a definite perk.

I met the love of my life, Wendy LaGrande, at a local watering hole called Billy Jacks. Funny how close I came to staying at home and working on an old motorcycle I picked up that night instead of going out, but the boys wouldn't take no for an answer, so I decided to go with them. Wendy had been visiting a girlfriend for a few days, whom she had met at college. It turned out to be a trip that would change both of our lives forever. She was Prom Queen in her hometown and what she could have possibly seen in me was unfathomable. But, against all odds, we soon fell in love and were married at a little church in Arizona where her Uncle Morty presided. It was the kind of church where they kept an old bathtub with claw feet behind the altar for the flock members to be baptized in. It was decorated with the giant words of good old John 3:16, "For God so loved the world, he gave his only begotten son that whosoever believeth in him should not perish but have everlasting life" hung high overhead. Subtle it was not. Religion never is. After the ceremony, we took one of those all-inclusive trips to Cancun for a week. It was probably the best week of my life.

It all seems so far away now.

I found my sister and her boyfriend in her living room four days ago. Whatever was happening came quickly to some, while giving others time to die painfully and slowly. My sister, who had always been trim and fit, and a faithful mile-a-day jogger, rain or shine, laid on the couch with dead, cloudy, gelatinous-grey eyes. The expression on what was left of her once bright and sensual face, had turned into an expression of shocking intensity. It was almost as if she had seen something, only she could see, and was still staring at it. Her eyebrows were cinched back towards her hairline as if someone glued them to her forehead, and the veins in her eyes had grown thick with blood, bulging as if at any moment they would burst and run down her greying, pus-filled cheeks.

I had to quickly turn away as I felt the need to vomit. Between the sour-sweet smell coming from her and Mat, who was laying in her arms, hair matted with skin swollen and blackening, also with protruding veins, I ran into the bathroom.

What I found in there was worse and almost too unspeakable to say out loud. It seems whoever had used the toilet before me, left what looked like a lung or stomach part in the bloody bowl. What was that? I couldn't even imagine as I ran out of the house, unable to give them a respectful shroud over their lifeless bodies.

Sometime later, I noticed the sun had disappeared below the horizon. I wasn't sure how long I had been walking away from their home, but I realized I had gone about seven miles. I must have walked right past my truck that I left in the driveway with no memory of having done so, whatsoever. The thought of going back and getting it seemed impossible, so I just kept walking. There was no way I wanted to go back there. There was no way I could go back there. All I knew was that I had to get somewhere where I could sit and hash this all out. I also thought it strange that no one stopped me to ask if they could give me a lift. Could it be that no one was around anymore to help?

I have so many unanswered questions. What could have caused all this destruction to human lives so quickly? It came without warning. It came without cause. And why are there so many healthy children? How could they have all escaped this sickness?

I arrived home at full dark and realized Rusty wasn't barking behind the front door or scratching for me to hurry up and give him some attention. Rusty, aka Rustoleum, was a now middle-aged red Doberman I had rescued from a local shelter.

At the time Wendy and I found him, he was only a year old with a not-so-good track record. It seems he had gone through three owners, each giving him up due to "aggressive" tendencies. As we walked past his little caged area along the long cement hallway of the Humane Society, both sides lined with similar enclosures, I couldn't help but notice him. The other dogs barked their greetings and ran back and forth, hoping to win the hearts of someone and be adopted, but Rusty just sat. Ears erect, straight back, head straight forward with the only movement being his eyes, which followed each passerby intently and with great determination as if he could read their minds. He had such a royal and stately appearance, as Dobermans always do, that he caught me completely off guard and lured me to him immediately.

When it was my turn to have my mind read, I stopped and looked him in the eye. Giving him plenty of time to judge me, I walked toward his fenced area and quietly asked him if he was a good boy. His response was priceless. He licked his lips and lowered his head just enough to make me think he was actually going to answer me. Wendy and I immediately asked the attendant if we could see him in the exercise area. It was love at first sight. He was playful and sweet, with no sign of aggression. He seemed to get along with other dogs in the exercise area, as well as the other prospective adoptive families. About half an hour later, we were walking through Pet Smart, picking out toys and food. Naturally, he would sleep on our bed, but Wendy insisted that we also pick out a nice pillow if the bed or couch wouldn't be the first of his choices. I had a feeling that I knew who would be ruling the roost in the future at our house.

My heart took a full header to my stomach as I grabbed for my house keys. "Oh please, God. Let him be ok. Please, please, please . . ."

He was. I guess he must have been taking a nap and hadn't heard me approach. Once inside, I stretched out on the bed with

Rusty plopping down next to me almost immediately, his head across my stomach as I tried to think.

There was no one of authority to call about my sister. The Police Department only provided an automated answering machine message that was basically a crock of shit. Hospitals rang busy, and funeral homes were packed, or dead themselves, unable to answer. Either way, Rusty and I were on our own now.

Up until about a week ago, things seemed fairly normal. Traffic moved at a steady pace, and stores were open. People seemed to be living their usual lives, doing what they always did. Normal, normal, normal. Looking back, it could have been wishful thinking on my part, but I don't know anymore.

I'm embarrassed to admit that I don't watch the news with any regularity. It's so biased and political these days you just don't know what to believe. Everyone has their own agenda, and the media lies in order to get us to believe what they are being paid to feed us, so I don't pretend to play their games. I just turn the channel. Maybe that is the problem with this world today. Everyone just turns the channel. It's easier to pretend bad things aren't really happening rather than put forth effort and search for the truth ourselves. We tend to remain happy when we hibernate in our own little make-believe worlds.

Chapter 2

A day or so before Kep found his sister and Mat non-ceremoniously splayed out on the couch in their own feces, Millie Davenport was mixing up her third cosmopolitan in her two-bedroom, seventh-floor condo in Puerto Penasco,

Mexico, also called Rocky Point to those who live just over the U.S. border in Arizona. Millie had quit using the fancy French Baccarat crystal martini glasses that her husband's family had given them on their first wedding anniversary – they were just too damned small. She had switched to a high ball tumbler instead.

"That ought to do it," she thought. "Much more efficient."

Considering the recent and strange occurrences that had been affecting her husband's business, he had flown back to their Ocean City estate in Maryland to be closer to the company that had treated both him and Millie so well over the years. Who would have thought cat litter would put them on the Forbes 400 list? They surely had not. Although anyone that knew Branson Davenport knew that whatever he found himself doing in life would take him to the moon. He was just one of those lucky guys who could turn anything into gold, and this was exactly what Millie had hoped for. She just never imagined that cat shit would be the cement that held her life together.

She sat on her massive, oversized balcony overlooking the beautiful Sea of Cortez, but instead of enjoying the view, her mind kept worrying about Branson. She had the feeling something awful was happening that no one had any control over.

Things were getting weird in Mexico. She first noticed the absence of planes. There were no advertisements stretched out behind little Cessnas because there were no little Cessnas. Where were the ultralights that constantly flew around with tourists strapped inside? Those passengers that had one hand white-knuckling their movie camera and the other hand death gripping the pilot's shoulder? And birds—where were the Reddish Egrets, Ospreys, and Snowy Plovers? She had come to love watching the birds while here. They always seemed to calm her nerves and put her at peace. Maybe later she would walk the coast and see if she could spot some. Millie stopped dead in her thoughts as she realized there was hardly anyone on the beach. Even the people seemed to have taken a vacation from their vacations.

It was a bright, warm, sunny day. The beach should be busy with sunbathers and children digging for clams and the like. Jet skis should be twisting back and forth along the waves, and kayakers should be playing in the breakers—but there were none of those either. Maybe there was something going on poolside that was more exciting. Her balcony didn't face the pool, however. She decided to pour herself number four and get ready for room service. She would also try to get a hold of Branson, who was bound to be landing soon in Maryland. Millie wanted to know how things were there, and for some reason, she didn't know why, she wanted to hear his voice and tell him she loved him.

The next morning, Millie went down to the lobby to speak with the concierge about having someone bring her car around. Soft Spanish music resonated through the speakers in the lobby. The melodies were always so happy and fun, she thought, as she walked up to the concierge's desk.

Millie was working off a stiff hangover, and her legs and body ached. On a scale from one to ten, her head pounded at about a six. This was unfortunately normal for Millie, who enjoyed her cosmopolitans a little more than she wanted to admit. She enjoyed them even more after Branson left town for business. She had thought about going back with him, but she had been so looking forward to this trip to Mexico. The day he left, she knew everything at the company would be all right, and Branson would fly back in a day or two, but now, she wasn't so sure and felt a little uneasy when she thought about it. Therefore, she planned to head to downtown Puerto Penasco today in hopes of getting the bad thoughts out of her mind.

There was an excellent wharf nearby where vendors sold everything from t-shirts and tourist souvenirs to fresh fish in coolers along the roadway. She thought about picking up shrimp and lobster to cook a feast for herself for dinner. There was a new recipe she happened to come across on the internet and was dying to make it, so she could get the kinks out before serving it to Branson. Her cooking skills weren't the best, and she didn't want to subject Branson to a disaster if she didn't have to, and with him out of town, this was the perfect time to give it a go.

The concierge was not at the desk. In fact, there was no one behind the large lobby desk either. The only person she saw was a child no more than ten years old who was obviously looking around for someone. Millie didn't get very worried until she saw three military soldiers carrying their machine guns. They stood in the lobby's entrance driveway, but Millie knew they were heading inside the hotel and would be coming through the doors at any moment.

Millie casually jumped into the elevator and hit the button. She would return to the lobby after running up to the condo to get her driving glasses. She supposed she would simply get her car from the lot herself; she could use the exercise, after all, and her hangover would have to deal with it. By the time she came back down, the soldiers had moved on, and she was on her way.

As Millie went outside and got into her car, she noticed that the place was deserted. No one was outside except for a few random kids, and this terrified her. They weren't playing in the pool or running around getting into mischief like most kids; they seemed to be wandering. Heads down and body movements slow. As she climbed in her car, she looked at the gas gauge and made a mental note to stop for some as soon as she got out of town, which was fifty miles or so. By then, she would be hungry for lunch.

Her cell phone wouldn't work when she was off the hotel property, which was normal for out of the country travel, especially in Mexico. But today, being without it made her feel a lot more uncomfortable.

She turned onto the main highway, immediately noticing that a bus had overturned. People were lying on the ground. There was no police or rescue service, or anyone offering assistance. As she got closer to the accident, she realized that everyone was either dead, or twitching in strange, uncontrollable movements that seemed to Millie to indicate some type of poisoning. The only sign of life was a small crowd of kids that must have been on the bus with their parents or relatives. They were huddled together as if listening to a story or saying a prayer. As Millie drove past, feeling guilty for not stopping to see if she could help, the children didn't even acknowledge her. They continued what they were doing without looking up.

Millie knew at once she'd made a terrible mistake by not heading home with Branson. Oh, how she wished she had! Now her main thought was how to get out of Mexico. If the shit was hitting the fan, her sole objective was to get back into the United States as soon as possible. There may be knowledge of what was happening, more people, and most importantly—safety.

Millie went back to her condo and gathered some clothes and as much non-perishable food as she could carry from the kitchen. She also made a call to Branson to fill him in on her plans to leave.

She threw everything into her Cadillac Escalade and headed out of town. Even though it was mid-Spring, it was still unusually chilly outside for Mexico, and she wasn't sure how the weather would be in the States for her long drive to Maryland. Having a breakdown, or something worse, wasn't in her plans, and she thought of stopping to buy a jacket or shawl, just in case. One thing Branson had always told her when preparing for a long trip was to hope for the best but prepare for the worst. For the first time, she finally understood what he had meant.

As the morning turned into afternoon, Millie was on her way out of Mexico and heading for the wonderful Land of the

Free. She knew she was only about an hour from the border, but with so much drama, she was dreading to make the drive alone. She had always considered herself a strong and resilient woman, and she supposed the next few hours would be the test.

Ten miles from the border, she realized she hadn't seen any cars pass in either direction. It was a Saturday afternoon, so typically the place would be packed with cars, campers, and buses. Finally, about three miles to the border, she saw cars. A lot of them. And they were all stopped.

"So, the traffic finally begins," she thought. Millie only hoped she could get through the border patrol and into the U.S. quickly.

After sitting in the slow-moving traffic and coming up to the gates, a Border Patrol officer approached Millie and asked to see her travel documents. She gave them to him as directed, then noticed the officer was sweating profusely and had weird marks on his face. She couldn't help but stare at him, and he took no notice. He seemed to be having a great deal of trouble with his motor skills, and the simple task of holding the papers in his fingers was too much for him. He dropped her passport on the pavement, and when he bent down to pick it up, he almost rolled right over on top of it, but caught himself by quickly putting both of his hands down on the ground. He stood up slowly and with great effort regained his composure. Then he returned the papers to Millie and waved her on.

When she took hold of her documents, she noticed they were slimy and wet from his sweaty fingers. She tossed them onto the passenger seat as quickly as she could with a grimace.

"Holy shit, that was nasty," Millie said to herself as she gassed the engine to life.

She phoned Branson as soon as she was a couple of miles north of the border. He didn't answer.

"What the heck? He always answers the phone. What could he be doing?" she thought.

Branson knew she was on the highway and trying to get out of Mexico. She had told him how worried she was and felt something was very wrong in Rocky Point. She explained about the lack of air traffic and no one being on the beaches. She also explained that the town was practically deserted, and she was going to drive out of there as soon as she could. As soon as she mentioned the armed soldiers, he seemed to believe what she was saying, but she still had the feeling he thought she was overreacting.

Millie flipped on the radio to catch the news. She was not at all shocked that she couldn't get anything on the radio. After all it was Mexico, but thought for sure it would wake up once she crossed the border into the States. Instead, all that came through was static with a heavy buzzing sound occasionally.

She pulled over at a slightly run-down Gas-N-Go and was pleased to see people inside. When she walked through the door, they looked at her and backed away as if she had the plague.

"Hello," she said as she turned and walked toward the cold case section. She was so thirsty, and finding this store was perfect timing. She was desperate for a huge water and maybe a slice of pizza or something. Her planned seafood feast had never happened, and she hadn't eaten in hours.

Branson would probably want to kill her for eating in the Escalade. He was always so anal about spilling anything on the leather seats. "He isn't here, and I'll be careful," she thought and headed for the check-out.

When she got to the register, the cashier looked at her cautiously and asked if there were many tourists or sick people back in Rocky Point. He must have seen her driving into the lot and knew she was coming from that direction. Rocky Point was really the only place behind her. His question scared her. Her fear must have looked obvious to him as he followed by telling her there had been a lot of talk about people getting sick there, too.

"What do you mean there, too?" she asked.

"People seem to be getting sick everywhere. You haven't heard?"

Millie suddenly felt a little faint and let the counter hold her up. She thought about the weird feelings she'd had about the soldiers in the lobby, and the bus wreck along the highway. Most importantly, she remembered the border patrolman who'd almost passed out at her car.

"I haven't been able to get a station tuned in on my radio. What is happening?" Her pulse suddenly quickened.

The counter guy looked at her, and she noticed his drawer was sitting out as if he may have been counting the money. Could he be getting ready to close for the day? That would have been weird since it was only afternoon and the store was right off the busy highway. Something strange must be going on. Maybe he was just as scared as she was.

"We have a TV in the employee break room," he told her. "I hear it isn't bad in Mexico, yet, but the tourist traps are worse than the communities."

"What the fuck are you talking about? You are scaring me!" she gasped.

"I'm sorry lady, but evidently people are suddenly collapsing all across the U.S. I'm not sure of the details, but the news is crazy with stories. New ones every hour it seems." He added, "I don't know what's going on beyond that, but things are getting pretty terrifying pretty fast. They say people may be dying."

"Well, thank you—I didn't mean to get upset with you. This has just caught me off guard," Millie said breathlessly.

"Yeah, you and everyone else. If I were you, I'd get to wherever you're going and turn on the TV" the cashier suggested. "My shift is over, and that's what I'm going to do. I'll be home in 15 minutes."

"Yes, that's exactly what I plan to do, too," she said. "And thanks for the information."

Millie almost left without grabbing her items off the counter. When she got out to the Escalade, she called Branson immediately. Still no answer. "Shit," she muttered. "I bet he's just in a meeting or something."

In her mind she thought this was crazy. This stuff only happens in movies, not real life.

"Branson is just having a normal day dealing with meetings and warehouse drama." She said to herself. "I'm sure he will call me as soon as things settle down. In the meantime, I will just head towards Tucson and catch a flight home in the morning instead of driving any further. I'll have the service drive the car back to the house, and all will be well once I get back home. No problemo."

As she gassed the Escalade up to seventy, she didn't look back. Although, for some reason, she found herself biting a nail, which she hadn't done in years.

CHAPTER 3

Three teenagers sat in a booth at a local pizza place, talking. "The media is telling us the Department of Economic Security has so many children on their hands that they don't have enough foster homes to take care of them all. Do you ever remember hearing about that happening before? I thought everyone wanted little kids. Especially, the white ones," Maddy announced.

"Why do you think everyone wants the white ones? I mean everyone knows the non-white kids bring in more state money," Hunter said, mouth full of Pizza Hut's meat lover's pizza.

They laughed to the point of almost choking.

"You guys are really fucked up, ya know? What's happening is really sad, and all you can do is eat and laugh about it. And by the way your humor is sick and wrong." Miranda chimed in.

"Well, it's easy to laugh when it's not happening to you," Hunter exclaimed. "Besides, you know the media these days. It's probably all crap. They are just after donations or something."

"Maybe. But I really don't think so. They are saying it's because a lot of people are dying of head tumors and brain aneurisms and shit like that. Also, these people seem to be fine, and within a few weeks, BAMM! They're dead." Miranda added.

"What are you talking about, Miranda? Where is this happening?" Maddy asked, her attention quickly focusing on this news.

"Haven't you been watching the news or anything? You really need to get your mind off Facebook and check back into the real world. The doctors and scientists are trying to figure out what is going on. They aren't sure what's causing the tumors, but they know it's not a virus or some kinda bug, or something viral," Miranda said. "It's getting scary. Almost, 97% of the people affected are over thirty years old and most seem to live very healthy and active lives."

"What about the old people? Are any of them dying?" Hunter asked, still not taking the news very seriously and jamming another massive wedge of pizza into his mouth.

"Yes, but not as much. The scientists really have no idea what's happening yet." Miranda added.

Maddy and Miranda had been friends since the third grade. Hunter joined them in junior high when his father was transferred from the "big ole Windy City" to Tempe, Arizona. His company had felt the crunch of the recession in 2008, and his branch had to downsize. Hunter adjusted quickly to Arizona, and now he and the girls were in the twelfth grade together and inseparable. They were even talking about applying to the same colleges.

Since hearing Miranda speak of the health issue that seemed to be all over the news lately, the three of them retreated into their own thoughts without realizing it.

"Do you think we should really be concerned about all of this?" Miranda asked them. "I mean, do you think it's just more fake news hype or is it really something bad?

"Well, there isn't much we can do at this point except wait and see what happens," Hunter suggested. "I wonder if we should be worried for our parents, though."

"I think I'm going to go home. I've had enough of you guys trying to freak me out. Y'all are a bunch of bummers," Maddy said, packing up her belongings and leaving.

When Maddy got home, she found her mom in bed with a bad headache, which was unusual. She telephoned her dad right away, who was still at work, and told him what Miranda had said about what was on the news and then said Mom was home, sick. He told her he'd be there as soon as he could. It was Friday, so he would be off the next couple days, and not to worry. He asked Maddy if there was anything special she wanted at the store and said he'd cook dinner when he got home.

Later that evening, they ate cheeseburgers and hotdogs on the grill with some Hormel Chili heated up in the microwave. Maddy's mom never got out of bed that evening and couldn't eat a thing. The next morning, she heard her mom crying.

She called Hunter and Miranda as soon as she had showered and dressed.

Chapter 4

Kep finally turned on the TV after what seemed like days. He had come to a kind of reckoning when he realized he had exhausted his attempts to find out what was really going on. No one could, or would, give him any information about the recent deaths multiplying daily.

His wife, Wendy, was dead. Kep knew it in his heart. She called him the week before to tell him that both her parents had caught whatever it was, and they were failing quickly. She said there was nothing she could do for them. The hospitals had been filling up with other sick people, and after calling and calling and not getting through, she tried to drive them to the ER herself. Wendy told Kep that she couldn't even get within a block of the hospital. Parking lots and roads were packed, and traffic was at a standstill. She told him she had no choice but to turn around and bring them back home. Even the pharmacy was cleared out of necessary drugs; the shelves empty except for hemorrhoid creams and laxatives.

Kep knew that if his wife was still alive, she would have tried to get a hold of him by phone by now, but she hadn't.

He had heard some crazy talk about the government shutting down cell towers everywhere, and they were urging people not to use their phones. He wasn't sure what that was about but figured it was just more misinformation going around to scare people. As if people weren't scared enough already.

The next day his cell didn't work, and as far as he knew, no one else's did either.

His plan was to drive north to Wendy's folk's farm, and if he couldn't make it, he would die trying. The roads were closed in many places and a lot of the small towns had closed completely to keep some order or set up quarantine areas to prevent becoming infected.

By the end of the week, Kep learned that most adults between thirty and sixty in the United States were dead or close to it due to brain hemorrhages, brain stem strokes, and other acute head trauma. The first symptoms were headaches, hand and arm numbness, loss of muscular coordination, and loss of sight.

CHAPTER 5

Millie felt wonderful being back in the States, and terribly annoyed that her cell phone wasn't working at all. It was normally very dependable and had never given her a worry. She planned to stop at the nearest Verizon store she could find to see if someone could fix it, or simply get a new one. She was always impressed with how most people could use their cell phones for anything, but she was a little bit old school and didn't want to be tied to it every second of her day like everyone else. She used the calculator from time to time and the camera, but rarely got on it to gab the day away. Millie thought it was very rude when people would talk to her while using their phones at the same time. She refused to be like that, and she hated all those social media sites. Facebook she could definitely live without, and she still didn't know what a "tweet" was. To her, cell phones were ruining the family unit, and who needed to talk to people they hadn't spoken with since kindergarten anyway?

After driving and store hunting, she realized that most of the stores were closed. In fact, there was hardly anyone out and about. The only foot traffic she saw were mostly kids who looked dirty and way too young to be out without an adult.

It seemed to Millie that everything had gotten so quiet. The streets were practically deserted, and as she looked up at the sky, she realized there were still no planes. Where had all the planes gone? No exhaust trails above either.

She decided she didn't want to go into Phoenix or Tucson to check the airports. She thought it would be safer to stay on roads and out of the more populated areas. The world was getting spookier every minute, and she decided she needed to move on and head East. Homeward bound, Millie got on the I-10 E. and jacked the Escalade up to seventy-five. She knew it was going to be a long drive now that the radio was dead, along with her cell phone. But she had no fear of falling asleep at the wheel due to boredom. Boredom was the last thing she was worried about.

She was thankful she had a full tank of gas and a lot of munchies for the ride. She wasn't planning on stopping unless she had to and just wanted to get home as soon as she could. Hopefully, she'd make it in a couple of days. There was little traffic, and it was smooth sailing. Creepy, but smooth.

Millie had no idea that almost every one of her friends was dead or dying, and that her husband was at home on the terrace chaise lounge, rotting in the sunshine like an unpicked tomato on the vine.

Chapter 6

The Center for Disease Control had announced, "This is an emerging, rapidly evolving situation, and the CDC will provide updated information as it becomes available." The CDC also noted that "Due to the type of related deaths that have recently occurred, it has been determined that the prolonged use of cellular phones may be directly related. Therefore, it is advised for everyone to avoid the use of these products immediately until further notice."

This made sense, given the surviving individuals were elderly or were children. Most elderly do not catch on to modern technology like the savvy, younger generation, and oftentimes do not even use cell phones at all. At least not as often as younger adults, and children simply haven't had years of radiation waves penetrating their heads from holding a cell phone day after day.

Cell phones emit low levels of non-ionizing radiation when in use. This type of radiation is also referred to as radio frequency ("RF") energy. Up until now, it has not been proven that this level of radiation is dangerous. Although cell phones became popular in the mid-80s, only time would tell if long-term activity would be harmful. And what is "long-term"? It seems a lot can happen in thirty-five years. It also seems fair to say that the length of "long-term" had just been determined.

The sad thing was, by the time the CDC realized what was happening, most of the adults who would normally watch the news were dead, and the people televising the news were also dead. It was believed by those unaffected that not many heard the news at all, or only learned of the information through street gossip.

Chapter 7

Maddy's mom's cries ended that morning when she had a brain aneurism burst in her frontal lobe. Death came swiftly and was seemingly painless. She was one of the lucky ones.

Maddy and her father assumed she had fallen asleep and went into the bedroom to check on her later that afternoon, and to offer her some tomato soup and a grilled cheese sandwich. They had hoped she would be up for eating a little something.

Upon discovering her mom was dead, Maddy dropped the tray of food, and the dog ate the sandwich. The circle of life continues, just not for Maddy's mother.

Maddy's father would soon follow his wife, except his death wasn't quite so pleasant. The miserable thing about his departure from this world was that he didn't get sick at all. He was just walking out to drop a letter in the mailbox when the nice gentleman who lived down the street had a corneal eruption in his left eye. In other words, his eye exploded from deep inside. The man, stricken by pain and confusion, hit the gas instead of the brake and pinned Maddy's father between the front of his car and the beautifully crafted, brick mailbox he had built the summer before. It's design matched the house exactly and he had always enjoyed admiring it when he had to make a trip to get the mail. He died from massive internal injuries and loss of blood, all while holding Maddy's trembling hand.

Hunter and Miranda comforted Maddy as best they could. But their lives were also falling apart. Both of their parents had also died quickly, along with various other relatives and friends who were middle-aged and otherwise healthy.

Chapter 8

Millie made it to Maryland in two and a half days. She slept at rest areas and was lucky to find most of the fast-food restaurants along the way had remained open. Probably because the employees were young and able.

She started noticing fewer vehicles along the highways. It was about one-hundred miles outside of Maryland when things got really disturbing.

It seemed those people who had jobs that took them outdoors, or had very busy, labor-intensive positions, lived. Those people, who obviously did not use their phones quite as often, or mainly used the speaker feature, were also survivors.

It was a fine line, and, of course, the strength of each person's immune system or natural ability to fight was also a factor.

The CDC were as helpful as they could be. But it had all happened so fast and so abruptly. There had been no warning. No matter how intense an agency's emergency plan was, until something awful happened, no one could ever really be prepared for things to fall apart.

In hopes of avoiding the disease or whatever it was, people retreated from one another not knowing or understanding what passed it on.

The most important duty to continue life at this point is to care for the children - the children of the world. There are certainly enough shelters and homes. The old will need to be stronger than they ever thought they could be and the young, well the young will have to be more understanding and considerate than they ever have been. People will need to learn to work together in many ways.

Chapter 9

Millie was about fifty miles from her home in Ocean City when she stopped at a rest area to do the obvious and walk the dog she'd found wandering along Interstate 50. It was a little dog, well taken care of, and probably a Shitzu/Maltese mix. It was well trained and very scared, and Millie thought, considering the recent events that had taken over the country, or maybe even the world, she had to save the poor thing. Printed on the collar's tag was, "I'm WeeWee. I'm lost!" along with a provided telephone number. The dog was about as endearing as anything she had ever seen, and they soon became fast friends. Millie learned that it was very easy to fall in love with something so cute and innocent and found herself wondering why she had never adopted a dog before.

About ten miles past St. Michaels, Maryland, Millie saw a motor home on the side of the road. On its roof was an MIA flag flapping in the stifling afternoon air and what looked like an older couple standing outside trying to change a tire. Millie thought these people looked as tired and as emotionally drained as she was and felt immediate compassion toward them. She pulled the Escalade over in the breakdown lane to at least try to offer a little assistance.

Millie shut off the engine and climbed out of her car. She had barely cleared the driver's door when the impact of the bullet dropped her in the street. It hit her square in the face and she was knocked backwards, thus shutting the door, leaving little Wee-Wee to die thirty minutes later trapped in the Escalade in the sweltering July heat.

CHAPTER 10

The wind is whispering to me like I am a child. I wish I could make it stop because the sound is hurting my head. I feel something warm on the side of my neck, and I think it's blood. How much blood have I lost, I wonder, as I lay here in this dark place? I'm getting cold now, which is not a good sign, and I want to sleep.

Kep was surely dying. No one was going to come and help him, and no one would be coming to write anything down for him.

"If only my cell phone still worked," he said to himself as his last breath escaped him.

A New World

Is this what dying feels like? There is no pain. There is no light urging me ahead. There is no path. I've heard there is a white light, but I can't find it. Maybe I need to be patient and wait a little longer. Maybe I'm not where I need to be. Oh, how I wish I could get out of this decaying place.

I am still breathing. I know because I see my chest rising. I can see Vivian, my faithful dog, lying next to me. Every time I hear myself moan her head rises as she checks on me. She is and always has been such a comfort to me.

I am not sick. I am not insane. The voices in my head are not crazy or unkind. They are simply telling me the way things are—telling me the way the world will end. I will lie here and wait because I am obedient.

The area I am in must be a hospital room. I am sure that in all of this chaos rules have been overlooked as Vivian remains here with me. The walls are filthy and white and there is a television mounted on the wall in front of me although its screen is cracked and dirty. The curtains are also white and block little of the sunlight streaming in. I enjoy the light. I am afraid there will be little, if any light, for me soon. I don't want to be in the dark now—not here in this place.

I am not sure what I should be doing right now. Maybe I should pack and tell others to do the same. I wonder if I should be looking for someone in charge, or at the very least, notify my friends on Facebook what is happening and tell them it is time to get ready for the end.

I believe it is time for a reckoning. I believe I should tell you why I am talking this way. I should tell you what happened to me and why I am in this place. How I wish I could! How I wish this horror would end and life would go back to normal.

Life has always been wonderful for me. I was a cheerleader all through school, most years the captain, in fact. I was popular and had many friends, and my early years were full of fun and parties and boyfriends. I had everything a young teenage girl could dream of. I am Gabby Monroe, not even forty-four years young and I should not be here. I have been married for the last twenty years and I have a family that needs me. I would be home this minute if I didn't have to drive into town to pay the damn electric bill and pick up a few things for tonight's dinner. I should not be here in this god-awful place, completely unaware of what is happening around me. I should be home where I am safe, and life is familiar. But nothing and nowhere is safe today and nothing is familiar.

The air has changed somehow. When I breathe I feel like I'm drawing exhaust fumes into my lungs, and it burns as if a thousand bees are stinging me inside, inside where I cannot swat them away or defend myself and it's so loud. It's so fucking loud, I cannot think anymore.

I am in a room and my memories of my life are being torn away. This isn't fair. I suppose I am one of the lucky ones. Reality comes in and out in little, confusing bursts. Vivian looks at me with those sympathetic, canine eyes. If she could only help me. If I could only help her.

The last thing I remember was a group of people in the grocery store who had congregated around the aisle of the express lane.

It seemed the folks who had gathered in line were talking about political agendas and something weird about trying to get home as soon as possible and that traffic outside was becoming worse by the second.

I wonder if something happened along the lines of a civil war, or maybe a terrorist attack? I only know something awful has happened.

Now there are loud explosions and I smell the acrid scent of dirt and heat, and something I've never smelled before; a pungent odor of feces and rotten eggs stings my eyes, and oh my God—Sweet Jesus! People are screaming! Please make them stop! I just want to relax here in this bed until someone comes for me and takes me home where I'll be safe. Yes. Home. I'll be safe at home. I have to get out of here.

My daughter will be here soon. Unless . . . unless something has happened to her in all this drama. Does she even know where I am? Oh, please let her be okay. I need to find my cell phone and call her. Where is it? I don't even know where my clothes are. If only I could get up out of this bed. My God, I can't get up. I can't move. It's as if I am being held down although I don't see any straps or anything restricting me.

In fact, I can't feel anything. My chest rises and falls as I breathe, but I cannot see anything beyond my chest. Am I paralyzed? I think I am. I must have been brought here to recover. Is that it? Maybe there is nothing left of me beyond my waist. I need to stop thinking such things. This way of thinking will not improve my situation one bit and it will only make me crazy. I am going to live, I know it. I am going to get the fuck out of this place soon.

The door flies open, and I see a woman, I think, but I can't be sure. Where her face should be is nothing more than melted skin and smeared blood. Tendrils of what must be muscle tissue sways loosely from misshapen matter I cannot describe. The holes where her eyes once were oozes a creamy, mucus-like substance that is red in color with chunks of white desperately clinging to that awful mass of flesh. I think the white chunks are parts of her eyes that must have exploded in their sockets. As she feels for the entranceway to my room, obviously searching for a loved one or possibly an escape from the ongoing horror, her body drops and limply succumbs to the inevitable death that is so abundant around us.

No one should have to endure this revulsion. I cannot stop the vomit rising in my throat.

Oh Lord, if this was some kind of chemical attack, I know I will begin to feel the effects at any moment.

Where is my daughter? If only I could get some answers. The last time I saw her she had been in the kitchen organizing a few papers for school. She always did so well in school. I was so proud of her and . . . and . . . I'm talking about her in the past tense. Oh my God—knock it off! I have to stop this.

The light coming in the window has now taken on a softer, creamier hue. Not the usual daylight of a normal day. This light is dimmer, as if there is a storm brewing. By the feel of things, I would say a large storm, and by the looks of it, I'd say the storm has already arrived.

The screaming has stopped. I am thankful I am still with Vivian who seems to be hanging on to my very thoughts. If dogs have souls, I know she is more human than anyone else I could ever have hoped to be with at this moment. It's quiet now except for a very low humming and the constant beat of my heart. The humming seems innocent enough, but it is also frightening and strange—otherworldly. I've never heard a sound quite like it. And it is getting closer.

Vivian leans up closer to me. She begins a muted, soft growling noise. Thank God she is healthy and seems unhurt. Without her I doubt I would have the strength to go on.

Footsteps are coming, steady and soft. They do not appear to be from someone who is hurt or injured. How can anyone not be hurt or injured in all this chaos? Maybe I am saved, after all? I can only hope the door will swing open and a friendly face will appear on the other side. Yet, I am frightened.

I want to hide.

If only I could move. I can only turn my head and close my eyes. Maybe the footsteps will continue past my door, which barely hangs from its hinges. I think an earthquake hit. I hope an earthquake is all that's happened.

There is a shadow on the floor on the other side of the door, and an energy of whatever is on the other side. It lingers as if trying to decide if it should enter.

I want to shout, "Just go away!" and as I realize I can no longer stand the suspense, the door sways. I know I am either going to live or die. I want to live so desperately, but I do not want to live as a paralyzed woman unable to care for myself and unable to do the things that make me who I am. I refuse to live under those circumstances, and I certainly don't want to live imprisoned by some strange and unknown enemy.

As the door slowly opens, I see a figure.

I am aware of another figure following closely behind. I say nothing. I have no words, but words don't seem necessary right now.

I realize I must have a sad, empty look. I am physically wasted. I cannot move and I feel I am teetering on the edge of panic. Although I must have slept, it wasn't a good sleep. It was the sleep of the burdened and emotionally drained.

The figures walk over to me and stand beside my bed. I feel a sense of release, like all the tension in my body has let go and extreme contentment overwhelms me. I stare at them and feel myself smile. How weird is that? After all that is happening around me, in all the devastation and obvious destruction, I just smile.

The first figure is tall and walks over offering their outstretched hand. I see no reason to doubt their humanity, yet I know they are different. Is it a man or a woman? The hand is neither masculine nor feminine, yet sensitive and quite pale. There are no lines like we have on our hands, and there doesn't seem to be any reason for fear.

I slowly outstretch my hand to meet theirs. My God, I can move my arms now. In fact, I can also move my legs.

Vivian, who has been very scared, and with great reason, now seems incredibly calm and mellow. She isn't trying to protect me, and she is, in fact, very receptive of the new strangers.

As I let their hand take mine, I am pulled to a sitting position. Soon on my feet and led away. I let them escort me through the building and away from the destruction.

Whatever had taken place has suddenly stopped. It is quiet now. There is smoking debris everywhere and it is hard to believe my room is left undamaged. Charred remains of what I know are people lie strewn about. Most are burned and melted so badly, I felt a sudden nausea swelling inside my throat. It takes great effort to not be sick.

How is it I've been spared? I should be dead or burned alive like all these others. What is it these figures want or need from me? I am just a simple person with no great knowledge of anything special. What do they possibly want with the likes of me?

A moment later, I am through the chaos and led upwards, slowly rising into the air. I look down and see everything below me—the smashed buildings, the crushed and burning vehicles, the parking lot, which looks as though it has been cracked apart with huge fissures separating the cement from the ground. The higher I am led, the more I see. Vivian is at my side, seeming to float right along with us. I am so relieved she is still by my side, her face full of expression and wonder not fear. I had almost forgotten about her in all the excitement. I don't think I could have handled it if I lost her. I reach for her, and she gently wafts upwards into my arms. I hold her as I would a newborn baby, caressing her gently. Her eyes wide and brilliant yet peaceful.

We finally arrive at a structure. It is silver, grey, and blue, and it immediately strikes me that it's been painted this way to help hide it from sight, like camouflage in the sky. It is a magnificent ship. My thoughts are it could not be from this earth as it is hovering and not making any sound except a soft humming as I float toward it.

I should be frightened but I am not. I only feel calmness and serenity.

Great doors open, and as we enter, we are greeted by others, who are also tall and very pale. Their faces are intelligent and civilized. I try to speak, but when I begin, they turn their heads and motion to keep moving onward into the ship. I follow unquestioningly.

They lead me through an immense corridor about fifteen-feet wide and lit by recessed lights in the floor, not too bright, but comfortably soothing and a pale blue color. There is a quiet humming sound I assume to be the ship's motor or operating system, and there are no windows or doors. I think, normally I would feel trapped, as if entering a cave or tunnel. I am not fond of tight surroundings, and I have often thought that people who commute to work every day via the Metro must be insane. However, instead of panic I have a great feeling of being safe.

After a few moments, the corridor broadens into a large room. In front there are three large desks, long and intricately carved with designs that I have never seen before. No one from my planet has seen them before. They are unimaginably elaborate and delicately engraved.

There are others seated in a group and I can tell by their faces they are human beings. Everyone has an intense expression of wonder, yet great reluctance. I am so glad I am not alone and as I am motioned to join the group, a myriad of thoughts flits through my mind. I am thankful that fear isn't one of them.

As we sit, others enter and join us. Some begin talking to those beside them and are quickly hushed; not in a harsh way, but in a way that you dare not resist. We all wait patiently in silence. This strange place offers a sense of peace compared to the nightmare we've escaped back on the ground. I find myself reluctant, but also happy to be here.

After some time, maybe an hour or two, the tall, pale figures that first greeted me as I entered the ship come into the room and sit down at the desks. My heart pounds as I wait for them to speak.

Their voices, through unmoving mouths, come to me strong and clear, as if I am wearing headphones. They are monotone, yet their faces are full of emotion. Clearly, they only intend good will and have offered us a choice.

They tell the others and I that our planet was facing destruction. These beings had monitored our news broadcasts and military developments over a long period of time, hoping we would solve our difficulties among ourselves, but things had not gone well. Their intervention was now necessary.

The destruction turned our atmosphere into poison and the magnetic field was deteriorating. Time was short and everyone knew it.

Our choices are simple. Stay and die or remain on the ship and live. Some of us would be taken to other planets and some would stay on a ship and learn the duties of working on board.

Could this really be happening? I look around the room. The expressions on everyone's faces mirror my own. As if our minds can't comprehend all that has been told to us. The fact that these beings stepped in to help our world is amazing.

There are tears and confusion. So many unanswered questions that may never be answered. Our new friends can offer no emotional help, only a new life.

These beings saw what was happening and came to our rescue without asking for anything in return.

They came for humans and animals alike, and without prejudice. To them, a life is worth saving no matter what the species. I look at Vivian, watching the aliens with an intelligence I find amazing, and I have never before seen. Does Vivian understand them? Are they speaking to her in a language that is understood by a dog? I believe so.

The skills involved in communicating with us and the love they show is unbelievably heartfelt by all.

I will choose to relocate to another planet and begin a new life for myself. There will be water, an atmosphere like Earth's, and the companionship of others.

We will all learn to exist again. We will all learn to deal with a new life, and new ways.

Can we, will we ever know exactly what happened to our world? Will we ever come to grips with such a travesty? Our families, our friends, and loved ones are likely dead or being relocated as I am now. We will never know who has been killed or who has been spared, and where they've chosen to live out the rest of their lives. All I can think of is my daughter. I pray I will see her again soon, that I will see her smile and hear her laugh, again.

There is so much to learn and so much to consider. No time to think, no more time for anything except moving forward.

As our new friends lead us to where we will sleep—as if anyone could really sleep after all of this—it is a chance to finally let all of this sink in.

Tomorrow will be a new day, and as I hear the engines hum louder, I know we are leaving what is left of Earth and we will never see our homes again. We are entering our future and our lives up until now will be nothing but memories. How I wish I could go back and take one last look at my family. How I wish I could hold them in my arms one last time and tell them I love them.

Each day is a blessing. Hold onto it. Life is what matters, and off I go to live it.

Unless you have skipped forward to the end of this book, I will assume you read it in its entirety and sincerely hope you enjoyed it. That being said, if I can ask you to do one more thing, it would be greatly appreciated. As you may or may not know writing books is not necessarily a get rich quick scheme. In fact, most writers still have regular jobs – though some may not mention them. I would like you all, as hopefully satisfied readers, to please take another second of your valuable time to give this book a review, preferably a good one, as it will help other readers locate "When Hearts Bleed" easier when searching books for their future purchases. With more reviews – hopefully, they'll be more happier readers. Not to mention more exposure for me, which as a new writer is always a good thing.

I'd also like to quickly mention that as this book was in its final editing phases, so many people came out of nowhere to offer kind sentiments, advice and general words of wisdom which touched my heart in many ways. Some of these people go back to my early school days when life wasn't full of responsibilities and fun was all we had. In gratitude, I hope I was able to offer you a little more fun as you read this book.

B.J. Lawyer
Humboldt, Arizona

Printed in Great Britain
by Amazon